Greetings & Farewells

Cover art by Julien Giever.

ISBN: 978-0-615-25603-0

CONTENTS

'TIS THE SEASON

Chapter 01.01

Kyle sat unmoving in the chair, staring down at the floor of the dimly lit room. His wrists and ankles were bound to the metal chair with duct tape, and the side of his head still throbbed from the blow he had received the one time he tried to cry out for help.

To his left was a young man with long blond hair by the name of Thomas, who Kyle had just met a short time ago, and was the reason they were currently sitting in this dark room. On the other side of Thomas was his servant, Harry, a man in his early fifties who sat calmly bound to his chair, eyes shut.

It had been an amazingly crappy day.

After taking a week off to oversee renovations on his Grandmother's house Kyle had returned to work on Monday, thirty minutes before the day shift started, which was his normal routine. That way he could go through the emails and catch up with managers before the onslaught of support calls started streaming in.

This day was different. He noticed the haphazard stack of Post-It notes piled next to the keyboard, which after being gone a week he knew would have covered both of his monitors. Instead there was one planted in the middle of his main screen from his IT Manager simply asking for him to come over when Kyle got in.

Pulling the note from the monitor he got a bad feeling when he noticed his Maneki Neko statue that sat at the front of his desk, the little white cat with one paw raised to greet people coming in, was lying on its side. As he exited his office he set it upright to face the entry.

Quickly making his way down the hallways covered in imitation hardwood the President of the company had installed to make them look more professional, Kyle stopped suddenly and knocked on the open door.

His boss, Jerry, sat on the other side of his desk and looked up.

"Ah, um, Kyle, come in," he said while avoiding eye contact, staring at the screen of his computer. "Close the door."

Kyle stepped into the office slowly and closed the door behind him. Jerry continued to stare at the screen intently but touched neither his mouse nor his keyboard, not a good sign. Pausing slightly, Kyle watched him for a moment before sitting down in the chair.

"Wait," said Kyle. "Oh crap, please tell me you read my report. Upgrading all of our Windows machines right now would be so bad in so many ways."

Staring down at his keyboard for a few seconds, Jerry looked up and gazed at Kyle's chest.

"Of course not, Kyle. How was your vacation?" he asked.

"Rather non-eventful in a construction kind of way," said Kyle. "If it's not about the upgrades then what's up?"

"Oh, well, um..." said Jerry trailing off. "Well, you see, ah, while you were gone some things happened. Well mainly our company became acquired by another company, and it was finalized just yesterday." He paused a moment, fidgeting with the pen in his left hand. Looking up, but not at Kyle he said, "Unfortunately we're letting everybody go except for upper management."

Kyle managed one word, "But..."

"I understand the inconvenience of this, you're a real genius but they wouldn't let me take you on in this merger. You are a great employee, but it's all a done deal now. Everybody is locked out of their computers, but if you have anything personal on yours I can log in so you can get the files."

Jerry was staring at the pen in his hand again.

He looked up into Kyle's eyes, his feelings obvious.

"So that is it," said Kyle in a voice devoid of emotion.

"Look, Kyle," said Jerry, "I tried, I really did. It's just..."

Another part of his life gone. Again. Just when everything seemed to be going so well.

Kyle tried to calm himself and sound normal as he stood and extended a hand to Jerry and said, "You've been a great boss. This must be difficult for you, I don't have anything on my computer so I'll just grab my things and be off."

Hesitantly Jerry shook his hand while wishing Kyle the best of luck.

"If you ever need a letter of recommendation or anything,"

started Jerry, but Kyle simply turned and left the room, not saying a word.

Kyle walked slowly, calmly, to his office, in a very controlled manner, and then pulled out his phone to check the time. Grabbing an empty box from a recent new computer he had set up before he went on vacation he quickly tore through his office and filled it with any personal belonging he had. Pausing for just a moment he looked around before slinging his satchel over his shoulder and picking up the box.

Ten minutes before normal employees were scheduled to report for work he was in his car and exiting the parking lot just as the first of the early birds started to pull in.

In a daze Kyle drove toward home, taking side streets. He had no care to deal with traffic right now, and as he drove he suddenly remembered a small café him and his Grandmother used to visit all the time. Never being a morning person it had been a while since he had been there, but he made a sudden right off the road he was driving.

It was a small mom and pop place that his Grandmother had taken him to several times a week when he was growing up. She had been going there for over forty years. The familiar sights and surroundings would be a nice comfort, after everything that had happened today.

Ten minutes later he stood next to his car, the engine still running, door ajar, facing the boarded up building.

Turning, he watched the people going about their daily business. Something he should have been doing right now. After standing there for a while in the empty parking lot, Kyle got back into his car.

He stared at the boarded up building for another moment then reached over to turn up the volume of the Industrial song that was blaring on his speakers, lying back in his seat and letting the intense beat fill him. Sitting up and letting out a long sigh, he reversed slowly, then inched his way onto the main road. As the song began to intensify he pushed the throttle down and began weaving in and out of traffic on his way home.

A mile later he found his rear view mirror filled with bright lights.

Fifteen minutes later, and a speeding ticket on the passenger seat, he slowly merged into traffic and found his way home.

Julien Giever

The remainder of the day was blissfully free of unfortunate circumstances. This was probably due to the fact that he sat himself in front of the television and started watching an anime series that always made him laugh, except for today.

He heard his roommate Ed come into the living room and stand near the corner of the couch, but Kyle said nothing.

"For us poor souls who don't speak Japanese the least you could do is put on the subtitles," said Ed sitting on the arm of the couch, inches from Kyle.

"You weren't here," the words came out in a slow dry monotone.

Ed looked down at Kyle who paused the DVD and continued to stare at the image on the television.

"Check out Mr. Cranky. Somebody blow up their computer at work? Wait, what are you doing home now?"

Kyle took a deep breath, exhaling slowly he sank into the couch and dropped his head a before looking up to the television again. "As of today I am gainfully unemployed."

"Byaaa what the?" asked Ed almost falling off the couch and barely managing to stand.

"Guess there was a merger when I was on vacation. Lucky me."

Scratching his bald head Ed then started stroking his goatee. "A week before Christmas?"

Kyle nodded.

"Damn, that's harsh."

"Yes it is."

"Hey, I could get you a job at Guitar Center!"

Kyle slowly turned his head and glared at Ed.

"OK, no on that," said Ed. "Taking you want to be alone and mope?"

Kyle nodded.

"No prob." Ed stood and walked toward the kitchen.

Kyle pressed the play button to continue the series he had been watching. He heard Ed's footsteps coming back into the room, and his thumb hovered over the pause button as he silently hoped more conversation was not necessary.

A Corona was placed on the coffee table. Kyle looked down at that and shook his head slightly.

"Thanks," he said grabbing it.

Ed just nodded his head and left the room.

Some time later, right after beginning of an episode of the series had been watching, the ringing of his cell phone brought him out of his reverie. Glancing at the clock on the wall he saw that it was five thirty. Normally he would be leaving work at this time. Looking at the display of the phone he saw one word, KEIKO with the phone number beneath.

Pressing the button to answer, he did his best to sound happy and said, "Hey, how's the shoot?"

There was a moan from the other end. "Ugh... Good news, we finished a day ahead of schedule, so I'm back. Bad news, that shoot was hell. I'm so exhausted."

"Ah," he said.

"What, no witty or sarcastic comments?"

"No."

"You alright, Kyle?"

"Um, no."

"What's wrong?"

He had met Keiko through Ed's girlfriend back when Cynthia and Keiko were seniors in high school. Kyle and Keiko had become really good friends, even though he was five years her senior.

And Ed had been dating Cynthia since that time.

Kyle had been there for Keiko from the beginning, when she first said she was interested in modeling, the first time she had photos taken and now numerous magazine covers and fashion shows. All these years and they had remained the best of friends. That was all. He tried not to think whether that was good or bad.

"Hey, you there?"

"Sorry," said Kyle.

He told her everything that had happened so far today.

There was silence on the other end.

"Kind of makes the crap I had to deal with in some exotic shoot seem pretty lame," she said.

He chuckled.

"So, hey, you want to go out to some dinner thing with me tonight?" she asked.

"Some dinner thing?"

"Well, see, there is this Christmas Charity Dinner I had been invited to, but couldn't go because I wasn't supposed to be back until tomorrow, and maybe if you got to be around a bunch of people you'd

5

feel better?"

"Keiko," he said slowly. "Being around those types of people won't cheer me up, and you know it."

She sighed. "I know, just you know how much I hate going to those things by myself. I fit in about as well as you do."

Kyle thought briefly about a recent article whose headline was *"Keiko Nakamura, Snob or the Most Anti-Social Model in the Scene"* and leaned back into the couch.

"Yes, but you're famous, so you should fit in."

"Ugh, most of those people are so fake, making contributions for tax breaks and good PR. But this is a charity that I've been giving to for years though, and they asked me to come and were kinda disappointed I couldn't make it."

"Huh? Wait, the one you used to volunteer for back when you were in High School?"

"Of course, what other charity do I work with?"

Kyle took a deep breath. "What time should I pick you up?"

"Really?"

"Yes, really."

"Damn, I love you Kyle, you're the best!" she exclaimed. "Let's see, it starts at seven, think you can be here in thirty to forty minutes?"

"See you then," he said.

"Hey, Kyle?" she asked.

"What?"

"Thank you. I know you've had a bad day. I really appreciate you doing this for me."

"What are friends for, right?"

"You know you're more than that to me," she said in a barely audible voice.

Kyle froze, grasping the bottle of Guinness and staring at the floor as the single word he hated most in the world came through his phone. The word that always carved his heart from his chest every time he heard it. The one word he would do anything to remove from the Japanese language.

"You're my onii-chan," she said.

Her brother, in Japanese.

Closing his eyes against the word, he summoned the best of his fake happiness and said, "I will see you soon."

"Hai!" she exclaimed.

Kyle pressed a button and ended the call. He stared at the phone for a few minutes.

"Great, like a brother. Nothing changes," he said. Taking another deep breath he let out a long sigh and went upstairs to change, after finishing the Corona.

Twenty minutes later he emerged from his bedroom in a designer tuxedo that Keiko had bought for him several years ago.

Somehow he always ended up going to these things with her. Several times Kyle's photo had appeared in magazines, he was always named as "Keiko's childhood friend" which was stupid because he had only known her for six years.

Ed always found great amusement in this for some reason.

The hard soles of his Italian dress shoes echoed loudly on the hardwood floors and down the hall. He paused at Ed's door and knocked lightly. There was no response. Leaning close he could hear faint music and the clicking of the keys on an electric keyboard, which meant Ed was composing a song.

On the message board in the kitchen Kyle scrawled out a note that he was going out with Keiko. He paused a moment, staring at the note, while considering calling her back to cancel. Unfortunately he knew how she could be when she felt abandoned, so gave up and put the pen back, then walked out into the cool night air and looked up and the crescent moon.

"Baka," he said to himself. "You've been unemployed for less than twenty-four hours. Things will get better."

Fishing the remote out from his pocket he opened the garage door and got into his car, draping the long coat over the back of the passengers seat. Smiling he popped out the MP3 CD of Industrial music and put in a J-Pop and anime mix that Keiko liked. He started his car and began to slowly back up, humming to the song that was playing, then paused. The steering wheel was pulling heavily to the right.

Putting the car into park he got out and walked around to look at the tire on the passenger's side. He turned around and walked back into the garage a few feet, then dropped his head in defeat.

Bending down he tried to pull the nail from the flat tire but had little success. Standing and kicking the tire twice he turned around and stepped from the garage, taking out his phone to make a call.

"Hey onii-chan, what's up?" asked Keiko.

"Bad news, I have a flat."

"Seriously? Or are you trying to back out?"

"No, I really have a flat. But there's a tire place near here I've been too before who are open until seven, so if I get over there quick they can fix it tonight."

"Damn, then we'll be late," she said. "Do you really want to go? I can call it off if you want."

"No, no, it's OK, I know how much this means to you. Can you get a ride there and I'll just meet you after I get this fixed?"

"Yeah, sure. It's at..."

"Hold on," he said pulling out his Zaurus PDA. He flipped it open, thumbs hovering over the keyboard he said, "Go ahead."

She told him where the event was being held and he typed it in.

"Got it," he said. "See you there."

"Thanks."

Walking back into the garage, he turned off the car and popped open the trunk.

Chapter 01.02

Keiko hung up and stared out of the bay windows of her living room.

"Damn, he's had a bad day," she said to her cat who was lying on the cushion in front of the window. "What do you think? Should I just cancel? No, then I would just look stupid, and I really should go, right?"

The cat glanced up at her and went back to sleep.

"You're no help. Or are you just pissed off at me that you had to go away mom's again while I was on another shoot, neko-chan?"

Her cat opened one eye at her then closed it.

Sitting down next to the feline and petting it, she stared at her phone. Scrolling through some names she pressed the dial button.

The ringing stopped and she heard silence on the other end.

"Cyn?" she asked.

"Good evening, Keiko," came a quiet voice.

"Listen, can I ask you a favor? Kyle has a flat tire and I'm supposed to be in downtown LA in less than an hour."

"Why?"

"Well it's for that charity I used to volunteer for back in High

School, but I didn't think I could make it, and Kyle has a flat, and I really don't know what to do."

"Are you at your house?" came the monotone voice.

"Yes."

"I will be there shortly."

"Thank you!" said Keiko as the line went dead.

"See Tomo," she said picking up her cat and rubbing his face with her own. "Everything will work out like always."

Her cat suddenly spun in her hands and sprung away from Keiko, running to the back of the house, and into the bedroom.

Keiko sat there, staring at the empty doorway.

Chapter 01.03

As Kyle got out of his car he took the ticket from the valet and walked around to the entry of the hotel, whose management had forsaken the normal political correctness and had only decorated the interior for Christmas. Walking into the lobby he looked around. Spotting the elevators he made his way quickly over to it and stopped next to a young man with long blond hair and an older man who were staring and waiting for an up arrow to appear.

There was a ding and the doors to one of the elevators opened, people exiting. As he stood there, waiting, three large men came up and stood behind him. Kyle glanced over his shoulder and thought they seemed like mafia, then realized he was in Los Angeles and had been watching too much television, mafia was east coast of course. He thought about taking the next elevator, but remembered how Keiko could be if she thought he had abandoned her.

The young man with blonde hair held the doors open with his arm as the group of them entered the elevator. His eyes locked with Kyle's and a smile crossed his face.

"Thanks," said Kyle.

As the doors closed he draped an arm over Kyle's shoulders and said in a thick British accent, "Of course my friend."

"And what floor might you gentlemen be going to this evening?" asked the grey haired man who seemed to be with the young man who had a sudden interest in Kyle.

"Thirteen," said one of the three men in pin-striped suites staring at the door, in a very distinct New Jersey accent.

"Top floor," said Kyle, uneasily looking around.

"Excellent," said the older man, pressing one button, then another button for the top floor.

"I am Dunne, Thomas Dunne," said the young man, stepping back and bowing slightly. He was dressed in a loose fitting suit with no tie, the top two buttons of his expensive purple dress shirt were unfastened. "And this is my Man Servant, Harry."

Harry closed his eyes at the title then said a brief hello.

"Ah, my friend," said Thomas placing an arm around Kyle's shoulders again. "From your dress it seems and that we are going to the same floor, so it would seem that we are both heading to the festivities above. And who might you be?"

Kyle had tried to casually pull away from Thomas' grip, but to no avail. Smiling hesitantly he said, "Kyle."

"Good to meet you Kyle," said Thomas grabbing Kyle's hand from his side and shaking it.

Placing his free hand on Kyle's chest he continued, "This shall be a grand night indeed. Fine women, fine drinks. The spirit of Christmas filling everybody's hearts with joy. Are you not looking forward to this evening, my friend?"

"Uh, sure," said Kyle who shot a pleading glance to Harry, who only sighed and looked at the numbers of the panel going up. Kyle tried to pull away from the arm that was suddenly around his shoulder, again, unsuccessfully.

The elevator slowed, then a light ding sound filled the small space.

On the display the number 13 was glowed in red as the doors opened. Two of the men in pin-striped suites stepped forward to block the doors from closing as the third one, in the middle, turned around and faced Thomas.

"Mister Dunne," said the large man, smiling slightly.

"We are representatives for Mr. Shoemaker. He would like to ask you about the money you were supposed to pay back four days ago. And about your interactions with his daughter."

"Oh, well, that, sorry, I must have lost track of time," said Thomas turning to him. "No need to worry. I shall pay it back post haste. And all I did with Alice is have a few pleasant evenings of conversation. So there is no need to worry."

"Mr. Dunne, if there was no need to worry, we would not be here."

The two men on either side simultaneously moved their free hands enough to show that they had semi-automatic pistols hidden just beneath their suit coats.

"Listen," said Kyle raising both hands. "I have no idea who this guy is, I was just going upstairs to meet a friend, so if you just let me go I won't remember anything that happened here."

"For all we know you are some gay escort."

"I'm not gay," said Kyle and Thomas in unison.

This reaction did not seem to persuade the three men.

Kyle sighed and leaned into the corner of the elevator. "Really, I don't know him."

"Well then, this is your unlucky day," said the man in the middle turning around and stepping out.

The two others stood on either side watching them closely.

Thomas, Harry, then Kyle, filed out of the elevator and followed the lead man down several hallways until they reached a room. Pulling out a key-card, the large man opened the door and stood aside, arm raised for them to enter.

They walked down a hallway, past the bathroom, and into a large, finely decorated room with a television, a couch, and two plush chairs. The cherry wood coffee table had been moved aside and in the middle of the room were four metal chairs.

"Please have a seat," said the lead man.

"I am Frank," he said. "This is Guido and Lefty. We will be your hosts this evening. Don't expect any kind of service."

Feeling a gun barrel in the middle of his back, Kyle walked slowly to one of the chairs and sat down, feeling that this was the culmination of the universe doing something unmentionable to him, without any type of lubricant.

"So, my good man, why then are there four chairs?" asked Thomas strolling over to one and sitting down with a casual flair.

"Because you usually have a couple chicks with you," said Frank. "Had no idea you were into boys."

"Hey," said Kyle.

"How dare you. I adore the female. I worship them. For you to insinuate that I would be interested in men..."

His sentence was cut short as the silencer, attached to a semi-automatic pistol, was forced into his mouth.

"I really don't know these guys," said Kyle.

Frank walked over and knelt down. "You know, buddy, if you don't, it kinda sucks to be you right now."

"Tell me about it," said Kyle.

"No matter to me," said Frank. Pulling out his pistol and aiming it at Thomas' head, he said, "Please, restrain them."

The other two men in dark pinstriped suits grabbed rolls of duct tape and fastened Kyle, Thomas, then Harry to their chairs.

"Now then, Mister Shoemaker has business to take care of, so he'll meet with you tomorrow morning, after he has breakfast with his Mother. Until then, please make yourselves as comfortable as possible."

Smiling at the three of them, Frank clicked the safety of his pistol on and off several times. "And just so you know, we own this hotel, so if you give us a problem or try to escape, please, rest assured that we will be long gone before the cops arrive and find your bodies. If they find any bodies that is."

Frank let out a chuckle reserved for those who know that their prey has no way of winning, then walked into the bedroom with Lefty, closing the doors part way behind them.

Everything was silent for a while. For reasons that defied common sense, when Kyle heard some people walking by in the hallway outside the room he started to scream out. Perhaps this was some primordial will to survive, or some stupidity brought upon by the situation.

This was cut short by a blow to the side of his head with the butt end of a pistol. He had not realized that Guido was behind him.

"Sorry, sorry," said Kyle. "Stress and all."

To be honest, inside, he was contemplating the fact that he should have finally spoken up to her and declined Keiko's request, then finished the anime series he had been watching, and finally topped it off with a bottle of Bourbon to numb out the day's experience. Instead he found himself staring at his arms which were duct taped to a metal chair, and came to hate his life, yet again.

Guido came around the chair and squatted down, looking into Kyle's eyes. "Do that again and I won't be so nice."

Kyle nodded his head and said, "I understand."

Guido stared at him for a minute before standing and walking back to the table. He sat down and placed his pistol on the table top. Sneering at the three of them he sat down. Pulling out a worn deck of cards he started to play solitaire.

Kyle looked to his left, at Thomas, then at the still, almost meditative form of Harry.

"Well, well, well," said Thomas. "Not an evening of fine women and fine drinks, but an interesting evening nonetheless."

"Shut up," said Kyle.

He felt something vibrating against his chest. It took a few seconds for him to realize that it was his phone. He had turned the ringer off right before he got to the hotel.

Kyle knew who was calling.

He stared at the floor, then at the two other men taped to the chairs, then to the man sitting at the table, then at the ceiling, wishing there might be some deity out there not distracted with running the universe to notice his situation. Unfortunately realizing how the universe usually worked, he sighed again and stared at his knees.

Chapter 01.04

Keiko listened to the beginning of Kyle's voice mail, then hung up her phone.

"He should have been here by now," she mumbled to herself shoving the phone back into her small purse.

She was sitting alone at a circular table in the back corner of the room. This afforded her little reprieve as the men at these types of functions seemed to operate on five minute failure interjections.

Somebody would approach her with two glasses of whatever they thought she was drinking. They would flash their award winning smile as they sat at the empty table and tried to engage her in conversation. Some of them knew who she was, but mostly they saw an attractive person of the opposite sex sitting by herself at a table.

To each was a curt response of, "Thank you, but I am expecting my boyfriend."

Not that Kyle was her boyfriend. She could only wish. But it was a convenient excuse. And after they left, leaving her a drink, five minutes later another would approach. And Keiko would spout off the same line. She found it interesting how this transpired, though. It was always the young, powerful types who approached her first, and as they failed the age would gradually increase until she had balding men with grey hair coming over.

"Hey beautiful," came a voice to her left.

Keiko put on a bored smile while looking up.

And saw a girl who was at best eighteen, sitting in the chair next to her.

"Nani?" said Keiko, slipping into Japanese, not even thinking.

"Huh?"

The girl was wearing a long white dress, very sleek and stylish in its design, probably from a top-line designer judging from the cut, style, and fabric. She had long blond hair and she stared at Keiko with intense blue eyes.

"You don't really fit in," said the girl, slowly shaking her head with a slight frown.

Keiko was mostly prepared to deal with all of the men here. Engaging in any semblance of an actual conversation was something she was not prepared for.

"Um, is it that obvious?" asked Keiko, glancing away.

"Well, no, but I am very perceptive," she said smiling and bouncing slightly in her seat.

"I'm Lucy," said the girl extending her hand.

"I'm Keiko," she said taking the hand.

She felt the hand go limp.

"Eeeeeeeee! The Keiko Nakamura?" the girl exclaimed jumping forward and putting both arms around Keiko's neck. "I loved the cover you did for FHM, and the interview was even better! I mean, for somebody who is so famous, you are surprisingly down to earth!"

"Um, thank you," said Keiko trying to pull away.

"Ah, sorry. Unhappy place. What's wrong?" asked Lucy letting go and sitting back down, but keeping a hand on Keiko's arm.

A waiter walked by with a tray of drinks. Lucy grabbed his coat-tail and gave him a disarming smile. "Excuse me sir, but we seem to be out."

He smiled at her and placed two glasses of champagne on the table, then walked away.

"Are you even legal to drink?" asked Keiko.

"Oh, yes," said Lucy. "I'm much older than I look, which can be a bother at times."

Nodding, Keiko pushed her empty glass to the side and grabbed the new one, taking a practiced dainty sip and suddenly realizing she was more buzzed than she had thought.

"Sorry for being so intrusive, but you don't seem happy," said Lucy.

"Eh, nothing I guess. My friend was supposed to meet me here hours ago but he never showed."

The girl in the white dress paused a moment, then turned to Keiko and said, "That's probably not good."

"I'm kind of worried," said Keiko. "He hasn't been answering his phone, which is unusual. But then again he had a really incredibly bad day. Got laid off, pulled over by cops and such. I kind of forced him to come here, so can't really blame him that he didn't show."

Keiko looked up as two men started to approach the table, and turned away as Lucy glanced at them. From her peripheral vision she saw them pause, then walk past them as if not even noticing the two women.

"Is he your boyfriend?" asked Lucy suddenly.

"No, just a friend I guess," said Keiko leaning both elbows on the table and drinking her glass of champagne. "I shouldn't have asked him here tonight. I was being selfish again. I should have spent the night at his place watching movies or something trying to cheer him up."

"Ah, well, too late now for regrets," said Lucy. "Why are you here? Like I said earlier, you don't seem to fit in, and from the interviews I've read you really don't seem the type to show up just for PR."

"True," said Keiko smiling. "When I was in High School I used to volunteer for this charity. On this side, seeing everybody else seems kinda hollow."

"Nah, it's a good group," said Lucy. "Don't let the idiots dissuade you."

Keiko shook her head slightly, wondering why she was suddenly telling a complete stranger parts of her personal life. Inside she recoiled in fear this might be some reporter, but for some reason could not help answering.

"So why you here?" asked Keiko, trying to turn the tables.

"An old friend of mine," said Lucy. "I'm here for moral support. Lot of politicians and the like are attending, and my friend is trying to get more funding for after school activities, especially for inner-city kids."

"Oh, sounds like a noble cause," said Keiko.

"Somebody has to watch out for the children, society as a whole does a rather poor job of that," said Lucy staring out at the crowd. "Anyway, what I want to know is why you're doing modeling when it makes you so unhappy?"

"What did you say?" Keiko's eyes opened wide for a moment before narrowing, her fears of this blonde girl being a reporter suddenly resurfacing.

Lucy seemed totally oblivious to the look and only cocked her head slightly, staring into Keiko's eyes in a way she found discomforting. "Sorry, but it just seems that you're doing something you really don't want to be doing."

Smiling widely Lucy poked Keiko in the arm and said, "Or am I wrong?"

Keiko said nothing and stared at the drink grasped tightly with both hands. Shaking her head slightly she downed the last of the champagne and put the glass on the table. The cacophony of all the conversations surrounding her was beginning to weigh down on her mind. She looked up at the ceiling, wondering where Kyle was right now.

Lucy watched her and asked, "Did you drive?"

Keiko looked down at her quickly and almost fell out of her chair. Holding the edge of the table, shaking her head to try and eliminate the fuzziness filling her mind, she said, "No, was going to catch a ride back with Kyle."

"Well then, I'm staying at a hotel down the way," Lucy said leaning forward. "Why don't you spend the night?"

"Nah, I think I'll just call a cab," said Keiko.

Lucy stood up and walked behind Keiko, leaning down and wrapping her arms around the model's neck as she placed her cheek against Keiko's.

"Come on, you're just going to go home and sit around with your cat, right?"

Keiko reached a hand up and put it on Lucy's arm, closing her eyes for a minute. The embrace, though light, was comforting.

"It's not everyday some cute girl asks you to spend the night with her, is it?" asked Lucy. "So what will it be? Come on, answer, answer, answer..."

"Fine, I'll go with you," said Keiko, her fear of being alone overtaking her fear of being around new people.

"Happy," said Lucy giving her a hug and letting go. "Ready to go?"

"Sure."

Grabbing her hand, Lucy led them through the crowd toward the back of the large room. Turning her head slightly she yelled over the din, "We have to find my friend before we take off."

With amazing deftness Lucy wove her way through the crowd without once touching anybody. It was almost as if people were moving out of her way without even knowing she was there. The crowd became denser as they neared the back.

Somebody slammed into Keiko with enough force that she let go of Lucy's hand and almost fell over.

Keiko looked up and saw a tall man, dark hair, with a moustache and beard. He was wearing a black Armani suit. Looking down at her the man said, "Watch where you are going." Two men dressed like he was stood on either side.

"Oh, hi Mikey," she heard Lucy say.

The bright blue eyes of the man became slits. "You... I have nothing to say to you." He turned on his heel and walked away, the two who accompanied him paused a moment before following.

Lucy grabbed Keiko's arm and pulled her close before starting to walk through the crowd. "You'll have to forgive him, he is pretty drunk and not happy to see me."

"Enemy?"

"Nah, nothing like that. He used to be like a brother to me long ago, but we had a big falling out and he hasn't really talked to me since then." Lucy stopped and started jumping up and down waving an arm. "Hey Bee, over here."

A man in his late twenties came over to them. He had sharp features and light brown hair that came to his shoulders, on his face were lines usually reserved for somebody much older. He looked over at Lucy's companion and did a double take. "Is that?" he asked.

"Sure is."

"It's a pleasure," he said. "Hi, you can call be Bee." He extended his hand.

She took his hand. "I'm Keiko."

"Wow, the guys at the office will never believe that I met you.

Mind taking a photo of her and me with my phone?" He asked Lucy. That smile quickly faded with a quick punch to his gut from her.

"Alright now you perv, we gotta go. It's getting late and I have a lot of work to do tomorrow, as always," said Lucy.

Bee had a look of disgust on his face. "Feh, don't remind me. I think I made some progress tonight, but nothing near what is needed. Damn system."

Lucy leaned over to Keiko and whispered, "He's a social worker."

She nodded and Lucy began to pull her through the crowd again. The man called Bee was walking beside Lucy and seemed to have the same skill at avoiding contact with people, one that Keiko wished she had. They wound their way through to the front of the room, then down the elevators. Eventually they arrived outside and were greeted by cool air, which was a relief from the stuffiness and unusual aromas from inside.

A man in a burgundy suit approached, looking over his shoulder he snapped his fingers at someone dressed in a black vest and white shirt. "Ah, Miss Lucy, I trust you had an enjoyable time?"

"Yes, I did, thank you. How are you and your wife doing now?"

"Wonderful," he said, eyes lighting up and smiling widely. "Thank you so much for the advice last time, I think it saved our marriage."

Ruffling the sparse hair on his balding head Lucy said, "No prob, you just keep treating her right and being open and I think you two will be just fine."

An old white Cadillac pulled up and the man in the burgundy coat opened the rear door so that Keiko and Lucy could get in while Bee got into the driver's seat.

Keiko stared out the window as they pulled away, slowly shaking her head at the situation. Her mind wandered to Kyle again and she looked at her hands clasped in her lap.

She heard Lucy begin to sing softly in Japanese. Keiko could not exactly place the song, but it reminded her of one that her Mother used to sing at night to put her and her sister to bed in a life that seemed very far away. She closed her eyes, listening to the tune. Keiko was tired, so tired of so many things. Keiko felt a hand on her shoulder, pulling her down. Listening to the song, Keiko laid her head in Lucy's lap, feeling small hands stroking her hair as she faded

Chapter 01.05

Keiko stirred from her slumber, pulling the sheets over her head to block out the morning light from the window on the other side of the spacious room. She was lying on her side and pulled her free hand around the pillow. *What happened last night?* she wondered to herself, the whole evening seemed rather hazy. There was movement behind her, and Keiko felt an arm wrap around her and a warm breath on her back.

Kami-sama, please not like this. Oh crap, dear Kami-sama, don't tell me I screwed up. Did I tell him? Please don't tell me that we got really drunk and I told Kyle everything!

Panic raced through Keiko and her eyes opened wide, staring at the sheets covering her head. This was not how it was supposed to be, if her Mother found out she would be furious.

Keiko cursed herself silently.

The breath on the back of her neck was sending tingling sensations up and down her spine. Her hand shook as she took Kyle's hand and pulled it to her chest, letting out a soft sigh, resigning herself to a future of truth and not lies.

The hand she held was much smaller than it should have been. Keiko noticed something pressed against her upper back that Kyle did not possess.

Throwing the sheets off her Keiko sat up in bed and looked down to see Lucy, arm now wrapped around Keiko's lap.

Opening one eye Lucy hazily looked up at her. "Morning, cutie. You should really tell him how you feel." Yawning Lucy rolled over and cuddled her pillow.

Keiko began to shake. That's not how things were. She was just fooling herself anyway. She was lucky that he even talked to her, let alone Kyle was her best friend after what she had done. So it was not like that. It was not. Pulling her knees up she placed her forehead against them, wrapping her arms around her legs. She tried to focus, cursing how stupid she was. No luck. Sitting cross legged she tried to focus, to meditate, to do anything to stop her mind from racing.

Keiko let out a scream of frustration and fell backward into the bed.

Lucy, eyes still closed, flipped over and wrapped one leg over Keiko and an arm over her chest. Keiko suddenly realized that although she was wearing a white shirt that was very tight, Lucy was completely naked.

Resting her chin on Keiko's shoulder, Lucy ran her fingers through the dark hair and placed her lips near Keiko's ear. Whispering she said, "If you don't listen to yourself, who will?"

Pulling her head away she turned to look at the semi-asleep face that was smiling at her. Sighing deeply Keiko pulled away slightly and turned away from Lucy. "You are a very strange girl."

Lucy smiled and nuzzled Keiko's neck. She pushed herself up and straddled Keiko, putting her hands on either side of her head and leaning down until her face was inches away. Looking deeply into her eyes she said, "I already told you silly, you don't listen to yourself, so somebody has to say it."

Keiko looked away shyly. "I'm not into this kind of thing, you know. Is that why you're naked?"

"Hmph, avoiding the obvious as always," said Lucy, pressing her finger into Keiko's forehead.

"Whatever, I really appreciate your support, but really this is going a bit too far. I'm straight, so thank you for being a fan but really I cannot go any further," said Keiko, opening her eyes, but making sure to not stare into those intense blue eyes.

In an amazing move of agility Lucy propelled herself several feet into the air, flipped, and landed on her back next to Keiko with her hands behind her head staring up at the ceiling and with her legs extended and crossed at the feet. "Interesting," she whispered.

"Huh?" asked Keiko.

"I need to take a shower, so I call first dibs. You just sit here and think about your life. OK?"

Keiko wanted, for some reason, to argue with the figure closing the bathroom door. Pulling the covers over her, Keiko wiggled her head into the pillow and stared at the ceiling thinking.

She must have fallen back asleep, because a moment later a wet Lucy was shaking her saying it was Keiko's turn.

She took a quick shower and emerged from the bathroom.

Lucy was watching the television and turned it off.

"Hey, Keiko," she said coming into the bedroom with a large paper bag. "I popped out and picked up something for you to wear. Figured you wouldn't want to go around in an evening gown."

Keiko looked at the side of the bag and frowned. "This store is in Beverly Hills, how did you get there and back in fifteen minutes?"

"Come on, I want to see how you look in this," said Lucy.

Keiko's cell phone rang and she jumped onto the bed and grabbed it, looking at the name, quickly flipping it open to answer.

"Kyle! Are you OK?"

Chapter 01.06

The darkness of the room was fading as the sun rose outside. Kyle and the other two men were still taped to the chairs and their captors had said nothing all night long.

His phone had stopped ringing some time before midnight last night, which meant Keiko was probably pissed off at him and Kyle was not looking forward to the aftermath of not showing up at the party last night.

Provided he was alive.

His arms pulled with no success at his bindings and he wanted to kick something, yet unfortunately his legs were bound as well.

Frank had been sitting in the room watching infomercials on the television for several hours from the comfortable chair next to them. Every ten minutes or so he would pull out his pistol unconsciously and play with the safety a few times before putting it back in its shoulder holster.

A phone rang and Frank pulled out an older mobile phone.

"Morning, boss," he said.

Frank looked up at the three men and smiled, nodding his head.

"Understood, sir."

He stood up and kicked their legs, making sure they were awake.

"Guido, Lefty," he yelled. "Get out here."

A minute later the two sleepy men wandered in from the bedroom.

Turning to his bound captives he said, "Well, gentlemen, it would seem that my Boss is in a bad mood today because his Mother is not feeling well. And he only really needs to have a discussion with Mr. Dunne here."

"But you're not letting me or Harry go, are you?" asked Kyle.

"You're pretty bright," he said smiling. "You two, get the duct tape and plastic bags from our little box of fun."

"Sure thing, Frank," they said.

Frank looked down with a solemn face and said, "Don't worry, this won't be painful, you'll just sorta fall asleep while slowly suffocating."

The two men walked into the bedroom at the back of the suite.

There was a cracking noise, followed by a low moan and a thud.

"Hey you ca..." they heard Lefty begin which ended in a scream that was quickly silenced.

"Guido? Lefty? Stop screwing around," said Frank nervously pulling out his pistol.

There was no answer.

Kyle strained to see what was going on, but could only see the body of one of the men lying crumpled on the ground in the bedroom.

Clicking off the safety and holding the gun out Frank cautiously walked over to the bedroom and peered in. "Stop screwing around and get up."

He looked closer at Guido and saw that his head was completely turned around, looking up with glassy eyes at the ceiling while the rest of his body was face down. Frank took a few steps into the room and was pulled out of view with the sound of a sickening crack and a scream of excruciating pain.

Kyle strained to hear Franks pleading words, but could not make them out. There was another cracking noise and the muffled sound of Frank screaming.

A few minutes later Frank came out of the bedroom. His right hand was completely smashed, fingers protruding in directions they were not supposed to, and he was severely limping. As he approached the three men in the chairs he pulled out a knife with his good hand, slightly fumbling to open it.

"Get out of here," said Frank cutting them loose, his words slurred from the injuries to his face as blood poured from his mouth.

"Hold on there, what happened?" asked Thomas standing and shaking his arms and legs.

"I said get out, now," screamed Frank, waving the knife at them.

"But I want to...." Began Thomas.

Kyle and Harry did not even hesitate as they rushed forward and grabbed Thomas' arms on either side, pulling him across the room at a run, opening the doors and sprinting down the hall toward the elevators.

Frank collapsed onto the floor.

"My boss ain't gonna like this," he said.

A woman with long red hair and pale skin stepped out from the bedroom. She slowly walked over and closed the door to the hallway with a towel, taking care to rub every bit of the brass handle, and the wood around it.

"Listen, we was just doing our job," he pleaded.

Her bright green eyes narrowed and she was suddenly standing right in front of him. Placing one hand on his neck she pulled him up off the floor and held him there. He put his good hand around her wrist, trying to pull it away.

"Please," he said in a hoarse voice.

With a quick motion of her arm his head snapped forward then back, the cracking sound of the vertebrae in his neck filled the room, followed by a soft sigh from his body, which she dropped to the ground.

She grabbed the arm of the body on the floor and pulled it into the bedroom.

Thirty minutes later there was a knock on the door, and a gruff voice on the other side said, "Hey, why you buffoons not answering your phones."

The door opened and he stared at the woman on the other side.

"Oh, what, my guys got some entertainment?" he asked, laughing a bit. "I'll give you some extra cash to not talk about those two other idiots they had to take care of."

He pushed past her into the hotel room and began to reach for his wallet.

As the door closed he looked down in shock to see a blade emerging from his chest. He slid off the blade and fell to the floor as a hand covered his mouth to silence his screams of pain.

When he stopped moving the woman stood and looked over her shoulder at the door to the hallway, listening for a minute. All was quiet outside.

Grabbing the towel off the floor she wrapped it around her hand then grabbed the open bottle of whisky from the table. Pouring its contents on the chairs and over to the newest body, she dropped the bottle and towel. Stepping away she pulled a matchbook and lit a single match, tossing it into the awaiting liquid.

The flames began to spread as she closed her eyes and faded from the room.

Chapter 01.07

As the doors of the elevator closed Thomas pulled free from their grip and tossed his hair back with a motion of his head in a manner that seemed well practiced.

"I want to know what happened back there," he said.

"No, I want to know what the hell happened, period," said Kyle glaring at him.

"Oh, sorry you got involved in all that," said Thomas smiling and leaning against the back of the elevator. "I borrowed some money from Mr. Shoemaker a bit ago because my dad is being stingy with funds right now. Should have paid him back, but alas, the horses were against me the other day. Plus for some reason Shoemaker thinks I am having an affair with his lovely daughter. We just talked, really."

Mumbling something under his breath Kyle turned and stared at the doors of the elevator, waiting for them to open.

"And you," said Thomas looking up at Harry. "You, Mister ex-special forces. Why the hell did you let them capture us anyway?"

"Thought it might teach you a lesson," said Harry.

Thomas raised a hand in the air and exclaimed, "I got it."

The other two men looked over at him.

"The way those attacks were so silent, there is only one thing that could have happened. Some Chinese guy borrowed money from Shoemaker, failed to pay it back, and got whacked. Now, his brother who is a monk from the deep mountains of China and knows ancient fighting techniques no one else in the world has ever seen has come back to avenge his death! Lucky for us. Oh, that would make a good story."

Pulling out a pad of paper from his suit coat he jotted down some notes.

Kyle looked at Harry and asked, "Is he on something?"

Harry's weary face frowned. "Unfortunately Master Dunne is

always like this."

"Creative genius," said Thomas tapping the end of the pen against his forehead.

The doors to the elevator opened and they walked into the lobby and towards the doors that led outside.

"I wonder if there is a girl?" asked Thomas. "Bullocks, of course there is. And he befriends her without knowing that she is Shoemakers daughter. Oh, yes."

Kyle walked outside to the valet counter and handed them his ticket and some money.

"But the man who killed his brother, on Shoemaker's behalf, is none other than his childhood rival from school. And this rival is in love with Shoemaker's daughter too."

"That doesn't sound too original," said Kyle.

Thomas paused his writing and looked up. "Nothing is, my friend. But it is how you tell the story that can make it original."

"Um, yeah, of course," said Kyle as his car pulled up and he walked to the other side to get in.

"Hey, want to go get some breakfast?" asked Thomas. "I'm starved."

"I think I'll pass," said Kyle getting in and closing the door.

He put the car into gear and drove down the driveway a bit before stopping suddenly. He pulled out his phone and saw that he had missed twenty-three calls and had nineteen voice mails. Pressing a button it called back the last incoming number.

"Kyle! Are you OK?" asked Keiko desperately.

"Yes, thankfully," he said.

"What happened?"

"It's a long story. Where are you, at home?"

"No, actually at a hotel down the road from where the party was last night."

"Which one?"

"Hold on, not sure," said Keiko.

"Good morning, Ky-Ky," said the voice of a girl he did not recognize. "Keiko's been worried about you."

"Uh, hello," he said. "Who's this?"

"Lucy," said the cute voice on the other end. "I met Keiko at the party last night."

"Right. What hotel are you in?"

25

The girl told him the hotel and room number.

"Got it, I'll be there in a few minutes," he said hanging up the phone.

Chapter 01.08

He had been running down the hallway. By the time Kyle arrived at the room he was breathing heavily. Typing on a keyboard and basking in the rays of a monitor were not legitimate forms of exercise, and the sparring sessions where Keiko had tried to teach him some of her martial arts moves had become less and less as her career had skyrocketed. Putting his hands on his knees a moment he caught his breath before knocking on the door.

It suddenly opened and he saw a young blonde girl with blue eyes dressed in a stylish white shirt and skirt. A smile crossed her face and she jumped up, wrapping her arms around his neck.

"Ky-Ky!" she screamed. She brushed her cheek against his and laughed. "Mmmmm... Scratchy."

He had bent down at the waist a bit so that she was standing on her tiptoes, and his arms were extended straight out on either side as his mind desperately attempted to grasp the situation and why this unknown female was addressing him such and hugging him.

"What are you doing?" he heard Keiko's voice, cold and sharp.

"Nothing!" cried Kyle.

"Oh, just saying hello," said the girl letting go of Kyle suddenly. "I'm Lucy by the way. Come on in."

Lucy turned quickly and walked down the entryway into the room. When she got to Keiko she jumped up and wrapped her arms around her neck. "Keiko! See, now you don't have to be jealous."

Kyle slowly walked in and closed the door behind him.

"I wasn't jealous," said Keiko glancing away from him.

Lucy dropped to the floor, looked up into Keiko's eyes for a second and walked over and sat on the edge of the couch.

Kyle walked into the living room area Keiko began to run toward him, but stopped.

"What the hell happened to you?" she asked walking over slowly and putting a hand on his arm.

He looked down and realized he still had pieces of duct tape on his tuxedo coat and slacks. Shaking his head he walked past her and sat down on the couch, sinking deeply into it and let out a long sigh. He opened his eyes and looked to his left and right at the two staring at him.

"Well," he said, trying to smile while pulling off the silk bow tie and unbuttoning his shirt slightly. "Um, well to top of a crappy day I was kidnapped and almost killed last night."

"What?" exclaimed the females on either side of him simultaneously.

A few minutes later he had brought the two of them up to speed on everything that had happened from the previous night until right now.

"Kyle," said Keiko, sliding over and holding his arm. "This is all my fault, if I hadn't asked you to come out last night... I'm so sorry." She wrapped her arms around his waist and buried her head in his chest. "I was so worried, this is all my fault, I'm so stupid, I'm sorry."

"Keiko," he said putting a finger under her chin and leaning her face up so he could see her eyes. "It's not your fault, so don't worry about it."

She smiled but did not look convinced.

"I just had a run of bad luck or something, so forget about it. We have Christmas and New Years coming up, right? After that I'll find a new job. It will be ok."

"You sure?" she asked.

"Yes."

"You two make a cute couple," said Lucy.

Both of their eyes opened into full circles and Keiko was suddenly sitting on the other side of the couch, far away from Kyle who had moved in the opposite direction but only ran into Lucy. They raised their hands in the air, shaking them.

"No, no, you have it wrong, she says I'm like a brother to her," Kyle said while Keiko simultaneously said, "No, no, you have it wrong, he doesn't like me like that."

Lucy blinked several times, then looked back and forth between them. A smile crossed her face. Standing on the couch she stood over Kyle and sat down in his lap, facing him. She crossed her arms against his chest and looked into his eyes.

"So Kyle, you had a run of bad luck, but you have a good outlook and a good heart, I think you will be just fine."

Kyle, meanwhile, was frozen in place, his left hand on the cushion and the right hand still against the back of the couch. As she talked she moved against him and he began to tremble slightly. He could feel the burning eyes of Keiko staring at the two of them.

"Um, Lucy, could you please get off me?" he asked.

"No," she said raising a hand and stroking her chin. "Hmmmm, let us see. Know what you should do?"

"Heh, uh, what?" he asked. He was quite sure that the far end of the couch was about to burst into flames.

Lucy put her hands to either side of his head and leaned closer. "You should do freelance work, like consulting," she said. "I bet if you call around you probably know enough people who could help you find other contacts."

"Eh, consulting, great idea," he whispered. His body was still frozen in place.

Lucy leaned forward, kissing Kyle on his forehead, then stood and took a few steps backward, looking at the both of them with a slight smile.

"Anyway, both of you think about what I said, got it?"

The two on the couch nodded.

Lucy picked up a small white suit case and purse. "I am going back home," she said. "Just make sure to be out of here by noon, alright? See you later."

She raised her hand and walked to the door and left the room.

"Wait," yelled Keiko running across the room and opening the door. She looked up and down the long hall but it was empty. She stepped out into the hall and looked up and down it again but there was nobody around. Shrugging her shoulders she walked back to Kyle.

"Let's get you home. You had a long night, I'll drive," she said grabbing her phone and the bag off the bed.

Chapter 01.09

Kyle felt himself being shaken from his slumber.

"Onii-chan," he heard mixed with the dream he was having about a blue cat, a supermodel, and a surreal desert with two moons.

He felt a pillow slam into his head.

"C'mon, we're all waiting for you."

Fade on the aliens as his mind meandered in a groggy manner to comprehend where he was and why this sixteen year old girl was currently beating him with a pillow.

"Okaa-san, get the ice water," she yelled out for her Mother.

Kyle managed some semblance of consciousness and sat up, knowing full well that she would douse him with the water given half a chance. Running a hand through his hair he yawned, "Morning, Kami."

"Merry Christmas, Kyle," she said grabbing his arm. "You going to lie in bed all day or come and open presents?"

Looking down at the clock he focused on the numbers. Falling backwards into the bed he moaned, "All day? It's five thirty in the morning!"

"Not my fault you stayed up late playing video games and drinking sake with my sister. Now get your ass out of bed you lamer."

He was then forcibly pulled from the bed and dragged stumbling from the room into the hallway and then to the living room.

"Keiko, get down here," he heard Kami yell up the stairs as they entered another room. She deposited him in the middle of the living room close to the Christmas tree.

"Lazy wannabe supermodel," said Kami. "I'll be back."

Kyle looked up and saw their Mother and Grandmother half asleep on the couch, sitting up very straight, though he could tell that they were trying not to fall over and back asleep.

"Ohayo," he said wishing them a good morning. He bowed forward out of respect and almost fell onto his face, barely catching himself with both hands.

"Koohii?" said Grandmother who only spoke Japanese and had stood to offer him a cup of coffee.

"Arrigato," Kyle said, thanking her, and taking the cup of coffee. The aroma wafted up and his sense of smell sent signals to his brain indicating that a much needed dose of caffeine was about to hit his bloodstream. The first sip of the rich dark liquid confirmed this signal and consciousness was bestowed upon him.

There was a commotion upstairs, some muffled yelling, and then stomping feet coming down the stairs. Kami was walking behind Keiko, arms crossed, while Keiko had a look usually reserved for people she was about to annihilate.

Keiko walked over to Kyle and waved a little hello with a small motion of her hand before turning and bowing to her Mother and Grandmother while wishing them a good morning and a merry Christmas.

"By the way," said Kyle to their Mother. "Thank you for having me over."

She smiled and said, "It is my pleasure, Kyle. With the recent passing of your Grandmother and you being a close friend of our family I could not allow you to be alone today."

Closing his eyes he bowed his head and thanked her.

Everybody turned to look at the sudden outburst.

"No, over here!" exclaimed Kami as Keiko began to sit next to Kyle. She was motioning to the loveseat next to the couch. "Can't have you getting a flat butt, bad for shoots, and anyway, I called first dibs on sitting next to Santa."

"Flat butt?" asked Keiko looking behind her unconsciously.

"Santa?" asked Kyle.

"Sure, you're the only boy here, so you get to be Santa," said Kami ignoring her sister's imminent strike and grabbing a bag next to her. From it she pulled out a Santa hat and put it on Kyle.

He sighed, took a long drink of coffee, looked up at the white fuzz that was above his eyebrows, and then glanced over at Kami. "You are unusually cheerful today."

Leaning over and whispering in his ear, Kami said, "Listen, if you got a problem with me liking presents or being happy for one day out of the friggin year I will gladly remove that mouth of yours if you say one more lame-ass comment. Now smile and laugh."

His eyes opened wide, and he almost spit out the mouth full of coffee. She pulled back and looked up at everybody smiling as he swallowed, paused for half a second and said the first thing that came to his mind. "Yes, 'tis the season and all."

"You're such a loser," she whispered sideways to him.

"If the two of you are finished flirting perhaps we should open presents?" said Grandmother in Japanese, with a slight smile.

Kyle opened his mouth and managed an 'ahhhh' sound, Kami stammered something incomprehensible and Keiko, who had sat down a few seconds earlier, had both hands on the edge of the cushions about to launch out of the loveseat.

"Children, please," said Mother.

Managing a forced laugh, Kyle reached over and grabbed the first present. The distribution of presents continued, with openings and thanks, until there was only one left. This is the one that Keiko had told him to save for last. A large smile crossed his face as he took it and handed it to Grandmother.

Bowing her head and thanking him she took the long thin box and began to open it, carefully pulling back each piece of tape so as to not damage the wrapping paper. When she was about half way through unwrapping it he saw Kami begin to move forward, mentioning helping, but this motion was halted by a glare from their Mother. Kami sighed and sat back down.

The wrapping paper successfully removed, Grandmother opened the side of the white box and pulled out a picture frame. She looked at the picture for a moment, it was a recent picture of an old house. She smiled and nodded, looking over at Keiko and displaying the photograph to everybody.

"I remember this fondly. This is where I grew up. It had been in our family for generations before my father had to sell it because of the war. Did you take this yourself, Keiko?"

"Hai," she said. "I was in Japan recently for a photo shoot."

A sad look crossed Grandmother's face for an instance and she smiled again. "Thank you, it is a wonderful present."

"No, Grandmother, that is a picture of your present," said Keiko in Japanese.

Grandmother's eyes opened wide.

Keiko nodded and said, "It is back in our family now."

Tears began to stream from Grandmother's eyes as she pressed the picture to her chest. She placed the frame carefully on the table and stood, walking slowly over to Keiko who had stood also.

"You honor our family so, this day is indeed a great day," she said bowing to Keiko.

ROOMMATES

Chapter 02.01

It was the middle of January and Kyle was staring at his main monitor trying to be proactive and figure what email card to send to Keiko for Valentine's Day. Something kind of happy, but not sappy, and not leading to innuendos and such. He found one with a kitten, thought about it for a minute, then closed the browser window, pounding his palm into his head.

"How difficult can it possibly be?" he muttered to himself.

Kyle spun around in his chair several times and hopped out, wandering over to the bed and turning to fall backwards onto it. He stared at the ceiling hoping for some inspiration that would allow him to send something that might possibly bridge this hopeless title of being 'like a brother'.

In frustration he rolled over and hit the pillow.

Lying back he tried to think of anything. His extreme inability started pissing himself off to the point that he hopped off the bed and started up a game that always managed to relieve frustration.

Kyle had the enemy lined up in his sights and was about to issue a satisfying death when there was a knock on the door. In the space of Kyle pausing to recognize this and say, "Come in," he found himself dead.

"Baka!" he cried tossing the mouse to the side.

Ed opened the door slowly and surveyed the room. "Mess up your game?"

"Don't worry about it," said Kyle.

"Cool. But I think you shouldn't spend twenty-four seven in front of a screen," said Ed.

Kyle stopped spinning in his chair and asked, "What's up?"

"Sorry to bother you, but I buzzed in some kid with long blond hair and an older guy who say their old friends of yours, and they want to talk to you."

"What did you say?"

"I think his name started with a T. Maybe a C.," Said Ed.

Kyle sunk into his chair and grimaced.

"A guy named Thomas?" asked Kyle.

"Yeah, that's it. You know them?"

"With long blond hair?"

Ed nodded and cocked his head. "Dude, you drunk or some-thing?"

"No. No, no, no... Completely sober, but that may change very soon," said Kyle. He stood and walked past Ed and down the stairs. The only two people he had told about the unfortunate events ending the worst day of his life had been Keiko and that Lucy girl. Ed obviously would not know.

Opening the front door he saw Thomas and Harry standing on the other side. Behind them were a stack of various sized suit cases.

"My friend," said Thomas stepping in and giving Kyle a hug. "How have you been?"

"What are you doing here?" asked Kyle pulling backwards and taking a step away. "How did you find me?"

"Well then, those are two completely different questions, are they not?" stated Thomas. "I seem to have run into a bit of a financial problem and need a place to stay. Gads, do you know how many female police officers I had to seduce until I could finally get one to run your license plate?"

"Financial problems?" asked Kyle. "Sorry, can't help, last thing I need is a bunch of thugs kidnapping me again."

"Oh, that," said Thomas laughing and holding out both hands, palms up. "Did you not see the news the next day? Shoemaker and his three employees were found dead in that room that very day, some terrible fire or the likes. And without him around everything is cleared up. I still suspect it was the Chinese gentleman set on revenge."

"Of course," said Kyle, hand on the door, ready to close it.

"Unfortunately the reason I am here now is because my stingy father recently decided that I need to be more responsible, and as such for no reasons I can comprehend has cut off all my funds. He even terminated my cell phone! How can somebody exist without a phone

I ask? Alas, he is a business man and cannot comprehend a creative genius such as myself."

"Creative genius?" came a soft voice next to them.

Startled, but not exactly surprised, Kyle had jumped slightly to the side and knocked a table with a vase that he barely caught before it fell to the floor. Meanwhile Harry had lunged forward, grabbing Thomas and pulling away from the opening of the door, swinging the young man behind him as he raised his hands in a defensive position.

Standing next to where Kyle had been was a young woman with black hair that flowed over her shoulders. She was wearing a black dress with black lace, black boots, and her gloved hands were crossed at her waist. She looked at the three of them silently and did not move. In her dark eyes was a glint that was deeper than even the night.

"Cynthia," said Kyle. "What are you doing here?"

"I came over to visit with my boyfriend."

Kyle stepped away from the table and toward her, pointing toward the two men standing outside. "Ah, well. This is Thomas and his friend Harry. I kind of met them back before Christmas."

"Keiko told me about that incident," she said quietly.

Stepping from behind Harry and back into the house, Thomas walked slowly toward Cynthia.

"Such darkness, such beauty," he said smiling and reaching out his hands. "I have been consumed lately with the need to paint, and I cannot think of anyone on this planet that I would want to paint more than you, my dearest Cynthia."

He was lowering his hands to place them on her shoulders. Kyle tried to warn him, but was too late. Thomas was flung backward ten feet into Harry who barely managed to remain standing.

"Do not touch me," she whispered, her eyes becoming slits.

Thomas leapt up and grabbed Harry's arms. "Did you see that? Neither did I. She was so fast I did not see what hit me."

Harry glanced quickly down to Thomas then back to the young girl in black, still in a defensive position, trying to determine the treat level apparently.

Walking back into the house Thomas bowed slightly and said, "My apologies, dearest Cynthia, I was overzealous and apologize for trying to touch you."

Turning to face the stairs she said quietly over her shoulder, "I do not see a problem with this, Kyle, as long as they pay rent. You should not allow them to stay here free."

Kyle paused a moment, waiting to see if there was more she would say, but was only greeted with her silent ascent to the top of the stairs.

"Anyway, come in," said Kyle motioning for them to go down the hall.

"What was that just now," asked Harry placing a hand on Thomas' shoulder to prevent him from going further.

"Huh?" asked Kyle looking over to Harry who seemed either agitated, paranoid, or both. "Oh. That's just Cynthia. She's kind of quiet so nobody notices her half the time. You get used to it. So come on in."

"Thank you so much," said Thomas, walking away from the firm hand on his shoulder. "Would it be too much of a bother for us to at least bring our things inside?"

Kyle looked past them at the suitcases. "Not right now, we need to talk first."

Thomas seemed to pale a little, stopping, then was pushed forward into the house by Harry as Kyle closed the door behind them. He walked past and they followed him to the living room.

"By the way, beautiful place you have here. Reminds me of my father's summer home," said Thomas sitting down on the couch, leaning back, and stretching his legs.

Harry sat next to him, and Kyle sat in one of the chairs to the side.

"So you don't have anybody else you owe money to or has a cause to harm you?" asked Kyle.

Thomas cocked his head and looked at the ceiling. "None that I can think of off-hand, can you Harry?"

Harry shook his head.

"And why are you here exactly?" asked Kyle.

"You seemed like a nice guy," said Thomas. "After all, most blokes would have punched me square in the face after we got out of there. But I am truly desperate. My father locked my savings and checking accounts, canceled my credit cards, and revoked the lease on my car. He even took away my cell phone! Can you believe it?"

"Why not just go back home?"

"And admit defeat?" cried Thomas. "Never! I came to California to fine tune my creativity and make it big. I cannot give up now!"

"And there isn't anybody else you can stay with?"

"Well, no," said Thomas. "To tell you the truth I was living the life of a playboy since I came out here and it is amazing how when all of my money is gone so were my friends. So what do you say?"

"I'm still thinking," said Kyle.

Ed came down the stairs and walked into the living room, stopping next to the couch.

"By the way, I'm Ed," he said raising a hand, the chains on his tattooed arm jingling.

Thomas stood up and grabbed Ed's hand out of the air, shaking it enthusiastically. "Pleasure to meet you, my good man. I am Dunne, Thomas Dunne, and this is my Man Servant, Harry."

"Hi," said Ed pulling his hand away.

"Yes, of course," said Thomas standing there for a moment before sitting back on the couch.

"We are going to get some drinks, would any of you like something?" asked a soft voice next to Thomas.

Standing in the space that had been empty moments before was Cynthia. Both Thomas and Harry jumped slightly and made a startled exclamation.

"I'll take some wine," said Kyle. "You two want anything?"

Flipping his long hair back Thomas said, "Cognac if there is any available."

"Harry?"

"I rarely drink, but thank you for the offer," he said.

Kyle pulled out some money and handed it to Cynthia, who nodded her head slightly and then left the room with Ed.

"She seems like a very interesting person," said Thomas. "I still want to paint her, mind you."

Standing up Kyle walked over to the coffee table and grabbed the remote. He turned on the television and tossed the remote over to Thomas, who was staring down the hall Cynthia had walked down, so it bounced off his chest and onto the cushions.

"Harry, will you come with me for a moment?" asked Kyle.

"What about me?" asked Thomas sitting forward quickly.

"Watch TV for a bit, we'll be right back."

Thomas nodded uncomfortably and glanced at them a few times before he grabbed the remote.

The two of them walked across the living room to the sliding glass doors, then out onto the stone patio. Kyle closed the door behind them and watched Thomas for a moment before turning and walking to the edge of the patio, stopping just short of the grass.

He looked across the lawn and then up at the sky. "What do you think, Harry?"

"Honestly, sir?" he asked walking over and standing behind him. Kyle nodded his head.

"Thomas is a good kid, at heart, albeit a touch eccentric," said Harry. "And he does have a tendency to act without thinking."

"What about his situation, is all that true?"

"Unfortunately it is," said Harry. "He is not very responsible with money, but never had a reason to be so. I have raised him since he was a child, you see. His parents are too busy to bother with such things, and they are the type who believes if you throw enough money at a problem it will be solved. It would seem that Sir Dunne has come to the conclusion that is not working with his son."

He paused a moment. "Please forgive me, but to speak honestly, if Thomas goes back, his father will crush any bit of individuality out of him and make Thomas just another corporate suit. If you are going to do that to him, you might as well just put a bullet in his head.

"I understand that we did not meet you in the most hospitable of manners, and I do so apologize for that situation, as I am partially to blame. I had no idea they would take it that far, otherwise I would have intervened when those men first showed up. But he is in a bind, and does need a place to stay. This is at your discretion of course, and if we become a nuisance, please inform me and we shall leave immediately."

"Thank you, Harry," said Kyle. "I will be back inside in a few minutes."

"Thank you for giving me the opportunity to clarify matters, Master Kyle," said Harry bowing his head and going back to the living room.

Kyle walked over and leaned against one of the wooden beams that held up the roof over the patio, thinking about Harry's words. Thinking about the present. A little over a year ago all was quiet here. It was just himself and his Grandmother, living in this large house of empty dreams. All those rooms and his grandparents had only one child, his Mother, before his Grandfather had died.

Kyle smiled in a melancholy way, thinking back. He would work at the company during the day, tending the computer needs of misguided employees and executives, then come home and help his Grandmother cook dinner, do work around the house. If Keiko was in town he would go out with her once or twice a week, this was right before her simultaneous covers of FHM and Maxim which seems to have been the push she needed to make it big. Ed would drop by on occasion and pester him, saying Kyle needed to get out more and get a real girlfriend. Sometimes they would go for drinks at this small pub hidden behind a parking lot down in Old Towne to catch up. Of course Ed usually did most of the talking because nothing much happened in Kyle's life.

Then, in a matter of three days, his Grandmother was gone. And he was alone in the house. Ed had never exactly asked to move in. He had basically announced he was going to six weeks after the funeral. Looking back Kyle knew why now, but at the time he was too numb to object. And in time Ed and Cynthia convinced him that it was a bit morbid to just leave his Grandmother's room as it was, that he should take over the master bedroom. Back then he was still pretty much an automaton, but something in his subconscious pushed him to do so. In time he did his best to accept what had happened, accepted that he was the one who owned this house now and lived in the master bedroom. Accepted that she was gone and he had no more family.

So life continued, but different. Then a little over a month ago he was sitting in a hotel room duct-taped to a metal chair with Thomas and Harry. It was morning and he was sure he was about to die, and Kyle had wondered to himself if he should have done more with his life. Tried harder, had some dream or anything normal people seemed to have or want for themselves

And yet he still did not have any answers to the questions that had had come to his mind in that horrible situation. Perhaps he was only an automaton living life now as a consultant, still with a girl he wanted to be with who thought of him only as a brother. A life devoid of meaning.

Kyle covered his face with both of his hands and let out a long sigh.

A few minutes later he heard the door slide open and looked over his shoulder.

"Yo, we're back," said Ed.

"Hey, Ed, come here a minute," said Kyle turning around. "I

want to ask you something."

Ed stared to walk forward and saw Kyle's hand motion. Reaching behind him he slid the door shut.

"So what's up?" asked Ed.

Kyle told him about Thomas' request, his conversation with Harry, and his decision.

"Ah, well, dude, it's your place and all," said Ed. "He seems pretty cool. But I agree with you, give him a chance and if it doesn't work just give him the boot."

"Thanks," said Kyle opening the door.

As the two of them were entering the kitchen they heard a loud crash and a cry of pain. Rushing through the kitchen to the bar area they saw Thomas lying on his back, the stool next to Cynthia lay on the floor by his feet.

"Ha ha, you tried to sit next to Cyn, didn't ya?" asked Ed reaching down and helping Thomas up.

Thomas stood then raised both hands defensively. "I was just going to talk, I swear. I was not trying to hit on her."

"Dude, if you had put the moves on her we'd be covering your body with a blanket right now, so don't worry about it. Here have a seat."

Ed led Thomas to the other end of the bar and sat down next to him.

"What would you like?" asked Harry who was standing behind the bar.

"Woah, why are you back there?" asked Ed.

"I do not drink, so I shall take care of your needs. Is that permissible, Master Kyle?" he asked.

"Sure."

"Oh, in that case can I have my Corona?" asked Ed.

"And I'll have a double Cognac, straight up."

"And I need a lime," said Ed.

"Right away, gentlemen," said Harry.

As the three of them were talking they did not notice the chair lift up from the floor and return to its spot. Kyle pulled it out slightly and sat next to Cynthia who had remained unmoving this whole time.

"Thanks," he said.

She inclined her head and slid a glass of wine in front of him with one of her hands clad in black leather gloves.

He took a sip and said, "Excellent taste as always." Kyle reached out and turned the bottle to inspect the label. Lifting the bottle he said, "I'm going to head upstairs, do you mind?"

"Please," she said, barely audible over the others talking. "There is another one."

Walking to the other end of the bar he set the bottle down.

"Thomas, Harry," said Kyle.

"My friend, this is excellent cognac," said Thomas. "Thank you."

"This is my decision," said Kyle taking a sip of wine and looking at the two of them. "You have two weeks here. If at the end of those two weeks you are not working, unable to pay rent, causing problems, or it is just not working out you will have to leave. Understood."

Tears began to form in Thomas' eyes as he jumped up and gave Kyle a hug.

"Thank you, thank you, thank you," he said. "You're a life saver, you truly are. When I become famous and write my autobiography, this moment will stand as one of the pivotal points in my path to fame."

Kyle pulled away from him. "You can use the room next to Ed's. There's not much in there except for a few dressers and a desk, but it should serve you fine. You'll find two futons in the closet, along with sheets and pillows."

"Futons? Those couches that pull out?" asked Thomas raising an eyebrow.

"No, like the mattress part," said Ed. "It's a Japanese thing."

Thomas grabbed Kyle's shoulders and looked intently into his face. "You look more European than Japanese."

"That is because I am of Irish descent," said Kyle. "I just have a deep respect of the Japanese culture."

"There you have it then," said Thomas as he let go and sat back down.

"Well then, I'm out," said Kyle grabbing the bottle of wine and starting to walk away. "Have some work to do. Night."

"You know," said Ed spinning around, "I wonder if you are really that busy or you just use work as an excuse to not have a social life."

"It is his choice if he does not want to be around people," said a soft voice at the end of the bar.

The three at the bar jumped slightly and looked over, partially because they had forgotten she was sitting there.

Kyle paused for half a second then continued to the door, "Have a good evening."

He heard the farewells behind him but paid little attention.

Ascending the stairs he went to his room and closed the door. Sitting down in the computer chair he moved the mouse to clear the anime screensaver and opened a new browser window. He had failed at finding an e-card, so now the mad search for a Valentine's Day present was now on. If he took care of this now then he would not end up at a twenty-four hour drug store at one in the morning on Valentine's Day frantically trying to find something to buy.

He scrolled through pages and pages of products. Got bored of looking and pulled up the Asahi Shinbun website since he had not checked the news today. He was reading through the current articles when he finished off his wine and went to pour himself another glass. As he did so an empty glass appeared next to his with delicate fingers, clad in black leather, holding the stem.

Cynthia was leaning against the edge of his desk, holding out her glass.

Kyle smiled and shook his head. "What's on your mind?" he asked.

"Ed," she said barely above a whisper.

"Good or bad?"

"Unknown."

He regarded her a moment.

"Well, that's probably not good," he said filling their glasses.

"Most likely."

Cynthia stared out the large windowed doors that led to his balcony, beyond which was a small valley and above the star filled sky. She sat there and sipped her wine in silence.

Kyle typed in the URL to a different store and looked through a few pages. He sighed.

"That horrid day of hearts approaches," whispered Cynthia.

Kyle nodded his head. This site had nothing of interest. He went to another store's site and started browsing what they had to offer. There was a new figurine of a character from one of the anime series Keiko liked coming out next week, the mouse cursor hovered over the buy button.

"What indeed to buy a supermodel who has almost everything?

41

And what should you buy so as to not look like you are really attracted to her?"

"Bah, tell me about it. Sucks."

Cynthia fell silent again for a few minutes. Kyle continued to browse hoping inspiration might hit.

"Did Ed tell you about Germany?" she asked, her glass dropping slightly.

"The tour? Yeah, earlier today. That what got you in a funk?"

She did not move. "Perhaps, all things change."

Cynthia made a slight movement with her hand toward the other side of the room. Kyle saw this out of his peripheral vision and nodded, standing as she walked across the room and pushed the handle of the door down, stepping out onto the balcony that overlooked the valley. Closing the door behind him, Kyle walked across the balcony and leaned against the railing with his back, looking into the room.

Cynthia stood near the railing. She was perfectly still, with the wine glass held before her, looking down and watching a car drive along the road at the bottom of the valley. "Do you think he loves me?"

"No, he has been with you for six years because he hates you," he replied.

"Kyle..." the word was spoken slowly, the temperature around them seemed to drop fifteen degrees.

"Sorry," he said glancing at her. "But you know damn well he does."

"It would seem so." She took a drink of her wine. "Does he have an interest in other women?"

Kyle shrugged. Turning around and leaning against the railing he said, "Ed's a guy, and yeah, he makes comments about other girls sometimes. But mainly to tease me. Like, 'wow, she's cute, maybe you should go ask her out' type stuff."

"But when I am not around does he flirt with other women?"

"Cyn, you know he flirts with everybody. Boy, girl, gay, bi. That's just Ed. I don't think he cares about stuff like that."

Cynthia was silent. She was looking into the darkness of the trees that lined the side of the yard.

"Look, if what you are asking is if Ed will cheat on you in Europe, then I would say no."

She looked sideways at him.

"The few times you haven't been at one of his gigs there have been groupie types who were seriously trying to get him, but Ed completely ignored their advances, actually seemed oblivious to them. You are his love and his muse."

Cynthia turned her head and looked at Kyle for a moment. He glanced over at her. The normally emotionless eyes seemed to betray something, but in a flash it was gone and replaced by cold darkness.

"I wonder if that is a good thing," she whispered.

Kyle frowned at her. "How do you mean?"

Cynthia stared into his eyes for a short time before looking back into the night. Slowly she looked down at her glass and then took another sip of wine.

"Are you alright?" asked Kyle.

She did not answer. Kyle watched her for a short time, expecting a response, but when none came he turned and looked out into the night also, watching the stars above. In the distance was the sound of the freeway, and the insects of the night.

After a few minutes he looked over at her and said, "Need a refill?"

But she was gone. Kyle stared at where Cynthia had been standing, then walked across the balcony and opened the door, crossed the room, and sat back down at his computer.

Chapter 02.02

Kyle awoke to the alarm and after a time dragged himself out of his comfortable bed, slowly. Opening the door he shuffled down the hallway. As he approached the stairs a scent registered. The smell of coffee.

Navigating the stairs he went to the kitchen and found Harry standing next to the stove wearing one of his Grandmother's floral print aprons. This alone caused Kyle to stop and stare.

"Good morning, Master Kyle," said Harry. "How are you this morning?"

"Ugh, fine," said Kyle.

"I have prepared some coffee," said Harry. "How do you take it?"

Kyle sat down at the kitchen table, finding the situation of having somebody awake and ready to serve him coffee somewhat surreal.

"Black."

"Very well then," said Harry walking over to a cupboard and opening the door. "Might you have a preference in cups?"

"Uh, larger the better," said Kyle, rubbing his eyes.

"As you wish," said Harry pulling out a very large coffee cup and pouring the coffee into it. Placing it before Kyle he said, "I hope it is to your satisfaction."

"Thank you."

"Please forgive me, Master Kyle, as I realize it is still probably early for you, but might you have an idea of what you would like for breakfast?"

Kyle stared at him.

"Or should I choose something for you, if you do not mind?"

"Uh, Harry?"

"Yes, Master Kyle."

"You're just renting a room here. I didn't hire you to be a chef or anything."

The smile on Harry's face faded.

"Sir," he said. "May I be honest?"

"Sure."

"I am not quite sure if Master Thomas has any redeemable job skills to procure any type of work so that he may pay rent. The least I can do in the interim is contribute my skills to your household."

"Oh," said Kyle. "Um, ok, sure. Can you make waffles? I haven't had those in over a year, if it's not too much trouble."

"Absolutely no trouble at all," said Harry smiling again.

"I know we have one of those waffle maker things around," said Kyle.

"No need to worry, Master Kyle," said Harry. "I tend to wake early, and have already have performed a full inventory of the kitchen."

Walking over to a cabinet, he opened it and reached to the far back, pulling out the dusty appliance. Harry opened it, and said, "If you please, I can clean this and prepare your breakfast so that you can catch up on the morning news or whatever morning routine you usually have."

"Harry?" asked Kyle.

"Yes, sir?"

"Sorry, but this is a bit strange to me."

"Worry yourself not," said Harry. "Would you also like some eggs and bacon with your breakfast?"

"What?" asked Kyle. "We have bacon and eggs?"

"Well, no, sir. I went out and picked some up earlier this morning."

"Oh, sure, I guess," said Kyle. "Do you need any help? I'm not bad at cooking."

"Master Kyle?"

"Yes?"

"Please, enjoy your morning. I shall prepare breakfast."

"Thank you, Harry. I really appreciate it."

"Might I inquire as to how you would like your eggs?"

"Scrambled will be fine," said Kyle.

Harry nodded and then started making a motion with his hand for him to leave. Grabbing the exceedingly large cup of coffee, Kyle went into the living room and turned on the television. He flipped through some stations. He had never been inclined to watch the news because of the blatant bias it tended to have, so opted instead for what was on the Discovery channel.

A short way through the show Harry stepped from the kitchen and said, "Your breakfast is ready, Master Kyle. Would you like to eat it there, in the kitchen, or the dining room?"

Flipping off the television Kyle said, "The kitchen should be fine."

"Very well, sir, at your convenience."

Kyle leaned forward and grabbed the coffee, taking several long drinks now that it was not at a temperature reserved for residents of hell. He finished off half of the cup quickly before he stood and made his way back to the kitchen.

And there, sitting upon the table, was a plate with fresh golden brown waffles, butter slowly melting into the squares, surrounded by bacon and scrambled eggs. Kyle stared at the plate for a moment, filled with a moment of melancholy.

"Is everything fine, Master Kyle?" asked Harry with a concerned note in his voice.

Sitting down Kyle said, "It looks very good."

Grabbing the knife and fork he took a sample of the egg first. Then the bacon. After that he gabbed the cup of syrup, which was warm, and poured it onto the waffles before cutting off a piece and eating the bite. His mouth turned into a smile.

"Harry," said Kyle. "This is delicious."

"Thank you," said Harry.

"Please, enjoy your breakfast," said Harry. "If you need anything, please call for me." With that he excused himself and walked out of the kitchen.

As Kyle was eating his breakfast he heard the heavy steps of boots coming down the stairs, then they approached the kitchen. Ed walked in and surveyed the area.

"What the hell? You suddenly get inspired or something?" asked Ed.

"No, all Harry's doing," said Kyle taking another bite and waving his fork in the air.

Harry appeared in the doorway of the other end of the kitchen.

"Oh, my, gawd," said Ed seeing Harry in his floral print apron. "Look at Mister Homemaker there. Damn you look pretty sexy in that."

Harry paused a second, looking at Ed before glancing furtively around the room.

"Dude, she's gone, left last night, had a meeting this morning or something," said Ed.

"I did not hear her leave," said Harry. "And I am a very light sleeper."

Kyle and Ed nodded their heads.

"But how?"

They shrugged their shoulders. Ed went to the coffee maker and grabbed a travel mug out of the cupboard, filling it up and adding several spoonfuls of sugar. Snapping his arm up, he checked the time on his spiked watch.

"Been fun, but have to go push musical equipment on budding wannabe rock stars," he said heading toward the door.

"Have a good day," said Kyle.

"Ciao," came the response as he walked out of the room with a hand raised.

Kyle finished his breakfast and had begun to wash off the plate when Harry had intervened and insisted he take care of it. Reluctantly Kyle went back to the living room to flip through channels before meeting with his client in a few hours.

He still found it odd, after working so many jobs in his life, that he was his own company now, and doing rather well, even though it had been only a month now. As Lucy had predicted, he had gotten up the nerve to make a few phone calls and was now making more per month doing freelance work than he had ever made before at a normal company.

Hearing somebody come into the room, Kyle saw Thomas, who walked over and suddenly gave him a hug for no apparent reason. The young man's hair was in a braid that almost reached his waist, and he was wearing a dark blue silk bathrobe with the letters TD surrounded by a heart on the left side, in pink.

"Good morning Thomas," he said hesitantly pulling away.

Thomas raised his left hand and placed it firmly on Kyle's shoulder, smiling. Glancing around the room he raised his right hand and said, "Good morning indeed! A wonderful morning. A spectacular morning. A new morning. Who knows what fruits this day may bear us, but we shall dine upon their succulent juices and enjoy every moment of it."

Harry appeared in the doorway of the kitchen and said, "Good morning Master Thomas. I see you are as jovial as always. Shall I prepare some breakfast for you?"

Letting go of Kyle's shoulder, Thomas leaped over the couch and ran over to Harry.

"Good morning to you also, Harry," he said giving Harry a big hug. Pulling away and placing his hands on Harry's shoulders he said, "Indeed. Indeed I am ready for another one of your beautiful morning creations."

"Very well then. The usual, Master Thomas?" asked Harry.

"Excellent idea," said Thomas dropping his hands and turning around. Walking across the room to the couch he said over his shoulder, "Thank you Harry."

"My pleasure, Master Thomas," said Harry returning to the kitchen.

Sitting down, Thomas asked, "And what might you be watching this fine morning?"

Kyle sat down on the other side of the couch and said, "Not much. Nothing on really. Just burning some time before I have to go see a client."

"How interesting," he said.

"Your breakfast is ready, Master Thomas," said Harry behind them several minutes later.

"Wonderful!" he exclaimed. "I shall eat it here if Kyle does not mind."

"Knock yourself out," said Kyle.

Harry walked across the living room and around the couch, then placed a plate on the table containing three Pop-Tarts along with a glass of orange juice on a coaster.

"Ah, thank you my good man," said Thomas grabbing the plate and starting to eat.

Kyle watched as Thomas started devouring the contents of the plate.

"Breakfast of champions?"

"Mmmph," he replied swallowing a large bite. "Indeed it is. Nothing fuels the creative spirit like sugar."

"Or alcohol," added Harry.

"Quite true, quite true," said Thomas taking another bite. "But a bit too early for that."

"By the way," said Kyle. "I forgot to mention this, but down that hall off the living room, the last room to the right is Keiko's. She stays here from time to time to get away from everything, so don't be alarmed if you hear somebody enter the house and go in there."

The two nodded.

Leaning forward Kyle grabbed the remote and set it next to Thomas.

"Well, need to get ready for my meeting," he said.

There came a high pitched buzz from the front door. Kyle looked over to the clock and saw that it was a little after ten, and he was not expecting any visitors this morning. Going down the hallway to the entry he pressed a button.

"I am looking for Kyle," came the voice from the speaker.

He did not recognize the voice. "And you are?"

"Jonathon Williams."

"Jonathon Williams?"

"Yes, Jonathon Williams." There was a note of irritation in the voice.

"Sorry, whatever your sales pitch is I am either saved, already have it, or not interested."

Kyle let up on the button and began to walk down the hall.

The box buzzed again.

Narrowing his eyes he turned around and pressed the button to talk again. "Persistent?"

"No, Keiko's agent."

Kyle paused a moment as the name registered. "Oh, sorry, please come on up." He pressed a different button to open the front gates.

Running down the hall he came up to Thomas and Harry who were standing several feet away. "Listen, its Keiko's agent, and I don't know why he's here, so why don't the two of you go watch TV in your room."

Thomas smiled. "Do we have to?"

"Yes, now," said Kyle pulling him up from the couch.

Kyle ran upstairs to his room, threw on a pair of blue jeans, and a T-shirt before he dashed into the bathroom to quickly brush his hair. The doorbell downstairs rang. Running back to the front door Kyle opened it.

The man on the other side of the door was slightly taller with a professional haircut and a dark blue designer suit under a designer tan trench coat. Smiling with teeth that were a bit too white he extended his well manicured hand.

"Kyle," came the name with artificial sweetness. "Jonathon Williams, so good to finally meet you."

"Same," said Kyle extending his hand. The handshake he received was one of those well practiced firm, but not too strong, lasting exactly three seconds, pausing for a half second, then a slight squeeze before releasing, that seemed to be standard protocol amongst suits.

Kyle decided to let him stand there.

Jonathon's smile widened as he glanced past Kyle to the inside of the house.

He stood there a second before saying, "Would you mind if I came in, I would like to talk to you for a few minutes."

Flashing a quick half-smile, Kyle took a few steps back and motioned with his hand to enter. As Jonathon closed the door behind him Kyle motioned to the coat rack.

"Oh, how wonderful, a coat rack. You rarely see these here in California these days," said Jonathon taking off his trench coat and hanging it.

"Not really a California thing," said Kyle.

Turning around and raising a finger, Jonathon said, "You know, I bet you are right." Big smile.

"Anyway, this way," said Kyle walking down the hall into the living room. Motioning to the couch he sat down in the chair.

Jonathon sat down, crossed his legs, and placed his hands in his lap.

"Quite a beautiful place you have here," said the agent.

"Thank you," said Kyle.

"Amazing that somebody in your line of work can live in a place like this, but then again I understand you inherited this house," another smile.

A red flag went up. "Oh, so Keiko has told you about everything?"

"That is neither here or there," he said with another smile. "I just wanted to talk to you about a few things."

Kyle nodded.

Keiko's foray into modeling had begun innocently enough with a small company that on occasion was lucky to land its models in ads or catalogs for chain clothing stores. During a spring fashion show in the Glendale Galleria she had been approached by Jonathon, asking her to join his agency.

Shortly thereafter she had signed on with them, seeing it as her chance to achieve her dreams. They had several big name models on their roster. He remembered the day she had come back from signing the contracts. Keiko had a talk with Kyle about not wanting to drag him into this business if she ever became a professional model. In her words, their friendship would be theirs, and her new modeling company would not know of him. At that time he had offered her a place to stay, with his Grandmothers blessings, if she ever needed a place to get away from it all.

"Well," said Kyle, leaning back in his chair and eyeing Jonathon cautiously. "I hate to be brief, but I do have an appointment shortly. What may I help you with?"

"I understand, busy busy busy," said Jonathon. "I wanted to talk to you about Keiko's career, to tell you the truth."

Kyle said nothing and just watched the man on the couch.

Shifting his position slightly, Jonathon raised his hand, pointing his index finger up, and said, "You see, Keiko's career is right on the cusp. She is doing incredibly well, and is poised to join the top ranks of Super Models."

"I am glad to hear of this," said Kyle.

"Yes, it is wonderful news, isn't it? Unfortunately, in this business image is, really, everything. And she has this habit of disappearing at times. After some inquiry I discovered that she usually comes over here." Flash of a smile. "Now, please understand that this business is quite fickle, and that image is really everything."

"Yes, you just mentioned that, twice" said Kyle.

Jonathon seemed lost in thought for a moment before he uncrossed his legs, then crossed them again, before he repositioned his hands in his lap. "So if it were to get out that she was secretly seeing a, please forgive the term, computer geek, that could have a negative effect on her career."

"Seeing?"

"Yes."

"As in?"

"Dating, involved with, doing who knows what behind closed doors," said the agent. "If the tabloids or magazines found out about this they would have a field day."

"Keiko and I are only friends, that is all," said Kyle leaning back into the chair.

Jonathon paused and smiled again. "Of course you are."

"No, really, we are just good friends," said Kyle.

"Call it what you will, I still think that you should consider her career." Jonathon shifted his position again, raised his hands, uncrossed then crossed his legs, and put his hands to his sides on the cushions of the couch.

Kyle cocked his head, paused a moment and said, "I do, but what does the two of us being friends have to do with her career?"

Grabbing the edge of the couch Jonathon leaned forward and said, "Listen, she is mine. I mean she is my client," he said as his shoulders rose and his eyes narrowed. "I am not going to have you destroy her career over some petty friendship."

Raising a hand, Jonathon pointed a finger at Kyle and said, "Let me make this perfectly clear, whatever relationship you two have is over. I cannot manage somebody that disappears like that, how can I manage her properly if I do not know where she is? If you care about her then just let her go and live her life. Because a model of her caliber should not be involved with somebody like you."

Kyle stared at him, partially in shock, partially in anger. Jonathon seemed to realize that his hand was still in the air and returned it to his lap, then slowly leaned backward and smiled.

"Mister Williams," said Kyle slowly. "This is her career, and her life. If you have concerns with either, then you should talk to her about that, not me."

A vein started to visibly pound on Jonathon's temple. He stood and looked down at Kyle.

"It would do you good to consider my words," said the agent. "Because I really do not want this matter to become... Messy."

Kyle looked up at the suit. Standing he raised a hand toward the exit and said, "Thank you for your visit, Mr. Williams. But I have a client to tend to soon so I must ask you to leave."

"And another thing," Jonathon said.

"Yes," said Kyle yawning on purpose.

"You do not mention this meeting to Keiko."

"Because?"

"It would not be good for you."

"Of course it wouldn't," said Kyle nodding.

"This is not over," said Jonathon who stared at him for a moment.

Flashing his own smile Kyle said, "It never is."

Jonathon sneered and walked down the hallway. A minute later the door slammed shut.

Chapter 02.03

Keiko focused her camera on the broken foundation leading to the church, zooming out slightly to catch the half broken bottle hidden partly behind the grass growing from the cracks, long shadows forming from the bright lights set about for the photo shoot. Pressing the button she waited a moment and checked the image on the display of the digital camera. Liking what she saw she pulled out her 35mm SLR camera and recomposed the shot, taking a few pictures with different settings.

Somebody came up behind her as the last shot was taken. "Excuse... you," came the broken English. "Makeup made ready... five minutes."

Bowing her head Keiko said, "Thank you."

The photographer's assistant excused herself.

Packing up her camera gear Keiko checked her watch and calculated the time back home, guessing it would be morning there. Taking a chance she dialed Kyle's number and it was answered on the third ring.

"Keiko?" came Kyle's voice.

"Wake you?" she asked.

"Nah, been up for a while."

"Any idea why my mom wants to talk to you?"

"Nope, she didn't say when I talked to her, only that she wanted to talk to me in person about something important. You're her daughter, you should know."

"Yeah, right, I have no idea."

"How's the shoot going?"

"Going to start in a short bit. Morning there?"

"Yes," said Kyle.

Keiko heard a male voice say Kyle's name, and the mic being covered and muffled talk. "Sorry about that," he said.

"Tell Ed I said hello," she said.

"Oh, he left a bit ago for work," said Kyle.

"Then who was that?" she asked.

"Long story, but you have a shoot to do, I'll tell you about it when you're done there. Give me a call, and I'll fill you in on your mom and some... some other stuff."

"Fine," she said coldly, then realized her tone. "Sorry, I'll call you later. Miss you."

"Miss you too," said Kyle.

"Bye."

The connection terminated and she looked at her phone for a moment before putting it back into her pocket and picking up her camera equipment.

Chapter 02.04

Kyle was not sure how many times he had rolled over and smashed his fist into the alarm clock, attempting to hit the snooze button the next morning, but for some reason he could not locate the large button. There was no feasible reason his mind could grasp as to why the alarm was going off at this time on a Sunday morning. Propping himself up on one elbow he successfully found the button and pressed it, bringing the incessant beeping to a halt.

Lying back in bed he closed his eyes. Stupid clock. There were no meetings with clients today. Ed was working this morning, but no reason for Kyle to get up. Thomas and Harry were here, again no reason to get up. Keiko was away on a shoot. Keiko...

He sat up in bed and looked at the clock, remembering the reason the alarm had been set was because her Mother had asked to come over and talk to him today. Throwing the covers off him Kyle stood hesitantly, his body beckoning him to return to the warm bed. Somewhere in the back of his mind it registered that he needed to do some straightening around the house before Keiko's Mother arrived, so with a tremendous amount of will he began to walk across the room.

Several hours later Kyle, Thomas, and Harry had completed straightening up the house. The two British men had excused themselves and left for the afternoon at Harry's insistence that Thomas needed to find a paper and start looking for a job. To which the Creative Genius had grudgingly agreed.

Kyle had just finished setting down the tray of tea and cups when the buzz came from the front door. He ran to the front door and pressed the button to open the gates and opened the front door.

He heard the car pull up and park, and its occupants get out and approach.

Coming into the entryway of the house Keiko's Mother, Grandmother, and Kami said hello simultaneously, bowing. Returning the greeting he motioned for them to enter. After they had removed their shoes and donned the guest slippers near the door, he led them into the living room. Mother and Grandmother sat on the couch, Kami in the chair, Kyle stood before the chair opposite and motioned to the table.

"I have prepared some green tea, if you would like some," he said motioning to the steaming ceramic pot and four empty cups.

"Yes, that would be nice," said Mother.

Grandmother nodded.

"Got any soda?" asked Kami.

Kyle nodded as he began to pour three cups of tea. "I shall get it for you in a moment."

"Don't worry about it," she said jumping up and going to the kitchen. She returned a moment later with a can of soda and sat back down.

Handing over two cups, he took the third and sat in his chair.

Mother sipped the tea and said, "This is quite good."

"Thank you," said Kyle bowing his head toward her.

"No, actually I must thank you for seeing us this afternoon, Kyle," said Mother.

"What is on your mind?" he asked.

"We have come here today to ask you a favor," she said, pausing. "The renovations on our family home in Japan are almost finished. After much consideration, I have decided to accompany my Mother in the move to help take care of her."

"Really?" asked Kyle.

"Yep, but I don't want to go live out in the country back there," said Kami.

Her Mother looked at Kami who bowed her head and apologized for interrupting.

"As I was about to say, Kami would like to stay here in California. Unfortunately Keiko is gone too frequently for her to stay with her sister. I understand that you have several rooms here not being used and would like to ask if Kami could stay here. Rent and other expenses shall be paid, of course."

Kyle sat back in his chair and took a sip of tea. "Kami, what are your thoughts on this?"

"Gee, duh, let's see. I can go live in the boondocks in Japan where they think broadband is a group of female musicians or I can stay here and entertain myself making your life hell. It wasn't a hard choice." She ended the sentence by smiling menacingly.

"Great," he said.

"Do you think this would be possible?" asked Mother.

"Yes, of course," he said looking back to the couch. "But just so you know, I have two new roommates who are staying here. British gentlemen I met back before Christmas, a man in his early twenties and his guardian. And of course Ed is still living here."

"Oh, how is Ed?" asked Mother. "Is he still doing music and seeing Cynthia?"

"Yes, they're still together, and his band was recently signed. He has done a few performances on the west coast and is going to Germany in a month for a small tour."

"That is good to hear. Well then, would this Saturday be too soon for Kami to move in?"

"This Saturday?" he asked.

"Yes, if it is not too much trouble. We have already begun to pack the house, and with your agreement I can work on transferring Kami to a school near here. This would allow her time to settle in before the two of us leave the country."

"Sure," said Kyle. "I have an appointment with a client that evening, but I could help you move during the day."

"Thank you," said Mother. "Your help in this matter is greatly appreciated, and I owe you a debt of gratitude.

"After all you have done for me over the years, it is the least I can do," said Kyle, bowing his head to her.

Smiling she said bowing her head slightly, "Please forgive me, but there are many preparations to be made so we should really be on our way."

"I understand," said Kyle standing as everyone else did.

"When I have more details I shall call and we can make the remaining arrangements," said Mother bowing.

"Very well," said Kyle and he escorted them to the front door which he opened after they put on their shoes.

The two older women stepped outside. As Kami passed she stopped and pushed a finger into his chest. "Guess big brother gets to be big daddy now." She turned and walked past her Mother and Grandmother.

Kyle closed the door and went back to the living room, sitting on the couch. He closed his eyes and sighed. Opening his eyes he looked over to see Cynthia sitting in one of the chairs.

"You know," said Kyle. "My life was very quiet and non-eventful. Now, in the space of several days I have a spastic Brit and his guardian living with me, a psychotic agent who thinks I'm banging his model, and her sister who is going to be living with me, whom," he said raising a finger, "absolutely hates me for some reason."

"It would seem that the gods of boredom have abandoned you," said Cynthia, unmoving, other than her eyes that slowly looked over at him.

"Lucky me," he said slouching into the couch.

Chapter 02.05

"Mom was joking right?" asked Keiko.

"No, Kami is going to be living here," came Kyle's voice through the airwaves.

"Shit, wonderful. So much for me staying there being a secret," she said.

"Well about that," said Kyle.

"What?"

He paused a moment. "You're probably right. But then there's the other thing I wanted to tell you about."

"What now?" she asked harshly.

"Um, well, I have two other roommates living in one of the rooms upstairs, the one next to Ed's."

Silence on Keiko's end.

"Remember that night I got kidnapped by thugs? Well Thomas and Harry showed up on my doorstep needing a place to stay."

More silence.

"What the hell are you thinking, letting those two live there?" she screamed into the phone.

"Well, they really needed a place and had nobody to turn to. It's a long story," he said.

Keiko groaned. "Kyle, your problem is that you are too nice sometimes."

"Yeah, I know," he said. "And..."

"What?" she asked in a terse voice.

"Your agent, Jonathon, came over the other day to talk to me, talking about your future and stuff. I thought you said you'd never tell him about me."

Silence filled the air.

"What's going on Keiko?" he asked. "You said you would never tell him about me, and yet he shows up on my doorstep. What exactly is going on?"

"I... I... Um..." she started. "Honestly I never mentioned you to him."

"Then why was he here in my house threatening me?" asked Kyle.

Keiko's mind raced, unsure of what was going on. "Look, just give me a few to figure out how he found you, you know I would never betray you, Kyle."

"Fine, I just don't want him showing up here again, really creepy guy. I can't believe he's your manager."

"Don't worry about it onii-chan," she said, trying to sound happy.

"You sure?" he asked.

"Of course," said Keiko.

"OK, maybe I'm just being paranoid. Have a good shoot and I'll talk to you later."

"Take care, miss you."

"Miss you too," he said. Then the line died.

Resisting the urge to throw the phone across the room she simply let it drop to the floor and fell back into her bed, wrapping her arms around herself and staring at the ceiling, trying not to shake.

There was a knock on her hotel room door. Keiko ignored it, but it came again. Frustrated she stood and kicked the phone out of her way before going over to the door and wishing she could at least see who was on the other side.

With what she just heard about her manager she just opened the door, not caring if it was a crazed fan here to rape and murder her. Much better than dealing with life.

As the door flew open somebody leaped into the air at her. Keiko was forced backward and caught herself against the wall, looking down at the girl hanging from her neck.

"Hi Keiko," said Lucy.

"Wha... What are you doing here?" asked Keiko.

Lucy dropped to the floor and took a step back. She had on a long white coat, trimmed with white fur and white boots, the long blond hair was pulled back into a single pony tail.

"Ah, funny that," she said. "I was here in Prague, visiting some friends, and the news had a short interview with you. The report said that you were in town doing a shoot for something or another so I decided I'd pop in for a visit and see how you were doing."

"Wait, how'd you find me?"

"So you want to go get a few drinks and relax?"

Keiko blinked a few times then slowly nodded her head.

BLIND DATE

Chapter 03.01

Kyle double-checked to make sure he had everything for his meeting.

As he was sorting through the bags for one last check something hit him in the back of the head and landed by his feet, a ball of newspaper.

"Hey, boya," he heard Kami from the door to his room. "We're taking a break from unpacking to eat dinner. Wanna join?"

He checked the time. "Sorry, I have to take off soon."

"Whatever, suit yourself," she said, and bound down the hall to the stairs.

Grabbing his bags he went downstairs and deposited them near the door before heading into the kitchen. Kami's Mother and Grandmother were cooking while Kami was opening some boxes in the bar area.

"I'm taking off," he said raising a hand. "If you need anything give me a ring."

"Very well then, take care, and thank you for helping earlier," said Mother. "By the way, I was hoping to meet your new roommates today, where are they?"

"They are at a job interview, actually," said Kyle.

"On a Saturday?"

"Yes, small mom and pop kind of shop I think," he said. "Anyway, if all goes well with my client's upgrade I should be back in a few hours."

"We shall see you then," she said. "If not I will call you tomorrow."

"Great," said Kyle. Looking down at Kami he said, "Good luck unpacking."

She groaned. "You should be helping me unpack, onii-chan."

"Why?" he asked.

"Because this is so not fun," she said.

"Heh, all the more reason for me to leave," said Kyle turning around and walking through the door.

"Baka," she muttered under her breath.

"I heard that," said her Mother.

"Sorry, sorry," said Kami opening a box with more force than was necessary.

Kyle chuckled as he walked down the hall and grabbed his things.

Chapter 03.02

"Must you drive so recklessly?" asked Harry holding the dashboard with his left hand while the other one held firmly onto the handle on the door.

Cynthia's black Jaguar, with heavily tinted windows, was weaving in and out of traffic through the four lanes of the highway. She said nothing.

A diagonal opening appeared and she cut across four lanes of traffic to the exit.

"Where are we exactly?" asked Harry grabbing the dashboard again as she came to a quick stop at the red light.

"Pasadena," she said.

"Well then, seems that this is rather close to where Kyle lives, is it not?" asked Thomas. He was sitting in the middle of the back seat, leaned forward so he could talk over the loud music.

An opening in the traffic opened as she came onto the main road, and she accelerated quickly, turning right onto a street.

"He lives in Pasadena also," she said, the car suddenly swerving into another lane.

"Ah, that would be that then," said Thomas rubbing his head from where it had been slammed into the window a moment ago.

Harry continued to occasionally mutter under his breath as Cynthia sped down the street and he let out a faint growl as she slammed on the brakes, engaged the parking brake, and somehow drifted the large car into a small driveway with a fence on either side.

Nestled between a large grey store and a gas station was a small nondescript one story house at the back of the lot. They drove down the deteriorated paved driveway, as they neared they could see a small sign hung above the porch, 'Corin's Occult Shoppe' in paint that was mostly peeled away. Pulling behind the house the car came to a stop next to a run down Morris Minor.

Turning the engine off she tossed the keys into her coffin shaped purse and said, "Please exit the vehicle."

"Wonderful, we are here," said Thomas, jumping out. "Are you not excited Harry, getting a real job, having the chance to interact with people and find out about their hopes and dreams?"

"I have a job," said Harry stepping out and squinting against the morning sun as he closed the door. "Unless, of course, you would like to relieve me of my duties so I can return to England."

Laughing uneasily, Thomas said, "No, no, that will not be necessary."

Cynthia was standing before them, a black parasol between her and the sun. She stared at Thomas, then at Harry.

Leaning forward slightly she whispered, "Do not ruin this opportunity."

"Of course..." they said, taking a step back.

"Good, then follow me," she said turning on her heel and walking around the house to the front.

Stepping up the stairs, which groaned and creaked under their weight, the three of them crossed the porch. Cynthia closed her parasol while she opened the door, causing a bell to ring, and entered, standing to the side as Thomas and Harry stopped next to her. The door slowly closed, ringing the bell a second time.

The main room was lined with shelves of glass containers full of dried plants and other oddities, several long tables occupied the center of the room with books. At the far end of the room was a counter behind which stood a man in his late fifties, greying hair and slightly obese.

Sitting on the counter was a young girl with long blond hair wearing a white dress.

Both of them stopped their conversation and looked to the doorway.

"May I help you?" asked the elderly man.

"I'll stop by later," said the girl hopping off the counter to the floor. She shot a glance back at them and walked through a curtained door behind the counter.

"Hello, and welcome to my shop," said the man leaning both hands against the counter. "May I help you?"

"They are with me," said Cynthia, who was suddenly standing next to him.

She was standing beside the counter, both hands holding her purse and parasol behind her back.

"Aaaahhh, Cynthia," said the man stepping toward her and smiling. "So wonderful to see you again."

Taking off her sunglasses, she inclined her head slightly while saying, "It is good to see you also, Corin."

Adjusting the glasses perched on the end of his nose he looked back at the two men who were still near the entry, both of them staring in shock at Cynthia.

"Oh well then, might these be the people you were talking about the other day?" he asked.

"Yes," said Cynthia.

"Ah, brilliant, very well then," he whispered. Speaking louder he motioned with one hand toward them and said, "Come here gentlemen."

Harry had Thomas behind him, his stance defensive as he stared at Cynthia. Thomas, oblivious, ran across the room and held out his hand. "Dunne, Thomas Dunne," he said smiling. "Thank you so much for this opportunity."

"A right pleasure to meet you, my good man," he said shaking hands. "I am Corin, curator of this fine establishment."

Thomas nodded and motioned to the person who cautiously walked up to stand next to him.

"And this is my faithful Man Servant, Harry."

Harry winced at the title and shot his charge a look.

"Sorry, sorry, just joking, anyway Corin, this is my guardian, Harry," said Thomas smiling and putting an arm around his mentor's shoulders.

"A pleasure to meet you," said Harry greeting Corin.

"Good to meet you. But anyway, why again are all of you here?"

"You have been seeking help for your Shoppe," said Cynthia. "I think that Harry and perhaps even Thomas would be able to assist you with organizing, taking care of the grounds, or any other tasks of your choosing."

"A wonderful idea, excellent, then you are hired, gentlemen," said Corin pounding the counter with his fist. "This calls for a celebration."

"Corin?" said Cynthia.

"Yes, my dear," he said.

"Is it not a bit early to be drinking?"

"Oh, well said, well said. Business has been slow these last twenty-five odd years or so. Not many people into the arcane arts these days, well, not compared to the eighteen hundreds. Now there was a grand time, let me tell you." He paused. "Bah, damned kids and their new age wish wash. And those who think they're following the old ways are reading contrived derivatives of derivatives of something somebody once glanced at. I tell you, it is a sad state these days."

"Corin," said Cynthia.

"Yes?"

"You seem to be ranting again."

He blinked several times and relaxed against the counter. "My apologies Harry and, and..."

"Thomas," he said.

"Thomas. Thomas, Thomas, Thomas," said Corin. "Right. Got it."

"Beautiful," said Thomas. "Remember my name well, because though I have been dealt a cruel hand this round, I shall prevail."

"That is wonderful to hear," said Corin somewhat confused.

"Oh, and that reminds me," said Corin raising a finger. "That book you were waiting for finally came in, Cynthia." He turned and walked through the curtained doorway.

He returned a moment later carrying a long wooden box about as wide as his shoulders. Setting the worn wooden box sideways on the counter he lifted the top portion off and looked around a moment. Laying the box on its side he slid out the large leather bound book and stepped aside.

Cynthia approached the book and ran her fingers over the cover, a smile briefly crossing her lips. Carefully she opened it and glanced at several pages, then flipped through more, staring at the illustrations and text. Her hand, clad in a black leather glove, rested upon a page for a moment.

"Excellent," she said. "Thank you. I will have the funds transferred to your bank account later today."

"Of course, of course," said Corin, watching her place the book back into the wooden box.

He stared at the ceiling for a while, then seemed to suddenly realize there were other people around him.

"Well then," said Corin looking at the two men on the other side of the counter. "Do either of you have any knowledge of the occult, magic, sorcery, necromancy, et cetera, et cetera?"

"Only what I have seen in movies," said Thomas. "Oh! And I had one of those boards with letters on it that spirits use to communicate with the living. But it never seemed to work. I left that little pointer thing on it for days and it never moved around like in the movies. I was terribly saddened at this. Would have probably led to a good story or something if it had worked. And now that I think about it I think I read a book on ESP when I was a kid. But some friends and I tried it and had no results whatsoever."

Corin stared at Thomas, seemingly unsure what to exactly say.

"As for myself, sir," said Harry. "When I was serving the Queen in the Intelligence Agency back home, there was a fellow Agent whom I worked with by the name of James, who had studied such things for many years. We would often have debates during missions, and though I must admit that though I do not necessarily agree that such things could exist, I also have to confess that I may have a general knowledge of what you were inquiring about."

"Well then, that is a start indeed," said Corin. "Just a moment," he said walking back through the curtains.

Several minutes passed, filled with the sounds of boxes falling, some muffled swearing, and things being moved around. He returned with three thick books which he placed on the counter and he opened the top one to reveal a page of handwritten text.

"I had a similar situation with my last assistant. Wonderful chap. All bright eyed and wanting to learn, but little experience. And just when he was starting to gain some comprehension, bang, First World War breaks and he gets drafted and killed. Damn shame. Kept his spirit around for a bit after that, mainly because he was so disheartened about being dead and all, and I did not mind the company either."

He adjusted his glasses, blinked a few times. "Where was I? Oh,

yes, so here are some notes in here that should help you understand some of this."

Thomas grabbed the top book and opened it while saying, "What a wonderful opportunity. This is great, thank you. Imagine the works of genius I could create by reading these? My heart is beating so fast right now."

"If you will excuse me, I have some business to take care of," said Cynthia.

"Of course, of course," said Corin smiling at her. "Thank you so much for bringing them by. I am quite confident they will be of great help around here."

"I hope so," said Cynthia turning to Harry and extending her hand.

He took the business card.

"That is my number, on the back is Kyle's," she said.

"I understand," said Harry placing the card in the pocket of his vest.

"Thank you, Cynthia. You honor me with your generosity," said Thomas bowing his head.

"You need to pay rent, Corin needed assistance," said Cynthia taking the large box containing the book under her arm. "I will return later to pick you up."

Thomas let out a small laugh and looked over at Corin who was flipping through the pages of one of the black books. Turning back to Cynthia he saw an empty space. Startled he spun around and stared out into the empty store as Harry suddenly became spooked again and dropped to the floor, looking around.

Chapter 03.03

Kyle had met Heather about six months before his Grandmother had died. He was working part time, temping back then, and struggling for cash. When his Grandmother had said that there was somebody who was an old family friend of theirs that needed help with her computer, he had readily accepted the job. Even though it was obvious that Heather had money, Kyle had never charged her for his services, only asking that she pay for the hardware.

Maybe he was too old fashioned, but he felt it was wrong to

charge family or friends for his help with computers. Or even charge friends of family for that matter. Kyle had explained this to Heather at their first meeting, emphasizing that he felt uncomfortable asking for money for his services. Instead a nice bottle of wine would cover the expenses for whatever work needed to be done.

He still remembered her reaction, because it was so odd.

"Not a response I would expect in this day and age, especially from one of your age," Heather had said.

Which was strange, because she seemed to be just a few years older than him.

Kyle had just shrugged his shoulders. "Just do me a favor and don't tell my Grandmother about this? She'd probably be pissed I was doing this work and not getting money."

"Agreed," Heather had said.

He could not prove it, but the fact that a week later he received a phone call from a company stating they had heard of him and were looking for somebody of his talents had always made Kyle suspicious that Heather had pulled some strings. But when he had asked her, right after being hired, she had claimed ignorance. Accented with a slight smile.

Heather was an artist, a painter, and she owned several galleries around the Los Angeles area, and at least two in Orange County. She lived in an old-style house on the beach in Newport, at the end where there was actually space. Which was nice when they sat outside on her deck drinking. Because a short distance away all of the houses and apartments were, at best, spaced three feet apart. Rarely did any-body come this far down on the beach as they sat there enjoying the night air and pleasant sounds of the waves.

He drove up to the gate and pressed the button.

"Hello?" came the voice from the box.

"It's Kyle," he replied.

There was a faint buzz and the tall gates slowly opened.

His headlights illuminated her standing at the entry as he pulled up to the large house and stopped. Turning the car off he stepped out and he heard her yell a hello over the wind. He closed his eyes and breathed the cool ocean air, soft mist sprinkling his face. Pressing the button on the remote he opened his trunk. Waving back he pulled the bags from his trunk and closed it. Crossing the beautifully sculpted lawn he walked up the steps and smiled slightly, looking into those deep green eyes.

"Have you been well?" she asked in her thick Irish accent as he came to stand next to her. Heather had a paint smeared lab coat on, over long black skirt and a dark green shirt, her long red hair was pulled back into a pony tail.

"Been OK," he said stepping inside and putting his things down. "Company I was working for restructured last month and I got laid off."

"That's horrible," she said.

"Ah, it's fine," said Kyle. "I've been doing freelance work since then to make ends meet, and doing pretty well I might add."

"Good to hear, I've been thinking about you," said Heather catching his eye and then glancing away.

Kyle frowned and said, "Just out of curiosity, what happened? I haven't heard from you in over a year."

"Sorry about that," she said closing the door and smiling sadly at him. "After your Grandmother passed away I needed to take care of some things in Ireland and Europe. Just got back into town a few weeks ago. Have you really been well?"

He glanced at the ground, "Yes, well, the best I can. My old friend Ed moved in with me shortly after she... You know, and in the last week I have three other roommates, which has made life interesting."

A silent pause filled the room.

With a half-hearted laugh Kyle said, "But anyway, that aside, I'm guessing you haven't given up on the computer?"

"No, not yet," she said laughing. "I still have no comprehension of technology, but I need to at least try to keep up with the times or I shall get left behind."

"So true," he said.

"Well then, if you want to start on the upgrades I shall begin dinner," she said motioning toward the stairs down the hall.

"Deal," he said heading upstairs as she walked into the kitchen.

Ascending the stairs he walked down a ways and then into the room where she kept her computer. He began to flip on the light and stopped for a minute, watching the waves crash on the shore outside the large windows, moonlight reflecting off the waves. He really did not like the ocean during the day, but always found it soothing at night.

Turning the light on he saw the computer, sitting on the long oak desk, was covered in plastic dust covers. Walking over he looked on top of the monitor and saw a pen sitting there on the plastic covers. It was the pen he had put there the last time he had come over, before his Grandmother had died. He sighed and shook his head, wondering why she wanted to upgrade her computer if she had not even turned it on in so long.

Pulling off the covers he fired the computer up. Everything was just as he had left it. Grimacing he started up the dial-up connection. After the shrieking of the modem stopped he typed in the address for a site he visited every day, then in the time while waiting for it to load pulled out his Zaurus PDA and made a note to advise Heather to upgrade her internet connection.

Shutting it all down he pulled the computer out from under the desk and took off the cover. A while later the new motherboard, processor, RAM, and DVD burner were installed and he fired it up, crossing his fingers.

It lived.

He smiled. There was a part of him that missed the jumpers, IRQ and DMA headaches of his childhood, but the fact that hardware worked sixty percent of the time without problems was a pleasure every once in a while. After booting he installed the new drivers and her system was ready for another length of time underneath plastic sheets.

Shutting everything down he put the computer back under the desk, covering up all the equipment with the plastic covers.

"Giving up or are you finished already?" she asked from the doorway.

"Pretty much finished," he said turning around to look at her. She had taken off the lab coat, and the dark green silk shirt was untucked over the long black skirt.

"Wonderful, dinner is finished as well if you would like to join me."

He nodded, pushing the chair back and walking over to her. As he approached Heather turned around quickly, the long hair of her pony tail swinging around and almost hitting him. He leaned back to avoid the near impact. Smiling he followed her down the stairs.

In the dining room, the cherry wood table, surrounded by eight chairs, had two place settings with their dinner. The plates were not on the ends of the long table, but on opposite sides. A large thick piece of steak, baked potato, and carrots were upon the fine white china set between brightly polished silver utensils.

Heather walked around to the other side of the table, put her hand on her chair and looked up at him.

"Please," she said motioning to the chair he stood next to.

He sat down and waited for her to sit before reaching for the glass of wine next to the plate.

"Cheers," she said raising her glass to his.

"Cheers," he said clinking their glasses before taking a sip. It was a dark red wine, somewhat musty in flavor, with a thicker viscosity than most wines he had tried, but having a very strong almond-like taste which he found odd. "Very good," said Kyle nodding his head.

"Thank you, it is a special vintage from Germany," said Heather smiling.

"Ah, have never had any German wines," he said, pausing slightly to try and remember if Cynthia had ever given him any wine of German vintage.

"Enjoy then," she said raising her glass and taking another sip.

Kyle raised his glass and smiled, taking another sip.

He put down his glass and grabbed the silverware, cutting a portion of the Filet Mignon, savoring the bite. It was a bit too underdone for his tastes, but this was same meal she had prepared for him the other times he had been here, and being a friend of his Grandmother's he had no room to complain. Smiling he said, "Excellent."

"I'm glad you like it," she said and picked up her silverware.

They continued through their meal with very little words, for which Kyle was thankful. He did not follow the news, or current trends, and had always been sadly lacking in any means of small talk. Heather seemed a bit sad, but he was not quite sure. Whenever he seemed to notice her melancholy, she would smile at him and slowly nod her head as her green eyes seemed to hesitantly linger on him before looking back at her plate.

After the meal was finished they cleared the plates and she poured the last of the wine for them. Kyle was feeling strange. Not exactly drunk, he felt pretty clear headed, but he was very warm, and there was this vague and constant throbbing in the back of his head.

"I was wondering if you could show me how to do email again. Many of my friends have been harassing me about not being, what is the term? Connected?" she asked smiling slightly.

"Oh, yes, sure," he said.

"Well, then, could you show me how to do it?" she asked.

Kyle nodded his head and motioned with his hand toward the stairs.

Heather turned and went up, Kyle following. He sat down in the leather computer chair as she pulled a carved wooden chair over to the desk and sat down.

After the computer was running he started the dial-up connection. The quiet room was filled with the sound of the screeching modem as it connected. He moved the mouse to the icon he had created on her desktop.

"First you get online, of course," he said. Kyle paused, looking at his hands and feeling an odd tingling sensation in his fingers.

Shaking them he said, "Then to get your email you double click, with the left, remember, the left mouse button, on this icon here."

Kyle looked up and caught her eyes.

Suddenly he felt nauseous, dizzy, and grabbed the desk to steady himself. He had no feelings in his hands and he fell forward onto the floor convulsing. Kyle could not control his body, as much as he tried, and terror filled him. He vaguely felt himself being turned onto his back and looked up helplessly into Heather's eyes as she looked down at him.

"Kyle?" she asked.

He tried to respond but he could not even open his mouth as everything went dark.

Slowly Kyle opened his eyes. He was surrounded by warmth. And even though he could only open his eyes half way, he saw that he was lying in a large bath tub completely naked. Remnants of his dinner seemed to be floating on the surface of the water. Spikes kept striking his brain, and he fought the urge to close his eyes against the pain.

He tried to take a deep breath but could not breathe. Trying to move his arms or legs resulted in a slight splashing of the water.

Looking up, at the far end of the room he saw a thirteen year old girl with red hair pulled back into two braids. She was leaning against the door and stood up as he noticed her.

"Heather," she said in a faint Irish accent.

Kyle heard a motion to his right. He could not move anything except his half-opened eyes, he looked over and saw Heather turn around and stare at him. She was wearing the paint-smeared lab coat, and it was completely buttoned.

"No," said Heather. "Caitlin?" she asked in a pleading voice.

"Deal with it," said the girl.

"But," said Heather.

Kyle tried to say something but only managed a series of coughs that forced him forward. He slowly felt himself sinking into the warm water. Heather and the girl were arguing about something, but he was more concerned with the fact that his nose was about to go beneath the waterline and he could not move his arms or legs to prevent this.

"No!" screamed Heather.

He felt one hand grasp him underneath his left arm, and the other hand cradle his head, pulling him up.

"Why, why, why is this going so wrong," she asked.

"Poor planning," said the girl with braids.

"Caitlin?" asked Heather in a harsh tone. "I need your help."

"No," came the answer. "Not for this thing."

Kyle managed to glance from Heather to the girl who shook her head and stepped outside, closing the bathroom door behind her.

His body was completely numb, but he felt the tug as she pulled him part way out of the water, letting his head flop onto her shoulder. She held him close for a minute before setting him back down in the water.

Tears were streaming down her cheeks.

She grasped his face and turned it up to look into his eyes.

"You should have had a choice," she said, choking on the last word. "But I made a promise."

Pulling his head forward she kissed him on the forehead.

"Dearest Kyle, I shall make you forget this... I do not want you to suffer, you have suffered enough. But..."

The voice trailed off.

She pulled him close to her and whispered in his ear.

"Please forgive me," she said slowly, choking back tears.

Kyle felt a slight pain against his chest.

Her left hand held his head, which she pulled back. Half-opened eyes tried to look at hers.

"Forgive me," she said as she started to chant words that he could not comprehend.

Pain exploded in his body like nothing he had experienced before. He tried to jump back, to pull forward, to do anything to escape the agony. His head fell back and made a dull noise against the marble tiles, his body was uncontrollably thrashing, making the water splash against the side of the bathtub.

All he could hear was more words coming from Heather, some old language that in a way began to resonate within him.

His head fell forward. He saw what looked like a dagger embedded in his chest, through his heart.

A hand around his left arm kept him from sliding down into the water. Long, delicate white fingers grasped the handle of the dagger and pulled it from his chest. He watched as this dark red liquid began to pollute the clear water of the bath tub.

He tried to scream but trying to take a breath to do so was too painful. All he could manage was a slight moan.

More words filled the air as the terror completely overcame him.

Staring down at his naked body in the water, there was a part of him that was amazed at how quickly the clear liquid became a murky dark red substance, so dark it was almost black. He had little time to appreciate this, because as the sight of his legs in the water became obscured and his vision began to dim, eyes closing against his will.

Then, from what seemed to be inside of him, he felt this glow. This pulsating red light that seemed to fill his body, wiping away the pain, wiping away the agony, wiping away everything. Filling him. Filing him more than any meal he had ever eaten. The warmth and the light spread, filling him even more. The terror faded away in this fine red mist that filled him, and expanded to every part of his being.

Kyle's eyes snapped open and he looked up to see Heather kneeling over him. Glancing around he saw that he was lying on the floor near her computer.

He paused for a moment, his mind racing, before he remembered that he was showing her email. Jumping up quickly he got back into the chair, his mind racing with the images he had just seen.

"Are you alright?" asked Heather, who was looking at him with her head cocked to one side.

Kyle looked into her eyes, down to his shirt, over to the computer, then at the floor, his hand unconsciously massaging his chest, seeming to check for damage that was not there.

"Uh, yes, fine, fine, fine," he said managing a small laugh.

"Good, you had me worried for a moment," Heather said. She was leaning forward, her long red hair hanging over both shoulders. Sitting up in the chair she pulled her hair back and tied it into a pony tail with some ribbon. "Actually I wanted to talk to you about some important matters."

"What?" he asked staring blankly at the screen because suddenly everything around him had suddenly become surreal and intangible.

She paused momentarily, looking at him, before staring out the window.

"Actually you seem a bit tired," she said. "And I need to review some things for my galleries, so let us do this some other night. Though I was wondering if it would be possible to meet maybe once a week or more, because I need to learn this God forsaken contraption and you seem like a good teacher."

"Sure," he said, staring at her and wondering why she was surrounded by various colors. Shaking his head, Kyle said, "I'm sure we could work something out."

"That would be very nice," she said. "It is somewhat embarrassing to have computers at work and I have no idea how they work."

He laughed. "That is kind of sad."

"I know," she said smiling. "And listen, I know you don't charge friends or family, but please consider this a contract job. I enjoy cooking dinner, but this will take a bit of time I am sure, considering how many years it took me to set the clock on my VCR."

Kyle hesitated, "Well... Wait, you have a VCR?"

She raised a finger, ignoring the question. "Listen, you're just doing freelance work right now. When a beautiful woman with a lot of money tells you she is going to pay you for your services you should nod your head and say 'Yes Ma'am'."

Kyle looked at the finger, then to the face which broke into a grin, and nodded his head. "Yes, Ma'am," he said.

"Good boy, I may be able to teach a new dog some old tricks after all."

Chapter 03.04

Kyle parked his car and walked into the house, closing the door slowly behind him, relieved he had made it home alive. Ever since his collapse at Heather's he had been hit sporadically with aches and pains throughout his body, huge bursts that lasted only a second or two and then faded away. And neither his ears nor his eyes seemed to work properly anymore, as both the lighting and volume of his surroundings seemed to increase and decrease randomly. Which made driving back home rather perilous.

On the way home he had considered stopping by an ER, but getting medical insurance for himself was one of those things that he had been pushing to the bottom of his 'to do' list since he had been laid off. The idea of sitting in a room for several hours waiting for some doctor in training to tell him he just had the flu made him wince.

"Hey, Kyle," he heard Ed call from the living room.

He put the bags on the floor next to the stairs and walked down the hallway. Ed was sitting on the couch, beer in hand, watching some reality show. Thomas was sitting next to him drinking cognac, and Harry was in the chair, brows furrowed, reading a book with a plain black cover.

"Have fun over at that chick's house?" asked Ed winking.

"Not really," said Kyle sitting in the chair next to the couch. "Just an upgrade to her system."

"Must have gone bad, considering how late it is, or where you introducing your hardware to her software?"

Kyle had not really paid attention to the time since leaving Heather's house and saw that it was after eleven. He blinked a few times, the room seemed brighter than usual, even though the normal lights were the only ones on. Shaking his head and ignoring Ed's comment he said, "Just a normal upgrade, showed her how to use some of her programs and stuff. Must of lost track of time."

"Ah well, anyway, what are you doing tomorrow night?" asked Ed.

Everything in the house went dark for a few seconds, then came back on. Kyle shook his head at the illusion the three men in the room had glowed slightly in the dark as Kami ran in from a side room.

"Sorry, my bad," she said. She was wearing overalls over a white shirt and had a utility belt around her waist. "Oh, look who decided to come back."

"Hey, Kami," said Kyle looking her up and down.

"Perv," she said making a disgusted face and walking across the living room.

"Just wondering what you're doing," he said.

"Rewiring. When I plugged everything in I blew the circuit breaker for my room."

"We could call an electrician," said Kyle.

Ed laughed, turning the television back on, and said, "Same thing I suggested."

"No need, it's all done," she said over her shoulder as she walked into the kitchen.

"I tried to call, but you didn't answer, and she is a bit... Stubborn."

"Wanna die?" asked Kami coming back into the room.

"Oh, no," said Ed flashing her a smile. "Stubborn is a good quality in a girl if you ask me."

"Nice cover," she said crossing the living room. "I'll be in my room," she said exiting into the side hall.

Kyle smiled and pulled out his phone and saw that he had missed one call. "Sorry I didn't get your call, but it's ok, she rewired her mom's place for the same reasons and it never burned down."

"So as I was saying, tomorrow night?" asked Ed.

"Not much planned," said Kyle.

"Good, then you're going out on a date," said Ed smiling.

"Wh-what?" Kyle stammered staring at his roommate. Out of the corner of his eye he noticed that both Thomas and Harry had looked up in his direction.

"A date," said Ed. "You know, leaving the house, spending the evening with somebody of the opposite sex in a non-work related environment. I know these are foreign concepts to you but I think you should get out more."

"A date?" asked Kyle, the words seemed foreign as he spoke them.

"Yes," said Ed finishing off his beer.

Harry stood and took the empty bottle from the table, going to the kitchen. Thomas watched him leave, shook his head and took another sip of the tan liquid in his glass, smiling as he did so.

Ed draped an arm over the back of the couch and said, "Listen, you know damn well you will never meet somebody sitting in your room pining away after some supermodel who thinks of you as a brother, so we set you up on a date."

"A blind date?" asked Kyle. "I'm not that pathetic."

Ed dropped his head, looking to the floor before looking back up at his friend. "Right. This from the guy who, whenever I take him out to a club or something, always ends up and the end of the bar watching people, drinking, and not talking to anybody. You realize that if you don't talk to people you can't meet them, don't you?"

Kyle shifted his position in the chair and watched the television. "You won't let me get out of this, will you?"

"Nope," said Ed.

"Great..." Kyle looked at Thomas who was intensely watching the drama unfolding on the screen. Taking a deep breath he asked, "Who is she?"

"A friend of one of Cyn's friends," said Ed.

"Huh? Cyn has friends?" asked Kyle.

"Shhhhh..." said Ed raising a finger to his lips. "She's reading in the study, don't encourage her wrath, I've had a long day."

"Sorry, but, well, a friend?" Kyle asked.

"Not really a friend really, but she's a friend of somebody Cyn talks to at the clubs once in a while."

"I am Jack's lack of enthusiasm," said Kyle.

"And I'm Jack's colon. Anyway, look, she isn't one of those, you know, big Goth girls. And she likes some anime, overall sounds like a nice person. Grew up in Sacramento and moved down here to attend college a few years ago, likes computers, plus there, right? She's just kind of shy so has a hard time meeting guys. Then there's you, the epitome of stand in the corner, hello I am the God of All Wall Flowers. So thought you two might hit it off."

Toward the middle of Ed's rant the voice had become somewhat distant and tinny, then amplified to the point where Kyle had to forcibly keep his hands on the arms of the chair and not put them to his ears. He shook his head.

"I'm not feeling too well," said Kyle. "It's been a long day with moving and work and all. Fine, I know you won't let me back out of this, I'll talk to you about this more tomorrow."

Kyle was staring at the floor, but looked up when he saw Harry return and hand his roommate another beer before sitting down to read again.

Thomas was slowly swaying left and right watching the music videos that had come on the television after the previous program had ended a minute ago. Something moved to his right and he looked up to see Cynthia standing next to Harry.

He looked into her eyes, which narrowed slightly as a small frown pulled at the corners of her delicate lips.

"What happened?" she asked.

Harry, literally, jumped several feet in the air, tossing the book he was reading to the side as he spun half way up and landed on the floor in a fighting position facing Cynthia. Thomas tried moving quickly, jumping backward with enough force that he bounced forward and ended up falling to the floor. Ed raised an eyebrow and looked over at his girlfriend.

Kyle said, "I was just telling them that I wasn't feeling well."

Cynthia looked at him. Her gloved hands were held in front of her, at her waist. She tilted her head, staring at him, and placed her hands behind her back. "Interesting," she said. Cynthia turned, then was no longer in the room.

Harry was frantically looking around the room. "Where did she go?"

"Who?" asked Thomas trying to stand but only managed to fall onto his side. "I'm done, flip me over."

Ed nudged him with his boot. "Hey," he said. "Maybe you should go to bed."

Cautiously Harry knelt down, all the while checking every section of the surroundings, and grabbed Thomas, quickly pulling him to a standing position.

"You must rest now, sir," said Harry holding Thomas close to him and backing toward the stairway. He reached the stairs and slowly ascended them, looking behind him, and down, until he reached the top.

Hearing the door close to their room Kyle looked over to the couch and said, "I need to go to bed too."

"See you tomorrow," said Ed grabbing the remote and flipping through the channels.

"Night," said Kyle standing and walking out of the room and up the stairs.

Closing the door to his room he passed the computer while pulling off his shirt and tossing it to the ground near the closet. Pulling off his shoes he crawled into bed and stared at the ceiling. He wanted desperately to think about all of this, but unconsciousness overtook him.

Chapter 03.05

The sounds of the New York night came through the open sliding glass door of Keiko's hotel room. She turned over in bed again and stared out at the balcony, then glanced at the clock. Unhappy with the time displayed she cursed under her breath and closed her eyes again, trying to will sleep upon herself.

Ten minutes later she sat up in bed and grabbed the pillow, holding it to her chest and rocking slightly backward and forward.

"This isn't good, Keiko," she said to herself. "You have a live broadcast on some stupid morning show and instead of sleeping all you are doing is thinking."

She rolled out of bed, still clutching the pillow and walked over to the table in the corner. All of this because she had made some stupid promise to some producer that she would do this show. She hated promises. They destroyed so much sometimes.

"Stupid girl," she said throwing the pillow onto the bed in a fit of anger. "If one word should be erased from your stupid vocabulary it should be the word promise."

She slumped into the chair next to the table and grabbed her phone. Pressing a few buttons she saw Kyle's name on the display, then cancelled it remembering he had an evening appointment with a client today. She started to flip through the names stored on her phone, hesitated at Cynthia's, then at Ed's and ended up back at the A's again.

She dropped the phone into her lap. After a few seconds she picked it back up and called Cynthia's cell phone.

"Hello, Keiko," came Cynthia's soft voice.

"Hi there, how you doing?" she asked trying to sound happy. Keiko picked up the pen on top of the hotel letterhead and started fiddling with it.

"Reading," said Cynthia.

"Anything interesting?"

"Possibly."

"Oh, well, couldn't really sleep and wanted to see how things were back there," said Keiko.

"All is the same, except for Kyle."

Keiko dropped the pen. "What do you mean?"

There was silence on the other end for few seconds. "Thomas, Harry, and your sister are now living here, and Kyle just returned from his client's house and something happened."

Keiko stood up quickly and started pacing. "You don't think he..."

"No, I do not think he had intercourse with her," said Cynthia.

"Oh, good," said Keiko standing still and relaxing.

"You are there again."

'There again' was Cynthia's term for loneliness when talking to Keiko. "Oh, no, not really, just wanted to see how things were."

"Do not do that."

"What?"

"That," said Cynthia.

"Sorry," said Keiko, knowing 'that' was 'lying'.

Keiko walked back to the table. "Um, listen, just tell everybody I said hello. I'll be back in SoCal tomorrow."

"I will let them know."

"Thanks," she said. "Have some morning show tomorrow so I need to go."

"Enjoy yourself," said Cynthia with a leer in her voice.

"Yeah, right, anyway, goodnight."

"And a good evening to you as well." The call ended.

Keiko held her phone in both hands, squeezing it. She resisted the urge to throw it across the room and smash it against the wall. Resisted the urge to toss the table aside and throw the chair into the fake oil painting above the bed.

Letting out a long, slow breath she put the phone carefully onto the table, walked over to the bed, and laid back down, staring at the ceiling.

"Fame, fortune," she said aloud. "Nobody ever wishes for happiness, do they?"

She grabbed the other pillow and held it close.

Chapter 03.06

There was a knock on his door and Kyle looked up from his computer. Ed stepped in, "You almost ready?" He had on a black fishnet shirt, black leather pants and boots, numerous chains, necklaces, bracelets and piercings that jingled as he moved.

"Sure, just let me grab my coat," said Kyle standing.

"You're kidding, right?" asked Ed.

"What?"

"Blue jeans and a white anime T-shirt?"

Kyle looked down at himself. "But it has a demon-like thing on it," he said pointing to his chest.

Cynthia let out a sigh, shaking her head slowly and giving him a look of severe irritation. She was wearing a black Victorian style dress and her long black hair was styled from the same period.

Feeling extremely self conscious, Kyle looked to the floor then back up at them and said quickly, "All I have are jeans and T-shirts, or dress pants and dress shirts. I don't have anything black except my shoes," he raised his foot. "I mean, even my leather jacket is brown."

"You have a black pair of jeans, correct?" asked Cynthia.

"Oh, yes," said Kyle "Oh, maybe even a black T-shirt."

"Get them, I will be back in a minute," and she walked into the hallway.

Hanging his head, he walked over to the dresser and pulled them out. Cynthia returned a few minutes later and handed him one of Ed's black leather trench coats.

"We'll be downstairs," she said and the two of them exited, closing the door.

Kyle walked into his bathroom, tossing the shirt and coat onto the floor, and looked into the mirror. "L four M three," he said to himself slowly. Grabbing his head he whispered, "What is wrong with me?"

This girl Janice seemed nice, and she was pretty. Ed had emailed him the link to her MySpace page this afternoon and Kyle had gone through it, looked at her photos and read the last few weeks of her blog.

She was kind of young, just turned nineteen, but seemed to be interested in some of the same things he was and at least did not come across as a vapid shallow bitch. Which was good.

He changed his clothes and went back to the bedroom, looking at the picture of himself and Keiko in front of the Eiffel Tower. It had been her first big shoot for a major magazine and she had flown him to Paris for a few days to enjoy the sights and lend her moral support. That was a week before she had told him how she really felt about him.

There was a part of himself that had always wondered, or more appropriately, constantly questioned his actions back then. Or lack of action, in reality.

Sitting at some café drinking coffee late at night with the Eiffel Tower filling the sky before them, he had almost said something. The night had been so perfect, and even though she had started modeling Keiko was still Keiko with Kyle. There was a specific moment, a specific choice he had made which had consumed him since then.

She had looked over at him and said, "This is so much fun, thanks for coming out to spend some time with me. I was really nervous about this shoot, but having you around really made me feel better."

And then her next sentence.

"No matter what happens with this modeling thing, I hope we can always be like this."

There were two responses that flashed into his mind. Nervous, he had chosen the second and said, "That would be nice."

The first response would have been a confession of his feelings toward her, how much he loved her, how he always wanted to be with her. How much she meant to him.

But those words never passed his lips, and a week later he had a new title.

"You're like a brother to me, onii-chan," that was it. "I hope you are always there to support me, onii-chan."

And for over five years he had wondered what would have happened if he had been honest and told her how he really felt. But it was pointless to think of such things. So he tried to live his life. Since then he had dated a few times, all ending quickly and disastrously. To the point that he never even thought about relationships anymore.

He looked at the picture again, then placed it face down on the nightstand. Standing slowly he leaned over and placed a hand on the back of the picture frame, letting out a deep breath.

He went downstairs.

"Ready?" asked Ed.

"Sure," said Kyle putting his hands into the pockets of the trench coat.

"Well, well," said Ed nodding approvingly. "Dressed all in black and depressed, a consummate Goth."

"Shut up," Kyle said to his roommate.

"I shall drive," said Cynthia.

Kyle and Ed glanced at each other, and then attempted to look glad about her offer.

"Hold on a sec," said Kyle walking away. He went to Kami's room and knocked on her door.

"Come," he heard from the other side.

He opened the door and stepped in. The room was dark, aside from the candles that flickered on her nightstand and the electronics. Kami was sitting in front of four large computer monitors on the other side of the room, each displaying a different operating system, and to the right an action movie was playing on the television.

She spun around in her computer chair and paused briefly looking at him. Blinking several times her relaxed face became irritated and she asked, "What do you want?"

"I'm heading out to the club, not sure when I'll be back," he said.

"So I hear that you are actually going out on a date," she said with a look of amazement.

"Blind date, but yes," he said.

"Blind date, figures," said Kami pushing herself up with her arms and pulling her legs up beneath her. "Not that you could find one if you tried. And if, miracle of all miracles, you did find somebody good you'd probably just screw it up, like you always do."

Kyle let out a sigh and said, "Your confidence in me has been noted."

"Well, have fun then," she said grabbing the desk behind her and spinning around.

He stared at the back of her head.

"That means get out," she said over her shoulder. "And close the door."

Walking back to the hallway he closed her door and went to the entry.

"I wish I knew why she hated me so much," said Kyle.

"You do not know?" asked Cynthia.

"What do you mean?" asked Kyle.

She said nothing and turned around, opening the door and walked outside.

"Don't worry," said Ed putting his arm around Kyle's shoulder. "We're not meant to understand them, just one of those things you have to accept."

Chapter 03.07

Keiko closed the door to her house and dropped her suitcases to the floor, one of them falling onto its side. Kicking it out of her way she went into the kitchen and poured herself a glass of juice and, grabbing some cookies off the top of the fridge, wandered into the living room and sat down on the couch.

Reaching over she took the phone off the end table and dialed her sister's cell phone number.

"Hello," said Kami.

"Hey there," said Keiko. "How did the move go?"

"Pretty good, got all the important stuff hooked up," she said. "You back in town?"

"Yes, just got in a few minutes ago," said Keiko.

"Cool, did the shoot go well?"

"It wasn't horrible," she said, "But having somebody around who knew more than twenty words of English would have been nice."

Kami laughed. "I can imagine. Oh, you should probably call mom tomorrow, I think she wants to talk to you about me or something. Knowing her she will ask you to play mommy seeing Kyle is already playing daddy."

"He seemed kind of shocked about the whole thing," said Keiko stretching and lying down on the couch. "Then again, so was I."

"Well, he's a complete idiot, but, honestly, I'm really glad he let me move in here," said Kami quietly. "I would have gone insane living in rural Japan."

"Ugh, understandable," said Keiko. "He upstairs?"

"Nah," said Kami. "They left a few minutes ago. Ed set him up on a blind date so he's out at some club, probably trying to figure out how to talk to a girl."

"What?" asked Keiko sitting up on the couch. "He's on a date?"

"Um, yes."

"Where?"

"Some fetish Goth type club in Hollywood," said Kami.

Keiko knew exactly which club they were at. "Listen," she said standing. "It's been a long flight and all and I'm kind of tired. I'll talk to you later."

"You're gonna go spy on him, aren't you?" asked Kami.

"No, no," said Keiko shaking her head. "Just going to go to bed."

"Liar."

"Goodbye," said Keiko hanging up.

She sat back down on the couch. Kyle was single, so it was probably good that he was going out on a date. But then again, considering how bad his other relationships had gone there might be the need for her to run interference. No, no, he can take care of himself. But, what if they did not get along at all, and he's stuck at the club with nobody to talk to? Or it all goes horribly wrong and he needs a friend? It would be good if she was there, just in case.

But she didn't want to be too obvious about it. A disguise? That would work, especially at that club. That way if nothing happened he would never know she was there.

"Right," she said aloud standing and racing across the room and down the hall, pulling off her coat and shirt.

Thirty-five minutes later she stood in the bathroom.

"Shit, I look like an anime character," she said looking into the mirror. She was wearing black PVC pants, top, and stiletto boots that came up to her knees, and had donned a blue wig and a white mask.

"At least I don't look like myself. Ah! Need accessories."

In a box under the bed she grabbed a studded leather belt, then attached several small whips to it, along with a large silver cross. Checking herself in the mirror again, she threw her keys, ID, money, and phone into a brushed steel box that doubled as a purse and ran out the door.

As she was pulling out of her driveway she heard the faint sound of her phone ringing. She put the purse in her lap, tossed the mask onto the passenger seat, and pulled out the phone as she exited her driveway onto the quiet street.

"Hello?" she said trying to think of the best way to get to the club.

"Where are you going?" asked the voice on the other end.

"What? Who is this?" she asked not really hearing what he had said.

"It's Jonathon," came the reply.

"Oh, hey, I'm back in town, but I'm kind of busy right now. I'll give you a call tomorrow."

"I need to talk to you," he said.

"Fine, fine, we can talk tomorrow," said Keiko coming to a stop light and trying to figure out if she needed to go straight or turn right.

"I was hoping we could talk now," said Jonathon. "I am near your place."

"Sorry, I'll be on the highway in a minute and I hate talking on the phone and driving," she said. "Like I said, we can talk tomorrow. I'm gonna let you go. Bye."

He started to reply but she had pulled the phone away and ended the call. Tossing the purse and phone onto the passenger's seat she turned onto the on-ramp of the highway.

Chapter 03.08

The three of them stood in line for the club in Hollywood, waiting for the doormen to check ID's. It was cold out tonight, and the people around them chatted idly. Ed would occasionally shout out a hello to somebody he knew, but the three of them were silent through the wait. Finally they were able to prove their drinking age and received wristbands, were frisked, and were inside.

Ed handed money to the person behind the cash register, holding up three fingers. Taking the change they began to walk toward the thick black velvet curtains when Cynthia's phone rang.

Pulling it out of her purse she said, "Hello?"

Not moving she listened to the person on the other end, then said goodbye. "Your date is running late," she said.

"Oh, um, ok," said Kyle.

Ed shrugged his shoulders at him and pushed Kyle through the curtains.

The main room was huge, and packed with people. The half closest to them had several stages, a bar along the right side, and the far half of the room was a dance floor whose people formed an undulatlating mass that moved in time to the Industrial music blaring from the speakers.

"I'll get the first round," yelled Ed over the noise and walking to the bar.

Cynthia followed in step with him. Kyle looked around again at the people in all manner of attire and caught up with them at the bar.

"What you want?" asked Ed leaning over to Kyle so he could be heard.

Looking up at the glass shelves that reached to the ceiling, filled with bottles, Kyle said, "Bass."

Nodding Ed leaned forward said hello to the bartender, apologized to her for not being around lately, then ordered a Bass, a Corona, and a glass of Merlot. When the drinks arrived he handed them out.

"Cheers," said Ed clinking his bottle into Kyle's

Smiling uneasily Kyle said, "Cheers."

Bill, one of the members of Ed's band came up and started talking to him. Cynthia stood quietly watching the people. Kyle tried to act like he belonged there. After a few minutes of conversation the band member left.

Turning around and leaning forward to speak to both of them, Cynthia said, "I'm going to the back room." It was strange, even though her voice was as quiet and subdued as always he had no problem hearing it over the overwhelming music that was playing.

They nodded and Kyle watched her walk away slowly, moving through the crowd of people as if she was not even there.

A new song came on and Ed leaned over, "Gotta dance, you ok?"

"Fine," said Kyle forcing a smile and raising his beer.

Slapping him on the back Ed strolled through the mass of people toward the dance floor.

Kyle let out a small sigh. Looking behind him he saw nobody standing at the end of the bar closest to the exit and walked over there. Leaning his right elbow on the bar he finished his beer and raised it to the bartender on the other side. Getting another he gave her a dollar tip and leaned against the wall behind him.

He knew very little of the Fetish scene, or the Gothic scene for that matter, and so he watched the people around him, taking it all in. Maybe he could make this date thing work and it wouldn't crash and burn as violently as previous relationships.

His face contorted for a moment. If this Janice girl was into all of this, he might as well get used to it, if they hit it off, or if she even liked him, he could make himself like this type of thing, he was sure.

Ed came back several songs later. "You doing OK over here?" he asked, shaking his head slightly as he noticed where Kyle was standing.

"Sure, just waiting for Janice," said Kyle.

"Ah, she should be here soon. Gothic Standard Time and all," said Ed. "Back in a few," he said and was gone again.

Kyle finished his second beer and ordered a third. As he was paying the bartender a tall woman in a shiny black outfit and blue hair came up to the bar next to him and pointed at his drink to the bartender. Tossing some money onto the bar she took the bottle and turned slightly. He noticed her staring at him.

He glanced up at the white mask she was wearing, it had the shape of a tear, drawn in black, next to the left eye, and was formed so that only the mouth showed. Smiling, she raised her Bass.

He clinked his bottle against hers, but she said nothing. Kyle was starting to get a bit weirded out. Especially noticing the whips on her belt. The woman with blue hair smiled again with her blue lips and turned around quickly, lost her balance and began to fall forward.

Kyle reached out and grabbed her waist, pulling her into him and stopping the fall. She spun away from him quickly, nodding her head and looking into his eyes. Smiling briefly she raised her beer and walked past him, disappearing into the crowd.

Four songs later Kyle finished his beer and ordered another one. He was desperately trying to not go insane standing at the end of the bar waiting for somebody who might eventually show up.

Taking a sip he decided to wander around a bit. After all, his date knew Cyn, and if she was around Cyn would probably be able to track her down. He also felt that if this date came in and he was not standing against the bar in the corner waiting for her would be a big plus against his inherent lameness.

He walked through the crowd and the right side of the dance floor to the hallway that led to the back. The other room was much darker, and had a center area for dancing, surrounded by a ring of people watching the dancers. Almost everybody was wearing black.

He scanned the room, looking for Cynthia, but could not find her.

Cutting across the room he went down a different hall and back into the main room. Standing to the side of the doorway he looked over the crowded dance floor and saw Ed toward the middle, dancing and lost in the music. Shoving his hands into the pockets of the coat Kyle started walking toward the entrance.

Passing the first stage he glanced up and saw a woman with her arms stretched above her head, hands tied by rope that was attached to metal pipes above her. Her legs were tied at the ankles and she was being whipped slowly, seeming to derive great pleasure in it. The second stage had a girl in a white devil outfit whipping an obese man strapped to a large wooden X. The third stage had some contraption on it but was empty otherwise.

Passing the second stage he noticed that there was a space relatively devoid of people right behind the performance, everybody was watching from the sides. He entered the area and leaned against the metal railing that kept people away from the stage, letting out a combination of a growl and a sigh. Between the waiting and there being too many people here he was ready to leave and get a cab home.

Standing he turned to go back to the bar and ran into a girl looking down at a piece of paper. She looked up at him, adjusting her glasses and said an apology, then looked back down at the paper and back to Kyle again.

"Kyle?" she asked.

"Yes, Janice?" he asked recognizing her. He saw the paper she was holding was the printout of an email with his photo on it.

She shoved the paper into her purse quickly and extended a hand. "Nice to meet you," she said. "Sorry I'm late, had some problems with my contacts so had to wear my dorky glasses."

"Don't worry about it," said Kyle smiling, his mind racing, trying to figure out something to say.

"So, you come here often?" he asked. As he finished the last word, the cliché of what he just asked hit him and he wanted desperately to walk over to the wall and smash his head against it. Instead he tried to not look dumb.

"No, not really, only a few times," she said stepping closer so she wouldn't have to yell too much over the music. Her left hand was playing nervously with a small Hello Kitty doll that hung from a zipper on her purse, and she was still shaking his hand. Suddenly realizing this she let go and put her hand in the pocket of her jacket.

"I usually stay in the back room though, some of the stuff out here is kind of scary, you know?" she said. Then quickly she added, "No offense, I mean, if you're into this kinky stuff, it's just I meant that for me anyway it..."

He held up a hand and she stopped. "No, it's ok, never been here, and never been involved in this scene."

"Sorry," she said making a weird look. "I'm just kind of nervous, you know?"

"Yeah, well, me too," said Kyle.

"Really?" she asked, face brightening.

He nodded. "I have no idea how to talk to people without a keyboard in front of me," he said.

She smiled, then started laughing.

He realized how pathetic his last sentence made him sound and could not help laughing with her.

The strange woman from earlier, in the mask with blue hair, walked by. She paused for a moment and turned back to look at Kyle before disappearing into the crowd.

"You want a drink?" he asked Janice.

She raised her arm and frowned, "No wristband."

"How about a Coke?"

"K," she said smiling.

As she started to turn around there was a loud smack followed by a groan from the man on stage next to them. Then creaking and the sound of wood splintering. Looking up Kyle saw the large X with the man strapped to it falling backward, he and Janice were directly in its path.

Moving quickly he grabbed Janice and pulled her into himself while spinning to shield her, stepping to the side. One of the 6x6 beams of the X smashed into his shoulder before the whole thing came to a rest on the floor, angled up over the metal railing. The man strapped to the wood looked dazed.

Letting go of Janice he winced at the enormous amount of pain in his shoulder. Trying to move his left arm provided both increased pain and the sound of something grinding that should not.

"Oh my God," screamed Janice, "are you ok?"

"I think so, just clipped my shoulder a bit," he said.

He grabbed his shoulder, involuntarily squeezing it as another wave of pain coursed through him, forcing him to close his eyes for a moment. The pain was replaced by a feeling of warmth and numbness. Which was probably not a good sign.

"Dude, you ok?" asked Ed pushing his way through the crowd.

The familiar voice caused him to open his eyes and he saw his roommate stop next to him.

There was no feeling of anything now. No pain, no warmth, no numbness. Kyle's brows furrowed he let go of his shoulder and slowly lifted up his arm. It was fine, he swung it around in a circle.

"Guess it's OK," said Kyle, shrugging.

"Damn, that's hardcore. I saw it hit you and it looked painful," said Ed.

"Maybe it just popped out and then when I grabbed it I popped it back into place?" asked Kyle.

"Dunno," said Ed. "Damn, I'm sorry. First time bringing you to a place like this and you almost get killed by a fat guy strapped to a Saint Andrews Cross."

"Would have made an interesting note in my obituary," smiled Kyle laughing lightly.

Janice had both hands wrapped around Kyle's arm and was pressed against him. Looking up at Ed she said, "He saved my life."

Ed nodded.

"Nah, just saved you from being maimed at worst," said Kyle subtly trying to pull away from her. Which in the back of his mind he could not figure out because it had been so long since he had been this close to a girl, well , except for Keiko, but she did not count obviously.

"Listen," said Kyle to Ed, "I was going to grab some drinks, want the usual?"

The bald head nodded up and down, pausing to stare around them.

Kyle pulled slightly and Janice looked down at the arm he was holding and quickly let go, putting both hands into her pockets. "Sorry," she said.

Turning around he ran into the back of the small white devil girl who was watching a couple men help release the man on the wooden X from his bonds. The twin blond pony tails set on either side of the white horns on top of her head spun around and the blue eyes looked at him. A smile crossed her face.

"Ky-Ky!" screamed Lucy loud enough that everybody around them looked over. She jumped up, wrapping her arms around his neck to give him a hug. Nuzzling his neck she whispered into his ear,

"Been a while, hasn't it?"

Kyle tried to pull back in shock and said, "Lucy, what the hell are you doing here?"

She let go and dropped to the ground. "Trying to do a show, but it seems that Mister Jerry is not in the mood to play anymore." She motioned back to the overweight man wearing only a leather thong and black mask who was holding his head, and after seeing Kyle suddenly closed his eyes.

"You want to stand in for him?" asked Lucy winking.

Raising both hands Kyle said, "No, no, that's alright."

"So who's the cutie giving me looks of death and the guy in a daze?" she asked.

Looking to his left he saw Ed staring at them with his mouth slightly opened, and to his left, arm placed firmly around his, was Janice glaring at Lucy.

"Oh, this is Janice, my, um, date for the evening, and this is uhhh Ed, my roommate," said Kyle, slightly at a loss for words. "Guys, this is Lucy."

The little devil girl walked up to Ed and ran her fingers across his chest, then stood on her tip toes to rub his bald head. "Hello Ed, you are a musician, aren't you?" she asked.

Ed shook himself out of his daze and looked down at her asking, "Yes, er, how did you know?"

Placing a finger on his lips Lucy said smiling, "Just have an eye for talent I guess."

She walked over to Janice and pulled her off of Kyle, giving her a big hug.

Pulling back, but keeping her hands on Janice's arms she said, "Date? Really? Guess Kyle and Keiko didn't work out, oh well. But you're cute and smart, which is a good sign."

"Who's Keiko?" asked Janice looking at Lucy, then Kyle.

Kyle started to say something but Lucy interrupted.

"Doesn't really matter, now, does it?" she asked.

To which Janice glared up at Kyle who stared at both of them, shocked.

Turning Janice's face back with one hand Lucy said, "But you two make a nice couple indeed."

"Really?" asked Janice smiling and grabbing his arm, pulling him closer to her. "You really think so? You know he saved my life."

Julien Giever

"I saw," said Lucy smiling at the girl. She reached out and grabbed Kyle's hand. "Come on, I need a break."

Her grip was firm and he had little choice than to follow. On his other hand was Janice as the three of them snaked their way through the crowd, through the dance floor, down the hall, and through a double set of doors next to the Goth room. They stepped outside into the smoking area which was part of the alley that was blocked off on either end by gates. Taking them back to the far corner Lucy stopped and let go of his hand.

Ed had followed them out and stood opposite Kyle.

"So Kyle, how have you been?" asked Lucy pulling out a cigarette.

Moving quickly Ed produced a Zippo and lit her cigarette, then fished around his pockets and lit one for himself.

"Anyway," said Lucy flipping her hips so her long white barbed tail swung up and hit the back of Kyle's leg. "You ever take my advice?"

"Advice?" asked Kyle.

"Doing freelance work?"

"Oh, yes, have like fifteen clients now and doing pretty good," he said. "Thanks, sure beats the hell out of trying to find a normal job, and I get to sleep in most of the time."

"Always a plus," said Lucy.

She looked at the young woman holding onto Kyle's arm.

"How about you, Janice?" asked Lucy.

"What?" she asked.

"What about you?" asked Lucy. "What's your story?"

"Oh," said Janice. "I'm in college, working toward a PHD in Bio-Chem, I think. Not really sure. Classes are kind of boring, and it's not what I really want to do, but it will pay good when I'm done."

Nodding her head, Lucy said, "Uncertainty. It seems you are studying the wrong thing."

"What do you mean by that?" asked Janice. She stepped forward slightly, as if being drawn to the question, but still had a hand holding onto Kyle's arm.

"Honestly?" asked Lucy smiling and leaning against Kyle. "You just seem to be going after something that you don't want, even though you know what you want to be doing."

Kyle felt himself be pulled away from Lucy, into Janice as she

92

took a step behind him almost as if using him as a shield against the words.

Janice paused momentarily, resting her head against Kyle's arm. Wistfully she said, "That is so true. But I'm not smart enough to do that stuff."

"Who says?" asked Lucy.

"My tests," answered Janice.

Stepping past Kyle and placing a hand on Janice's shoulder, Lucy said, "Silly, you'll be fine. If you don't follow your heart, you'll just end up like all those people you hate so much."

Janice seemed to be unable to respond.

"And Ed," said Lucy, suddenly turning around. "You seem to be pretty true to yourself, music is your life as much as your Muse is. Though you should be cautious... Oh." Lucy stopped, suddenly noticing Cynthia standing next to him.

"Muse?" he asked.

"This beautiful dark creature," said Lucy taking a step sideways and putting her hands on Cynthia's waist.

Cynthia stared silently at Lucy. Everybody took a startled step backward as if Cynthia had just appeared out of thin air.

Ed's girlfriend stared at Kyle for a moment and then looked back to Lucy.

"Oh, god, you are so serious," said Lucy. Reaching up one finger she pressed it against Cynthia's nose and said, "Beep."

Cynthia did not move or say anything.

"No fun," said Lucy removing her hands from the dark girl's waist.

"Perhaps," said Cynthia, staring past the devil girl and into Kyle's eyes for a moment before looking behind him, her eyes narrowing slightly.

"Kyle?" asked a voice with an Irish accent.

He turned around and saw Heather standing behind him.

"Heather? What are you doing here?" he asked.

"Funny, same thing I was about to ask you. But, more to the point, and to answer your question, several of my artists come here, so I show up every once in a while," Heather said smiling.

"Please, pardon me for interrupting," she said nodding at the circle of friends.

"Oh, no, don't worry about it, Heather," said Kyle. "Everyone,

93

this is Heather, one of my clients and a friend of my Grandmother."
He raised his free arm toward her. "Heather, this is Lucy, Cynthia,
Ed, and Janice."

"A pleasure to meet all of you," said Heather bowing her head
and taking a step forward to join the group.

Heather looked at Lucy and said, "Are you?"

Lucy nodded.

"Well then, it is a pleasure to meet you," said Heather.

"Don't believe the rumors," said Lucy smiling while twirling her
tail.

"Ah," she said, hesitating and staring at his shoulder for some
reason. "By the way, Kyle, we never set our next appointment. My
week is rather busy. Are you free tomorrow?"

Kyle pulled his PDA out of the pocket of the trench coat and
turned it on. Checking his calendar he said, "Yes."

"Morning would work best for me. Ten?" she asked. "I tried to
get my email today and it was not working for some reason."

"Did you turn the computer on?" he asked teasing.

Narrowing her eyes she said, "I know how to do that much, you
wretch."

He typed the appointment into the calendar. Placing it back in
his pocket he said, "Ten it is."

"Excellent, I shall see you then," said Heather. "It was a pleasure
to meet all of you, even if briefly. Have a good evening all."

Heather wandered back into the mass of people.

A man in a black shirt, with the yellow word SECURITY on the
back was leaned over talking to Lucy. She nodded her head.

"Sorry, but they have everything set up so I have to go do my
next set," she said.

She hopped up and gave Kyle a hug, then Janice, Ed, and finally
Cynthia, who closed her eyes, almost in disgust of the farewell. Stopping with one hand on Cynthia's shoulder Lucy said, "Have a good
night everybody!"

Her hand was raised in the air, and her face was that of a three
year old who just found a butterfly. Dropping her arm she spun
around and followed the man with the black shirt back into the building.

Janice's left hand suddenly swung up as she quickly checked the
time on her watch. Sighing, she said, "Actually, I need to take off too,

have class tomorrow morning."

She looked up at Kyle and said, "Listen, we really haven't had time to talk much but it was good to meet you."

Reaching into her coat pocket she pulled out a piece of paper and handed it to him, saying, "I was probably a dork, but I'd really like to talk to you again. Here is my number and email addy."

Not even waiting for a response she said, "Thank you for saving me tonight."

She squeezed his arms and ran into the crowd.

Kyle looked at the piece of paper and said, "Night," even though she was gone.

The remaining group stood in silence for a few minutes.

"Strange night," said Ed.

"Tell me about it," said Kyle.

"Agreed," said Cynthia softly, barely audible over the music coming through the doors to the smoking area.

"Actually, we should take off too," said Ed. "I have to be at Guitar Center in the morning."

"Then we should leave," said Cynthia.

"Homeward bound we go then," said Ed throwing his cigarette onto the ground and stomping it out with his boot.

Ed turned around and started walking toward the doors. Cynthia was looking at Kyle.

"What?" asked Kyle, looking at her.

"You have no idea," she said walking up to him and hooking her arm around his, pulling him through the crowd.

Kyle looked down at her in shock, but she just stared forward. As Ed turned to ask them a question she let go and placed both hands behind her back.

Chapter 03.09

Keiko leaned against the bar, staring at her reflection in the mirror, sipping on the Long Island Ice Tea she had just ordered.

Somebody bumped into her, then pressed against her side. Expecting another man desperate for a conversation, or worse, Keiko looked over and saw Lucy dressed up in a white leather devil outfit.

"Hi there, long time no see," said Lucy.

"Wait, what are you doing here in the States?" asked Keiko.

"The usual," said Lucy raising a hand to one of the bartenders. A moment later she had a bottle of water in front of her.

Keiko shook her head, "Wait, am I that obvious?"

"Looks, no, mood, yes," said Lucy opening the bottle and drinking it all in one take.

"Later!" yelled Lucy waving at Kyle, Ed and Cynthia as they passed.

Unfortunately due to the music they did not hear her. Lucy shrugged and looked at the person next to her at the bar.

Setting the empty plastic bottle on the bar, Lucy turned to the shiny black girl with the blue hair and asked, "You never told him, did you?"

"No," said Keiko taking another long drink through the straw. "I've fucked up his life enough as it is, should I really add to that?"

"Have you ever wondered," asked Lucy spinning around and leaning her back against the bar, "what this world would be like if there were more honest people? If we were all honest with each other, we'd all feel good. I think even rice would taste better."

"What?" asked Keiko looking down at Lucy.

"But that would go against human nature."

Keiko nodded her head and took another long sip of her drink.

PROMISE NOT AGAIN

Chapter 04.01

There was a knock on his door.

"Come in," said Kyle glancing up from his computer.

Kami opened the door and walked in, closing it behind her.

"Ohayo, onii-chan, I wanted to ask you about..." she started, then paused. "Oh my god you look like shit. Do you have a hangover? Are you OK?"

"No, only had a few beers," he said trying to smile, attempting to focus on her face.

She sat down in the other computer chair and wheeled over to him, pressing the back of her hand against his forehead. "You're sweating, but your skin feels really cold."

"Yes, freezing, throbbing head, nauseous, hurts to even move," he said. "I was feeling kinda sick Saturday night, so I probably shouldn't have gone out to a dumb club last night."

"Maybe you're just allergic to girls," said Kami. "Got any cold medicine in your bathroom?"

"I don't think so," said Kyle pulling the blanket around him more.

Kami went into his bathroom and flipped on the light. She was amazed that, for a guy, the bathroom was pretty clean. Checking the medicine cabinet Kami found it bare except for a first aid kit, toothbrush, and some aspirin. There was nothing of note in any of the drawers either, aside from an unopened box of condoms hidden beneath some towels. She picked it up and noticed the expiration date was almost three years ago. Shaking her head she tossed it into the trashcan.

"I couldn't find anything," she said coming back into his bedroom. "I'm gonna check the downstairs bathroom."

"Thanks," he said, looking back to the monitor whose brightness and contrast seemed to be changing every other second, but Kyle realized all of his vision was doing the same thing.

Kami returned a few minutes later with Cynthia.

"She wanted to look at you," said Kami.

Cynthia walked quietly over to Kyle and bent down, looking into his eyes. Her expression remained as blank and unmoving as always. A gloved hand lightly touched his face as she stared into his eyes for a few seconds. Slowly she stood back up, placing her hands behind her.

"I will be back," said Cynthia to Kyle with a slight nod. Walking past Kami she said, "You stay here."

Kami began to retort with something but stopped seeing the look in Cynthia's eyes. Shivering slightly Kami sat down and watched her leave, then muttered, "Creepy girl."

"She's just Cynthia." Kyle tried to laugh but coughed instead. "Ugh, sorry, so what did you want to talk about?"

"Oh, that," she said leaning back and draping one leg over the arm of the chair. "I just wanted to ask you about Thomas and Harry."

He stared at her, his eyes wandering from her face to her neck, then down to the one bare leg hanging in the air, feeling an odd sensation, then shook his head and asked, "What about them?"

"Well, Harry seems nice enough, I guess. But Thomas really bothers me. He's a freak, as in the mentally not quite all there kind. He never shuts up and is constantly ranting on about his art and crap, yet when I asked him why he was staying here he never would answer the question. Like he's hiding something."

"He's a little eccentric, but a good person," said Kyle.

"How do you know?" she asked. "From what I've gathered he's some guy you met back before Christmas and he suddenly showed up on your doorstep. I know you're pretty dumb and way too nice to people, but letting a couple strangers live here? Especially in this day and age? I mean I don't feel safe with him, the way Thomas is always going off about the beauty of the female form and stuff. Kinda scares me, especially yesterday because tried to hug me. Doesn't he know it's illegal to do stuff with minors?"

"Kami, I understand why you're concerned," said Kyle. "Truth is, Thomas was having some family and financial problems and asked to stay here for a bit. But I did specifically tell him if he caused problems or didn't pay rent that he would have to leave. I'll talk to him, and make sure he understands that you're family and if he doesn't quit harassing you he's out of here."

She smiled slightly and said, "Thanks. Sometimes you have your moments."

"Wow, a compliment?" he asked.

"Baka, shut up," she said spinning the chair to face away from him.

"So, you start at the new school tomorrow?" asked Kyle.

"Yes," she said letting out a groan, shoulders dropping. "I was hoping for at least a week off to get situated here, but lucky me... Mom got me in to a new school so quick. I am so not looking forward to a new school."

"Yeah, switching schools sucks," said Kyle. "I remember what it was like when I was a kid and had to move out here. Not only had to deal with culture shock of California, but new people. I don't think I talked to anybody for the first two years."

"How old were you again?" she asked, turning around slightly to face him.

"Ten," he said. "If I'm still alive tomorrow do you need a ride there?"

Kami stared at him a few seconds, then said, "No, mom's gonna take me in, has to fill out the final paperwork and stuff. Oh, and you're finalizing all that guardianship stuff with her Wednesday, right?"

Kyle nodded his head.

"Wow, so weird. You're gonna be my official guardian. That means if I blow up the school or hack into the Pentagon you're the one who has to deal with it."

He frowned at her and said, "Not funny."

She stuck her tongue out and said, "It is a child's intrinsic duty to do everything possible to drive their parents insane, and you will be the closest thing I have to a parent-type figure, so I get to have fun with you."

"You realize, of course, I could just pull you out of school, lock you in your room, and declare that you were being home schooled," Kyle said flashing her a menacing grin. "Or better yet, send you to live in the country with your mom."

Kami frowned over at him, then jumped backward in her chair seeing Cynthia standing next to her. "Where'd you come from?" she asked.

Looking down at the teenager, Cynthia said, "Downstairs. Could you please move the keyboard?"

"Uh, sure," said Kami putting the wireless keyboard on the top shelf of the desk.

Cynthia set down the tray and looked into Kyle's eyes, saying, "Eat this. All of it."

Kyle looked into the large bowl and saw a red-brown liquid. A grimace crossed his face as he put the spoon into the foul smelling thick liquid.

"What is this?" he asked.

"Something that should make you feel better, I hope," she said.

Reluctantly he took a spoonful and swallowed the foul tasting concoction. After the third one he started to feel some energy returning, the nausea abating suddenly. Fighting back his body's reaction to the taste of the strange mixture he felt this soft red wave start to flow through him, but there was something else, a lingering taste of darkness that seemed to wrap small tendrils throughout every part of his being. Finishing it off he leaned back in the chair.

"Thank you Cyn, at least the nausea is gone," he said standing. "But I need to wash that taste out of my mouth."

Cynthia raised her hand and placed it on his chest. "No, nothing to drink. Now you rest."

He looked at her black leather gloves and was about to argue when a wave of exhaustion washed over him. "Oh, maybe that's a good idea," he said.

She guided him over to the bed and he laid down, closing his eyes as his head sunk into the pillow. Then his whole body went limp, head tilting to one side, and he began to snore.

"What did you do to him?" asked Kami standing a few feet away.

Turning slowly Cynthia looked at Kami a moment before saying, "I gave him what he needed to get better."

Kami crossed her arms, looking at the sleeping figure on the bed. "Should I stay here with him?"

"No, he will be fine, let us go," said Cynthia raising a hand toward the doorway.

Kami hesitantly turned around and started walking, as she reached the doorway the room behind her fell into complete darkness. Looking back she saw Cynthia closing the last of the thick curtains of the room. In the dimness she could barely make out Kyle's sleeping form on the bed. She frowned, then ran downstairs to her room.

Chapter 04.02

JadedKitty411: mornin QT

DarkRoseQueen: ::yawns:: Hello.

JadedKitty411: howd date go?

DarkRoseQueen: He was sooooo cool. He saved my life.

JadedKitty411: WTF??

DarkRoseQueen: Really!! Theres this big x thing with a fat guy tied to it, and it fell, and he pulled me into his strong arms, out of harms way.

DarkRoseQueen: Thing even smashed his shoulder. I could see he was in pain but he played it off like it was nothing!!

JadedKitty411: wow. was he cute?

DarkRoseQueen: Yessss... OMG he was soo nie too!

DarkRoseQueen: *nice

JadedKitty411: so you going out on another date?

DarkRoseQueen: I wish. I was a dork and couldnt figure out what to wear, got there late, had to leave early.

DarkRoseQueen: But I gave him my number.

DarkRoseQueen: I wish I wasnt such a Loser. :(

JadedKitty411: lighten up. do you have his contact inf?

DarkRoseQueen: Yeah, his roommate sent it to me.

JadedKitty411: then drop him an email

JadedKitty411: maybe can make up last night ad start talking via email or im?

DarkRoseQueen: Thanks, that's a great idea!

DarkRoseQueen: gotta run to class.

DarkRoseQueen: Bye

JadedKitty411: SYL QT!!

JadedKitty411: call me after class

DarkRoseQueen: k

Chapter 04.03

Keiko was still lying on the couch where she had fallen asleep after returning from the club the night before, her outfit lay in a pile on the floor near her. She was wrapped in a blanket watching Cartoon Network. The sounds of neighbors going about their morning routines filtered through the open windows, fighting with the audio of the television.

She was not even sure if she had slept last night. All she could remember was constant tossing and turning, checking the time every once in a while. Part way through the night she had considered going back to her bedroom, but had decided against that, the living room was free of photographs.

Slowly she sat up on the couch, pulling the blanket tight. Mustering determination she stood and walked to the kitchen. Grabbing a short glass she opened the freezer and pulled out the large bottle of Grey Goose and poured herself half a glass. Placing the bottle back, Keiko leaned against the counter and took a few long sips from the glass. Shaking her head she walked out of the kitchen into the hallway and started toward her bedroom, stopping several steps from the doorway. Turning around quickly she returned to the kitchen.

Keiko opened the freezer and looked over the sparse contents. Closing it she opened the other door, looked at the almost empty fridge, and closed that door, returning to the freezer for a couple of frozen waffles. Putting them in the toaster she stared at the dripping water of the faucet as she waited for them to cook. The two waffles popped up, one of them just enough that it flipped over and fell onto the counter.

She bent down and looked at the tile of the counter which had not been cleaned since she was last home over a week ago and made a gagging noise. Tossing that waffle into the trash she grabbed the other one and started munching on it.

Grabbing the glass of vodka with her other hand she walked back into the living room and watched some more cartoons. She simply stared at the television, not seeing what was on.

"Stupid girl," she said aloud.

Clenching her fists she stood, grabbed her drink, taking another long gulp, and walked quickly to the bedroom. Slowly she entered the room and walked to the bed, sitting on the edge. On the nightstand two grinning faces stared at her, the Eiffel Tower behind the smiling forms.

Keiko stared at the ground, ignoring the image as best she could. Finishing off her drink, she looked up and tried to focus on the frame that surrounded the picture but, she could not stop looking at the captured memory itself. Her and Kyle, in Paris, her first big shoot. When they were happy. When the future seemed so certain. When he was the most important thing in her world.

Tears welling in her eyes she ran back to the living room, jumping onto the couch, and laid there staring at the moving images, trying to let them burn the picture of the smiling people out of her mind. Everything eventually became fuzzy.

She must have fallen asleep, because a noise came from the front door and caused her to jump up, suddenly awake, though pleasantly buzzed.

Grumbling she stood, wrapping herself in the blanket, and walked over to the intercom. Pressing a button down she asked, "Who is it?" in a bitter tone.

"Good morning, Keiko, it's Jonathon," came the chipper voice.

She moaned and pressed the button to talk again.

"What are you doing here?" she asked.

"You said on the phone yesterday that we could talk today, so I am here to talk," he said.

"Um, Jonathon, have you ever heard of calling ahead?" she asked wryly. "I had a long flight back, had a full evening, and am not even really conscious yet."

"Then now isn't a good time for you?" he asked.

"No, not really," she said.

"But, well, are you sure?" he asked, pausing before saying the last word.

"Yes, Jonathon," said Keiko. "If you want to come back after noon to talk, that would be fine, though."

She heard some muffled swearing, and when Jonathon spoke again his voice was deeper and sharper in tone. "Fine. But I have to be in the office. Come by my office at two. Do you understand? Two o'clock. We will talk then."

"Fine, I'll be there around two," she said leaning against the wall.

"No, not around two, at two," screamed Jonathon. "Do not disappoint me."

Keiko reflexively looked at the ground and took a deep breath, then said, "My apologies, Jonathon. I will be there at two."

"Good," he said.

The sound of his car reversing, then the squealing of tires as he departed, came through the open windows.

Keiko leaned against the wall motionless for a minute, trembling slightly. Letting out a scream she grabbed the umbrella from the corner next to the door and began smashing the wall with all her strength.

The long metal umbrella was bent, cloth shredded when she stopped, deep gouges in the drywall stared back at her. Throwing the umbrella down the hallway it shattered a vase of flowers as she dropped to her knees and began sobbing uncontrollably.

Chapter 04.04

Even though he was standing barefoot in the snow wearing just jeans and a T-shirt, Kyle was not cold. He was staring at the ground, watching the flashing red and blue lights illuminate the white powder that covered his ankles.

A short distance away was a mass of paramedics, firemen and police officers surrounding a small car that was smashed almost all the way underneath the back bumper of a semi truck's trailer. From the passenger door nearest him a dark red liquid dripped into the snow, staining it.

"Any survivors?" asked a cop to one of the firemen.

"Unlikely, two adults were in the front, not much of them left obviously, and there's a kid smashed in the back," he motioned to the car.

The shower of sparks from the giant saw faded and a group of men pulled off the back door of the car. Another tried to get into the back seat but was unable to, he reached up a hand to the child.

"We have a live one here!" he screamed.

The gathered men swarmed on the crushed car and began to work at getting the boy out of the back seat.

Kyle turned his back to the scene, looking to the snow again, and began to walk away. After a few feet he stopped, seeing the black dress of somebody standing in his way.

"Cynthia?" asked Kyle looking up.

"Hello," she said bowing her head slightly. The dark eyes focused on him. "I thought you could not remember this?"

"I can't," he said putting his hands into the pockets of his blue jeans and looking to his left, over his shoulder. "At least when I'm awake. Sometimes I know I dreamed this but never can remember details. Not that I want to remember anything about the past."

"Understandable," she said.

With a slight motion of her hand they were standing underneath the stars on the beach, the full moon illuminating the night. She turned to face the water and sat down in the sand, pulling her knees up and wrapping her arms around her legs.

Kyle sat down next to her. He stared at the stars, then out onto the mist shrouded waters of the ocean. Looking over he said, "Can I ask you something?"

"You may," she said unmoving.

"Um, well, it's just," he began, then paused, shifting his position to extend his legs out and leaning back on both hands. "It's just I wanted to know why you've been acting so weird toward me over the last few days."

"How so?"

"Well, you never touch anybody," said Kyle. "Hell, I can't even remember the last time I saw you touch Ed. But putting your hand on my chest a little while ago, and that thing at the club before we left, it was just kind of…"

"Disconcerting?" she interjected.

"A little," he said.

She nodded, but said nothing.

He stared out into the dark waters.

"Does it have something to do with Ed leaving, or are you two having problems?" he asked. "You know if you need to talk I'm always here. Well, not here in a dream, but you know what I mean."

"That is not it," she whispered.

He watched the wind play with her hair, strands of black flowing around the side of her face.

"Then what?" he asked.

In one quick move she spun around, pushing him backward, and straddled Kyle. In shock, he could not move. She leaned down, her body pressing against him, her face close. Cynthia's dark eyes looked into his, her pale white face expressed no emotion and looked like a porcelain doll in the moonlight. One of her bare hands touched the side of his face.

"Even I am not sure," she said.

Kyle shot up in bed and looked around him, seeing the darkness of the room. He shook his head as he pulled his sweat drenched shirt off. Something about snow, and flashing lights, a beach and Cynthia. He struggled to remember but it slipped from his mind.

He looked at the clock next to his bed. Cursing at the time, 10:04, he jumped out of bed and ran across the dark room to his computer, grabbing his cell phone and dialing a number.

"Hello?" asked a female voice.

"Heather? It's Kyle. I'm so sorry I missed our appointment this morning," said Kyle.

"What do you mean?" she asked. "So you are running a little late, that is alright, so am I. How about we shoot for noon?"

"Noon?" asked Kyle.

"Yes," said Heather. "Or do you have an appointment later today with another client?"

He turned around and saw a small sliver of sunlight through the drawn curtains. Moving the mouse to eliminate the screensaver he saw the time displayed: 10:05 AM.

"Kyle? Are you alright?"

"What? Yes, yes. Didn't feel good this morning. Probably just the flu, or stress from moving all day Saturday combined with going out last night. A friend brewed something up for me and I feel much better now," he said. "Sorry, I fell back asleep and thought it was ten at night."

"What did she give you?" asked Heather.

"Dunno," said Kyle. "Cynthia is into herbs and stuff. Whatever it was I feel great."

Heather said nothing for a moment. "Are you sure, you seemed kind of drained at the club. Are you quite sure that you feel fine?"

"Feel like a million bucks," he said.

"Well then, noon?"

"Sure."

"See you in a few hours," said Heather.

"See you then," said Kyle hanging up.

He set the phone down and walked over to the curtains, pulling them open. He squinted at the bright scene before him and immediately closed the curtains. Turning around he grabbed some clean clothes and went into the bathroom to take a shower.

A while later he emerged and went downstairs. Ed was sitting on the far end of the couch, Kami was on the couch also, and both were watching television.

"Oh my god," said Kami seeing him. "What the hell?"

Kyle looked down at himself, "Huh?"

"I can't believe that you looked like death warmed over an hour ago and now you look fine," she said.

"Ah, well, you have Cyn and her spooky brew to thank for that, I feel fine now."

"Wow," she said.

"Hey," said Kyle looking at Ed. "What are you doing home, thought you had work."

"Eh," he said sighing. "Some stupid safety meeting this morning. But, lucky me, I get to go back in a few hours to work a full shift."

"That sucks," said Kyle.

"Tell me about it."

Kyle started to walk to the kitchen and stopped as Ed spoke.

"Kyle?" he asked.

"What?"

"Oh, go get your coffee," he said waving a hand.

Kyle went into the kitchen, paused to read the note on the board that Harry and Thomas were at work, then returned with a cup of coffee in hand and placed it on the end table, sitting down in a chair near the couch.

"What did you want?" asked Kyle.

Ed grabbed the remote from between him and Kami and pressed the mute button.

"What was last night all about?" asked Ed.

"Huh?" asked Kyle, trying to look innocent, hoping he had not seen the arm thing with Cynthia.

Ed looked at Kami and pointed a finger at Kyle.

"OK, check this out," said Ed to her. "Mister Anti-Social here goes out to this club last night for a blind date I set up. This cute college girl shows up, and they're talking. I'm being Mister Voyeur to see how He of No Social Skills is doing, when all of the sudden this big St. Andrews cross with a fat guy tied to it breaks and starts falling on them."

"St. Andrews Cross?" asked Kami.

"Like this big X made of wood you strap people to so that they can be whipped and stuff," said Ed.

"You people really need help," said Kami making a weird face.

"Anyway, this thing is falling, and faster than I can follow, Mister Kyle here jumps forward, grabs her, and pulls them out of harms way. Except that this cross smashes his shoulder in a serious way. I saw it, he went to one knee with the impact, but totally blows it off like nothing happened. Then Little Miss College Girl is enamored with him and clinging onto his arm espousing how Kyle here just saved her life."

Kami started laughing. "Oh, god, I can see it now." She stood and placed the back of her hand against her forehead. "Oh, Kyle my love," she said dropping to her knees and grabbing his arm, rubbing her face into it. Looking up into his eyes, her motions exaggerated, she crooned, "You are so big and strong and handsome, and you have saved my life, please take me."

"I think you read too much shoujo manga," said Kyle smiling down at her.

"No I don't! Onii-chan no Baka!" she exclaimed. "Let go of me," she screamed, standing and dropping his arm, returning to the couch and glaring at Kyle.

Ed reached over and poked her arm.

"What?" she asked glaring at him, raising a fist.

"That's not even the best part," he said.

"You know I'm right here," said Kyle. He raised a hand slightly and waved to Cynthia who had walked in and taken a seat in the chair opposite his.

"Later," said Ed ignoring his roommate, "This really famous Dom named Lucy grabs him and takes him outside, college girl still attached to his arm. And then, this hot Irish chick shows up, who is a client or something. So he's standing there with these three beautiful chicks."

"Four," said Kyle motioning over at Cynthia.

She bowed her head at him as the two people on the couch turned and jumped slightly at her presence.

"Oh, hey," said Ed. Turning back to Kyle he said, "Just how the hell do you know Lucy?"

"Lucy?" asked Kyle, his mind racing. He had never told anybody, except Keiko and Lucy, about the kidnapping incident. And had sworn Thomas and Harry to secrecy about it also, which they had agreed to, obviously.

"Uh, well, remember that night that I got laid off and disappeared for about a day? I had ended up driving around and ended up at this hotel and met her at the bar."

"You said you were at Keiko's," said Kami.

"Well, the next day I went over to Keiko's," said Kyle.

"Whoa, no way," said Ed. "You spent the night with Lucy at a hotel?"

"No."

"Who's Lucy?" asked Kami.

"She's this really infamous Dom girl..."

"Dom?" Kami asked.

"Like Dominatrix," said Ed. "You know, like S&M stuff."

"Ewwwwww," said Kami. "You're into S&M, Kyle?"

"No!!!" he screamed. "I just ran into her, she was dressed really normal in a skirt and a shirt, and I had no idea she was a Dominatrix. Really. We just talked, and it was some weird fluke that she was at the club last night."

"Not really, she performs there once in a while," said Ed.

"Oh," said Kyle.

"So how does some geek like you end up standing around with three, er, I mean four hot girls?" asked Ed.

Kyle shrugged his shoulders. "Luck?"

"Luck my ass," said Ed.

"Probably just a fluke," said Kami. "Considering how sick he was this morning it seems obvious he is allergic to girls."

"Anyway, enough with this gossip about me. I need to go do some stuff before meeting with my client," said Kyle standing.

"The Irish chick?" asked Ed.

"Yes, and her name is Heather," said Kyle turning around and going down the hallway.

"And what's with this Heather?" asked Ed.

"Indeed?" asked Cynthia softly.

Kyle ignored them and ascended the stairs.

Chapter 04.05

The bell above the door rang as Thomas and Harry stepped in.

"May I help you?" asked Corin adjusting his glasses and peering at them.

"It is I, Dunne, Thomas Dunne," he said tossing his hair back and walking across the store to the man behind the counter. "So good to see you again this fine morning."

"Thomas?" asked Corin. "Hmmm... You look awfully familiar, and so does the gentleman behind you. Ah! You're the ones who ordered that unpublished Crowley book back about ten years ago, aren't you. I have it around here somewhere, wondered what happened to you chaps."

"We are your new assistants," said Harry.

"Right then, indeed you are!" exclaimed Corin pounding the counter with his fist and smiling. "No wonder you looked familiar. Sorry, memory not what it used to be. Too many people over the years. And how are the two of you?"

"Everything is satisfactory," said Harry.

"Absolutely beautiful," said Thomas.

"How wonderful to hear," he said looking at his pocket watch. "I take that the two of you did not have any adventures this morning?"

"No, sir. We boarded the correct bus this morning," said Harry.

"Good, good," said Corin. "Well then, I need to get some papers together so I shall be in the back office. Take care of things out here until I am finished, if you please."

Corin disappeared behind the curtains.

Thomas and Harry both walked behind the counter. The younger man opened a drawer and pulled out a notepad and a pen, then sat down on the floor and started to write, talking softly to himself as he did so.

Pulling out one of Corin's black books, Harry deposited his briefcase on a shelf under the counter and sat down on a stool. He started to leaf through the pages and stopped. Closing the book he placed it on the counter.

"What's wrong?" asked Thomas stretching and leaning against the wall.

"Too many things to memorize for a situation that may not last long," he said.

"Ah, true, hopefully my dear father will have some luck with the ladies or something and get in a better mood so that things can return to normal," said Thomas closing his eyes and smiling.

"More specifically, Master Thomas, I was hoping you would change your ways to resolve that issue. Your father does have some points, as much as you may not like to admit it to yourself."

Letting out a long sigh, Thomas opened his eyes and looked up at his mentor. "I understand you are correct. That this is a product of my thoughtlessness. But I need to follow my dreams or I will die."

"Then follow your dreams, but balance it with some responsibility," said Harry.

"Your words, as always, ring true," said Thomas. "Thank you. You are a beautiful man and I do not know what would happen to me if you were not around."

Harry stared down at the young man, thinking that if his son was still alive he would be about the age of Thomas right now. He wondered what type of person he would have become.

"It is nothing, sir," said Harry.

Turning, Harry stared out into the room. Thomas began writing again, but after a short time leaned back and fell asleep against the wall. Several hours passed, Harry remaining motionless, lost in thought.

"May I speak with Corin?" came a soft voice next to Harry.

The stool went flying backward, bouncing between the counter and the shelves behind him as Harry instinctively jumped out of it and assumed a defensive position.

"Damn you," said Harry standing upright and looking down at Cynthia. "Please do not do that."

"Do what?" asked Cynthia tilting her head slightly.

"What is all the commotion out here?" asked Corin coming through the curtains and stepping over Thomas.

"Sir, I was watching the store and she suddenly appeared out of nowhere," said Harry pointing at Cynthia.

"She does that," said Corin.

"Do you have your paperwork in order?" she asked.

"Taxes?" he asked. "Right, I think I do this time."

Corin went through the curtains and returned a moment later with a large stack of folders which he handed to Cynthia.

"Thank you," she said taking them. Kneeling she opened the large case on the floor and placed the folders in it.

"By the way, Corin," she said standing. "Looking over your paperwork from last year it would seem appropriate for you to have this business inherited by a cousin or some other relative within the next two years. You have owned this building for almost forty years, and in this day and age, it would be best not to take any chances."

"Oh, my dear, I do not have any cousins," said Corin.

"Cousin being you," said Cynthia.

"Oh, indeed?" asked Corin. "Forty years, seems right, I guess, if you say so."

"I can make the arrangements for a new license, social security number, transfer of the deed, money, and all necessary papers if you like."

"Very well then," said Corin. "If you think it is best, let us make it so. How about a late lunch to celebrate?"

"My apologies," she said. "I have much work to do between you and other clients. I shall have to decline."

"Ah, very well then, I am off to the Pub," said Corin. "Harry, watch things while I am away."

"Is there anything you would like me to do?" asked Harry.

"No, not that I can think of," said Corin. "Back in a bit."

Corin walked half way across the room, stopped, started walking back, then turned around and left the store.

Harry let out a big sigh, then turned to Cynthia.

"What, exactly, is going on here?" he asked, his voice rising slightly. "What is this talk of cousins, and ownership and such? I am unsure who you people are, but there is definitely something not right with all of this."

The only part of Cynthia that moved were here eyes, which looked up into Harry's, as she said in a cold, clear voice, "These are not matters that concern you."

Harry took a step back.

She closed her eyes and said, "As for matters that do, one thing you could do is water and mow the lawn, or organize this room, seeing as nothing is in order."

"Regarding my previous question?" asked Harry.

"As I said, this matter does not concern you," said Cynthia staring into his eyes. "And I would advise not pursuing any questions along those lines again."

Harry paused a moment, this fear he had never felt before filling him. Then he said, taking another step back and trying to laugh, "My apologies, Miss Cynthia."

She simply stared at him with cold dark eyes, her head barely inclining forward.

"Eeeeeeerrrrrrrrraaaaaarrrrrgggghhhh!" screamed Thomas sitting up suddenly, panting heavily.

"Are you alright?" asked Harry spinning around quickly.

"I hate this place! I need a date!" exclaimed the young man.

"Master Thomas, I believe that there are more pressing matters to attend to. Perhaps you could even take a few moments from your writing to actually do some work around here so that we may keep this job."

"For the love of God I hate this," said Thomas.

"I would have to concur," said Harry.

Turning to Cynthia, Harry saw an empty floor. Glancing around he saw that she was gone. Sighing heavily he picked up the stool from the floor and sat down.

Chapter 04.06

Kyle followed Heather from the porch into her house, taking off the dark sunglasses he had purchased before coming over, and placed the bags at his feet.

Heather turned slowly and stared at him for a moment.

"What did that person give you to make you feel better?" she asked.

"Huh?" asked Kyle. "I don't know, like I said, she's into herbs and stuff so who knows what she might have given me."

Stepping forward quickly, Heather grabbed the shoulder that had been hit by the wooden beam the night before. Closing her hand with enough force to cause him discomfort she asked, "And what happened to your shoulder?"

"Hey, stop that," he said pulling out of her grip. "Just got dislocated and I popped it back into place. Why are you acting so strange?"

"Did you feel anything strange after it happened?" she asked.

Kyle paused, thinking back. Everything had happened so quickly he had not really paid much attention, more distracted that there was a female in his arms than the fact one had almost been torn off by a wooden beam.

"Well," he said. "It hurt a lot, which is when I grabbed it, and I couldn't really move it. And a shock of pain hit me and that's when I must have accidentally put it back into place, because that's when it got warm and kind of numb and then it was fine."

Heather stared into his eyes for a moment then turned away.

"My apologies, there is something else I need to take care of today, so we will have to re-schedule."

"What?" asked Kyle. "But I drove all the way down..."

She cut him off saying, "Your payment is in the envelope on the counter. Please see yourself out."

Heather walked out of the room, listening to the muffled grumbling behind her and the sound of the envelope being taken as the front door slammed.

Her mind raced and she ran into the living room and grabbed the phone, calling her sister.

"McClellan residence," came the dry male voice over the line.

"It is Heather, may I speak with Caitlin?"

"Just a moment, Ma'am," came the reply.

"Yes?" asked Caitlin.

"I need your help," said Heather, fighting back tears. "It is about Kyle."

"Not my concern."

The connection went dead.

Heather dropped the phone into her lap, staring over to the photo of her sister in-law, and then covering her face to stem the tears.

Chapter 04.07

Letting out the last of a series of punches Keiko stood and steadied the large punching bag that hung from the rafters of her training room. She had found that kickboxing provided both good exercise and a good way to relieve stress. Letting out a long breath she removed her gloves and tossed them aside, walking back to her bedroom.

Taking a quick shower she threw on some sweat pants, running shoes, and a baggy T-shirt, then grabbed a coat and went into the living room. Taking the keys off the coffee table she fished around in the purse from the night before and grabbed her wallet and cell phone, shoving them into the pocket of her jacket. Glancing at the time on her watch she let out a series of curses and ran out the door to her car.

Some time later she pulled into the parking garage underneath the large building of her agency. She checked her watch again and winced, closing her eyes. Taking a few deep breaths she got out and took the elevators to the top floor, walked down the hallway and into the agency. The floors were marble and the chairs in the waiting area were mahogany as was the desk behind which sat a woman in her early twenties.

"Keiko," said the receptionist standing. "So good to see you. How was the shoot in Prague?"

"It went well," said Keiko. "Is Jonathon available?"

"Let me check," she said pressing a button on the phone.

"Hello, Keiko is here to see Mr. Williams. Really? I'll send her back then." Pressing a button to disconnect the call she said, "He is expecting you."

"Thanks," said Keiko and turned to walk through the cubicles and corridors to the corner office.

As she approached a young man stood from his desk quickly and greeted her at the intricately carved double doors. Turning he opened them both and stepped in saying, "Miss Nakamura is here to see you."

The leather chair was turned around, facing away from them. "See her in," said Jonathon.

Motioning with an extended arm the young man followed Keiko in and made sure she was comfortable in the high backed leather trimmed chair.

"Would you like a refreshment?" asked the assistant.

"No, thank you, I'm fine," said Keiko.

"She will have a glass of ice water, with a splash of lemon," said Jonathon, his back still to them. "And bring me a scotch on the rocks. Now."

"Right away, sir," said the man who walked quickly to the other side of the room.

The young man returned from the bar a minute later, placing the glass of water on a coaster next to Keiko, and the Scotch on a coaster on the large desk.

"Leave, now, and close the door. Hold all calls," said Jonathon.

"As you wish, sir," he said leaving the room quickly, closing the doors behind him.

Jonathon sat in silence for a few minutes before he spoke.

"I said two o'clock."

"I'm sorry," she said. "I was working out, and I was only five minutes late."

"Did I ask for excuses?"

"No."

He slowly turned around. When he saw her a disgusted look crossed his face.

"What is this shit?" he asked.

Keiko looked furtively around. "What?" she asked.

Sneering he said, "Look at you. If you want to dress like a slob you do it on your own time, I run a modeling agency here, not an athletic club. How many times do I need to tell you not to wear such abominable outfits in my presence you stupid girl?"

Sinking back into her chair she looked at the floor and held her hands tightly in her lap.

"I'm sorry," she said.

"What did you say?"

"My apologies, Jonathon," she said.

He let out a deep breath and reached forward, taking the glass of scotch and sipped it slowly before placing it back on the coaster.

Trying to change the subject Keiko asked, "So what did you want to talk about?"

"That does not matter," he snapped. "This is all wrong. All wrong. Not how it should be. I will talk to you about that when the time is right."

"Um, OK," said Keiko.

"Though there is something else we need to discuss," he said standing and walking around to sit on the edge of his desk near her. He grabbed the glass and swirled the ice inside it before taking another drink.

"You disappear sometimes, and I used to never know exactly where you were," he said. "This has to stop."

"What's the big deal?" she asked. "I have a phone by my side constantly, it's just sometimes I need a break so I stay at a friend's houses and stuff."

"Ever hear of paparazzi?" he asked. "You are on the cusp right now, the last thing you need is some scandal. And the best way to avoid that is to make sure you stay out of trouble. Now, Keiko, how can I make sure you are staying out of trouble if I do not even know where you are? And what manner of incriminating photographs could they produce from your selfish behavior?"

"So you are telling me I can't even be around my friends?" she asked sinking farther into her chair.

"Depends on the friends," he said. "Those old friends you disappear with, definitely not. But being seen around town with friends who are prominent models, actors, actresses, producers and the like would be good for you and your career."

"Those aren't friends," said Keiko softly.

"All part of the game," he said flashing a smile. "You in or are you out?"

Keiko said nothing and stared at the floor near his feet, knowing better than to answer.

"You are in, whether you like it or not," said Jonathon coldly. "I have tired of your pathetic rebellious nature. You rarely go out to events, your career barely holds onto the photo shoots you do and the occasional interview. This is going to change. We will make a new Keiko, one who is seen around town. One who dates or is engaged to a worthwhile individual. One that people will say is the next Tyra or Claudia or Heidi."

He drank the last of his scotch and held the empty glass in his hands.

"So, from here out I will not only be managing your professional career but also your private affairs so that we can meet these ends."

Slowly she looked up at him, staring into those hollow grey eyes.

"And what if I say no?" she asked.

He smiled slightly and dropped his head a moment before looking back up into her eyes. Shaking his head several times he looked up to the ceiling and stared at the ornate tiling. Looking back at her he pulled his hand back and threw the glass at her. It passed several inches from her face and smashed against the floor near the doors.

"What if?" he asked standing and walking over to her. Staring down he said, "What if?!"

Kneeling next to her he placed one hand on the chair and leaned close. His other hand shot up quickly, grabbing her around the throat and he pushed her head back into the leather chair.

Instinctively she grabbed his wrist with both of her hands, trying to pull it away.

"Let go," he said squeezing her throat slightly.

Hesitating for a second she dropped her hands to the arms of the chair, grasping them so tight that her knuckles turned white. She looked sideways at him.

"Let me make this clear," said Jonathon in a soothing voice. "I pulled you out of that shit mom and pop modeling wannabe agency and have made you what you are today. You will do as I say, because if you do not, trust me, I will make sure that you never work around here again. Agencies will flee from the simple mention of your name."

She tried to speak but he squeezed tighter.

"Keiko," he said in a comforting tone, caressing her face with his free hand. "I am only doing this because I believe in you, because I care about you. You can be great with the proper guidance. Now is the time to make or break. And I will either make you or break you."

He smiled and leaned forward, kissing her lightly on the lips. "I would much prefer the former than the latter."

Tears began to well in her eyes.

"Don't," he said sternly.

A single tear traced down her face.

"You unappreciative bitch," he raising his hand to hit her. He paused and smiled. "You are distraught, that is understandable. Having the possibility to get everything that you wished, everything I promised you is probably overwhelming.

His free hand fished around in the inside pocket of his coat and produced a pill.

"Here, this will help you calm down," he said.

Her mouth was forming the word 'no' repeatedly.

Raising the pill to her mouth she pressed her lips shut.

"Stupid girl," he said standing while still holding her throat. The hand that held the pill formed a fist and he punched her in the stomach. She leaned forward, mouth open and he popped the pill in and covered her mouth with his hand.

"We can sit here until you swallow it or you can have some water to help wash it down," he said.

She closed her eyes, holding back the tears, wanting no more pain. Opening her eyes she nodded and looked at the glass of water next to her.

"Very good. I may be able to form you into the next top super-model of the world yet," he said raising the water to her lips.

He kneeled again, relaxing his grip on her neck slightly.

"Now then, seeing all this nonsense has been going on, I have booked a flight for you day after tomorrow for another shoot. An Australian magazine."

"But my Mother and Grandmother leave in three days," she said.

"I understand, I understand, which is why after that I have booked a flight for you to visit them in Japan. While you are off in that part of the world for a time I will work on getting you into some premiers and charity fundraisers and such so we can start on the next phase of your career."

Keiko stared out the window and watched a crow fly by. Flying, free, fleeting dreams. Taking a deep breath she relaxed every muscle in her body.

"Ah, there now, feel better?" he asked.

She nodded her head.

"Excellent," Jonathon said standing and letting her go. "Probably not safe for you to drive, those things are very strong."

He walked back to his desk and sat down in the chair. Picking up the phone he pressed a button. "Yes, Keiko isn't feeling too well, so I need a limo to take her home and somebody to drive her car back also. Thank you."

Keiko slouched even further into the chair.

"You alright my love?" asked Jonathon.

"I need to pee," said Keiko. Her words were slurred.

"Oh, of course, let me help you," he said.

Coming around the desk he carefully helped her stand and assisted her across his office to the bathroom.

"Sank you," she said stepping inside.

Closing the door behind her she purposefully made shuffled noises with her shoes, making her way to the toilet.

Opening her mouth she let the pill fall into the toilet. Turning around she moaned and slurred some words, made some fake fart noises, moaned some more and then waited a while.

Pulling a line of toilet paper off she threw it in the toilet. Then did the same thing several more times. Finally she flushed the toilet.

Keiko walked over to the sink and tried to look at her reflection, but could not meet her own eyes. Washing her hands, she splashed her face with water. Resuming her drug-induced stupor, she stumbled back to the door and fumbled with the handle to the a few times before opening it. Jonathon's assistant was there and he stepped forward to hold her up.

"Make sure she gets home safe," said Jonathon. His chair was turned with its back to them.

"Yes, sir," he said and led her out of the office and through the corridors to the elevators. "I will need your keys to your car, Miss," he said as they got in.

Keiko fidgeted around in her purse and gave him the keys.

"Thank you" he said. "The red Eclipse Spyder, correct?"

She nodded.

The doors of the elevator opened and there was a stretch limo waiting a few feet away. He guided her into the back seat, closed the door and ran away. A few minutes later she heard the sound of her car's engine behind them. She had sat in the corner of the seat unmoving. The limo started forward.

On the drive home she stared out the window. Wanting to be a part of that world that lay beyond the cold steel and tinted windows.

At her home she got out of the limo and keyed in the code to open the gates, stumbling back into the limo and lying on the back seat. It drove her up the hill to her house and stopped. The chauffer opened the door closest to her house and the assistant leaned in.

"Keiko, we are home now," he said.

"Osh Kshay, Kewwwell," she slurred pushing herself up and lurching forward into his arms.

The assistant pulled her up and assisted her to the door. He handed her the keys and she opened it.

"Sank yooo," said Keiko opening the door, he guided her into the house and to the couch in the living room.

He carefully laid her down and pulled the blanket over her.

"Listen," he said. "I know you probably don't understand what I am saying, and probably won't remember any of this, but please, trust me, he is going to pay, not just for you, but for all the others, especially my sister."

Keiko's mind raced, but she had to continue to play the drugged model, so she simply smiled and nodded.

"Yeer new. Wat isss yer ah nam nam name?" she asked.

"Greg," he said.

With that he turned around and left, closing the door behind him. She heard the limo speed away.

She sat up in the couch, slamming her hand against the cushions. Standing, she went into the kitchen and poured a full glass of vodka. Drinking half the glass in one long gulp, she strode into her bedroom and grabbed the picture from the nightstand with trembling hands.

"I know you really like Kyle," she heard her Mother speaking to her from the past. It was the day after Keiko had returned from her first shoot in Paris. "The two of you have been friends for a while. But you seem to be getting closer lately. Promise me you will focus on your career. I know you think you are in love. I thought I was in love when I was eighteen also, but you have this incredible opportunity with Jonathon and his agency. Please do not ruin your future."

Keiko's answer echoed through her consumed mind.

"Yes, Mother. I promise, I will focus on my career."

The picture fell from her hands onto the floor, the glass shattering.

A NIGHT OUT ON THE TOWN

Chapter 05.01

Kyle knocked on Kami's door.

"Come," she said.

He opened the door and leaned in slightly, one hand holding the doorknob.

"Just wanted to let you know I was back," he said.

She spun around in her computer chair. "Oh, and how did the date with the hot Irish lady go?"

"I drove all the way down there, and suddenly she remembered some other meeting, or something, I'm not quite sure," he said shaking his head and sighing.

"Big waste of gas," said Kami.

"Well I still got paid," he said. "Hey, Keiko was due back in last night, have you heard from her."

"Ah, oh, yeah, she called me last night, she made it back safe," said Kami who turned back to her computers quickly.

"That's odd, she usually calls me after she calls you," said Kyle. "You didn't tell her about the blind date, did you?"

"Baka, of course not," exclaimed Kami. "Like that's any of my business."

"You sure you didn't say anything," asked Kyle, suspicious.

"Get out of my room, you tentacle loving freak, before I call the police," she mumbled.

"Really?" he asked. "So you're the one who's been borrowing my Hentai without permission."

"Have not!" she said clenching both fists. "Just get out."

"Sure, guess I'll be upstairs," he said, his voice displaying how unconvinced he was.

"Whatever," she muttered as she started typing.

He began to close the door.

"Wait," she said spinning around again.

"Going to confess?" asked Kyle, raising an eyebrow.

"Oh you wish," she retorted, looking over to her bed.

"Figures, what's up?" he asked.

"What's behind those double doors that are always locked at the end of the hall? I saw Cynthia go in there yesterday."

"The study," he said.

"Why is it locked?"

"She keeps her books and stuff in there I guess, maybe some of her work. Haven't been in there since she took it over last year."

"You can't even go in there? That doesn't seem right."

"Well," he said. "I guess I could, haven't felt the need to. The room really wasn't being used anyway, other than storing books. And when was the last time you saw me reading something other than Manga? So really saw no harm when Cyn asked to set up shop in there."

"Can I go in and look? I hate not knowing what's in there."

"Um... no," said Kyle. "And anyway does Cynthia really seem like the type of person you would want to piss off?"

"Ooooh, I'm so scared," said Kami raising both hands. "What is she going to do, scowl me to death?"

Kyle crossed his arms and leaned against the door.

"Back when Cyn and Keiko were juniors in High School, there was this cheerleader who had made it her mission in life to eliminate the weirdoes and freaks, basically intimidate them into transferring to another private school or something. This girl did something really bad to Cyn, in front of the whole student body from what I heard. Two days later that cheerleader goes insane, almost kills herself, and has been locked up in a mental institution ever since."

"What did Cynthia do?"

"That's the thing, nobody knows if she did something or it was some odd coincidence."

"Creepy, creepy, creepy," said Kami under her breath.

"Exactly, so don't mess with her. Ever," said Kyle.

"Yeah, sure," said Kami, suddenly needing to attend to one of her computers.

"Talk to you later," said Kyle.

She just raised a hand.

Closing the door, he went upstairs.

Kyle sat on the corner of his bed and stared out the doors of the balcony.

Strange that Keiko had not called him. She always called Kami, then him when she got back into town. Unless... Unless Kami had actually told her about that blind date last night, and Keiko was mad at him again.

The last two times he had tried dating, Keiko had been both upset and distant to him, saying that he deserved better. Which was probably right considering how quickly the relationships had disintegrated.

He slid down the edge of his bed and took the picture that was still face down on his nightstand and set it upright. Staring at it for a while, he stood up and grabbed his phone to call Keiko.

"Hello," she said.

"Hi, missed you, how was the flight?"

"It was ok," said Keiko.

Her words were slightly slurred, which was never a good sign. He tried to choose his words carefully.

"Hey, you alright? Sound a little down," he said.

"Just got back from my agent, have to leave day after tomorrow for another shoot and interview."

"Wait, your mom and grandma are leaving in three days."

She sighed, "I know, but I'm going to visit them in Japan after the shoot."

"Oh, that's cool," he said.

"I guess."

"Keiko?"

"What?"

"You don't sound so good. I'm free the rest of the day, want to go celebrate your return?"

Celebrating her return was a term they had coined many years ago. After she got back from an assignment they would go out to dinner and spend the day together, going different places, talking, and having fun.

"I..." she trailed off. "I don't think I'll be able to do that."

"Well, maybe when you get back."

"I have to go," she said and the line went dead.

He stared at the phone and considered calling her back, then decided against it. Something was wrong, maybe just stress, but Keiko was extremely stubborn. He would just be wasting his time trying to

get her to talk, and would piss her off if he tried.

Walking across the room he sat down at his computer and checked his email. There was one from Janice. He stared at his monitor and blinked a few times, wondering how she got his address. Then he remembered how Ed could be at times and sighed. Slowly moving the mouse up to the email, he double-clicked to open it.

From: JaniceA   To: Kyle
Subject: Last Night

Kyle,

Hi there! I just wanted to thank you for being so nice last night. And I wanted to apologize for ruining the evening by showing up so late we didn't have time to talk

Its just, i Know I'm supposed to wait for you to call and all but and i hope you dont think I'm being too forward amd am making you mad but I wanted to see if we could possibly go out again maybe tno to a club cause I'd like to talk with you more.

Janice

"If I am not wrong, there should be a turtle civilization around here." --Seta

He leaned back in his chair and read the email again.

"Wow, she didn't think I was an idiot?" he asked his computer. "Ugh, then again we only exchanged maybe twenty words."

Clicking the reply button he began to compose an apology that he was really busy with work, that it had been nice to meet her, that maybe they could get together some time. The cursor hovered over the send button. Slowly he let go of his mouse and stood, then began pacing back and forth in front of his computer. A few minutes later he sat back down and went to click the send button, but stopped again.

Cursing under his breath he highlighted the message and deleted it.

"What's the worst that could happen, another quick crash and burn, right?" he asked himself.

Pulling out his PDA he checked his schedule. Setting it down he stood and paced in front of the computer for about ten minutes, sat down, stared at the screen, stood and paced some more, double-checked his schedule, then sat down and placed his fingers on the keyboard.

```
From:  Kyle                To:  JaniceA
Subject:  Re: Last Night

Sure, we could do that.  And don't worry about
being late, at least we got to meet, right?  As
for being forward, actually, thank you for
emailing me.  You're not being too forward.  I
get busy with work sometimes and lose track of
time, and may have missed the all-important
waiting two days to call (at least according to
what everybody says ^_^).

How's Thursday?

--Kyle
```

He hesitated for a few minutes before finally clicking on the send button. After which he debated in his head for about an hour whether he had done the right thing.

Lost in thought the sound of a new instant message startled him. It was Keiko.

Asuka_EVA97: your offer for today still stand?

Negima23: Sure, have a change of heart?

Asuka_EVA97: Sort of. Just want to forget everything for a bit. Go out and have some fun with you one last time before I leave.

Negima23: makes sense. You seem to be a little distant lately. Stress?

Asuka_EVA97: Yeah. work sucks in a lot of ways right now.

Negima23: Then its a date. When you want me to pick you up.

Asuka_EVA97: No, don't pick me up here.

Asuka_EVA97: Kindof a long story. Think there's a stalker around but not sure. Gonna slip out back. Meet me at that park about a mile from here. Remember which one?

Negima23: The one with the stream, right? We've been there a few times.

Asuka_EVA97: Right. Make it about an hour, OK?

Asuka_EVA97: And don't drive near my place ok?

Negima23: Got it. See you then

Asuka_EVA97: Baibai. Thanks

Chapter 05.02

Being overcast and cool outside there were not many people in the park. As Kyle pulled his car into the lot he saw Keiko sitting on top of a picnic table watching children playing with a ball some distance away. He parked and got out, hesitating to see if she noticed he had arrived. Closing the car door he walked across the grass and stopped next to her.

"So what's a nice girl like you doing in a park like this?" he asked.

She looked up at him, startled. The sadness that filled her face faded.

"Waiting for a guy like you, I guess," Keiko said smiling and hopping off the table to the ground. She wrapped her arms around him, giving Kyle a big hug, holding him close for a while. Resting her head on his chest she enjoyed the feel of his arms around her, the feel of his chest raising up and down slowly as he breathed, the feel of his cheek pressed into her hair.

She pulled away and looked up into his eyes.

"Have you been crying?" he asked, a concerned look crossing his face, one of his fingers wiping away a slight wet spot at the corner of her eye.

Punching him lightly in the shoulder she smiled and said, "Don't want to talk about it, and I don't want to think about anything right now, just want to have some fun like we used to have."

"Well then," said Kyle. "We have a bit before the sun sets, want to walk through the trails?"

She nodded her head.

Side by side they walked across the grass to the woods nearby, following the path next to the stream that wandered through the forest. Neither spoke of the things happening in their lives, only what was around them right now. Catching glimpses of birds, squirrels, and other denizens of the woods, they laughed and joked and talked.

"Damn," said Keiko. "The sun is setting, guess we better get back."

They turned around and started back.

"Wow, hadn't realized how far in we'd gone," said Kyle.

Keiko took his arm. "Tell me about it, can barely see the path," she said.

"It's not that dark," said Kyle looking around them, noticing that though everything had a slight bluish tint he could see very clearly. "Well," he said pulling her closer, "At least one of us can see."

After a long walk they emerged from the forest into the park. Everything was quiet. Behind them the faint murmurs of nocturnal animals, before them the sounds of the city. A tan truck with a green circular logo on the side pulled up as they got to his car.

"Hey, come on," yelled a man from the gates. "Park closed half an hour ago."

"Sorry," said Kyle waving his arm at him.

The two of them got into his car and he pulled out of the parking lot, turning to go down the hill toward town.

"I'm starved," he said.

"Me too."

"In the mood for anything?" he asked.

She thought for a few seconds then said, "Pizza."

"Oh, good call," he said laughing lightly. "Ummmm... Manny's in Old Towne?"

"Perfect," she said. "Pizza and beer, yum."

"Beeeeeeer good, fire baaaaad."

Keiko laughed at the dated joke, not a brief one, but one of those laughs where she felt like nothing really mattered anymore. As her laughter died she hit his chest with an open hand.

"Was it that funny?" asked Kyle.

"Shut up and drive," said Keiko turning her body slightly to look out the window and up at the sky.

There seemed to be more stars in the sky when she was a kid. This vast infinite universe out there that she could almost touch. The place where dreams dwelled. She had always felt that she could one day grasp onto one of those stars, one of those dreams, and make it her own. Now, looking up, the stars were faded, and there were far fewer of them than she remembered. And the dream that she had taken hold of and held onto so tight for so many years seemed equally as faded.

"We're here, space cowboy," said Kyle.

Keiko blinked her eyes and looked down, seeing the buildings around the parking lot they were in.

"Sorry, zoned out there for a bit," she said shaking her head.

"Don't worry about it," he said touching her arm. "Come on, let's eat."

They got out of the car and walked along the sidewalk a few blocks to Manny's Pizzeria. Holding the door open for her the two of them went inside and sat at a table.

"You know," said Keiko. "I kinda like the old place better, back when it was on Colorado."

"That's right, I remember you saying it used to be over on Colorado." he said.

"My mom used to take us there every once in a while when we were younger," she said. "Guess it was kind of dumb, but as a kid it was great. Me and Kam would get so excited when she'd say we were going out to Old Towne Pasadena. And we'd eat pizza, then shop at the stores, and walk around until the sun set. Then she'd take us for ice cream and we'd sit on a bench watching the cars and people go by."

She paused, "Sorry," she said. "Just stupid memories."

Kyle leaned forward, looking at her.

"Why would they be stupid?" he asked. "You should be happy to have memories like that. I can't even really remember my life before I came out here."

"Still?" she asked placing a hand on his.

"Guess there's no real point, all that's gone anyway," he said.

"Kyle?"

Pulling his hand from hers he sat back in his chair, closing his eyes. Something from this morning bothered him, but he could not exactly determine what it was.

With a melancholy smile he opened his eyes and looked at her. "But we're not thinking about sad things tonight, right?"

"Right!" she said, raising an arm and smiling.

"Hello, how are the two of you tonight," asked the young man in a white apron.

"Uh, Good," they both said at the same time, looking up in a startled manner.

He held out a menu.

"Nah, no need," said Kyle. "We'd like a medium pepperoni pizza with extra cheese and a pitcher of beer, please."

"Will do," said the waiter turning around and walking away.

He returned several minutes later with a pitcher and two glasses which he put on the table and filled. "Your pizza should be ready in about fifteen minutes."

"Thank you," they said at the same time.

Laughing at the expression on their faces he said, "You're welcome," and went to the next table.

Chapter 05.03

Harry sat on the stool staring out into the room for a while after Cynthia had left. Eventually he decided that her suggestion to organize the rows of jars and other merchandise might be a good distraction, if even for a short time. Thomas had offered to help, but after seeing the results of the first shelf he had told the young man to go back to writing.

Harry set about rearranging the jars in alphabetical order according to the handwritten labels attached with yellowed tape. Periodically he would check on Thomas who was sitting at a desk in the back working on a story.

An hour before sunset Corin had returned, reaffirmed that Harry was supposed to be in his store, and retired to his room upstairs. The glass jars in order, Harry checked on Thomas again and sat on the stool behind the counter, watching the door. He checked his watch and saw that the store would close in about fifteen minutes.

"Is Corin around?" asked a female voice to his right.

He tensed and almost shot out of his chair, but he had been preparing for this and did not move.

"He is upstairs, Cynthia," said Harry with a note of victory in his voice.

"Huh?" asked the cheerful female voice which sounded nothing like Cynthia's.

Turning his head slightly he jumped backward at the girl with long blond hair and bright blue eyes standing inches from him.

"Who are you?" he asked, arms raised defensively.

She took a step forward and placed her hands on his fists, gently pushing them down. Looking into her eyes he did not resist, even though every instinct and all his training told him otherwise.

"I'm Lucy," she said with a disarming smile, still holding his fists gently at waist level. "And you are Harry, correct?"

"Yes, I am, Miss, pleased to meet you," he said releasing one of his fists and taking her hand in greeting. His eyes blinked several times and he took a quick step back, pulling his hand from her.

"How do you know who I am?" he asked.

Lucy jumped up and sat on the counter, laughing lightly.

"Old friend of Corin's," she said smiling. "He mentioned he had some new assistants."

"My apologies, miss, I can be a bit jumpy at times," said Harry. "But Thomas and I were just about to close up shop. I shall go inform Corin of your presence."

"Thomas?" asked Lucy. "He's not here."

"What do you mean?" asked Harry taking a step through the doorway and pulling the curtains to the back room aside. Looking in he saw an empty room.

Rushing forward he glanced around the back storage room and called out Thomas' name. He ran around frantically searching for the young man before giving up and returning to where Lucy was sitting, flipping through the notebook on the counter.

"That impetuous brat," he said. "Why does he do this to me?"

Jumping down to the floor, Lucy smiled and patted his shoulder. "Unfortunately it's your lot in life."

Harry simply gripped the edge of the counter, lowering his head, swearing under his breath, trying to tame his rage.

"I'm guessing he went out there," she said pointing to a window that was partially opened in the storage room beyond the curtains.

"Miss Lucy, unfortunately I am not that familiar with this city. May I ask your assistance in finding him?" he asked.

"That sounds fun," she said. "Count me in."

Chapter 05.04

Thomas stood in the middle of a parking lot, spinning slowly in circles a few times, watching the scenery of the city twirl around him. He stopped and smiled. It had been a while since he had snuck out like this. Standing alone in the cold night air surrounded by a few cars and the sounds of the city, he closed his eyes and took a deep breath.

From the inside pocket of his suit coat he pulled out a small bottle wrapped in a paper bag and unscrewed the cap. Raising it to the air he finished off the last of the whiskey and let out a long sigh. Laughing to himself he put the cap back on and stuffed the bottle into his side pocket.

"This night shall be glorious," he said to himself, staring at the sky. "Such wonderful places, such beautiful women awaiting seduction, such glories that stories shall be told."

He heard hurried footsteps behind him and spun around to see a woman glancing nervously over her shoulder as she fumbled with the keys to open the door of her car.

"You there, Miss," he cried. "Are you having a wonderful evening?"

Opening the door, she quickly jumped inside and slammed the door shut, her fist pounding the lock. The engine roared to life and the tires of the old car attempted to make a squealing noise but failed as she pulled away. She did not even stop at the exit of the parking lot, but sped into traffic. The night filled with the sounds of horns screaming as a car slammed on its brakes and barely avoided broad siding her.

"Such a strange country," sighed Thomas. "But none can resist the lure and charm of the Creative Genius, Thomas Dunne!" He stood alone in the middle of the parking lot with his hands raised in triumph.

The night air around him was filled with the sound of crickets from a field nearby.

"Time to have an adventure," he said to himself, turning around.

Passing the dumpster he tossed the empty bottle inside. As he exited the parking lot he turned right and started walking along the sidewalk. What people he did run across did as much as they could to ignore his existence as he passed them, not even responding to his greetings or desire to engage in conversation.

Eventually he came upon a road named Colorado. Stopping for a moment he recognized this as one of the streets that Kyle lived off of. Doing his best to calculate his position in relation to where he was living currently he took a guess and turned right. After a few blocks he ran across a gathering of people in front of a bar named after a Scottish moose.

Thomas patiently stood in line until he reached the front door.

"ID, please," asked the man.

"ID?" asked Thomas reaching to his back pocket.

The pocket was empty.

He checked the other back pocket of his pants. Then the front pockets. Then his suit coat pockets. No wallet.

"Well, sir, I do not seem to have it on me," said Thomas.

The man sighed. "Sorry, I need to see a valid form of identification."

Thinking for a moment Thomas asked, "Really?"

"Yes," said the man.

"Will this work?" asked Thomas pulling out a twenty.

Last night, while Harry had been taking a bath, Thomas had found the hiding spot for the money that Corin had given them as an advance. The temptation had been too great, and he had taken it. After all, it had been weeks since he had gone out and had fun. And months since he had been able to dump Harry.

"Sorry man, but the rules is the rules," said the man pointing to a sign on the door declaring that one needed a valid form of ID and that they had to be over twenty-one to enter. Placing a hand on Thomas' grey suit coat he said, "Never know when boss or cops are watching, so the rules is rules."

Thomas was pushed out of the line and found himself standing to the side of the doorman. He let out a frustrated sigh as he began to walk along the streets again, wondering where his wallet might be. Trying to follow the flow of human traffic he crossed the street of Colorado Boulevard. A few blocks later he came across a building with neon purple letters, through the windows he could see many people gathered around, sitting at tables and around a bar. He stood in line for a while, then came up to the man in black, ear bud and mic on the side of his face.

"ID please," said the young doorman with medium length hair that went in all directions. He held out his hand.

Smiling and acting casual Thomas asked, "Sorry, but I seem to have left it at home."

The doorman glanced up at him and a look of shock crossed his face.

"No way," said the doorman staring at Thomas. "Didn't we meet at that heavy metal concert a few months back? You were in that British band, right?"

Thomas had no idea what the doorman was talking about, but laughed and grabbed his shoulders with both hands, saying, "Good to see you again. How have you been?"

"I have been very well," said the doorman. "I'm Frank, by the way, and I apologize, but I have forgotten your name."

"Dunne, Thomas Dunne," he said.

"Of course!" said Frank. "You guys were great."

Squeezing his shoulder, Thomas said, "My good man, I am so happy to hear that you enjoyed the show, to the point that you were moved by our music. It is for people like you that I perform."

Somebody in the line behind him coughed loudly.

"Sorry, sir," said Frank. "Please."

The doorman opened the door and Thomas walked through. He took in a deep breath and crossed his arms, surveying the room and picking out all of the beautiful candidates around him. He strutted over to the bar, happy to catch the eyes of a few women. Reaching the bar he leaned against it and smiled at the bartender.

"What will it be?" asked the man on the other side of the counter.

"Your best Cognac, please" said Thomas.

The bartender nodded and returned several minutes later with a small glass.

Disappointed with the feeble amount of liquid within it, Thomas let out a small sigh and handed the man a piece of green paper. The bartender returned with change, of which Thomas slid a twenty dollar bill toward him.

"Can you keep them coming? And perhaps a bit more next time?" asked Thomas.

"Not a problem, sir," he said taking the tip and rapping the bar with his knuckles.

Sniffing the liquid, enjoying the aroma, Thomas raised the glass to salute the potential conquests around him and drank the contents of the glass in a series of five slow sips. He placed the empty glass on the bar and in seconds it was refilled, Thomas handed the bartender more money, giving a generous tip from the change.

As he watched the people around him, Thomas drank the second glass slowly. When he was finished he put it down, received a refill, and exchanged more money. The warmth in his stomach began to spread and he relaxed, taking a slow sip of his drink and looking around him. Laughing lightly to himself he slid down the bar a few feet he brushed up against a woman who was talking with her girlfriend. She looked down at him.

"You are quite beautiful," he said flashing a smile.

"Gee, thanks," she said turning back to her friend.

Brushing against her arm again he said, "I was wondering..."

"No," said the woman.

Leaning forward he said, "You know, I am thinking of working on a film, and you would be perfect for the lead role." He caught her eye, nodded, and flashed her a smile.

"Lead role in a movie?" she asked which produced an outburst of laughter from her friend.

"Of course," he said.

She smiled at him and Thomas felt a warm spot in his chest and below his belt. His winning charm had worked once again.

Leaning forward she said with a smile, "Listen, there are two ways this can go. You walk away and don't bother me or my friend or I have security throw your pathetic ass out onto the street."

Thomas' smile faded. "Ah, well, sorry for bothering you and all. Have a good evening. Cheers." He raised his glass.

She turned her back to him.

He slid back to where he had been standing. Finishing off his third drink, he took the immediately refilled glass and tossed more money onto the bar. "Thanks, going to wander around a bit."

"Need anything, sir, I'll take care of you," said the bartender. "If you are new here, Pool is upstairs and dancing will start downstairs in about forty-five minutes."

Pool? The visions of beautiful women scantily clad in swimwear filled Thomas' mind. He wandered around until he found the stairs near the entry and ascended them.

Reaching the top of the stairs he sadly looked out over the room filled with only billiards tables and noticed a woman with long black hair who was sitting on a stool near him. The depression in her eyes, as she watched a man leaning over a table, caught his attention.

Taking a sip of his drink he walked up to her.

Women who were sad with their lovers were always an easy score. "Could I buy you a drink?" he asked.

She looked over at him.

"No, thank you," she said raising her beer. "Just got one. Oh, you suck."

"Eh?" he asked, then saw she was watching the table.

She screamed something in a foreign language to the man standing at the table, who had just sunk three balls in one shot.

It was Kyle, who started to say something in a foreign language then suddenly stopped.

"Hey, Thomas. What are you doing here?" asked Kyle looking at him.

"Ah, nothing really, just having a night on the town and all," said Thomas.

"I think he was hitting on me," said the dark haired girl, laughing.

"I was not," exclaimed Thomas, stepping back.

Kyle laughed and said, "No worries. Want to shoot a round?"

Thomas looked at the stairs behind him and said, "Thank you but, no. I shall have to pass. But I am going to go back down and check things out. Here, let me buy your next round."

Handing Kyle a twenty he quickly excused himself and returned to the first floor.

Back on the ground floor, Thomas attempted to entice several other women with absolutely no luck. Disheartened he returned to the bar and sat down in an empty seat at the far end.

"Doesn't seem you're having a good night, sir," said the bartender.

"Bah, I don't understand these women," said Thomas. It was so much easier when he had an endless supply of money, the claim to being of Noble English birth, with a castle to the family name, and a reputation for being an incredible lover. Trying to pick up women without any of these was proving very difficult.

"No offense, sir," said the bartender pouring another round and leaning slightly over the bar. "But perhaps you are being a bit too forward. Maybe a more subtle approach would work better?"

"Ah, thanks, I will keep that in mind," said Thomas tossing money onto the bar.

He drank the glass quickly, then when it was filled again spun in his chair at the bar and noticed a woman with short blonde hair and a little too much makeup was sitting next to him. She was watching the people playing pool on the billiards table near them.

Leaning forward he said, "You are quite beautiful, and I am rather lonely."

"What?" she asked blinking and looking at him, meeting his eyes she smiled and said. "Oh, I'm lonely too. Damn game."

"Really? Could I buy you a drink?" he asked.

"Oh that would be really neat," she said laughing lightly and touching his arm.

"Not a problem," he said raising his hand to the bartender who was suddenly standing near them. "Whatever she wants."

"Oh, I'll take a Coors Light," she said smiling first at the bartender, then at Thomas.

Tossing more money on the bar a bottle of beer soon appeared.

"You seem really nice," she said placing her hand on his knee. "My name is Monique."

"Monique? Well met then, I am Thomas," he said placing his hand around her back.

"So cool to meet you, Tom," she said taking a long drink of her beer. Finishing it she set the bottle down and gave him a look as he finished his drink.

Raising his hand another bottle appeared and his glass was filled.

"Actually, it is Thomas," he said taking a sip of his cognac.

"Wow, cool, neat," she said drinking the bottle of beer in a series of quick gulps. Placing the empty bottle on the bar she began to stroke his leg up and down, leaning against him and laughing lightly. "You seem like a really cool guy."

"Thank you," he said taking a deep breath and slamming his drink.

Raised hand, another beer, another refill.

Bringing the bottle to her lips she stuck out her tongue and licked the top of the bottle slowly, looking over at him with a grin as he slammed another double cognac between deep breaths.

"Who the fuck are you?" asked a deep voice.

Thomas looked up to see a large man with three men behind him, each of them holding pool sticks.

"Don't tell me you been flirting with guys again, Monique," he said looking at her.

"Oh, um, sorry Julio, sweetie, just you were like so like involved in, like, your game and I was like bored and lonely. But he bought me beer, so he's cool, right?"

"Cool my ass," said the large man walking up to Thomas. "Touch my girl, you dead meat."

Raising both hands and hopping out of his stool, stumbling

backwards, Thomas said, "Well now, see I did not know that she was with you, obviously, because how could I possibly compete with the likes of you?"

"Piece of shit," said Julio punching Thomas in the stomach.

Unfortunately this was not the first time that he had been in a bad situation like this, so Thomas was prepared for the punch. He absorbed the blow as best he could, while moving backwards to lessen the impact. The result was Thomas flying backward several feet and knocking over a table and landing sprawled on the floor.

As he tried to stand Thomas felt a hand on his shoulder.

"Sir, please, come with me," said Frank helping Thomas stand.

The doorman guided him to the back of the room and down a hall quickly as several men in black descended on Julio and restrained him.

Pushing a door open, Frank asked, "Sir, are you injured?"

"What?" asked Thomas straightening his suit coat. "Not at all, did not even feel it."

"Sir, you are a true man, and an inspiration," said Frank.

"Why thank you, my friend."

"Sir, I am sorry sir, but I would advise you to leave immediately, sir. The situation is not safe, and I do not want you to be here if the police show up, as it might create unnecessary rumors, sir. You can rest assured that you were not here this evening, sir."

"Thank you, Frank," said Thomas. "I will not forget this."

"Sir, you honor me, sir, but I must attend to the events inside, sir. Permission to leave, sir?"

Thomas nodded his head.

Frank walked back inside, the door closing behind him.

He was in an alley of sorts, and he turned to walk down the steps.

"Thomas!" screamed the all too familiar voice of his guardian.

"Hello," said a small girl with blond hair dressed in white.

He realized that the last several drinks had pushed him way over the threshold. What little control he thought he had over his bipedal form evaporated from him and Thomas' legs crumbled. He began to fall down the stairs.

Harry caught him mid-fall. "Are you safe?"

"For now it seems," said Thomas.

"We should get back home," said Harry.

"Indeed," said Thomas. "Who are you?"

"Lucy," said the girl.

"You do not happen to be lonely and in need of some princely loving, do you?" he asked trying to smile at her.

"Silly kid," she said messing up his hair.

As they came out of the alleyway Lucy ran across the road and raised a hand at a taxi that was passing. It squealed to a stop and they ran over to it, getting in.

"Lucy?" asked the driver turning around.

"Ardad!" she screamed leaping forward and wrapping her arms around his neck. "How have you been?"

"Good, good," he said flipping the meter off. "This one's on me, sis. As for me, just the same old same old with people and life. How you been?"

Kissing his forehead she caressed his face and said, "Same old same old on my front."

"Seems like an eternity," he said.

"Well that's our choice, isn't it?" she asked letting go of him and sitting in the back seat.

Ardad nodded his head slowly and looked into the rearview mirror at the sound of a car's horn. "So where you folks off to?"

Harry saw Lucy staring at him. "Aaaaah, that would be," he stopped. "I have no idea, I left my paperwork at the store."

"You don't know where you live?" asked Lucy.

"Er, well, sort of, I believe we live off a Colorado road somewhere, and I have to walk past a bridge to get to the bus stop."

"Just drive," said Lucy waving at Ardad and pulling out her phone. Scrolling through the names she highlighted one and raised it to her ear.

"Hello?" asked a male voice.

"Ky-Ky! How are you?" she asked.

"Lucy?"

"Yep."

"Uh, hi," said Kyle.

"Sorry to bother you, but I have one very intoxicated gentleman by the name of Thomas here, and his friend who is not exactly sure where they live."

Kyle laughed and told her the address which she repeated to Ardad.

"On our way," said the driver.

"Oh, hold on, Keiko wants to say hello," said Kyle.

"Hi Lucy!" came the slightly slurred voice of Keiko.

"Good evening, beautiful," said Lucy. "What are the two of you doing?"

"Ah, having fun like the good old days," said Keiko. "I wanted to have one last night of fun before I left for another damn shoot."

"Keiko?"

"Yes."

"Do yourself a favor and think about everything while you are away."

There was silence on the other end of the line. "I'm not thinking about stuff like that tonight."

"Well then, Keiko, think about it on the morrow," said Lucy.

"Um, yeah, sure," said Keiko with a note of irritation in her voice.

"I have to go, tell Ky-Ky I said goodnight," said Lucy.

"Hey," said Keiko. "Wish you were around more."

"I know, but you have to find your own path," said Lucy. "Bye."

Lucy shoved the phone back into the pocket of her coat.

"You know Kyle?" Thomas managed to slur.

"Sure do. Back before Christmas. I was at the party that Kyle never made it to because of you."

"Oh, well then, there you have it," said Thomas closing his eyes and slumping over onto Lucy.

She grabbed under his shoulders and lifted the long haired man without effort. "This is yours," she said handing the unconscious person over to Harry.

Gently taking hold of Thomas and laying the man's head in his lap, Harry looked over at Lucy.

"My lot?"

"Sorry to say, but yes."

"Wonderful."

"Never doubt a dreamer," said Lucy, smiling slightly and looking out the window.

Chapter 05.05

Kami was wandering around the house, bored and lonely. She went down the hall and tried the double doors to the study, but they were locked. Getting down on the floor she tried to look under the door but was only able to see a bit of floor lit by a faint orange light. Standing she turned around and looked down the empty hall. Ed was upstairs in his room working on music. At least he had spent a few hours watching TV with her. Kami thought Cynthia was here, but was not quite sure. Kyle, Harry, and Thomas were gone.

"Are you lost?" asked a quiet voice behind her.

Spinning around and slamming her back into the wall, Kami saw Cynthia staring at her from the open doors to the study.

"Ah, no, was just wandering around," said Kami rubbing the back of her head with one hand and letting out a nervous laugh. "Just wondering what was in there."

"The study," said Cynthia motionless.

"Really? Sounds cool. Can I go look?" asked Kami peering past her.

"No."

"Why?"

"I am in the middle of something, so you cannot go in there," said Cynthia stepping out and turning around, closing the doors.

The quiet house was filled with the sound of her locking the doors.

Walking past Kami, Cynthia looked over her shoulder and said, "Do you not have school tomorrow?"

"Uh, yes," said Kami scurrying down the hall and back to her room.

Even though Cynthia wore boots with thick heels she barely made any noise on the hardwood floors as she passed the bedroom door and walked into the living room. Sneaking out of her room, Kami hugged the wall of the hallway and listened. A minute later she heard the front door open then close softly.

Running across the living room she cautiously peered out the front window and saw Cynthia get into her large black car and start it up, turning on her headlights.

Kami walked slowly back to her room, pausing before entering to stare at the doors to the study at the end of the hall.

Kami sat on the edge of her bed. Grabbing the remote off the night stand she turned on the cable box and television, flipping through the stations for a while. Sadly she realized there was nothing remotely interesting on right now. Turning off the television she sat and thought, trying to remember where something was.

Jumping up off the bed she opened her closet and pulled out a cardboard box. Tearing off the lid she rummaged around inside it, then pushed it to the side, grabbing another box. Looking in it she found what she was looking for. A lock pick set one of her online friends from Arizona had sent her.

Smiling she opened her door and ran down the hall to the double doors of the study.

Thankfully this was an old house and the lock on the door was the type that used a skeleton key from what she could tell. Kami stopped for a moment, wondering why the keys were called that and decided she would look it up online later.

Kneeling she pulled out a couple of the tools and began to fiddle with the lock. In a few minutes she heard a satisfying click. Putting everything back she rolled up the tools and shoved it into the pocket of her baggy jeans that hung off her hips.

"Ha, you can't hide things from me," she said standing and placing a hand on the handle.

Turning the doorknob she pushed the door open and beheld a dark room.

Stepping in she fumbled around on the wall until she turned on the light. She saw that all the windows were covered by thick red velvet curtains. Kami took a few tentative steps into the room and stopped. She heard an almost inaudible deep growl for a second, but quickly dismissed it, knowing there were no pets in the house.

Glancing to her left she saw a bookshelf filled with fine porcelain dolls. There must have been over one hundred of them, from floor to ceiling, all of the exquisite female dolls dressed in fine clothing reminiscent of the eighteen hundreds. Each doll, though, had one distinguishing feature.

Their eyes were painted a solid, glossy black.

When this realization hit her Kami stepped backwards and hit a table.

"Creepy," she said.

Looking down at the table she had run into, she saw several human skulls, and several not so human skulls.

Screaming, she backed away and ran into a chair.

"What the hell is with this girl?" she asked.

Turning around she saw a long table with many chairs around it. On the table were many folders stacked in various piles, all of them arranged meticulously to one side with exactly one inch between each.

Grabbing the folder closest to her she paged through and saw multiple receipts and other financial paperwork. Looking to the empty end of the table she saw a large calculator with a spool of paper. Putting the folder down she looked around the room.

It was a massive study that reminded her more of a library, with many rows of books and leather bound chairs, stairs on either side of the room led up to another floor. On the far end of the long table was a tall stand upon which was a large book on a wooden podium. Walking over she looked at the book. There were some illustrations, and the text was written in some strange language whose characters she could not even decipher.

Kami marked the page with a finger and began to page through, staring at various diagrams and drawings that both confused her and made her skin crawl.

She heard another low, deep growl behind her. This was followed by a second, equally low, deep growl, behind her and to her left.

Slowly she put the book back to the page it had been on.

Growls behind her, closer this time.

Looking up and closing her eyes she swallowed hard and slowly turned around. Opening her eyes she saw two large black dogs with glowing red eyes. They were somewhat transparent, for she could see the floor through their ghostly black bodies.

Letting out a scream she ran past them, toward the doors to the study. There was no sound behind her of clawed feet hitting the hardwood floors. Just the sound of the growls growing lower in pitch, and worse, nearer.

Reaching the doors she ran through and down the hallway, slamming into somebody stepping out from the bathroom. Kami careened off of the person and suddenly saw the ceiling as she fell backwards, closing her eyes in preparation for the pain she was about to experience. Just before her head should have slammed into the floor she felt an arm around her shoulder and her head came to a stop inches from the hardwood.

Opening her eyes she saw a girl about her age with long blond hair and blue eyes, who smiled at Kami and said, "Hello, cutie."

Staring into those eyes she momentarily forgot what had been happening and smiled also, saying, "Hi."

Some low growls shook Kami from those eyes and she looked down the hall at the two semi-transparent black dogs that were pacing in circles just inside the doors of the study. Panic filling her again, Kami started kicking with her legs, trying to back away from them.

The girl holding her looked over at the two beasts and let out a small laugh. Picking Kami up while standing she said, "Wait here."

Kami would have collapsed if the girl had not leaned her against the wall. Every fiber of her being was telling her that she should flee, yet she was enraptured by this girl dressed in white who calmly walked down the hallway toward the doors of the study.

The growls intensified as the girl approached the two dog-like creatures. Stopping inches from the threshold she looked down at them and said, "Go," waving her hand in a dismissing manner. They paused momentarily and then turned and walked back into the study.

The girl in white closed the doors, then turning around she walked down the hall to Kami and pulled her forward, holding the terrified girl with a supporting arm.

"I am Lucy, by the way," said.

Kami was still staring at the doors. Letting out a scream of panic she pulled away and ran back into her room, slamming the door shut.

"Miss Lucy," asked Harry stepping into the hallway from the living room.

"Yes?" she said.

"Is everything alright?"

"Yes, nothing to worry about."

"Ah, very well then. Master Thomas is no longer feeling ill, so we shall retire to our room now," he said with both hands clenched in fists at his side. Bowing slightly Harry said, "I owe you a debt of gratitude for your assistance this evening, Miss Lucy. Please have a good night."

"Good night to you as well, Harry," she said waving a hand at him.

Harry turned and left the hallway.

After slamming the door to her room, Kami had leapt onto her bed and grabbed her Cait Sith, holding it close, staring at the ceiling.

There was a knock on her door.

"I'm sleeping," said Kami.

"It's me," said Lucy.

Kami did not say anything.

The door opened slowly and Lucy stepped inside, closing the door quickly behind her, shutting off the screaming match echoing from the living room. Thomas seemed to be yelling something about a wonderful idea for a new story and Harry was replying at an equal volume that they should be going to bed.

Letting go of the doorknob Lucy asked, "And what is your name."

Kami did not respond, but continued to stare at the ceiling, hoping this girl would just go away.

After a while she sighed and said, "Kami."

"Guessing you have never run into something like that before?" asked Lucy.

"Look, I'm stressed about my mom leaving and starting a new school tomorrow, and have been spending much too much time on the net, so it's only natural that I might see things that aren't there," said Kami.

Lucy sat on the edge of the bed and watched the girl holding the stuffed animal for a few minutes. "And you really believe that?"

"I have no idea who the hell you are, and I didn't ask for your opinion," said Kami turning onto her side away from Lucy.

"Well, you are right there," said Lucy laying down next to Kami who visibly tensed.

"What the hell are you doing?" growled Kami in a low voice. She felt Lucy touch her shoulder gently and swung backward with all her might. The strike was blocked by a hand that gently held her fist. She resisted, but could not fight back, so she pulled it away and pounded on the pillow.

"You have no idea what's going on, so just leave me alone," said Kami. "Just get out of here."

"I am guessing that you were not supposed to be in that room," said Lucy.

"What does it matter?"

"And it would be natural to assume that is the room Cynthia uses," said Lucy. "I know of her, not somebody one such as yourself should cross."

"Are you finished? Will you leave now?" asked Kami.

Lucy started stroking Kami's hair. She wanted to pull away, but the touch was soothing.

"Who are you?" asked Kami.

"I am Lucy. I met your sister before Christmas, the same night Kyle met Thomas actually," said Lucy. "But Thomas went off on an adventure tonight and I had to help Harry find him, and now I am here."

"Thanks for not answering the question," sneered Kami.

"I am just me," said Lucy. "And I try to help people whenever I can."

"That's so lame," said Kami.

"That is the choice I made," said Lucy in a somber tone. "People are too precious to just give up upon, for any reason."

"Wonderful," said Kami wanting to pull away, but at the same time not. "Will you just leave now?"

Laughing lightly, Lucy said, "You seem to be having a hard time."

"Tell me about it," said Kami. "Everything has fallen apart lately. Mom is leaving with Grandma to go back to Japan, my sister is becoming more and more distant, and I've been tossed to the side and have to live here."

Trying to contain her emotions, she muttered, "And even worse, this house is full of freaks, and I have no place else to go."

"You're right where you need to be," said Lucy. "You always are. Sometimes that is hard to see though."

"Easy for you to say, you're not some ugly freak worthless sister of a supermodel who continuously screws up her life."

Lucy let out a small laugh and gently turned Kami's face toward hers with a gentle hand. "You're sixteen, my love, you can't do everything correct. And you are not worthless, you are a beautiful, unique individual. You just have to be true to yourself and do your best."

"Ugh, now you sound like my Grandmother." Kami said turning over and lying on her back, staring at the ceiling.

Lucy, on her side, leaned over her slightly.

The pale, smooth skin was inches from Kami, the long blond hair falling over her shoulder brushed lightly against her cheek, and she was keenly aware of Lucy's body pressing against hers. She felt the warm breath on her neck, the fingers still touching her cheek, and Kami swallowed forcefully, blinking several times into the intense blue eyes that stared into hers. Lucy smiled down at her and brushed the hair from Kami's face.

There was this belonging there, in the depths of those eyes where she could see her stark and lonely soul surrounded by a circle of blue that seemed to form this shield that held out all of the bad things that were around her.

Kami pushed herself up slightly with one arm, staring into those eyes, her other hand caressing the blond hair as her lips touched Lucy's. As they did, she closed her eyes and leaned back, pulling Lucy down with her, lost in that sphere of blue protection.

This person did not pull away from her, did not exclaim she was a horrible person for doing such a thing. All Kami felt was the warmth of her lips and a gentle embrace as she slowly relaxed.

She felt Lucy pull away slowly and her eyes shot open.

Placing a finger on Kami's lips, Lucy said, "Shhhhhh, tomorrow is a big day for you, it will be a good day, but you must sleep."

Kami wanted to protest, wanted to sit up, but staring into those eyes she found herself overcome with the feeling of security and acceptance. Fight as she could, Kami could not help slipping into a deep slumber.

Chapter 05.06

Opening the front door to the house Kyle stepped in, closing it behind him with his foot. Taking off his coat he tossed it over the banister of the stairs, then took off his shoes, before walking down the hall toward the living room where he heard the television. Stepping into the room he looked around and saw nobody.

Shrugging his shoulders he went over to the TV and shut it off. As he was standing back up he heard something behind him.

"Ky-Ky!" said a familiar voice.

Startled, he spun around and suddenly found himself standing about fifteen feet from the television, behind the chair next to the couch.

Lucy was standing in front of the television, arms raised, and turned to look at him, leaning her head slightly and saying, "Wow, impressive." Then with a running jump she leapt over the chair and had her arms around his neck. "Ky-Ky!"

"Whaaaa? Uh, hi Lucy," he managed to blurt out placing his hands on the arms around him.

"Ha, I'm faster than you are," she taunted, dropping back to the floor.

"Bah?" was all he managed.

"Everything OK with you?" she asked.

"What?"

"Nothing, just looks like you haven't had any today," she said walking around the chair and hopping onto the couch. Spreading her arms over the back cushions and stretching her legs to rest her bare feet on the coffee table, she said, "No big really, not that you need to, but not a bad idea being new to this and all."

Kyle walked around the chair and sat in it.

"What are you talking about?"

Lucy stood and walked over to him, grabbing his hand and pulling him to the couch, against his mild resistance, and then pushed him down. She looked at him then said, "I see, never mind."

Raising a hand he said, "Listen, Lucy, it's been a long day. I'm assuming that you got Thomas back here, right?"

"Indeed we did," she said turning and sinking into the couch, examining the hand within her own. Looking up into his eyes she said, "Though in an unrelated matter Kami tried to break into Cynthia's room and got rather freaked out by what she found."

Kyle paled, not wanting to imagine the consequences.

"Oh no, was Cynthia here?"

"No. Kami is alive. Perhaps Cynthia let her in as a warning?"

He started to stand but a hand on his shoulder pushed him back into the couch forcibly.

Calm down," she said looking in the direction of her room. "Kami will be fine."

He was about to say something when Cynthia walked into the living room from the entry of the house. The two of them watched her move without motion across the room and sit in the chair next to the couch.

"Interesting," said Cynthia. "Could it be that Janice is too tame for your tastes?"

Her tone was colder than normal.

"What?" asked Kyle as Lucy threw her arms around him. "It's not even like that, I hardly even know her," he said pointing down at the person holding him.

Lucy shook her head and winked at the dark girl.

"I understand," said Cynthia. Looking up at Kyle she said, "How was your evening?"

"It was OK I guess," he said.

He tried to ignore the girl next to him, who was poking his chest and asking, "What happened, Ky-Ky, what happened?"

He tried to push Lucy away, with no success.

"Went out to dinner with Keiko, then went to shoot pool, ran into Thomas, who was pretty drunk, then dropped Keiko off a ways from her place because she seems to have a stalker and needs to sneak into her place, and well, that was about it. So actually not very interesting."

The sound of a door slamming and quick footsteps down the stairs caused them all to look down the hall.

Ed walked in with a smile and said, "Hello, all," waving a hand. The motion caused him to lose his balance and he caught himself on the corner of the hall that entered into the living room. "Bah, new song not going well, need more Corona."

"You sit," said Cynthia in a voice barely above a whisper. "I shall purchase the Corona you need."

"Oh, well, cool, thanks, sweetie," he said.

She narrowed her eyes at the last word.

"Sorry, sorry, sorry," he said stumbling over to the chair and sitting down.

Standing, Cynthia said, "If you will excuse me," and walked across the room and down the hall.

"Dude, F me still, I can't believe that you know the infamous Miss Lucy, let alone that she is in our house. So you decide to skip over the sweet nice Janice and become Lucy's S&M sex slave?"

"Christ, no! Why the hell is everybody asking that?" exclaimed Kyle trying once again to pull away from Lucy and failing.

Pulling him closer Lucy said, "Sweet Ed, you have it all wrong. I enjoy Ky-Ky but not like that. Hmmm, well, not yet anyway."

"What?" asked Kyle looking down.

"First I have to break him in," she said, then winked at Kyle.

"You're just joking, right?" Kyle asked actually trying to use force to push her away, but she did not move.

Lucy ignored him and grabbed the remote to turn on the television. She flipped through some channels until a movie came on.

Ed looked at them a moment, and shook his head.

"Do you want me to leave the two of you alone?" he asked.

"Ed?" asked Lucy.

"Huh?" he asked.

"Watch the moving pictures," she said.

"Oh, sure," he said leaning back in the chair and staring at the television.

Kyle's mind was bouncing all over.

Here was this cute girl cuddled next to him, her hair lightly brushing his chin, her body pressed close to his in ways that made him very aware of her presence. Yet he could not help worrying about Keiko. She had called when he was on the freeway, to say that she had made it back to her place safe, but there was still the note of sadness in her voice. And then there was Janice, whom he did not know very well, but found really interesting. And then there was Cynthia, who had started dating Ed the day after the four of them went on a double date. The four of course being Keiko, Cynthia, Ed, and himself. Ed became lucky and got a girlfriend, he got the status of brother. But now Cynthia was acting all strange toward him. Which made absolutely no sense to him. Sure they talked all the time, mainly him asking her questions, and if he was lucky getting more than a one word answer.

He suddenly became aware that Lucy was staring at him.

"What?" he asked.

"You should stop worrying so much," she said. "You love everything Japanese, perhaps you should study Zen."

"Wait, what?" he asked.

"Kyle is a Zen master?" asked Ed.

"Just watch the TV," said both Kyle and Lucy.

After a few minutes, he felt the person leaning her head against his shoulder ask something.

"Who is Heather?" asked Lucy, with a serious look on her face.

"Heather? Was a friend of my Grandmother's, owns some galleries around town, I help her with her computer from time to time. Why?"

Lucy frowned slightly, then said, "Nothing, just curious."

She turned and watched the television, pulling him closer, leaning her head against his chest.

As much as Kyle wished in his deepest fantasies to enjoy such a situation, he could not. Yet every time he started thinking about the situation, Keiko, or anybody else, his head was hit with a fist.

And Lucy would whisper, "Why cannot you enjoy the moment?"

To which he had no answer

Cynthia walked in a time later and handed Ed a bag.

"Here," she said.

"Cool!" Ed said loudly, standing. "Now I can finish the rest of the song, I'm sure of it! Night all," he said rushing across the room, down the hall, and up the stairs.

Cynthia watched him ascend the stairs, then looked to the floor. At the sound of the door slamming shut she turned to the two on the couch and nodded at them, disappearing down the hall to the study.

Kyle and Lucy continued to watch the movie until it ended twenty minutes later. Somehow during this time she had ended up in his lap, head upon his chest, arms wrapped around him, and both legs over his.

"You don't want to hear this," said Lucy in a soft voice as she pressed her head into his chest, "But you need to let it go so you can live your own life. It won't be easy, but a lot of things are changing for you right now."

"What do you mean?" asked Kyle.

Placing her arms around his neck she stared into his eyes a moment and said, "You'll see."

She leaned forward and kissed his forehead.

Somewhat shocked Kyle pulled back.

Pausing for a moment, Lucy stood.

Turning around slightly, over her shoulder Lucy said, "That goes for you too, my little dark one."

Kyle thought he saw a slight motion of something at the edge of the doorway of the hall, but heard nothing

Lucy seemed to chuckle, then said, "I must leave, please take care, my dearest Kyle."

Stammering he stood and walked her to the door. Lucy turned back to him with a look in her eye that Kyle could not exactly place. She bowed slightly to him, then turned and ran outside. He stepped from the doorway, about to offer her a ride, but saw only the empty driveway and yard before him.

Standing there a moment, he went back into the house and closed the door. Grabbing his coat off the banister he went to his room, his mind filled with too many thoughts to consider, in a way wishing that life was as nice and quiet as it had been living here with his Grandmother.

Kyle paused a moment.

A brief flash of pain tore through his heart, briefly remembering a vague memory of his parents before they were gone.

His Mother standing in the bathroom telling him he was not an ugly child. His father building a deck. Red and blue flashing lights as he opened his eyes to see a patch of snow filling with a thick dark liquid, looking up slightly to the one eye of his Mother staring at him, mouth open, head smashed in.

He grasped his head with both hands, shaking, as the memories attacked his mind. There was a car, and snow. But struggle as much as he could, the images escaped him. And everything faded away again.

Kyle sat down on the bed, stood, then sat down again. Pulling off his shirt he threw it in the general direction of the closet. He fell backward into bed and stared at the ceiling.

"What is wrong with me?" he asked aloud to the empty room.

"Nothing, Kyle," said a soft voice.

He pushed himself up onto his elbows. He could clearly see Cynthia in the darkness, even though the lights were off, sitting on the edge of his bed with a wine glass in her hand.

Looking into her dark eyes he asked, "What are you doing here?"

"Drink this," she said extending the glass.

"Why?" he asked, irritated.

"Because you need it," she said.

Kyle hesitated for a moment before he took it from her, looking into her eyes again. They were unmoving and darker than he remembered.

He took a tentative sip of the thick liquid and raised an eyebrow, the thick wine was that luscious. In four quick gulps he finished off the contents of the wine glass, letting the feelings of red and black wash through his system. She took the glass from his hand and filled it again with a bottle of wine that had no label.

After he finished the bottle, he sat there staring at her for a while.

"That was good, but I feel sleepy." he said, falling backward onto his pillow.

"Of course," said Cynthia.

Kyle pulled his legs up off the floor and onto the bed, lying on his back.

"You know," he said, "I think I had a dream about you and it was weird because you were touching me."

"I do not touch people," she said in a whisper, barely audible, placing her fingers cautiously upon the bare skin of his chest.

Kyle fell into a deep sleep.

LEAVING THE PAST

Chapter 06.01

Checking the time, Kami swore under her breath and finished fastening the last button on her uniform. Grabbing her bag she flung open the door to her room and ran into the kitchen, tossing the satchel onto the table before darting to the cupboard to grab two Rice Krispie Treats which she began to devour in between gulps of Code Red.

Her phone rang.

"Hello?" she asked.

"I am at the gate," said her Mother.

"K, open it in a sec," Kami said tossing the phone back into her satchel and finishing off the rest of her drink, leaving the empty can on the table.

She ran to the front door and hit the button to open the front gate.

"Ohayo," came a voice still half asleep. "Good luck at school."

She looked up and saw Kyle descending the stairs, one arm raised.

"Ohayo, onii-chan, thanks, bye," she said opening the door and stepping outside.

Her Mother's car pulled up and she got in.

"Well, I'm surprised you are actually on time for once," said her Mother driving back toward the gates.

Kami took a deep breath as they drove forward. "Guess I got a good night sleep or something."

"Hopefully you will keep that up," said her Mother, pressing the button on the panel outside the car to open the gates.

"You realize, of course," she continued, driving through the gates and turning onto the road, "that you will have to be up earlier to catch the bus to school, right?"

"Yes, Mother," said Kami gritting her teeth and holding the satchel tightly in her arms.

"Very good," her Mother said. "You know, your sister never had a problem waking up in the mornings."

"I know."

"Hopefully you can start pulling your life together. I will not be around to deal with your frequent tardiness and other problems. And I will not allow you to be a burden on Kyle. You are not a child anymore, Kami, in two years you will graduate from High School, then what will you do? These really are things that you need to start thinking about now."

"Yes, Mother," said Kami.

"I am serious."

"I know you are."

"Then act like it."

"What do you want me to do?" pleaded Kami, screaming. "I can't be the picture perfect super model who always woke up on time in the mornings and had a great GPA."

Her Mother shot a quick glance over at her, then glared at the road for a time, sullen but silent. "You can try. Just look at how wonderful Keiko's life is. No, you won't be a supermodel, but you can still achieve a great level of success if you were to try for once instead of playing those stupid games and wasting your time on your computers."

"Mom..." she began.

Cold eyes stared at her for a moment.

"Mother," she started again. "Computers are very important in this day and age."

"That is what I have heard in the news, but Kami, honestly, I really have not seen you do anything useful than just play around. You do not have any special talent there that I have seen. Maybe you should look into other options before deciding upon a college."

Kami opened her mouth to reply, then closed it and looked out the window.

"You see, you know I am right," said her Mother.

Neither of them spoke for the remainder of the drive.

They arrived at the school before classes started and finished up the last of the paperwork with the principal. He was a jovial man in his late forties who, after her Mother had left, showed Kami to her locker. Classes had started about fifteen minutes ago, so the halls were empty as he walked her to her first class.

"Miss Nakamura," he said walking with both hands behind his back. "I see that your GPA isn't exactly the best, but noticed that you had chosen computers and advanced math as your top classes. Tell me, do you tend to get bored in your previous classes?"

"Oh, well no, of course not," she said looking down at floor. "I guess I'm just kind of dumb."

The Principal stopped and looked over at her. "Are you? Or have you found yourself bored because the classes you have taken were not challenging."

Kami held her satchel in front of her with both hands and stared at his feet, her mind racing to figure out the correct answer he was looking for.

"You honestly would answer with a yes, wouldn't you?" he asked.

She paused a moment, then said, "Yes, Mr. Bellman."

He leaned forward slightly and said, "Kami, I try to run a good school here. And I try to look after my students. But you need to be honest with me. If you find yourself that bored with your classes, come see me or your counselor. You just may be in the wrong classes to suit your needs."

Kami looked up and stared at his chest, "Yes, sir."

Turning and beginning down the hall again, he smiled and said, "Wonderful." Then, stepping closer to her he whispered, "To tell you the truth I dropped out of high school because I was bored out of my skull. I decided to become a teacher to change things. Now I'm a Principal. Ironic, huh?"

"Um," said Kami, taking a side step away. "Yeah, I guess it is."

"Listen, this is your first day, so you're under a lot of stress. Come by my office Monday morning before class and talk to me. I want to hear your impressions."

"Sure," she said.

"Kami, this is one of the top rated schools in the state. That is why there are so few students and that is why there is a three year waiting list to get in. I made an exception with you, because your Mother was a close friend when we went to high school here."

She dropped her satchel, then quickly picked it up from the floor.

"Oh, she didn't tell you, sorry, my mistake," he said.

"No, she didn't," said Kami wiping off non-existent lint from her sleeve that had suddenly appeared.

"Well we should get you to class now," he said smiling, turning and continuing down the hall, whistling an old song.

Kami shook her head and caught up with him. He stopped at a door and her stomach began to dance.

That door would open and she would have to deal with a bunch of new kids and a new teacher, and she wanted very much to be at home, with her Mother and Grandmother, in the house she had grown up in. Or even the freak show house she now lived in. Anything but what was about to happen. She never could talk to people she did not know.

"Breath," said the Principal. "Not good to make your grand entrance all tense and stressed out."

Startled, she looked up and at his smile took a few deep breaths, trying to calm herself.

The Principle knocked on the door and opened it, leaning in and saying something to the teacher.

Taking another deep breath Kami tried to calm her nerves. She was holding onto the handle of her satchel with both hands in front of her, decided that was too proper and held it to her side, decided that might look too casual, and held it before her again.

"Here you go," said the Principal in a whisper opening the door and nodding at her.

Kami looked through the door and saw a woman with short grey hair standing behind the desk, smiling at her. Summoning all her will she walked toward that smile until she was standing near the desk.

"Good morning Kami," she said. "I am Miss Heit, your calculus instructor."

"Thank you," said Kami. She saw her instructor's eyes dart toward the class, and Kami hesitated a moment before turning to confront the new faces.

"Class," said Ms. Heit, "this is Kami Nakamura, she will be joining us today."

Everybody in the class raised their hands and said, "Good morning, Kami."

She raised her hand half way and said, "Uh, good morning."

"Would you mind telling us a bit about yourself?"

Kami almost dropped her satchel again. She looked up at the green eyes of her teacher, then back at all of the students. Hide-in-the-background was her modus operandi. Seeing all those eyes staring at her she fought the instinct to flee.

"Um, sure. I'm Kami," she said, gripping the handle of her satchel tightly with both hands, trying not to fidget. She turned back to the teacher. "I kind of like math, and am really into computers and anime and stuff."

"What kind of computers?" asked the teacher.

"Oh," said Kami, letting the satchel fall to her side. "I have a Mac G5, a Windows PC; XP Pro obviously, not that Vista abomination. Also I have a Debian box, and a custom Linux one that I've been programming on the side. The last three custom built of course."

There was an audible sound of students taking deep breaths.

"My, my, adventurous, aren't we?" asked Ms. Heit.

Kami suddenly became aware of all the eyes staring at her and looked to the floor.

"Where can I sit?"

"Anywhere you like, I do not have assigned seating."

Kami thanked her and walked as quickly as she could to the back of the class. She sat down and smiled a hello at the person to her left, the right desk was empty.

"Alright class, please we will go over the homework assignment from yesterday," said Ms. Heit. "Kami, I will go over what we are working on with you toward the end of class, but follow along as best as you can, please."

The door to the classroom was flung open and a girl with light brown hair to her shoulders ran in. She stopped several steps into the room, turned around, ran back to the door and closed it, then turned around and said, "Sorry I'm late."

"Why Stacie, so good of you to join us today," said Ms. Heit looking down at a notebook and making a mark. "That is your last tardy for the month."

"Is that bad?" asked the girl.

"Considering we are not even half way through the month, yes, that is bad," said the instructor.

"Oh, sorry," said the girl, laughing lightly, and then looked around the room. She ran to the back of the class, sitting next to Kami.

"And since you could not deign to be here on time, the person to your left is a new student. Her name is Kami Nakamura."

The girl looked over and Kami caught her eyes. "Kami!" she screamed standing and launching herself.

Unprepared for the sudden hug, Kami muttered a hello, somewhat confused.

Pulling back, the girl said, "Come on, we were so close and this is how you treat me?"

Looking up at the girl again Kami barely recognized the face and asked, "Stacie, Stacie?"

"He he he, well, duh," she said. "We were only the best of friends. Oh, well, then again that was about five years ago when I moved to London, wasn't it?"

Kami shifted in her seat, painfully aware that everybody was staring at her, Stacie's arms still around her, then opened her mouth to speak.

"Oh my God," said Stacie. "I can't believe it, after all these years we're back together again. So how you been?"

"Uh, good."

"Stacie?" asked Ms. Heit.

"Yes?"

"I have a class to teach now. Return to your seat immediately."

"Oh, sorry," said Stacie. "We were like old friends and all, you know?" She let go of Kami and sat down in the desk next to her.

"Very well then," said the teacher. "As I was saying, we shall go over yesterday's assignment."

Leaning over slightly Stacie whispered, "It is so good to see you again, when you didn't reply to my emails I thought you hated me. Wait, do you hate me?"

"No," said Kami. "I don't hate you. Just figured I'd never see you again. Sorry."

"Oh, I see, I think."

Kami stared at the desk, feelings of guilt filling her. They had been the best of friends, and she had always hated losing the one person closest to her, other than Keiko. She had stopped replying to Stacie's emails because it was too painful. Because any time she started to care about somebody they always left. That was just the way the world was.

Trying to focus on the instructor's words, Kami opened her satchel and pulled out her calculus book and a notepad.

She was keenly aware that Stacie was staring at her, but did not look over.

Chapter 06.02

"Wow, this is where you live?" asked Stacie as the car passed through the gates and drove up the driveway to Kyle's house. "Looks like he's doing pretty well."

"Not really," said Kami. "He inherited it."

"Is it the same Kyle your sister wanted to date back before I left?" asked Stacie. "Did they ever get together like you wanted?"

"Same guy, and no, he's a loser and never asked her out. So my sis has only been focusing on modeling since then. Pisses me off. But this is better than living in rural Japan to tell you the truth."

"Oh, sounds complicated," said Stacie.

"But you living here must be fate," she continued, suddenly switching gears. Seeing the questioning look on her friend's face she said, "I live less than a mile from here."

"Really?"

The car stopped and the two girls got out.

Leaning back in, Stacie told her Nanny, "I'll be just a few minutes."

"All right, dear, but not for too long."

Smiling she shut the door and looked up at the house. "Wow, this has been such a great day! Not only do we end up back together but you live in this huge mansion so close to my house!"

Turning and grabbing Kami, Stacie exclaimed, "I'm so happy!"

Kami smiled and grabbed her friend's hands. "You have no idea how glad I was to see a familiar face."

"Oh, that's right, this is the first time you've gone to a new school, isn't it?"

"Yeah."

"No worries, you'll be fine. I'll show you the ropes and fill you in on the teachers and students and stuff. Oh, hey, how are you getting to school?"

"I have to take the bus," said Kami, scowling at the last word.

Stacie made a hissing noise. "Screw that. I'll have my Nanny pick you up. It's sorta on the way."

"Really?"

"Close enough."

"Damn, thank you. I wasn't looking forward to taking the bus. Lot of weirdoes on them."

Stacie pulled back and shivered. "Tell me about it. I had to take one back home once in the morning, after a Rave I snuck out to. Never seen so many scary people before in my life! I mean, LA public transit really isn't like it is in most cities."

"I've heard."

"Dearest?" said the Nanny through the open window.

"Oh, sorry," said Stacie spinning around.

Turning back to Kami she said, "I'll call you tonight or text you and we'll work out the details for tomorrow morning."

"Thanks, talk to you then," said Kami.

Stacie flung herself at Kami and gave her a big hug. Squinting and smiling she said, "Bye bye."

Letting go she opened the door and jumped into the back of the car, waving at her friend as the car drove down the driveway.

"She's so weird," said Kami to herself. "And hasn't changed a bit, thankfully."

There were no cars in the driveway, so Kami walked over to the garage and opened the fourth door with her remote. The last stall was where some of her belongings and furniture were stored that would not fit in her room. She looked at the new stack of boxes at the front, which were hers, and the stacks of boxes behind them, then pushed her way through to the door at the back.

The other three stalls were empty. That meant an empty house, since Harry and Thomas were usually at work until after six.

Sighing she went back through and closed the garage door behind her, walking to the house. Stepping in she checked the alarm and saw it was off, as usual.

"Tadaima," she said to the empty house, announcing she was home, as she kicked off her shoes in the general direction of the coat rack, then picked them up and pointed them toward the door.

Slowly she walked to her room, her feet dragging, closing the door behind her. Tossing her satchel onto the bed, she tore off her uniform and put on a pair of shorts and a T-shirt.

Kami jumped onto her bed and grabbed her Cait Sith plush, holding it close.

Looking into the eyes of the plush she said, "Have I told you lately how much I really hate my life? Though I did run into an old friend, which makes it slightly better."

Holding the feline plush close she went over and scanned the shelves for something to watch. Something funny and light. Picking one she threw it into the DVD player and turned on her television, adjusting the volume low enough so that she could just barely hear it. Setting the plush on the desk next to the monitor she was working on she fired up her IM client and checked to see who was online.

Kami let out a moan. One ex-boyfriend and two ex-girlfriends were on. She was in no mood to deal with past relationship garbage and turned off the client. She fired up mIRC and cruised through some of her normal places, one after another, before quitting the program.

As lonely as she felt, she was not really in the mood to deal with people online or off. She stood in the middle of her room, surrounded by the hum of the fans of the computers that were always on. There was comfort there, in that sound, since she was a kid.

Her phone rang and Kami leapt onto the bed, opening her satchel to see who was calling.

"Hey Stac," she said, sliding the phone open.

"Long time no talk," said Stacie.

Kami fell back onto the bed and laughed uneasily.

"Listen, I know you just moved and are probably busy, but what are you doing for dinner?"

Sighing, she sat up and looked at her plush doll on the desk, then said, "Don't know, everybody's gone so probably a frozen pizza or something."

"Want to come over for dinner and work on homework?" asked Stacie. "My mom makes the best lasagna."

"I remember," said Kami thinking back to many years ago.

"And," continued Stacie, "I can bring you up to speed on class and stuff."

"That sounds so much better than sitting at home alone," said Kami.

"Yay!" screamed Stacie. "We'll be over in a few to pick you up."

"Thanks, Stacie," she said hanging up the phone.

"Maybe this school won't be so bad, ne?" Kami asked her Cait Sith.

Hopping out of bed she changed into some loose fitting khaki pants and long sleeved shirt before putting everything back into her satchel. Flipping off her monitors and the television, she wandered around her room until the buzzer of the front door sounded.

Grabbing her satchel she raced to the front door and pressed the button to open the gate. Opening the door and stepping out, she watched the car approaching. It stopped in front of her and Kami jumped into the back seat.

"Good to see you again," said Stacie leaning over and giving her a hug.

"Thanks for the invite," said Kami smiling.

As they pulled away from the house Kami said, "Oh."

"What?"

"Probably should call Kyle and let him know where I am," she said.

Pulling out her phone she dialed his number.

It went straight to voice-mail, and Kami said, "Hey, Kyle, it's Kami. Ran into an old friend at school today, so I'm going over to her place for dinner, then we're working on homework. I'll be back later."

"By Kyle!" yelled Stacie as her friend ended the call.

Chapter 06.03

The next day Keiko was walking in circles around the terminal, ignoring the stares of people around her. As she completed another circle she decided to sit town in a seat near the window, leaving several empty chairs between her and the people close by.

A song came on that she was not in the mood for. Pulling out her MP3 player she advanced several tracks to something more suitable for her mood, an angry Japanese metal band. She closed her eyes and lost herself in the music.

She was about half way through it when somebody started poking her shoulder. Pulling her fist back she opened her eyes and saw Kyle kneeling before her, still pressing his finger into her.

Her eyes narrowed as she pulled the ear buds out, they fell onto her lap.

"Baka," said Kyle. "You never bothered to tell me what time you were leaving so I had to torment Kami until she told me."

Looking over her shoulder, out the window, she said, "I didn't want to bother you."

Sensing something was wrong, Kyle sat down in the seat next to her, putting a hand on her shoulder. "What's gotten into you lately?"

"What do you mean?" she asked glaring at him and pulling away from his touch.

"Well," he said pulling his arm from behind her. "Just seemed like you were trying to force yourself have fun the other night, that's all."

"Oh, and you think you know me so well?"

Kyle pulled back.

"What?" he asked. "How long have I known you?"

Keiko unclenched her fists and put on a happy face.

"Kyle," she said smiling. "I've just been a little stressed from work and all. Don't worry about me."

"You are not even remotely convincing," said Kyle.

They stared at each other.

"Is it about your manager? He seemed a bit odd when he came over to my Grandma's house."

"No, no, of course not," said Keiko defensively. "And that's not your problem anyway. And it's your house now."

Both of them looked up at the announcement that boarding was about to begin.

"I have to go," she said standing.

He stood and pulled her into his arms. Her arms were limp by her side.

Pulling back and putting both hands on her shoulders Kyle said, "Have a safe trip."

Keiko looked to the floor and muttered, "Thanks."

"Um, Keiko?" he asked, she took a step back.

Keiko looked past him.

"Can we talk a bit when you get back?"

Shrugging her shoulders she turned around and walked toward the gate, pulling out her ticket.

"Not even a good-bye?" she heard behind her.

She raised a hand.

"First class only right now," said the flight attendant.

Keiko held out her ticket.

"Thank you, have a pleasant flight."

Keiko walked down the corridor of the plane and took her seat. As she sat down, she stopped, seeing the wires in her lap. Pulling them up she put the ear buds back and listened to the music. It was a sad tune from some shoujo anime she and Kyle had watched a few weeks back. Pulling out her player she forwarded to a different song.

Fastening her seat belt she leaned back in the chair and stared at her trembling hands that were clasped in her lap.

"Sorry, Kyle," she whispered. "But we can't be friends anymore. Thank you for everything. You have your life to live and I have this job I must do. Goodbye."

Chapter 06.04

Several days later, Kami was sitting alone in her room, working on homework. Kyle was her official guardian now, her Mother and Grandmother had left for Japan early this morning, and she was struggling to keep up with school, but somehow managing.

Kami was tapping the eraser of her mechanical pencil on a piece of paper, trying to figure out a math problem, when she heard screaming from just outside her closed door.

"Cyn, c'mon, it's not like I planned this," said Ed loudly.

Kami put her pencil down and turned her head slightly to listen. There was no sound for a minute, then she could barely discern the whisper of Cynthia's voice.

"Work? What do you mean work? Look, this was out of the blue. Least you could do is spend some time with me."

More soft talking that Kami could not hear. She stood from her desk and walked quietly to her door, opening it slightly to see them standing in the entry to the living room.

"I know you're busy, but c'mon," pleaded Ed.

"My apologies, Ed," said Cynthia, Kami could barely hear her voice. "I have much work to finish. I agree that it is indeed a good sign that your label has added performances, unfortunately I have clients who are not flexible. Understand that this is the tax season, and I am quite busy."

"And you can't even spare a few efing hours tonight?"

"No, not tonight, Ed. I am sorry," she said.

"Well, sorry, I better leave so I don't interrupt your work any more," sneered Ed turning around quickly and walking through the living room.

Cynthia looked over her shoulder, directly into Kami's eyes for a moment before walking down the hall to the study.

Kami quickly closed the door as the dark girl passed by. Then she heard the door to Ed's room slam shut.

She wandered over to her computer chair and sat down, somewhat sad. She had met Ed back when everybody hung out all the time. Keiko, Kyle, Cynthia, and Ed. How many times did they crash at her mom's house? And even though she was ten back then, she had developed a bit of a crush on the dark musician who lived upstairs from her now. Over all these years she never had figured out why he was with Cynthia.

Shaking her head to let loose meaningless thoughts Kami went over to her bed and began working on her homework again, tempted to call Stacie. But she had to figure this out herself so resisted the temptation.

Staring at the paper she picked up her pencil, stared some more, then wrote some equations. Knowing they were wrong she crumpled up the paper and threw it toward the trash can, missing. Re-reading the problem she started over, sighed, and put the pencil down, closing her book.

There was a knock on her door.

Kami looked up and said, "Come."

Ed opened the door and said, "Hey."

The sheer depression on his face made Kami look back at her notebook to avoid it.

"Um, come in," she said.

He walked in and sat down heavily on the corner of her bed.

"So what you up to?" asked Ed.

"Giving up on my homework, you?"

"Saw your door was opened a bit so am guessing you know a bit of the 411 of what's going on."

"Yeah, kinda."

"Want to go get some food or something? My treat."

"Sure."

"Kyle around?"

"Nah, he left a bit ago for a date with that Janice girl."

"Dude, hope he doesn't screw it up. You need to get ready?"

"Not really," she said. Grabbing her phone she shoved it into her pocket along with her wallet, then grabbed her combat boots and put them on.

Kami followed him out of the room and through the house and out to his car in the garage. They drove to a fast food joint, got some food and drove to a park close by.

"Looks closed," she said.

"Of course it is," said Ed smiling as he parked his car on the street. "Come on," he said getting out of the car with the food and his drink.

They walked down a short way to the entry and stepped over the chain that blocked off the entrance. He led them to a picnic table that was mostly hidden in the shadows and they sat down.

"Here you go, fries, burger," he said, handing them to her.

Kami thanked him and looked around at the dark surroundings. They ate their dinner without many words. As she was crumpling up the wrapper of her burger Ed let out a long sigh.

"Do you date much?" he asked.

"Not much, really. Some online relations, which mean jack, but not much real world people to people stuff."

"Ah well, just to warn you, it can get messy."

"Oh, trust me, I know that much."

Ed laughed. "Yeah, you probably do. Ah, just sucks. I wasn't supposed to ship out for six weeks and my agent calls me today saying that they nailed some really good concerts in Europe and that I need to leave soon. Cyn is all up to her eyeballs with tax season and such so I probably won't be able to spend much time with her if any before I leave."

"Sux0r."

"Tell me about it. Guess I'm just being stupid. Really can't expect her to sacrifice her job just because my schedule changed. But I never know what she's thinking anyway."

"Ed?"

"Huh?"

"I don't mean to pry, but why are you with her?"

Ed stared at the table for a long time.

"I don't know," he said. "We've been dating for so long now, she's just always been there. I don't even try to understand her, but I accept Cynthia. And she accepts me, she lets me do my things, doesn't ask anything of me. There is this part of her, this darkness that I can't even wrap my mind around, that inspires my music."

Julien Giever

"Oh."

"Well, it's not like that. Huh, maybe it is. I really don't think about it much. We have our routines. I do my music and day job, she does work for her clients and her spooky magic stuff."

"Magic?"

"Yeah. I don't even want to think about that stuff. I'm not the most religious person on the planet, but I get the feeling she deals with some pretty dark shit, if you know what I mean."

Kami shivered thinking back to the ghostly dogs from the study. "I'm sure."

"So how's school going?" asked Ed. "Haven't seen you much since you started the new one."

"Oh, it's ok," said Kami. "I ended up running into an old friend I knew years ago who lives close by, so it's not as bad as it could be."

Kami stared at Ed. He caught her eye and looked away, into the darkness of the park surrounding them. She stood and walked around the table, sitting down next to him.

He inched away a bit, glancing at her, then back to the darkness.

Grabbing his arm and pulling it around her Kami said, "I'm cold."

"Um, do you want my jacket?"

"No, you're fine," she said pressing close to him.

The arm that was around her was grasping the table firmly, and the rest of his body was equally as rigid. He did not move as Kami placed her head on his chest.

"I haven't even seen her touch you," said Kami.

"Ah, well, um, she's not really one much for physical contact and all," said Ed.

Her left hand moved across his back, pulling him closer to her while she placed her right hand on his chest and slowly moved it up to his neck, then the back of his head. She moved her face up, lips gently brushing his neck.

Ed was petrified.

"I am," she said pulling his head toward her and kissing him.

Chapter 06.05

Kyle had been sitting in his car for about twenty minutes, pulling

168

out his phone in three minute intervals to check the time. He was supposed to pick Janice at seven-thirty. Normally he was not too time-conscious, but had made an effort this evening to get ready early and allow ample time for possible traffic jams.

He had his head leaned back in his seat, listening to the music in his car, when the alarm on his phone went off. Jumping slightly he turned it off and double-checked the time before letting out a sigh. As he was going to turn off the electrical of his car he was hit with panic.

What type of music did Janice like?

He had been so out of it, with the concept of going out on an actual date, he had completely forgotten to ask Ed or Cynthia what type of music she liked. He turned up the volume and listened for a second, then skipped through the next few tracks.

Frowning he ejected the MP3 CD and grabbed the case from the glove compartment, putting that one back and then flipping through the rest. Kyle's mind raced. Time was up, he needed to get out of the car. But he needed to make sure that when they left sucky music was not playing.

He flipped through all of his CDs again.

Resting his head for a minute he looked through all the CDs a third time. Giving up he closed the case, held it in the air, and dropped it. The case flopped open and showed four possible candidates. Thinking back on what he knew of Janice, which was little, he pulled out one and put it into the CD player, then skipped three songs ahead and let it play for about forty-five seconds before turning off his car. Nothing was more obvious than being at the beginning of track one, and he did not want to come across as being lame or trying too hard to impress her.

Taking a deep breath he returned the case to the glove compartment, closed it, and got out of his car, clicking his remote to enable the security system.

The street was pretty quiet. He was in West Los Angeles, just off the 10 freeway. Kyle walked down half a block to her building and went up to the door, glancing at the directory and pressing the button for her apartment.

"I'll be right down," came her voice.

Kyle looked at the front door and tried to decide if he should be standing there or leaning against the wall waiting for her. He was still deciding when she suddenly walked into the lobby and opened the front door.

"Hi, Kyle," she said stepping out, shoving her hands into the long beige coat she had worn to the club.

"Hello, Janice," he said, half raising a hand in a pathetic attempt at a greeting. Cursing internally to himself he put his hand back into the pocket of his blue jeans.

Turning and leading them down the stairs they walked along the sidewalk.

"So where would you like to go to eat?" he asked. "I'll be honest, I really don't know this section of town."

"Oh, that's OK," she said pulling out a piece of paper and unfolding it. "I made a list of restaurants around here, all arranged by price range of course."

"Um great, any preferences?" he asked as they approached his car.

"Hmmmm...." she said holding the paper up so she could see it with the street lights. Pointing half-way down the list she said, "How about this one? It's just down on Pico and has pretty good food."

Kyle glanced at the name of the restaurant, and nodded his head, having no idea because he had never been there. Pulling out his keys he hit the button on the remote to unlock the doors and opened the passenger side for her. After she was in he closed it and got into his car, placing the keys into the ignition.

Just as he started the car, his phone began to ring. Pulling it out he saw it was Heather and let it go to voice mail. Putting his car into drive he pulled out onto the road.

"As I mentioned, I'm not that familiar with this area, you know the way from here?" he asked.

"Of course," she said. "Just go to that stop sign and hang a left, and I'll get us there."

"Cool, thanks," said Kyle as he turned left from the stop sign.

"Oh my god, I love this album," she said as the next song started.

Kyle was in shock for about half a second before he recovered and said, "Yes, it is pretty good. Though I didn't like their second album."

"Ugh," she said. "Tell me about it. It sucked. Er, the second one that is."

They drove to the restaurant as she flipped through songs, making comments and opinions on each one. After parking the car they walked toward the entrance and went inside, then were led to a booth.

The waitress took their order and left, returning a short time later with drinks.

Taking a sip of his red wine, Kyle said, "I think I saw another report recently saying red wine was good for you."

"That's such bull," said Janice. "Because if you look at medical surveys or studies, statistically most of them should be thrown out the window."

"What?" asked Kyle.

"Sorry, pet peeve of mine," she said smiling. "You know all those studies that say butter is bad for you, and alcohol is bad for you, then a few years later a new study reverses the other's findings?"

"Yes," he said nodding his head.

"First," she said raising a finger, her voice getting slightly louder. "First is the fact that you have this small group, usually less than two hundred people. And these two hundred people are supposed to represent over six billion? You couldn't even get a bet with odds like that in Vegas.

"Then," and she raised a second finger, "There is the fact that we cannot possibly calculate any of these studies accurately because of all of the possible elements that might skew the results. Like genetics, all the chemicals we intake, our psychology, the environment where we live, things like that."

She stopped and blushed slightly.

"Sorry, I just get a little passionate about stuff like that," she said. "It bothers me that people jump from trend to trend based off some study like that."

Kyle laughed and said, "Almost like a religion."

"How so?" she asked, frowning slightly.

"People need something to believe," said Kyle. "Because if you were to tell them that scientifically we really don't know what effects all these things have on us, they would be lost. So they jump from study to study, taking vitamins, aspirin, limiting their intakes of this or that, eating more of the stuff that might be good. And they are happy with their lives because they are living by the latest rules."

"Then bam," she said smiling. "As you're out jogging one day you get hit by a truck."

"Weird," he said looking over at her and catching her eye. "I was just about to say something like that."

"Really?" she asked. "Ah well, great minds."

"Heh, something like that," he said looking at her again.

The waitress came back with their food.

As they ate, Kyle glanced at Janice for a quick second then stared at his food. It suddenly struck him that after they had talked about the music in his car all airs of nervousness had dissipated within both of them.

Chapter 06.06

Closing the door of his bedroom behind him, Kyle let out a long sigh and closed his eyes, smiling.

In all the evening had gone well. After dinner he and Janice had gone over to the Sunset strip and had a few drinks by the pool in the hotel bar that he had seen in a movie called The Player once. One of his clients had recently recommended it to him as a nice place to hang out and relax on a weekday.

Over the course of the evening, Janice and himself had talked about a wide range of subjects, laughed, joked, and in general been really relaxed around each other. She had mentioned that she had not dated much, to which he had replied that he had not either.

He was amazed. Sitting there next to the pool, looking out over the city, they chatted away and enjoyed the evening. No hesitation on his part, no worries that he would say the wrong thing or do something stupid. And after he dropped her off he had been filled with this sense of happiness he could not quite remember ever having before, except once, in Paris.

Walking over to the computer chair he draped his coat over the back, then noticed somebody standing next to him.

Looking up he saw Cynthia, holding an unmarked wine bottle and a red wine glass that was half full.

"Hey, Cyn," he said. "Sorry, think I've had enough for one night."

"Kyle," she said intently. "Please, you should drink this."

He hesitated.

"You do not have to drive anywhere else this eve," she said taking a step forward.

"Fine, fine," he said taking the glass and sitting down in his chair next to the computer.

Cynthia placed the bottle on the computer desk and sat down in the chair next to his, crossing her legs under her long black dress. Leaning forward she pulled the bottle a few feet toward her, away from the keyboard.

Kyle smiled and said, "Thank you," raising the glass.

Taking a sip of the thick red wine he closed his eyes and enjoyed the slightly metallic after-taste as this feeling of a red mist wrapped around a black void spread from his stomach and filled his body.

"Every night lately you've been giving me this stuff," said Kyle. "What is it exactly? Doesn't seem like a normal wine."

"It is not," she said. Her hands were clasped calmly in her lap, as she stared at him.

"What is it?" he asked.

She paused for a moment before saying, "A special mixture of mine to help you."

"Special mix?" he asked. "Like with herbs and stuff? Prevent me from getting sick with the coming flu season?"

"You seem to have had a pleasant evening," she said, looking out toward the balcony.

Kyle smiled and took two more sips of the wine.

"It actually turned out really, really good," he said.

Staring down at the liquid in the glass he brought it to his mouth and finished the contents in three gulps, then felt guilty for drinking the wine so quickly.

"Sorry," he said.

"Do not worry yourself," said Cynthia refilling his glass. "As you were saying?"

"Oh," he said taking another sip. "I didn't screw up the evening that I know of, we had a nice dinner, then drinks at this other place. And the whole evening was relaxed and we seemed to get along pretty well. Had some good conversation with her."

Cynthia paused a moment and stared at the wine glass in his hand.

"That is good to hear," she said slowly.

"You bet it is," he said drinking some more. "She's kind of dorky like me, and I don't mean that as an offense. It's just Janice hasn't dated much, and has always been with, you know, typical guys who get weirded out because she's smart or other things that might conflict with their testosterone. And we talked all night, and I think I really like her."

He looked down at his glass.

"I hope I don't screw this one up," he said.

"Kyle?"

"What?"

"Did you spend the night worrying about what Keiko would think?" she asked.

Kyle sat back in his chair and pondered a moment.

"No, actually I really didn't think of her at all, I was just having fun and she never really crossed my mind."

"Interesting," she said.

They fell into silence. He finished off his glass and she refilled it for him. Kyle was lost in thought, then looked over at Cynthia.

"Cyn?" he asked.

"Yes?"

"Sorry for bringing this up, but it has kind of bothered me for a bit," he said. "When Thomas showed up and we talked later that night," he started, then stopped.

She waited for him to continue, but when Kyle did not she asked, "Yes?"

Raising a hand he said, "This is a personal question, so you don't have to answer, but I know that Ed loves you, but after we talked I was wondering if you loved him."

Cynthia stared into Kyle's eyes, then stood and turned her back to him.

Turning her head slightly she said, "I am not capable of experiencing love."

She left the room, closing the door behind her.

REVELATIONS

Chapter 07.01

"I do so apologize for not calling you sooner," said Heather.

Kyle set his bags down and looked over at her.

"Um, what do you mean?" he asked. "I was just here little over a week ago."

Walking past him she closed the door and leaned against it, brushing her long red hair from her face and staring at the ground. She stood there for a moment before taking a step forward.

"No, it is just that there are several important matters that I have needed to discuss with you that I have put off for a time," she said.

"Like what?" he asked.

Heather smiled in a sad way and then walked over to the bar, grabbing a bottle and pouring a glass for him. She held it up to him.

"First, drink this wine and tell me how it makes you feel."

Taking the glass he sniffed the dark liquid and a smile crossed his lips. Taking a tentative sip, the smile broadened and he took another full drink, feeling a familiar sensation.

"Ah, this is good," he said. "One of those special mixes, right?"

Her head shot up and she looked at him.

Kyle frowned slightly and stared at the glass, asking, "Just out of curiosity, Cynthia won't say, but what exactly is in this? Taurine, guarana or something to give me energy? Oh, like a Vodka and Red-bull? Poor mans eight ball? Except with wine?"

Heather suddenly took a step back and leaned against the edge of the bar, trembling slightly.

"What did you say?" she asked slowly.

He took another drink and leaned against the wall, enjoying the feeling that flowed through him.

"It's just that you and my friend seem to have similar recipes," he said. "She mentioned something the other night about it being a special mix to give me energy, or something like that."

Heather turned and stared at the bar, grasping it with both hands.

"And it tastes the same?" she asked.

"Pretty similar, but a different kick," he said walking forward so he was standing close. "Are you ok?"

"Why? Why is all of this going so wrong," she whispered.

Turning slightly Heather asked, "What is your friend's full name?"

"Huh?" asked Kyle. "Oh, Cynthia Hapsburg. Why?"

She closed her eyes for a moment, seemingly lost in thought. In a voice barely above a whisper she said, "Unfortunately I do not recognize that last name as one of us or one allied. Can you contact her?"

He had taken a few steps back, but said hesitantly, "Sure."

"Please do so, the three of us need to talk," said Heather in a coarse voice, holding back both fear and tears.

"She's probably at my place," said Kyle taking another step back.

"Then we can meet there," she said in a voice that was barely audible to Kyle.

"Yeah, fine, hold on," he said setting his glass down and pulling out his phone.

"Kyle," came the soft voice.

"Cyn," he said leaning his back against the wall. "I'm with Heather, the Irish client, and she says the three of us should talk," he said, then dropping his voice he whispered, "But she's acting very strange."

"It is about time. I am at the house," said Cynthia. "Knock on the study doors when you get here."

"About time?" he asked.

The line went dead.

Putting the phone back into his pocket he turned slightly and said, "She's at my place."

"Very well, you drive," said Heather.

"Heather?"

"What?"

"What the hell is going on?" he asked.

She closed her eyes and dropped her head for a minute. Then, turning to Kyle, she walked over and placed both of her hands on his shoulders.

"We will talk more of this when we arrive at your place," she said. "Until then, please do not ask me any questions. Now, we should go."

She let go of him and walked to the front door, opening it.

Shaking his head, Kyle grabbed his bags and walked back to his car, Heather was right behind him. He tried to start a conversation several times during the drive, but she would not reply. Eventually he gave up. When they arrived he parked his car in the garage and unlocked the doors.

"We're here," he said.

"Thank you for driving," said Heather in a monotone voice, opening the door and getting out of the car.

Kyle hesitated a second before pulling the key from the ignition and getting out of his car.

"Come on," he said walking past her, clicking the remote to close the garage door as they walked through the darkness toward the house.

Opening the front door they stepped inside. He heard the television from the living room. Kyle cursed to himself.

Walking down the hallway he saw Ed and Kami sitting on the couch, watching a movie. She was sitting cross-legged with a bag of microwave popcorn in her lap, Ed was sitting with his arms crossed.

As he entered the room only Ed looked over.

"How was the job with that hot Irish chick?" asked Kami with a sarcastic tone, staring at the television.

"Hey," said Ed, then added, "Oh, hello."

Kami's eyes widened slightly, looking over, and she let out a slight 'uh' sound before suddenly becoming interested in the television again.

He felt Heather inches from his back.

"Good evening," she said.

"Wow, check you out, Mr. Gigolo," said Ed smiling as Kami let out an uncomfortable laugh.

"Sorry, we really can't visit," said Kyle beginning to walk across the room. "Have to talk to Cyn."

"What?" exclaimed Ed and Kami simultaneously.

Kyle paused and turned to them, trying to think of something, then said, "Well... Heather had some tax questions I thought Cynthia could help with. Now, if you'll excuse us."

He and Heather walked around the couch then to the door that led to the hallway. At the double doors of the study Kyle knocked twice. As his hand was pulling away the locks clicked, and both of them opened.

He looked in and did not see Cynthia. Irritated he walked through the small hall and stepped into the study for the first time since before his Grandmother had died. Cynthia was standing on the other side of the room in front of a tall table, upon which was a large book she was reading. She raised a hand and the doors closed behind them.

Kyle jumped at the noise and turned to see that the doors were closed as he heard the locks click shut. Nobody was near them. Over the years he had become accustomed to Cynthia's mysterious entrances and exits, odd thing occurring or moving, and though Ed had mentioned she studied magic Kyle had always laughed it off, because things like that just did not exist in the real world.

Spinning around he stared at the girl in the long black dress who slowly looked up to the two at the entry hallway of the study. She stared at them for a moment. Her face and body language were as emotionless as always.

"Relax, Kyle, it will be alright," he heard Cynthia's voice in his head.

This did little to help him relax.

Heather took a step forward, seeming to study every inch of Cynthia, from head to floor. She paused then said, "What is the meaning of this? You are not…"

"No, I am not," said Cynthia raising a hand. "Please, this way."

Heather hesitated, glancing over to Kyle. He was staring blankly at his dark friend.

Grabbing Kyle's wrist, Heather pulled him along as they walked the length of the long wooden table stacked with folders to where Cynthia was standing. When they reached her, she led them through a maze of bookshelves to the center of the room.

There was a rectangular mahogany coffee table, upon which was an unmarked bottle filled with a dark liquid and two wine glasses. On opposite sides of the table were two couches, and two high-backed chairs, each of the same wood, whose cushions were dark red leather.

Cynthia motioned to the couch as she stood before one of the chairs. Next to her chair was an end table with a bottle of a California

Merlot, and a wine glass that was already filled.

Stepping forward, Heather said, "I am Heather McClellan, thank you for having us."

"Cynthia, and please forgive my rudeness but I do not shake hands."

"As you wish," said Heather, dropping her hand.

"Please, be seated," said Cynthia, sitting in the chair, resting both hands on the arms of the chair.

Kyle stared at her, because her poise and demeanor seemed different than how she usually was, almost elegant in a way. He lost his train of thought as he was pulled over to the couch and sat down next to Heather.

Looking at the unmarked bottle on the table, Heather asked, "Is this?"

Cynthia inclined her head slightly, and then took her own glass.

Pouring two glasses, Heather handed one to Kyle who grabbed it and took a long drink. As he did so his brows furrowed.

"Please do not mention that it tastes different," he heard Cynthia's voice in his head again.

He almost dropped the glass of wine as he looked up at her.

"Thank you," said Heather taking a small sip.

"You desired a conversation?" asked Cynthia, her words crisp as she stared at the woman with red hair.

In his peripheral vision, Kyle saw Heather's hands begin to tremble. She raised the shaking glass to her lips, took a long drink, then carefully set the glass back upon the table. Heather stared at Cynthia for a long time.

"You know of our kind?" she asked hesitantly.

"Obviously," came Cynthia's reply, her tone cold and hostile. "I have been caring for Kyle since you did this, and then simply abandoned him."

"I..." started Heather. "It is just that..." she said, faltering again.

"Wait, what did you do to me Heather?" asked Kyle.

She tried to speak a few times, avoiding his questioning stare.

Finally she managed, "May, may I get something?"

"Is it to help resolve this matter?" asked Cynthia.

Heather nodded her head.

Cynthia made a motion with her hand and Heather left the area.

Kyle leaned forward and asked in a whisper, "Cyn, really, what's going on? What did she do to me? Both of you are kind of freaking me out."

"Please be patient," she said softly. "I would like to hear what this woman has to say."

"About what?" he asked, almost standing.

She looked over into his eyes for a moment then asked one word. "Please."

Hesitantly he sat back.

Chapter 07.02

Kami was kneeling on the floor, with Ed above her. Both were peering cautiously down the hallway at Kyle and the Irish woman. The doors to the study opened, then closed as the two walked through.

"Weird," said Kami starting to stand and bumping into Ed.

He jumped back away from her, paused a moment as she stood, then said, "Taxes my ass, something's up."

"What do you think it is?" she asked walking toward him.

Ed nervously took a step back.

"Not sure, but Kyle has been acting kind of strange lately," he said.

"You're one to talk," said Kami glaring at him.

"Well, it's just, that, well…" he trailed off.

"Oh, jeez, we were just having some fun, don't make such a big deal," said Kami walking past him and back to the couch, sitting down.

Ed stood there for a minute, staring at her, then said, "I'm going upstairs."

"Whatever," said Kami.

He closed his eyes for a second then left the room.

"Guys," Kami grumbled grabbing the remote.

She flipped through some stations, became bored and turned everything off, returning to her room. Sitting down in front of her computers she fired up an IM client and logged in with a new name she had recently created.

Stacie was online and she popped off a quick hello.

Kami's cell phone rang, she grabbed it off the desktop.

"Too lazy to type tonight?" she asked.

"He he he, kinda," said Stacie. "Just suck at typing so easier to talk."

"Take it your family thing is done?"

"Thank God," said Stacie. "It was so boring. So what are you doing at home on a Saturday night?"

"Well, you know me," said Kami. "I had all these parties I was invited to, and just couldn't decide which one to go to. It's horrible being so popular."

Stacie burst into laughter.

"God, I wish we were that popular," she said. "Listen, I really need to get out of here. Could I spend the night over there?"

Kami looked at the state of her room and frowned.

"Please?" asked Stacie whining.

"Sure," said Kami. "Just give me about thirty to straighten up."

"You're so funny," said Stacie.

"Why?"

"I'm coming over to see you, not your room."

"I know," said Kami sighing. "But anyway, come over in about thirty, ok?"

"Got it, want me to bring anything over?"

"Dunno, have any good movies?"

"Hmm...." said Stacie. "I'll grab a few, and pick up some ice cream on the way over."

"Ooooh, you're a goddess."

"Yeah right, see you in a bit."

Chapter 07.03

Heather returned with an old book held before her with both hands. It was leather bound, and the leather was cracking. Sitting next to Kyle on the couch, she placed the book in her lap and leaned forward to grab her glass of wine.

"Heather, what the hell is going on?" asked Kyle. Cynthia had been silent since his last request.

Heather froze, and began to shake again. Closing her eyes the trembling of her wine glass calmed and she took a drink before opening her eyes and placing the glass back upon the table.

"Before we talk, I wanted to show you something," she said opening the book.

It was a photo album filled with black and white photographs, each of which was tinted yellow from age. Carefully Heather paged through the book, hesitating some times, until she came to one particular page. Grabbing her glass to take another drink, she slid the album into Kyle's lap and pointed at a photograph.

Kyle stared at the photo, searching his mind, because he had seen it before. There was a man and woman with their arms around each others waists, and another woman standing a few feet from them. Behind was a mass of men working on building something.

"Hey, wait," said Kyle. "This is a picture of my Grandma and Grandpa when they were building this place. Wait, don't you have this photo in your living room?"

Heather finished off her wine and poured another glass. She pointed at the other woman in the photo.

Kyle leaned forward, looking at the picture, then sat back in shock.

"Wow!" he exclaimed. "She looks almost exactly like you. Is that your Grandmother?"

Pointing at the woman Heather said, "That is not my Grandmother, that is me."

Kyle laughed. "Yeah, right."

"It is true," said Heather, staring into his eyes.

"Your Grandfather was my brother," she said, her voice faltering.

Chapter 07.04

Harry stood in an alleyway surrounded by four unconscious men who lay at his feet. Letting out a long sigh he turned and walked back to Thomas.

"Good show," said Thomas raising a fist into the air. "We showed them, did we not!"

"Master Thomas?" asked Harry.

"Yes?"

Grabbing Thomas' shoulders, Harry pushed him backward into the wall and glared into his eyes with the look that he had a few moments ago with the now unconscious men.

"Hold on there, Harry, that hurt," said Thomas, smiling.

"This is the last time," said Harry.

"What do you mean by that, my good man?" asked Thomas, patting Harry's shoulder with one hand.

"The next time you are on your own," hissed Harry.

Looking into his mentor's eyes, he paled.

"You have been cursed by your wealth and my presence," whispered Harry, leaning forward. "You fancy yourself to be a creative genius, and that may be so, but you need to learn how to be a man, not some pampered child."

Letting go, Harry took a step backward and stared intently at Thomas. "If this does not please you, Master Thomas, I shall tender my resignation and return home immediately."

Thomas avoided his eyes, instead staring at the Oxford shoes a few feet from him. Glancing over at the bodies on the ground, he looked up to the sky.

"You are not kidding around, are you?" he asked.

"No," said Harry, turning his back to him and walking away.

Thomas dropped his head and began to weep.

Chapter 07.05

"That's not possible," said Kyle.

Heather was staring at the couch on the other side of the table.

"It is," said Cynthia.

"Oh, bullshit, funny, whatever," said Kyle slamming the book shut and tossing it on the table as he stood. "I have work to do."

He began to walk away, but felt a tender hand upon his. Tears were streaming down Heather's face as she pulled his hand toward her.

"Please forgive me," she seemed to plead in a broken voice.

"For what" he asked, pulling his hand from her grasp.

"Please, just sit and hear me out, I promise I will explain everything."

Hesitantly he sat back down on the couch, making sure there were several feet between him and Heather.

"You probably know almost nothing about your Grandfather before he met your Grandmother, do you?"

Kyle started to say he did, but stopped at her words, thinking. Living with his Grandmother, he had heard many stories of the things that his grandparents had done after they got married, but now that Heather mentioned it, he could not recall any details about his Grandfather before then. Except for the once mentioned fact that he had been disowned by his family when they had gotten married.

"That photograph holds a lot of meaning to me," said Heather. "That was the day he told me his plans. And because of his decision our family severed all ties with him."

"What do you mean?" asked Kyle, looking not at Heather but at Cynthia.

She caught his eye for a moment, then looked away.

"Do you know how they met?" asked Heather.

"Yeah, at some party in Hollywood in the thirties. She always talked about it."

"No, he first met your Grandmother in Central Park, the year was 1922, she was a child" said Heather with a melancholy smile. "I still remember how disturbed he was when he came back home that evening."

She took a sip of her wine, Kyle was watching her intently.

"My brother had just finished enjoying a pretty young woman he had met that night. When he was finished he had wiped her mind of the act he had just performed, and let her wander off. As she left the cover of the bushes he looked over and saw a young girl of ten years staring at him."

"What are you?" the girl had asked.

Kneeling he had looked into her eyes and said, "You did not see anything this eve."

The girl simply stared at him.

"Nobody would believe me if I did tell them," said the girl. "What are you?"

"But he could not affect her mind," said Heather. "There are some Humans like that, that are immune to such things as changing current memories."

"Humans?" asked Kyle.

Raising a hand, Heather continued, "After he returned, we became nervous and left New York for California. All of that was forgotten..."

Heather wiped her eyes quickly with the back of her hand.

"Wait, you're telling me that my Grandmother, as a child, caught my Grandfather having sex with somebody?" asked Kyle, feeling a little disgusted.

"No that is not what happened," she said. "Allow me to finish."

"You're not explaining anything," he said.

"Allow me to finish," said Heather more forcibly.

"Fine," he said.

"Then, about twelve years later he ran across this young woman at a Hollywood party. She had approached him, actually unusual in that day, and begun to talk with him. They had many similar interests, so much so that he began dating her.

"He had no idea that this woman in her early twenties was the girl from Central Park. Never had a clue until the day he proposed marriage to her. That is when he found out that she was the girl, and that from the day she had seen him twelve years earlier, she had been searching for him."

She paused, then continued. "You see, your Grandfather was the youngest in our family, but he was always the romantic compared to myself or our older sister, Caitlin. He completely fell for this Human girl, and they got engaged. Our family, of course, was unpleased by this, because such relationships are not allowed."

"Wait, why wouldn't it be allowed?" asked Kyle.

"It is part of our ways, which I can explain later," she said. "Then came the day of that picture."

She leaned forward and grabbed the photo-album, flipping through to the photo of the three people in front of the construction. Her hand caressed the image of his Grandfather.

"After we took this photograph," said Heather. "After that, we walked through the woods, because there were not any other houses on this hill at that time. It was pleasant, up until that point when he spoke. We had wandered around the forest, enjoying everything around us when he told me."

Taking her wine, Heather took another drink.

"My sister," he had said. "I have made a decision."

"About what?" she asked.

"Before we wed, I shall go back to sleep. The fact she knows of us, please keep a secret, to the Council it will be necessary to ensure her life under our laws," he said.

Heather dropped the flowers she had in her hands.

"What do you mean by that, brother?" she asked.

"I am happy," he said. "And I cannot think of any worse horror than having the love of my life grow old as I remain unchanged."

"You know what they will say," said Heather.

"Heather," he said stepping forward and holding her arms. "True that it may be that we are gifted with the ability to live generations, but this is something that I have thought about deeply. And, even though my bride to be may argue, and even you, this is my decision."

"They will not condone this, you know that much," she said.

"That is true," he said. "But being so old and jaded they would not understand."

"Understand what?" asked Heather, pushing him away and taking several steps back.

"Love," he said, letting go.

"Love? You are barely over two hundred. How could you possibly understand love? This is not love!" Heather screamed at him.

"What would you choose, dearest sister?" he asked. "Hundreds of years of pointless melancholy, loosing track and becoming a bane to the current age, or a brief moment wherein you can find Love? Which would you choose? Eternal life, or a few moments of love?"

"But if you do this, and you die, you will not be able to even have the Returning ceremony, you will just be gone!"

"Unfortunately that is true, and yet knowing all of this I would choose the life of a mortal to be with my wife. Heather I plead of you, please accept my decision."

"I cannot stand the thought of losing you," she said, pausing.

"I know. My dearest sister, please let me do just this. Just one thing in my life with all our rules and decisions by Councils on high that would not even hear my plea. Let me do this."

Stepping forward, Heather took his hands and said, "My brother, though I know how they may react, please trust me that I will accept this, if it is truly what you want."

"Even if it means watching over my children, or their children, if I may die?" he asked.

"With my life, Jeoffry," she said.

Nodding he had smiled and stared out into the woods.

"Thank you," he said. "Though you are honestly being overdramatic about all of this."

Heather turned several pages to photographs of his grandparents holding a child.

Kyle was looking at the man in his late thirties wondering what she meant when she had said two hundred, doubting it was years.

"Shortly after they married your Mother was born," she said. "As predicted, our family cut all ties with him. But he was happy, Kyle. And he never regretted his decision. Your Mother grew up living a normal life, got married, you were born, and she never knew about her family history, of the power that lay asleep inside her."

Kyle stared at her, a look of confusion on his face, but he did not interrupt.

"But his choice had its consequences," said Heather. "Eventually he began to weaken and I begged him to return to us, to leave my sister-in-law and regain his power, but he was a stubborn man. Then he was gone."

Heather dropped her head, tears streaming down her cheeks.

"I remember," said Kyle. "That was a few years before my parents died. We flew out here for the funeral."

Reaching out she took his hand and squeezed it.

"Then that accident happened," she said. "And in a moment, she was suddenly gone. There is nothing I could have done for her, though, she died instantly. You see, with our kind, we are normal mortals until we are Awakened, and she never was. After the accident, that was something that your Grandmother regretted to the day she died. Because if I had performed the ceremony on her, she would have lived through that crash and you would still have a Mother."

"Ceremony?" asked Kyle, clenching the fists in his lap.

Painful flashes of images suddenly filled his mind. Images he did not want to remember.

"Stop!" screamed his Mother as he opened his eyes from the back seat in time to feel them slam into something. The sound of metal grinding and glass shattering, collapsed into half of a second, as he lay on his back, pinned by his Mother's chair, her blood dripping into his eyes.

Then he was lying in the bathtub of warm water, strange symbols painted in dark red on the walls. Heather holding a dagger and chanting words in a language he did not understand. A dagger in his chest. As everything went black the brief image of her arm, sliced open, blood pouring forth being raised to his mouth.

"Is that what you were doing to me in your bathroom?" asked Kyle.

Heather look at him in shock, dropping his hand and pulling away.

"You remember that?" she asked.

"Yes," said Kyle nodding slowly. "Though I thought it was just some weird delusion because after you stabbed me I was suddenly lying on the floor next to your computer."

"I am so sorry, Kyle," she said. "I should have told you all of this before then, but I could not take the chance that you might say no. Your Grandmother made me promise to Awaken you, to give you the chance at life that your Mother never had, to give you something that she, as a Human, could not give you."

Kyle looked over to the chair and asked, "You knew, didn't you?"

"Yes," said Cynthia. "I could sense the change in you the moment you walked in the door that night."

"And you didn't tell me?" he asked, raising his voice.

"Do you remember the day after the club, when you were ill?"

"Of course," said Kyle.

"Tell me then, what would your reaction have been if I had come to you, honestly, and said that you needed to drink my blood to get better?"

Kyle started to respond, then stopped, staring at the table. Suddenly he realized what the special ingredient in the soup she had given him that day was, and what was mixed with the wine. He closed his eyes, nausea filling him at the thought.

Chapter 07.06

After her photo shoot, Keiko had flown to Japan and spent a few days visiting with her Mother and Grandmother. They could tell something was wrong, but she would not answer their questions. Tiring of their concern, knowing she could not talk about what was happening with Jonathon, or her life, she had left in the middle of the night and set out to travel around and try to escape everything before she had to return to the nightmare that was her life.

This evening she was sitting in the hot springs of a remote Inn she had stumbled upon by accident, which was at the base of an old Shinto Shrine. Leaning back in the soothing warm water she tried not to think about her life, the one she had to return to at the end of the week. Instead she let the waters sooth her body as she thought instead of the wonderful people she had met journeying through the country, and all of the incredible pictures she had taken.

She heard the door slide open and turned slightly to see a Japanese woman in her mid twenties enter.

"Good evening," said the woman bowing slightly before carefully stepping into the water and sitting down a few feet away.

"Good evening," said Keiko.

"I am Iizuka Sayaka," she said bowing her head. "It is a pleasure to meet you."

"I am Nakamura Keiko," she said, bowing her body forward in the water. "It is a pleasure to meet you also. Are you traveling or do you live near here?"

"I live on the hill, Nakamura-sama," she replied.

"I understand, in the Shrine?" asked Keiko, somewhat startled at the honorific the woman was using.

"No," said Iizuka. "Please, pardon me for asking Nakamura-sama, where are you traveling from?

"A small village North-East of here," said Keiko. "I was visiting my Grandmother and Mother, and then I decided to wander the country for a while."

"Have you found what you were looking for?" asked Iizuka.

"What?" asked Keiko, forgetting formalities.

"Please, forgive me, Nakamura-sama," she said bowing her head. "It is just that most travelers who arrive at this destination are looking for something in their lives."

Keiko slid down in the water so that only her head was above and leaned it back against the rock, letting out a long sigh.

"No, Iizuka-san, I have not."

"If it would please you, Nakamura-sama, I would be happy to listen to your tale. Perhaps a fresh perspective may help your endeavor."

"Thank you, Iizuka-san," said Keiko.

She sat back up and glanced over before saying, "I made a promise to my Mother many years ago that I would focus on my career and do my best. But I am miserable doing that career, I despise my boss, and I am in love with a very good friend. I do not even know if he likes me that way though. In all I want out of my career so I can go and do something I enjoy. But I made a promise."

"Keeping a promise is very important, Nakamura-sama."

"I understand, Iizuka-san. Though I grew up in America my Mother and Grandmother raised me and my sister in a traditional Japanese manner."

Nodding her head slightly, she asked, "Nakamura-sama, have you talked to your Mother about this promise?"

"No."

"Perhaps you should. After all, she would be the only one who can release you from this promise."

Keiko stared into the waters, then smiled slightly.

"Iizuka-san, thank you, thank you very much! I had never even considered that possibility."

"Each of us has our own separate journey we must follow, yet at times one must stand up and declare that they desire a different journey. Though to truly do so means leaving your past behind, if you truly want to start anew."

Keiko looked over at her.

"Would you be willing to do that? To start a new life?"

Keiko thought about her own existence for a moment, then without hesitation said, "Yes."

"Well then, Nakamura-sama," she said, "Perhaps you can find what you are searching for after all."

"I hope so."

They fell into a silence for a long time. Keiko did not know what to say after the last conversation, and the woman seemed content to sit in the warm water with her eyes closed, softly humming to herself. Keiko closed her eyes and leaned her head back against the stones, relaxing and listening to the tune.

She lost track of time, but opened her eyes hearing the woman stand and stop her humming.

Iizuka bowed to her, saying, "Nakamura-sama, I wish you good fortune in your travels. Please have a pleasant evening."

"Thank you, Iizuka-san," said Keiko. "You have a pleasant evening also."

The other woman walked across the rocks and back into the inn as Keiko leaned back again and enjoyed the fresh, warm water, the cloudless sky above, and the stars that seemed to be shining brighter than when she first entered the bath.

Starting to feel drowsy a short time later, Keiko stood and stretched. Catching something from the corner of her eye she looked down and saw a glint from below the water where Iizuka had been sitting. Reaching down she pulled up a necklace with a charm on it. The Kanji etched into the silver circle was the symbol for Life.

Standing from the water, Keiko wrapped her towel around her and quickly made her way back inside. Iizuka was not in the changing room, but her wet towel was folded in a basket on the floor.

Sliding open the door Keiko ran down the hall into the entry of the inn and looked around, seeing nobody. Opening the front door she was hit with a blast of cold wind.

Staring out into the night she scanned the area for Iizuka, but did not see her. As she was turning to go back inside she caught movement to her right. Looking over she saw a fox near the stairs that led to the Shrine at the top of the hill. The fox had turned and was watching her.

Keiko held her breath, not wanting to startle it, silently wishing she had her camera. It watched her for a few seconds, then disappeared into the forest that covered the hill. Smiling to herself, she walked back inside and slid the door closed.

The manager had come out, a woman in her early sixties.

"Is everything alright, Nakamura-san?" asked the manager.

"Yes, fine," said Keiko. Lifting the charm she said, "By the way, the woman who lives on the hill dropped this in hot spring."

The manager simply stared at her and said, "There are only two people who live up there. Our Shinto Priest and his son."

"Sorry," said Keiko. "My mistake. I am most sorry to have disturbed you."

The manager smiled and then bowed, saying, "You have not, Nakamura-san. If you need anything, please let me be of service."

She turned and walked back behind the small counter and through the door behind it.

Shaking her head, Keiko returned to the changing room and dried herself off. Perhaps she had misunderstood what Iizuka had said. After all, the woman had a strange accent and used a lot of older Japanese words that were not commonly used these days.

Placing the charm down on the bench she looked over at the

towel folded in the basket.   Leaning slightly to the left she could see the wet footprints of Iizuka that led to the basket.

Keiko paled and collapsed onto the floor.

The wet footprints leading away from the basket were that of a dog. Or a fox.

Chapter 07.07

"No way," said Stacie pushing Kami's shoulder and almost knocking her over.

They were sitting on the bed watching a movie in the dark.

Nodding her head, Kami finished off her ice cream and set the bowl on the floor. She lay down on her stomach, facing the television, and Stacie did the same.

"What did your mom say?"

"Amazingly she was pretty cool about it, probably resigned to the fact that I am the failure sister," said Kami. "But she did give me the lecture about how even if I was in a relationship, getting good grades in school was more important."

Kami sighed, then said, "But it didn't last long. The girl's parents found out we were dating and flipped out totally. They made us break up and threw her into therapy, even going so far as to transfer her to a different school."

"That sucks," said Stacie. "Were you guys happy?"

"Yeah, but oh well, that's life," said Kami, trying not to sound sad. "How about you?"

"Me?" asked Stacie, somewhat startled, staring down at the bed. "Never been in a relationship. But then again I'm not really prime dating material, you know. I'm absent minded, not very smart, not athletic, and can't talk to people that good."

"That's not true," said Kami leaning into her, laughing. "You talk just fine with me, and you're pretty good at math in a scary kind of way."

"He he he," she laughed. "Well, I'd probably have better grades if I remembered to do my homework."

"Now that I'm around I'll make sure you get it done. Provided you help me figure it out."

Stacie blushed and looked to the television. "Thanks," she said.

"But don't give up," said Kami. "You'll find somebody sooner or later."

"That would be nice," said Stacie looking up into Kami's eyes.

Kami smiled back at her and then went back to watching the movie.

Stacie stared at her.

"What?" asked Kami.

"Just happy that we got to meet again," said Stacie. "It's nice... I... I really like being with you."

"I'm glad we ran into each other, too. You're fun to hang out with."

Stacie paused a moment, then quickly asked, "What do you think about dating?"

"Dating?" asked Kami laughing. "So over dating, not interested in getting my heart broken again."

"I see," said Stacie turning back to the movie.

"See what?" Kami asked.

But Stacie did not respond.

Chapter 07.08

Kyle fell into silence. He could feel Heather staring at him, he could feel her hand raising and reaching toward him. His eyes shot to her and she froze, withdrawing the hand and placing it in her lap.

Taking a drink of his wine, he slowly swallowed it, knowing now what that slightly metallic taste was. Closing his eyes, he felt the sensation issue through his body from the liquid. Opening his eyes he put the wine glass down and reached into the pocket of his pants, pulling out a knife. He opened it with his thumb.

"Kyle," said Heather.

"Shut up," said Kyle.

Pulling his shirt sleeve up on his left arm he turned it palm up and placed the knife against his wrist. The point of the blade dug into his skin, and he hesitated a moment. Clenching his teeth he pushed down with the knife and pulled it toward him. The pain caused him to drop the knife. He watched the skin from the deep wound open, blood welling.

Then he felt a warmth around the cut, followed by a slight tingling sensation as the wound closed. In two seconds he was staring at his wrist which showed no signs of ever being cut.

He picked the knife up from his lap and slowly closed the blade with one hand, placing it back in his pocket.

"Get out of here," said Kyle.

"But Kyle," said Heather choking back tears. "There are many things that I need to tell you."

"I said get out," hissed Kyle as his anger rose. He could feel this power within him welling, with something even more powerful veiled beneath that.

Heather had opened her mouth to protest, but involuntarily pulled back. Standing she looked down at him and tried to say something, but her voice faltered.

She faded from the room.

His anger rose even further. He began to tremble. Everything in his vision took on a reddish hue. To do this to him, betray his trust, to violate his life and his future without even giving him the opportunity to accept or decline. To turn him into some inhuman monster. To curse his life such.

He closed his eyes as his hands became fists, as his whole body began to shake from the anger. He heard the sound of glass breaking. Everything building up inside of him began to be replaced by this impenetrable darkness.

He felt two cold hands upon his face.

"Stop," came a soft voice.

Connecting the hands to the voice, the shock that Cynthia was holding his face hit him and his eyes shot open to see her leaning over him, her face inches from his. Her normally cold dark eyes betrayed something he had never seen before. Concern.

Everything inside of him began to dissipate.

"There now, calm yourself," she said calmly. "If you lose control the darkness can consume your mind."

He began to feel normal, though he was unsure what normal was anymore. She let go and stood up, her eyes cold again.

"Sit here, I shall return in a moment," Cynthia said walking away and disappearing behind a row of bookshelves.

Kyle leaned back in the couch and then sat back up seeing the scarred table before him. The dark red contents of the wine bottle were splashed across the table, shards of glass from the disintegrated bottle and the glasses radiated away from him. The couch on the other side of the table had multiple shards of glass embedded in the leather and wood.

Cynthia returned with a small metal trash can and some towels. Placing the trash can on the other side of the table she muttered something underneath her breath and made some motions with her hands.

All of the shards of glass began flying into the trash can. When the glass was gone she took one towel and wiped off the surface of the table, then took another and cleaned up what had dripped onto the floor or splattered on the other couch. Finished, Cynthia placed the towels in the trash can and picked it up.

"Would you like some more to drink?" she asked.

Kyle blinked several times at her and did not respond.

"Kyle?" she whispered.

Thinking about what he had been secretly drinking, he said, "Water."

"As you wish," she said bowing her head and leaving

His brain hurt. His very concepts of reality hurt. Bringing his wrist up, he ran a thumb over the smooth skin. Running his tongue along the roof of his mouth, he could taste the metallic remnants of the liquid that he had been drinking this whole time.

Cynthia returned with a glass of water, which she handed to Kyle. Turning, she walked back to her chair and sat down.

"This is so stupid," he said closing his eyes. "I don't even know what the hell is going on. What am I, some stupid creature of the night cursed to feed off the living? Sitting around listening to chamber music alone in my candle-lit room? Do I have to go out and buy a bunch of black clothing? Does this mean I have to stop eating Italian food?"

Cynthia let out a small laugh.

His eyes shot open and he looked over at the girl in black whose eyes were closed and mouth was turned up in a slight smile. Glancing to the ground, then back to her, his mind raced. He had known her for over six years and had never heard her laugh.

Her face became somber again, but her eyes still betrayed mild amusement.

"No, Kyle," she said softly staring down at the dark liquid in her wine glass. "Though your kind is a basis for those legends."

"What should I call myself then?"

"You should call yourself Kyle," said Cynthia glancing up into his eyes.

"Funny," he said glaring at her.

"In all honesty, that is who you are, no matter what you are."

"But what am I?" he almost screamed, barely containing himself.

"Do you want me to tell you what you are? I cannot do that. There are accounts saying that your race are the offspring of fallen angels and mankind, others say that your kind has always been here, yet they are all essentially folklore. From what I understand, your kind do not have many of the limitations from mythology. But you do need sustenance to live as such."

"Blood?" asked Kyle staring at the holes in leather couch opposite him.

"Yes."

He shook his head and closed his eyes.

"Now that you are like this..." she said starting off. "Never mind. It will be a decade or two before it hits you. Looking around to see that people and places you knew have changed over time but you have not."

Noticing the deep melancholy in her voice, Kyle leaned forward and asked, "Cynthia, are you?"

She looked away from him.

"Like you? No. I was Human. But there was an accident when I was fifteen."

"The year before I met you?" asked Kyle.

"No, the accident happened over forty years ago," she said.

"Forty?"

"Yes," she said tensing slightly.

"Wait that's impossible. You're trying to tell me that you're older than me?"

"We are here to talk about you, not me" she said coldly. "I am concerned. From what I understand, your kind has a very strict set of laws in how they function in this world and with Humans. And it does not appear that Heather is following any of them."

"How do you mean?"

"She did not tell you any of this in advance, Awakened you and then tried to wipe your mind of the experience, then just let you go about your life in that state. And still did nothing until she found out I was feeding you."

Cynthia paused for a moment, her left hand becoming a fist, before she said, "When you were severely injured in the club, your body healed itself. That is why you were so weak the following day. If I had not been here to help you, Kyle, you could have easily lost control and seriously injured the people living here."

Kyle frowned and thought back to that morning, to the feelings he had when Kami came into his room. He had fought them, thinking that he was just having inappropriate ideas about Kami as she had sat there with a leg draped over the chair. Now he realized that the urge to take her, to have her, were not of a sexual nature.

Kyle paled slightly.

"You might be right," he said, trying to sound confident but still unable to fully understand what was going on. "Thank you."

"If she is not following protocol, you may be in danger," said Cynthia standing and walking over to him. She sat down on the couch next to him. "So therefore I want to help make you stronger."

With deft fingers she unfastened the button at the wrist of her sleeve and pulled the black lace up to expose her delicate white arm.

She paused a moment and then calmly looked into his eyes.

"Cynthia," he said. "You don't have to do this, I'm sure I can find some other way."

"My apologies Kyle, I refrain from being close to people since..."

As the sentence suddenly ended, she pulled out a small dagger from the folds of her dress. Raising her exposed wrist to him she pressed the point of the blade into her skin.

"Cyn..." he began.

"Take it," she said, slicing open her wrist and pushing it up to his mouth.

He was about to protest when he saw the blood pouring down her arm from the wound. Instinctively he grabbed her wrist and brought it to his mouth. The shock to his system was a thousand times more powerful than the wine she had given him on many occasions. The red mist that seemed to fill his body was more intense. And layered beneath that was the blackness that expanded its dark tentacles through every fiber of his being. He became lost in that feeling, time came to a stop. There was only himself and Cynthia entering him.

He felt the wrist pull away.

Opening his eyes he saw a large wound where he had bitten

deeply into her skin. As he watched, the bleeding stopped and a black substance filled the wounds as they closed and disappeared, what blood was on her arm evaporated in a dark mist, and the deep indentations from his teeth filled out and disappeared. Within a moment her arm appeared normal.

She dropped her hand to his lap as the other one that was gripping the fabric of his shirt clenched tighter and sporadically pulled into him as she let out a low sigh.

Breathing heavily she held him closer as her body trembled.

"Are, are you ok?" asked Kyle.

She nodded slightly, eyes still closed. Cynthia's breathing slowed and became deeper as she fell asleep, still holding tightly onto Kyle.

ON THE MORROW

Chapter 08.01

Heather sat at her dining room table, hands holding her head.

"Thank you for coming," she mumbled.

Standing in the living room, staring out at the morning sun glinting off the waves, was her older sister, whose red hair came to just below her shoulders. She looked to be around thirteen, and currently had her hands on her hips and a scowl on her face.

"What is it now?" asked Caitlin.

"I wanted your advice, since you know more of these things than I do," said Heather as she stood from the dining room chair and walked into the living room to sit in a chair against the wall.

"The fact that you have even involved me in this situation irritates me more than I can say," said Caitlin crossing her arms and turning around slowly to face her. "Yet you have turned a horrible situation into an absolute failure that words cannot even begin to describe."

Heather tried to say something, but could not.

"What were you thinking?" asked Caitlin in a very low tone. "Awakening a line of the family that has been Exiled? Because of a promise to a Human no less?"

"I know," moaned Heather, her head dropping into her hands.

"You mentioned it went bad, again, last night."

Heather sat up and wiped tears from her eyes.

"Dear God Almighty, are you crying again?" Caitlin asked harshly. "If you want my advice, the least you can do is pull yourself together, child."

Heather pulled her face from her palms, trying her best to stop crying and looked up. Taking a deep breath she clasped her hands and leaned back in the chair, staring at the picture on the wall, while absently wiping her eyes. Fear was slowly creeping into her. Their brother had been Exiled, and by that right Kyle may not even be recognized.

Heather's movements suddenly stopped, and her heart froze at that thought. If everything had gone according to plan, she would have been able to train Kyle so that if his birth right was challenged he would be able to defend himself.

Now, Heather was unsure if Kyle would be alive by the end of the week.

Caitlin walked around the love-seat and sat down in it hard, crossing her arms again, and letting out a long sigh.

"So?" she asked.

"I..." began Heather, then looked away.

"Am stupid?" asked Caitlin feigning a cheery voice.

Heather closed her eyes at the jab, and then continued, "Last night I found out that somebody has been feeding him."

"You mean he has been feeding? That would be normal, provided you are training him properly. Not that I want that abomination to survive, mind you. So why did you even bother to call me here?"

"No, somebody was feeding him without his knowledge," said Heather. "Because he, um, did not know what he was."

"What?" asked Caitlin sitting up and staring at her sister.

"One of his friends knew the change in him and had begun to feed him," said Heather, closing her eyes while stating the next sentence. "And I had not told him anything yet."

Caitlin raised her hand and began to massage her temple with two fingers as she asked, "So you Awakened him, did not tell him, some Human figured this out, began feeding him... Then you met up with the two of them and talked about... Everything?"

"Essentially, yes," said Heather, after pausing a moment.

"Please," said Caitlin. "Please at least tell me that she is listed as one of our allies."

"No, just a Human with no ties to us from what I have been able to find out," she replied. "But she studies the Dark Arts, the really ancient ones from what I saw in the study. So maybe that is how she knew of our kind."

Caitlin closed her eyes for a minute, her head barely moving left and right.

"What is her name?" she asked, opening her eyes and looking toward her sister, but not at her.

"I was, I had a lot of things on my mind. I think Kyle said her name was Cynthia Hapsburg."

"Hapsburg? Does not sound familiar to me," said Caitlin frowning. "Continue."

"Then I went to Kyle's house and talked with him and that girl," she said.

Caitlin's silence was ominous.

Heather bowed her head, then said, "I did not know what else to do, honestly. She knows of our kind and could sense the change in Kyle the first day. She even knew to feed him after he got injured! So... Well, I did not know how to explain why I did what I did, and to try and keep him from being mad at me I told them about his family history."

Caitlin's fist slammed into the arm of the chair, the sound of wood splintering filled the room.

"Please let me understand this," said Caitlin. "Even though I have always had you remain in the shadows since my brother died, you who have no qualms killing anybody I ask, you who rarely ever speaks to any of our brethren, and have never spoken about our family to any of our kind. Obeying my orders without question. In this situation you simply told both of them everything?"

Staring at the floor, Heather managed a slight nod of her head.

Standing, Caitlin stepped forward and hit the coffee table with her shin, then mumbled something beneath her breath.

Leaning down she grabbed the edge and flung the coffee table across the living room where it skipped off the dining room table and smashed through the kitchen. Stepping forward she grabbed her sister's throat and lifted her off the chair, slamming her head into the wall with enough force to create a deep indentation.

"You told a Human about our kind, and my dearest brother's decision that cost him his life?"

"I was in a panic when I found out he had been feeding and wanted to find out who had been giving him... After I got there I did not know what to do and I just started talking."

Throwing her into the wall on the opposite side of the room, Caitlin walked away a few feet and stared out the windows.

"Heather, you know what my position is."

"Yes, but I wanted your help," begged Heather standing slowly, massaging her throat. The blood from the wounds on her head flowed into her eyes and blurred her vision. "If the Council were to find out I fear the punishment they would deal me, let alone what they would do to Kyle."

"Fix the situation immediately," said Caitlin in a coarse whisper. "If they find out I will do what I can for you, because you are my sister. He is of no concern to me."

"What should I do?" pleaded Heather.

"Correct the problem, obviously," said Caitlin.

She faded from the room.

Chapter 08.02

Kyle slowly opened his eyes and stared at the ceiling of the study. He was lying on the couch with his right arm and leg hanging off the edge of the leather couch. Looking down he saw Cynthia lying on top of him, her head resting on his chest, both arms curled close to her, still holding his shirt firmly. His left arm was around her waist.

Staring at the top of her head it suddenly struck him how small she was.

"You are awake," she said in a voice barely above a whisper.

"Yes," he said. Kyle leaned his head slightly and saw that her eyes were open.

"So strange, is it not?" she asked, eyes glancing up a few millimeters. "Two people who are dead, yet both have heartbeats."

"I think I am still in shock, actually," he said. "I have no idea what the hell is going on. None of this makes sense."

He paused a moment before saying, "Expect me to have a mental breakdown some time very soon. Perhaps within the next hour."

Cynthia chuckled lightly and said, "You will be fine."

"I don't know what is more disturbing."

"What?" she asked.

"Trying to accept what has happened to me, or the fact that in the last twenty-four hours I have heard you laugh twice."

She pressed her face into his chest and said in a voice barely audible, to him, "You do not know what it is like."

"What do you mean?" he asked, his hand coming up to rest between her shoulder blades. Suddenly uncomfortable, he pulled his hand off her back and placed it next to him, staring at the ceiling.

She did not say anything for a few minutes, then said, "I do not wish to talk about that matter."

He looked down at the top of her head and for some reason could feel how painful the subject was for her. "Sorry to pry," he said.

Pushing herself up, Cynthia stood, straightened her long black dress, and she put on her leather gloves.

"Can you sense them?" she asked.

"What? Who?"

"Close your eyes," she said. When he did, she continued, "Can you sense the other people in the house?"

He was about to respond that he could not when he noticed it. One person above to his left, two people down the hall, one further away to his right. As he concentrated on it he could tell who each one was. Slightly freaked out he opened his eyes.

"How?"

"In time."

She looked into his eyes and asked, "Would you like some coffee? A bit of normality might suit you at this juncture."

"Uh, sure," he said standing.

Hesitantly he stood from the couch, and followed her through the rows of books.

As they reached the doors to the study, he reached out to open the door. Right before his hand grabbed the brass doorknob he heard the clicks of the locks. Turning the handle, he opened the door for her.

"Thank you," she said, bowing her head to him before stepping into the hall and waiting for him to follow.

When the door closed the locks clicked back into place.

They were walking through the entry of the living room when Kyle looked down at her and asked, "Can I eat food?"

"What have you been doing these last few weeks?" she asked with a wry smile, looking up at him.

They heard the sound of something breaking and saw Ed standing near the doorway of the kitchen. On the floor near his feet was the shattered remains of his coffee cup, its contents splattered across the floor, and his boots.

He looked at Kyle, then Cynthia, then back at Kyle.

"So, so, so," he stammered.

"Those are the clothes the two of you were wearing last night. And my girlfriend is walking very close and smiling at you. The same girlfriend who won't even go out with me for a couple hours because she's too busy with work. And you obviously spent the night together in the study."

"Listen, Ed," began Kyle.

Ed ran toward him, pulling his fist back.

Never being the fighting type, unless you were to count video games, Kyle had started to close his eyes when he noticed everything around him slow down slightly. Ed's fist was two inches from his face, and moving in slow motion forward as Kyle stepped out of the way. Just as suddenly, the world returned to normal speed and Ed went flying past him, the momentum causing him to fall to the floor.

Standing and slamming his boot on the floor, Ed turned around and glared into Kyle's eyes, the hatred he felt obvious both in his stance and the low growling in his voice when he spoke.

"I knew something was up," he said. "Both of you have been acting strange lately."

The emotions Ed was feeling overwhelmed Kyle, who took a step back.

"We were best friends," said Ed, slowly, his voice trembling in anger. "How could you?"

Kyle began to say something but Cynthia interrupted.

"Ed," she said in a cold voice that pulled his glare to her. "If you are insinuating that Kyle and I are having sex, or any other type of relationship, you are wrong."

"Then what is it?" he screamed at her.

"That does not concern you," she said even colder.

Ed took a few steps back, glancing between the two of them. Turning around he walked quickly across the room and down the hall to the entry.

Kyle began to say something but she placed a hand on his extended arm, shaking her head.

The front door slammed shut, and a minute later they heard the squealing of tires.

"But, Cyn," he said.

"Each of us has their own path to follow now," she said.

"But," he began.

"Kyle," she said turning to him. "If that had been somebody else attacking, you could be dead right now."

"Yeah, but you said I cannot be killed," he said smiling.

"I said it is almost impossible to kill your kind. From what I understand. Almost. And I am not an expert on your kind so anything I say could be wrong."

He looked into her eyes, then away.

"Keep that in mind," she said.

"I will," he said nervously.

"Let us get some coffee," she said walking away from him to the kitchen.

Chapter 08.03

Keiko stirred from her slumber at another bump in the road. Dawn was breaking and she was slouched in the passenger seat of an old delivery truck heading North-East.

"Hey, you have a good rest, Nakamura-san?" asked the man in Japanese, who had a distinct Kansai accent. His hair, moustache, and beard were grey and he had on a pair of round-rimmed sunglasses that were a bit too small for his face.

"Eh, best I could," said Keiko stretching as best she could in the confines of the truck.

"Good, good," he muttered shifting into a lower gear to pass a slow car in front of them. "Damn country drivers."

Raising a fist he screamed out the closed passenger window, "I have a job to perform, you know!!"

Suddenly pausing with his raised fist inches from her head, he grabbed the steering wheel and asked, "Hey, you hungry?"

"A little," said Keiko.

"Great!" he exclaimed. "There's a good stop about ten kilometers ahead. Fishing village, nice fresh food."

"Thank you again, Noriyuki-san," she said bowing her head.

He waved his hand and said, "Not a problem, not a problem. Glad I could help."

Raising a fist and blaring his horn he passed another slow driving car and screamed, "Idiot! If you want to enjoy the scenery just pull off the road!!"

"Sorry about that Nakamura-san," he said blushing slightly. "Just these country drivers seem to have no concept of the speed limit."

Julien Giever

Keiko laughed and leaned forward to her right to look at the speedometer, asking, "And you are driving the speed limit?"

"Oh, well, maybe a bit over," he laughed and hit the top of the steering wheel. "But that is not important. What is important is a good breakfast. After that it will be about three hours to your Grandmother's house."

"Thank you."

"I still get that autograph, right?" he asked smiling widely.

"Of course," said Keiko.

"Oh won't the guys back at dispatch be jealous when they find out I got to give you a ride. I can't wait to see their faces."

Keiko nodded, then turned to watch the fields out the window, smiling to herself, playing with the necklace around her neck.

The night before, after she had pulled herself together in the changing room of the Inn, she had gone back to her room. There she had laid on the floor in her yukata, staring at the ceiling, remembering tales her Grandmother had told her of the old country and fox spirits.

A shiver had run up her spine, part of her convinced it was a delusion from exhaustion and stress.

The manager had announced through the sliding door that dinner was prepared. When Keiko had walked into the common room she saw the manager and a man in his late fifties sitting on the floor at the table. They ate dinner, then relaxed and drank some beer. He had excused himself so that he could continue his route. When Keiko asked, he answered that he was driving North-East.

Thinking about the words the woman in the bath had said, Keiko had immediately sat up and asked him if she could ride with him. Because that was where her Mother was.

"Yo, we're here," he said as the truck came to a stop in the parking lot in front of a small restaurant.

Pulling on the lever, the door opened with a loud creak and Keiko jumped down to the ground, stretching and enjoying the mist of the sea in the distance.

Noriyuki walked around the truck, kicking the driver side tires then checked the back to make sure everything was secure. Satisfied he walked around and kicked the two side tires. Smiling he slammed her door shut, went to the front of the old truck and patted the hood several times.

"They have the best miso here," he said as they went into the restaurant.

"Noriyuki-san!" exclaimed a young woman hurrying toward the entrance. She was wearing a dark blue kimono.

Bowing he said, "Shimizu-kun, good to see you. How have you been?"

Returning the bow she said, "Ah, Noriyuki-san, I have been well as has the restaurant. Who is your guest this morning?"

"Shimizu-kun, this is Nakamura-san, an Idol from America who is going to visit her Grandmother."

"Nakamura-san, welcome to my restaurant. I wish to serve you well this morning," she said bowing. "It is an honor to meet you Na-kamura-san."

"Shimizu-san, it is a pleasure to meet you and a pleasure to eat here," said Keiko bowing.

Seating them at a table near the kitchen, Shimizu took their order and left. She returned a few minutes later with a can of beer and two cups of steaming green tea, then excused herself.

Keiko reached out and held the cup of tea with both hands, warming them.

Opening his beer, Noriyuki leaned his head back and drank the entire contents in a series of quick gulps. Slamming the can on the table he exclaimed loudly, "Aaaaaah! That hit the spot!"

Keiko could not help but laugh.

"So, Nakamura-san, are you really thinking of leaving model-ing?" he asked.

"Yes," she said.

"Ah, that is sad," he said. "I will miss your pictures and your in-terviews."

"Thank you," said Keiko, bowing her head.

"Nakamura-san, may I ask why?"

"Yes, you may," she said taking a drink of her tea and setting the cup down. "But only as long a you promise to never speak of this."

He inclined his head.

Accepting this she continued.

"I am very unhappy with what I am doing. The business I work in is filled with people concerned with only their image and their ca-reers, and I am not that kind of person. Also there is this guy I like, but I am not sure he likes me the same way. I do not know, maybe I should just try harder at my career."

"Hey, let me tell you," he said leaning forward. "I was a salary man most of my life. Played by the corporate rules, had my little desk, small apartment in the big city. And I was miserable.

"Then several years ago, I had taken a vacation and ended up at that Inn where I met you. I was out walking around one night and, coming down from the Shrine, right there, half way down the steps, I met this lovely woman from the area. We talked for a long time, and then she looked at me and said that I would probably do well in the stock market."

He paused as another can was set before him and he popped it open, drinking the contents and slamming the empty container back on the table.

"What happened?" she asked.

He chuckled and shook his head.

"I was so desperate to escape my life that I took her advice. Gathered my savings and my retirement money, and invested it. Bought stocks, sold stocks, not even really sure how I did it, but ended up with enough money that I left the corporation, bought a nice house out here in the country, and then for fun went to work at a trucking company. Now I get to drive around the countryside, meet wonderful people."

"Really?" she asked.

"Yes."

"You are lucky," said Keiko.

"Maybe I was," he said, laughing so loudly that most of the people around them looked over.

Shimizu returned with two bowls of miso soup, steamed rice, grilled fish, rolled omelets, and several other side dishes.

"Looks delicious!" exclaimed Noriyuki raising his hand to pat Shimizu's arm.

Seeing something glint in the light, Keiko looked over at his wrist which had several leather bracelets. Hanging from one of them was a silver charm with the Kanji for the word Life on it, exactly like the one she had found.

She sat there, silently eating her food.

Chapter 08.04

Kami opened her eyes and squinted against the morning sun filtering through the curtains. Letting out a moan she tried to sit up.

"Ugh, get off me," she exclaimed, pushing Stacie off her and onto her back.

Stacie stirred slightly and mumbled something about cookies.

"What am I going to do with you?" asked Kami pulling her knees to her chest with both arms, staring at her friend.

After talking about relationships last night Stacie had become withdrawn and had not talked much the rest of the evening. Which had been draining on Kami, trying to cheer her up. She reached down and shook Stacie's shoulder several times, calling her name, but could not wake her.

Giving up, Kami quietly opened her door and walked to the kitchen. Grabbing a soda from the fridge, she was walking back through the living room and came to a stop.

Kyle and Cynthia were sitting at the table on the patio drinking coffee, which was very strange.

Going over to the doors of the patio she opened them and stepped outside.

Glancing back over his shoulder Kyle said, "Morning."

"Hey," said Kami walking up to them.

Looking down at Cynthia she said, "I though you would burst into flames if the sun is out."

Kyle choked on a mouthful of coffee and almost spit it out.

Cynthia turned her head slightly and said, "Good morning, Kami."

"Uh, yeah," she said shivering involuntarily from Cynthia's tone of voice.

"Hey, Kyle," she asked. "You still going out with that Janice girl this afternoon?"

"What?" he asked turning quickly in the chair and spilling half of his coffee on the ground.

"Maybe you shouldn't drink when I'm talking to you," said Kami.

Placing the cup on the table he slouched back in his chair and said, "Crap, I totally forgot about that. I don't know."

"Oh, well, just so you know I'll probably be spending the day with Stac, not sure what we're doing though."

"Have all your homework done?"

"No, papa Kyle, I don't" she said. "But there isn't much, I can get it done tonight."

"Better," he said. "I don't need a repeat of earlier in the week when the two of you went psycho because you forgot that math assignment was due."

"God, I said I would get it done," she said walking away.

"OK, have fun then," he said.

Kami went back to the living room, closing the door behind her. As she did, she watched Kyle lean both arms on the table and begin talking frantically to Cynthia.

Shaking her head she went back to her bedroom and tried to wake Stacie up again, knowing full well that if let be she would sleep past noon easily. Which is why Kami had to keep calling her, non stop, at five minute intervals, every morning to wake her in time for school.

Sitting on the bed she leaned forward and put both hands under Stacie's arms and pulled her up to a sitting position. Stacie let out a moan, almost opened her eyes, then flopped forward onto Kami.

Muttering somebody's name over and over in a whisper, she nuzzled Kami's neck with her lips.

Kami closed her eyes for a second at the feeling then shook her head and pushed Stacie away.

"Hey, Stac, wake up," she said loudly pulling her back and forth.

After a minute of this Stacie opened her eyes slightly and grabbed Kami's arms.

"Oh, hi," she said, then started to fall backward again.

"No you don't," said Kami, grabbing her. Using one of her feet she pushed Stacie's legs off the bed and pulled her to a standing position.

Stacie leaned against her friend and said, "I don't want to go to school."

"No school, come on," said Kami grabbing her friend's bag and guiding her down the hall to the bathroom.

Chapter 08.05

After Kami closed the door, Kyle leaned forward and said in a hushed tone, "What am I going to do? I forgot I had a date with her today."

"I would suggest you start getting ready," said Cynthia.

"What? How can I? Seriously? After last night, um, should I even, I mean, it's not like I can tell her. What if I try to bite her or something?"

Letting out a soft sigh, Cynthia placed her cup on the table and turned to him.

"Kyle," she said slowly. "You are still yourself. You have been like this for two weeks and did not even realize it. Knowing what you are changes little, you still have your life to live. Working, paying bills, and even... going out on dates."

He pondered her words for a few minutes.

"Guess you're right," he said.

"How late shall you be?" she asked.

"Not very," he said. "She has an early class Monday mornings."

Cynthia stood and looked down at him.

"Come see me after you are finished with her, there are several things I wish to show you."

Kyle nodded his head and Cynthia picked up her cup, then walked toward the doors.

He watched her walking away, and thought of this morning, blushing slightly. She stopped and turned to glare at him. Kyle smiled and spun around in his chair to stare at the grass in the yard. As he heard the door slam shut he suddenly felt stupid and guilty over what Ed had said a short time ago. And how he found himself this morning.

Kyle slid into his chair more.

His mind wandered for a while over everything that had happened, everything he had been told, the night before. And he found it impossible, and really amazingly retarded. What Heather had said could never be true, of course.

Even though he told this to himself, he had her and Cynthia insisting that it was. That everything he had known for over twenty something years about how the world worked was actually a lie. That somehow things like this usually reserved for B grade horror movies actually existed.

He had been drinking last night. This was something he kept telling himself. Like every night since this weirdness started. Some strange wine that Cynthia gave him. Every night.

And alcohol made one susceptible to suggestions. Perhaps this was some sick joke that Cynthia and Heather had decided to play on him, some hallucinogen mixed with the oddly metallic tasting wine.

Though the why for such perverse actions eluded him.

Even though he kept reciting all these things in his head, he had a sinking feeling in his heart that these repeated words would not change anything from the night before.

"Maybe I need Lithium or something," he muttered to himself.

Standing, he went to the edge of the shadows and paused. He reached his hand out into the sunlight hesitantly. He felt the warm rays strike his skin. Nothing happened. No pain, no smoke, no fire.

Kyle pushed all these thought to the back of his mind as he walked to the patio door and slid it open. He needed to figure out if he was even going to go out with Janice today. That was the most pressing matter at the moment.

As he was walking past Thomas, Kyle said hello, out of habit.

"Hi," said Thomas in a sullen voice.

Kyle paused, forgetting his problems, and walked around to look at his roommate who was slouched in the couch watching television.

"No cheerful morning greetings?" he asked, somehow slipping into his normal self.

"No," said Thomas.

Kyle looked around and could only sense Cynthia, Kami and Stacie.

"Where's Harry?"

"He went out for the day to relax," muttered Thomas.

Kyle sat down in the chair and asked, "So what's wrong?"

He suddenly felt that solving somebody else's problems would be easier than trying to solve his own.

Heaving a heavy sigh Tomas replied, "I got smacked along side the head with a good dose of reality last night, my friend. After phoning my father this morning I realize that this is it. This is my life. Nobody is going to bail me out. My dream is dying."

"You have that job Cynthia set you up with, that's a start," said

Kyle.

"Good God man," said Thomas. "That dilapidated old shop that has no customers? Unfortunately I have little choice because I have no redeemable job skills."

"You're a creative genius, right?" asked Kyle.

"I am not sure anymore."

"Why don't you use some of that creativity to help the shop?" asked Kyle.

Thomas raised a finger and tapped his lips.

"That might work," he said. "I could create a glorious ad to lure customers in."

"What do they sell?"

"Magic and Occult related items," said Thomas.

"Heh, figures," said Kyle. "Know much about that?"

"Not a clue."

"Well, I'm not an expert, but it usually helps to know your target audience before making an ad."

"Ah, damn," said Thomas sinking into the couch.

Pointing a finger, Kyle said, "Those books on the end table there. Are they from that shop?"

Thomas leaned forward, looking over, then jumped from the couch and grabbed one of the unmarked black books. He paged through it, then closed the book and sat in the chair opposite Kyle.

"I think you have something there," said Thomas smiling. "With these books I can gain the comprehension I need to create the ultimate ad to draw young and old alike into the arcane arts that Christianity has subjugated throughout the ages."

Kyle laughed and stood, saying, "Good luck."

He started walking to the hallway that led to the stairs.

"Kyle?" asked Thomas in a somber voice.

Turning around he asked, "Yeah?"

Thomas put the book aside and stood slowly, looking up at Kyle for a moment, then down at the floor.

"I know that I am an arrogant, pompous prick," said Thomas. "To be honest, I was expecting you to throw me to the curb the night I showed up here. Especially after how we met. But I asked for help and you gave me a place to stay. I have never met somebody like that before. I just wanted to thank you for giving me a chance."

Thomas looked up into his eyes.

Smiling slightly, Kyle nodded, then turned around and walked down the hallway.

Chapter 08.06

Heather was standing in her living room, staring at the framed photograph of her brother and his wife. She took a step forward and reached out a hand, tracing the contours of his face with a finger.

"I am sorry," she said. "I do not know if I am strong enough to carry out either of your wishes."

Her hand dropped to her side, listless as the rest of her body.

Wandering to her bedroom, she walked over to her bed and lay down on her side, staring out the large windows at the ocean. Debating whether to call Kyle, what to do about his friend. If there was anything she could do now. She had always stayed out of politics, and the closest link to the Council she had was through Caitlin.

Which meant there was no way to save him, if anything went wrong. Or if there were a challenge to his bloodline.

Cursing herself, she closed her eyes and tried to calm her mind. Two weeks. Two weeks had passed and she had done nothing. And this was after running away to Europe to avoid the situation entirely for a year after her Sister-In-Law had died.

Panic erupted through her again as she tried to think of some way to solve this problem.

Reaching over, she grabbed her telephone and dialed Kyle's number.

"Heather," he answered, saying her name slowly.

"Hello, Kyle," she said. "Are... Are you alright?"

There was a long pause on the other end.

"I'm still pissed off at you," he said. "If that's what you wanted to know."

"Again, Kyle, I must apologize for my ineptness in handling everything," Heather said. "To be honest we really need to sit down and talk, there are some things you need to know."

"I'm about to leave," said Kyle. "Maybe tomorrow, depends on how I feel."

"Kyle, please understand that there are important matters to discuss."

"Heather, please understand how I feel about what you did to me."

"But..." she began.

"I have to go," he said, hanging up.

Tossing the phone to her side she closed her eyes again before she went over to the dresser and opened one of the drawers, taking out a long dagger. Pulling it from the sheath she checked to make sure it was sharp and slid it back in, then tucked it into her skirt at the small of her back. Dropping her baggy knit sweater back into place she checked in the full length mirror to make sure that it was not visible, then faded from the room.

She appeared behind the tree line that circled the property and waited patiently. A short time later Kyle stepped from the house and left in his car. Waiting for the gates to close she crossed the lawn to the front doorsteps of her brother's house, pausing momentarily in sadness to correct the thought to Kyle's house. Raising a finger she pressed the doorbell.

The door was opened by a man with long blond hair who looked her up and down then smiled and said, "Well, well, well. Hello, how may I help you?"

"Is Kyle's friend here? The young lady who wears black?" she asked.

"Cynthia? I don't know," he said.

Stepping past her he looked down the driveway to the parking next to the garage and said, "Well, her car is here. Come on in and I shall try and find her for you."

"Thank you," she said following him inside.

"By the way, I am Thomas," he said extending his hand.

"Heather," she said extending hers.

He did not take it in a normal handshake, but held it as if he would kiss the top of her hand.

"A pleasure to make your acquaintance," he said with a flash in his eyes, his thumb softly caressing her hand. "Let me check upstairs."

Thomas ran up the stairs and knocked on Ed's door. He waited a minute and knocked again. When there was no answer he returned to her.

"She may be in the back," he said starting to walk down the hall, then let out a startled gasp.

Cynthia was standing in the middle of the living room calmly watching them.

Thomas let out a startled, "Ah!"

Heather rushed past him and stopped a few feet from Cynthia.

"May we talk?" asked Heather.

Cynthia nodded.

The two of them walked back to the study, ignoring the frantic questions from Thomas. As they stepped inside the opened doors, they closed and locked by themselves. Cynthia walked into the room and half way down the long table, then stopped to turn around.

Looking into the girl's eyes, Heather smiled and reached out with her mind to erase the memories from the night before. As she did so she came across nothing, actually it was more like a void of black. Heather focused harder, but could find nothing.

"No," said Cynthia in a soft voice that chilled Heather.

"You will not be able to affect my mind," she said. "Is this why you wanted to talk to me?"

"I..." Heather paused against the empty eyes staring back at her. "I am sorry, Cynthia, it is just as a Human I should not have told you about our kind."

"Obviously I was aware of your kind, that is how I knew what happened to Kyle that night. And why I knew how to help Kyle when you chose to abandon him."

"What do you mean by that?" asked Heather.

"You may see yourself out," said Cynthia turning around and walking across the room. She sat down in the last chair and began to page through the contents of a folder, typing numbers into the calculator.

Heather walked up behind her.

Cynthia did not look up from her paperwork as she asked, "Was there something else you wished to discuss?

"Yes there was, actually," said Heather as she quietly pulled out the long dagger. "I was planning on training him soon."

As she finished the last word, Heather brought her hand up and stabbed down quickly with the dagger.

She had to fix this situation, no matter what.

Not being able to erase Cynthia's mind left her with no other choice. She would have to kill this Human girl and dispose of the body so that nobody knew of their kind.

That is what her sister had said, or more appropriately insinuated.

Heather's movements were a blur as the dagger descended, then the tip of the blade suddenly came to a stop several inches from the back of Cynthia's head. She tried to jump back but her body would not move, she tried to say something but her mouth would not open. She could not even move her eyes.

"Acting out of desperation usually results in failure," said Cynthia, in a low, almost imperceptible voice.

She continued typing numbers into the calculator, the paper tabulation getting longer.

Heather tried to move again but was unable to. She tried to leave but could not. Trying to use any of her abilities failed also, again she tried to move but could not.

Cynthia tore the paper from the calculator and placed it in the folder, then closed it. She moved the folder several feet away and placed her hands on the table before her, staring out into the study.

Though quiet, she spoke words that seemed to be sharp blades coated with black poison as her voice slowly rose and Cynthia said, "The only reason I am going to allow you to live is because you have information that Kyle needs to survive."

Leaning to the right she stood from the table and faced Heather.

"That is the only reason," she said in a calm tone, tilting her head at the organic statue before her, a sinister smile tracing her lips for a brief moment.

"Exquisite dagger," said Cynthia, her finger caressing the blade. "Mid seventeen-hundreds, Spanish, typically given by royalty of that time period as a gift."

Heather could barely see the girl out of her peripheral vision. She disappeared, then came into sight again to her left.

"I want you to understand something," said Cynthia leaning slightly so that Heather could see her clearly. "You do not mention this incident to anybody. Your kind, Kyle, not one single individual upon this planet or anywhere else."

She raised a hand and removed the leather glove, then placed her bare palm on Heather's chest.

Heather struggled to pull away as she felt tendrils of something enter her, then wanted to scream in pain. She had never experienced anything like this before, it was as if her very soul was being ripped from her body in a slow, meticulous manner. Her vision began to dim. The excruciating pain became even more intense. Her mind was about to slip into shock when the pain suddenly ended.

"Do you understand? You are not to discuss this with anybody," said Cynthia in a harsh whisper as she pulled her hand away.

Heather wanted to scream, wanted to nod her head, wanted to run away, but could do nothing. Cynthia disappeared from her sight again.

"I have work to do, if you will excuse me," said Cynthia. "And I would like you to take this time to seriously consider what you can do to help Kyle."

Four strong hands grasped Heather beneath her arms and around her waist and she felt herself lifted up, but could not see who was moving her. She was carried to the center of the study and set down. Two humanoid creatures made of black mist came into her line of sight, and they transformed into two large dogs who looked back at her with glowing red eyes before they left the area.

The only sound in the study was that of the keys of the calculator, and the occasional shuffling of papers.

Chapter 08.07

As the credits for the movie began to roll, Kyle and Janice made their way through the throngs of people to the exit doors and into the hallway. They walked down the marble stairs to the main lobby.

Glancing over, Janice said, "Those bell-hop outfits are too much."

Kyle looked over at the person behind the information desk of the theater and nodded. As they stepped outside Kyle put on his sunglasses. The last time he had been in this area was ages ago when it had just been the Farmers Market on 3rd and Fairfax. Now it had been transformed into The Grove, a shopping complex whose many shops were derived from various architectural styles.

"We have some time until our dinner reservations, want to grab a cup of coffee or something?" asked Janice.

"Uh, sure," said Kyle.

They went over to the coffee shop that was connected to the theater. Inside they got two cups and went back outside because there was no place to sit. Janice pointed over at the grass on the other side of the fountain and they pushed their way through the crowd. Finding an empty place they sat in the grass next to each other.

"Hey, Kyle, are you OK?" she asked.

Shaking his head slightly he looked over at her.

"Yeah, why do you ask?"

"You just seem kind of distant today, is it something I did?"

"No," said Kyle. He thought a few seconds, "I had some problems with a client last night and didn't get much sleep."

"Oh, did you get it fixed?"

Looking down to the grass, he said, "No, still trying to figure it out."

"You computer people are so amazing," she said. "I can use the word processor, check email, IM, and that's about it."

"Look," he said. "Janice, sorry I'm kind of out of it. It's nothing you did."

"Thanks," she said putting her hand on his knee for a moment, then pulling it away.

"Um, Kyle?" she asked.

"Yeah?"

"I know you're tired, but can I ask you something?"

"Sure."

"I was wondering... Well, Valentine's Day is coming up in a bit... And I was wondering if you wanted to do something. Together?"

Everything that happened last night and this morning flooded back into his mind with so much force he almost fell backward as he closed his eyes.

Could he live like this? Was this even acceptable? It seemed that being involved with a person not of his kind was bad. Should he just end this now? Not to mention he had no idea what his kind was, whatever a kind could possibly be.

"Sorry, sorry, I shouldn't have said anything," she said, her voice filled with panic.

"No, it's just, no, it's fine, just let me think about it," he said.

Music began to play loudly behind them, and they both looked back at the crowd gathered around the fountain. Water shot up into the air in time with the music.

"You know, I heard that was designed by the people who did the water show for the Belagio in Vegas," he said.

"Really? Never been," said Janice.

"Never?"

"No point going to Vegas," she said. "I don't gamble and I'm under twenty-one. Plus I don't like traveling by myself."

"Oh right, anyway the water show in the pond in front of the Belagio is very beautiful, especially at night, with classical music playing as it goes off," he said. "Well if you ever get a chance you should go see it."

She nodded her head, looking away uncomfortably.

When the water show in the park around them was over he took a sip of his coffee and then pressed the tall paper cup into the grass so it would not fall over. Interweaving his fingers together he brought his hands to his chin and turned his head slightly toward her.

"Janice?" he asked. "Do you ever wonder what you will be doing in the future?"

"What? Oh, um…" she said, seeming surprised by the question.

"Well I was doing Bio-Chemistry," she said, smiling faintly. "But earlier in the week I changed my major to Physics. I'm not exactly great at it. But there's just so much we don't know about how the world, or even how the universe works, and I want to help figure out a part of it."

Kyle nodded his head.

"What about you?" she asked, leaning forward, placing her hand on the grass less than an inch from his knee.

"Don't know," he said. "Never really thought about it before. But a lot of stuff has happened recently and I have suddenly realized that I have no real goals in my life, no direction or any dreams I can think of off hand. What am I going to be doing ten years from now, or twenty?"

Then to himself, one hundred?

"You don't have any dreams?" Janice asked.

"Life always seemed like something that could end at any minute," he said.

Chapter 08.08

"Are you sure you cannot come in?" asked Keiko as the truck came to a stop.

"Sorry, but I have two more villages to hit before my run is over. Thank you for the invitation," said Noriyuki patting her shoulder.

"Well then, Noriyuki-san, you wanted an autograph?"

Smiling he reached underneath his seat and produced a Japanese magazine with Keiko on the cover. He held it out to her, pulling out a pen with his other hand.

"Thank you," she said taking both.

Pulling off the top off the pen she placed the magazine in her lap and wrote in Kanji, "Noriyuki, thank you for driving me back home. You are a wonderful man, and I sincerely wish you all the best in your life. -Nakamura Keiko," then handed it back to him.

He laughed out loud and held the magazine in the air.

"And thank you, Nakamura-san, it has been a pleasure meeting you," he said setting the magazine carefully on the seat between them.

"Can I ask one more favor?"

"What?" he asked.

"May I take some pictures of you? If you have time?"

"It would be an honor," he said. "Where?"

"In front of your truck."

"Gladly," he said throwing his door open and jumping out onto the ground.

Keiko hopped down and slammed the door shut. Dropping her bags to the ground she grabbed one of them and pulled out her 35mm SLR, then walked around the vehicle.

"No, don't pose," she said. "Be yourself. Inspect your truck, show me that part of you I have seen on this trip."

Noriyuki laughed and stopped his flamboyant pose.

Keiko shot a roll of film. When the last picture was taken, and the film began to rewind, she ran up to him and said, "Noriyuki-san, thank you for everything."

"I wish you the best," he said.

"You too, you are a wonderful man," she said.

"Ah, if I were but younger…"

"Pervert," she said laughing and hitting his arm.

"Have a good day, and a safe journey back to America," he said. "I hope you find what you are looking for."

"Thank you," she said bowing.

Noriyuki nodded his head and got back into his truck. It reversed a short way, then turned around and drove down the dirt driveway toward the road.

Laughing lightly to herself, Keiko pulled the roll of film out and put in another one. Putting the camera back, she grabbed her bags and turned around. Her Mother was standing on the porch watching her.

Keiko dropped her head and walked to the base of the stairs, then stopped.

"We were worried about you, disappearing like that in the middle of the night."

"I am sorry, Mother," said Keiko bowing. "I should have called."

"Are you alright, Keiko?" she asked.

"No," she said. "Mother, I need to talk to you."

"Put your things away, when you are ready we shall talk," said her Mother. Bowing, she walked back inside.

Keiko waited a few minutes before ascending the stairs and entered the house. Taking off her shoes she walked through the building, to the room she had been in before. Dropping her bags she sat on the floor and closed her eyes.

This was it.

This was her way out of the pain and misery that had consumed her life for all of these years.

Freedom.

That elusive word that she had not possessed for over five years.

And she would be able to do what she wanted, would be able to confess to Kyle, finally.

Putting everything away in the closet, Keiko donned the kimono that had been left out for her before pausing to survey the orderly room around her from where she sat. She raised a hand to her chest, her thumb rubbing the pendant, absently, as she silently questioned what she was about to do.

Standing, Keiko slid open the door that led to the back yard of the house. As she did the dull thud of the bamboo pipe that had filled with water, dropped, then returned to its previous position echoed through the air.

Walking along the covered walkway of wood raised above the ground, Keiko stopped at the door to her Mother's room and sat in seiza position before saying, "I am ready to talk."

"You may enter."

Keiko opened the door, slid in, and then closed it behind her before going to sit opposite her Mother. They sat on the floor, facing each other across the table.

"What is it you wish to speak of?" asked her Mother.

Keiko held her hands firmly in her lap and said, "The promise."

"Promise?"

"Shortly after I began modeling, you asked me to promise you that I would focus on my career, not Kyle. I am asking to be released from that promise."

Her Mother smiled slightly and said, "So you still have feelings for him?"

"Again, my Mother, I must ask to be released from the promise I made."

Her Mother did not move, but sat watching her daughter for a while.

"You have made me very proud, Keiko," she said. "I know it must have been difficult to make such sacrifices, but you have done so and honored our family with your achievements."

She paused. "You are released from that promise. Please, find happiness for yourself."

Losing form, Keiko's head shot up and she asked, "Really?"

Smiling her Mother said, "Yes, my dear, really."

Keiko jumped up and ran around the table, wrapping her arms around her Mother.

"Thank you, thank you," said Keiko burying her face into her Mother's shoulder.

Reaching up, her Mother put one hand on Keiko's head, and the other on her back, pulling her daughter closer.

Chapter 08.09

Kyle knew the cemetery was closed before he slowly drove past the gates that were locked. Pulling off onto a side street he parked his car and got out.

The silence in the night air was both disturbing, and refreshing, as Kyle made his way along the sidewalk close to the houses near the cemetery. Seeing no cars around he closed his eyes and reached out to sense if anybody was nearby, or near a window who might see him. He paused a moment as somebody a block away approached, then turned and went down a different street, walking their dog. Quickly Kyle bolted across the empty street and came to the iron bars of the fence.

Tossing his leather coat over the top of the pointed spikes of the fence, Kyle climbed up the iron bars, with more agility than he knew he possessed, and grabbed his coat as he fell to the ground.

The last time he had been here was a little over a year ago at his Grandmother's funeral. And before that he had been a frequent visitor when his Grandmother was alive.

Kyle paused before glancing around to make sure nobody saw him. Quietly he put on his jacket and surveyed his surroundings again. He could sense the man with a flash light, driving along the roads of the cemetery in a golf cart, but Kyle did not worry about because he was some distance away.

Kyle sprinted across the field of dead people, making sure not to step on any graves, his destination known.

He made his way through the cemetery until he came upon the building he was looking for. Even though the moon was crescent, everything was almost as clear as if it was daylight.

Pausing a moment behind the short wall, he looked across the pavement to the entry of the building he wanted to enter. Kyle stared at the doors beyond the wall, flanked on either side by palm trees, wondering why he was here.

His rational side simply answered that everything he had heard the night before was just either misinterpreted or not possible. Delusions created in his mind from lack of any social life, playing too many games, and watching more anime than he could keep track of.

The irrational side kept replaying scenes of a thick wooden beam smashing his shoulder, slicing open his arm to see it heal in seconds, and the realization he had been drinking blood for two weeks without his knowledge.

Plus there was the information that the friend of his Grandmother was actually his Grandfather's sister, who turned him into this.

And here he crouched, staring at the distant wooden doors.

Even though they were dead, some part of him wanted to confront them interned in the mausoleum. And with this realization he felt that perhaps his sanity was slipping.

He ran across the empty parking lot and came to the large wooden doors. He tried to open them, but found them locked.

"Damn it," he muttered.

Breaking down the large doors was something he could not do, plus even if he could, he was sure the noise would bring the security guard. So Kyle made his way around the building and found a side entrance with a normal door.

Without even thinking he kicked it in, the metal door buckling from the impact. Rushing in and closing the slightly bent door behind him he looked around, then paused a few minutes to make sure the noise had not alerted anybody.

It seemed to be a normal maintenance room, but there was a door to an adjacent room which was unlocked. Making his way through various rooms he found himself inside a long hallway.

Shaking his head he mumbled to himself, "Crap, I don't know this section."

He started to make his way through the halls. Yet this time he found it difficult to find his destination as he wandered the Mausoleum.

"Your parents are gone, and there is nothing to change that. I know you miss them, but a part of them lives in you, just as a part of your Grandfather does," said his Grandmother, many years ago, in this very place when they visited the grave, shortly after the accident that claimed his parents.

Kyle stopped and looked around to try and find his bearings.

"Sometimes you may not feel like you are normal," he heard his Grandmother say to him when he was a teenager, they were sitting in the living room at home. Then, with a pause, and a note of sadness in her voice, *"But please try to be. You will understand when you are older. Trust me, I will explain it to you."*

She smiled at him.

Back then those words had a completely different meaning.

His footsteps echoed through the hallow hallways as he remembered things he had heard here. Stories of the depression, various vague difficulties his Grandparents had after getting married, after the family disowned him, finding a place in California to build their dream house, how many children they had dreamed of having.

Words. Words. Words.

Nothing but words describing the life and times of his Grandfather who happened to not even be Human it would seem.

Words that were not lies, but words that never completely told the truth.

A truth that, if had been told, many years ago, perhaps his Mother would still be alive today.

And that truth caused him to stop, the dismay welling within him, his Mother would still be alive if she had only known, or had been given this same twisted gift.

"God damn it," he muttered to himself, suddenly realizing he was lost again, his train of thought gone.

He tried to calm his mind. But no matter how he tried to look at it, his Mother was dead because of this big something that he had no clue about.

And nobody seemed ready to provide answers.

Not Cynthia. Not Heather.

Looking around he mumbled, "This is so stupid, like my mom would be alive. Life isn't like that. People die all the time."

Eventually, after traveling through many corridors, he found himself in the correct wing, then after some more wandering of his feet and mind, in the room.

Staring at the bronze plaque that bore his Grandparents names, he stopped.

Kyle placed a hand upon the cold stone for a moment and bowed his head.

Pulling the slightly beaten flowers from where he had tucked them into his belt, he stood on his tip toes and placed two white lilies into the empty glass vase suspended from the wall. Taking a few steps back, he stared at the brass rectangle as if trying to interpret a different meaning from the letters etched there.

"So is it true?" he asked, his words echoing through the marble hallways.

Kyle bowed his head and asked again, clenching his fists, asking slightly louder, "So is it true?"

There was no answer. No sudden swelling of air. No spirits of them suddenly appearing to reply to his question, or even give him Council.

Only the silence one can find amongst the dead.

Standing there, alone as he had always seemed to be, he did not know when it started. But as he stood there he felt the warm rivulets of liquid streaming from his eyes and down his face.

He wanted to let the rage consume him. To slam his fists into the marble wall until every single decomposed body, including theirs was exposed. To level the entire building with his bare fists to just, for a moment, calm his pain. Kyle wanted to destroy absolutely everything. If only to make his hopeless life have some kind of meaning.

He was standing with one hand on the marble wall, and the other raised in a fist ready to strike.

"Why?" he screamed.

Kyle walked to the back of the room and stared at the bronze plaque for a while.

"Why?" he mumbled, sitting down on the marble floor and leaning against the wall behind him.

He pulled out his pocket knife and opened it.

"Honestly you two, I really don't get it," he said, taking off his coat and tracing the blade against his exposed forearm.

He sat there and listened to the silence.

"This doesn't make any sense, none of this," he said to the dead bodies around him as he slowly sliced his arm lightly and watched the minor wounds heal in seconds.

"No sense at all."

He paused his self mutilation and asked, "What is it you always said, Grandmother? It was some quote from my Grandfather who I never met, right? *'You cannot know who you are, or what you are, until you can accept both, and move forward.'* Didn't you tell me that once, here?"

The silence was overwhelming.

"So was this your dying wish? Strip me of my Humanity because you fucked up and let my mom die? Become the thing that my Grandfather was when you first met him in Central Park?"

Kyle could not help but stare at the brass plate.

"Then you have your sister-in-law turn me into this as your dying wish? You never told my Mother, did you, you never gave her this chance? Then she died, as a Human. Did you feel guilty about it? That my mom could be alive right now?

"And then on your death bed you made my Grandfather's sister promise to make me like him? Without even giving me a choice?"

Kyle paused, too many things racing through his mind.

"What kind of future does that leave for me? In that empty house of dreams that you left me?"

For half a second he sat there with the knife held in his right had, staring at his wrist. A quarter of a second later he felt his fingers grasp the knife tighter.

"You got your selfish little death wish, Grandmother," he said in a coarse whisper.

Kyle stabbed the knife into his forearm, near his wrist, the blade piercing through his arm, and pulled it toward him as far as he could until it hit upon bone.

He had been a suicidal teenager once, and from what he remembered studying various anatomy books, this was a very lethal way to end one's life, albeit slow and usually best performed in a bath of warm water. The angle of the cut making sure to sever both the major artery and vein, though the sinking feeling in his heart conveyed that it was most likely pointless.

He slowly pulled the knife from his arm and tossed it aside.

Blood sprayed from his wound, erupting from his arm, much like the garden hose his Mother once used to spray him with water as a child in the summer. He calmly looked up and watched the dark red liquid dripping from the wall to his right.

Then he felt it.

The warmth, the numbness.

And as he watched, the deep wound, which should have killed him, filled with a reddish-black substance and healed before his very eyes.

Looking down he saw the remnants of blood on his exposed flesh evaporate in a dark cloud, along with the blood on the walls and pooled around him, the mist flowing back into him in a way that felt both surreal and natural.

His fingers touched the flesh that had been bleeding moments before.

After sitting there for about half an hour, he stood and walked across the room, bending down to pick up his pocket knife.

"Great. And I have to live with all this now."

Kyle looked up at the brass plate again and slowly shook his head. He was still upset, and confused, but he thought that he had started to understand.

He had spent many years, after the accident, wondering what he could have done to save his parents. Many a time in church he had prayed to God to take his life and bring his parents back. Wishing he could go back and change things.

Now he wondered if he had the ability to Awaken his Mother back then, if he would, just to save her. So that she would still be alive now.

What would he do in his Grandmother's position?

Probably the same thing, he finally admitted to himself.

Kyle did not really like that realization.

Bowing to their grave, he said, "Goodbye."

Pausing at the entryway, he raised his left arm and stared and the skin that showed no damage after being cut twice in as many days. Clenching his hand he hit the wall with the side of his fist. The marble tile shattered and fell in chunks to the floor.

Closing his eyes he let out a long sigh.

"Baka."

Kyle walked out of the room and made his way back to his car.

Chapter 08.10

Kyle stopped at the double doors of the study, and hesitated before knocking. After he did, he heard the clicks of the locks and the door on the right opened up. Cynthia was standing on the other side.

Stepping forward she looked at Kyle and asked, "You had a bad evening?"

Stepping back and turning to lean against the wall, he let out a low moan and said, "That is an understatement."

"What happened?"

"Tried to kill myself, if that is an answer."

"The date was that bad?" she asked.

"No, the date was alright, just had a lot of things on my mind and broke into the cemetery where my Grandparents are buried to try and figure some stuff out."

"Why would try to end your life?" she asked, her head tilting slightly to the left.

"Hell if I know," said Kyle. "Not really in the mood to try again, or talk about it."

"I see," said Cynthia.

"We're not going to talk in the study?" he asked as the door closed behind her and locked.

"No. We shall conduct the training in your room," said Cynthia

Julien Giever

walking past him.

Kyle let out a low sigh as he began to follow her down the hallway.

"Ed stopped by to grab his things, and said he was staying with
his parents before he flew to Europe," said Cynthia as she slowed her
steps so Kyle was walking next to her.

"But he hates his parents."

"I know."

Kyle looked away from her, thinking about his best friend since
High School, feeling guilty, even though he had not done anything
with Cynthia. Except drink her blood. Which he could never tell Ed,
let alone anybody else.

Though having your best friend's girlfriend sleep on top of you
all night, after drinking her blood, even clothed, probably violated
some rule of friendship.

He massaged his temples for a moment, trying not to think of
everything.

"He is..." she started.

"Yes, I know, we are following our own paths," he said. "Whatever that means."

They entered the living room, and Harry, sitting and reading a
book, did not seem to notice either of them, as they walked past him
and down the hall to the stairs.

In his room, she shut the door behind her. Moving both hands in
a series of patterns, all of the walls, floor, and ceiling seemed to waver
for a second. Stepping forward she held out a hand toward the chairs
in front of his computer desk.

They sat facing each other.

Cynthia leaned her head to the side, staring at him.

"You agreed to this training, yet you do not seem ready. Are you
sure you want to continue?" she asked.

"Sorry, just distracted from earlier," said Kyle sitting up in his
chair and leaning forward a bit. "I'm ready."

"Very well then, the first thing I shall teach you is how to shield
your mind," said Cynthia.

"OK," he said smiling.

"This is serious, Kyle," she said staring intently at him. "There is
a part of me that you have seemed to acquire, and they cannot know
of it for both our sakes."

"Sorry," he said.

"Close your eyes."

Four hours later Cynthia was satisfied with his progress.

"Good," she said standing. "Just remember it is like a TSR program, you need to keep it running all the time or both of us may be in danger."

"TSR?" he asked. "Wait, Terminate and Stay Resident? How the hell do you know that term? That's ancient."

Smiling slightly she said, "About twenty years ago, when I awoke from my coma, my father bought me a computer."

"You were in a coma?"

"I am going to step outside, would you care to join me?"

Kyle grabbed his phone off the desk and checked the time. Strangely he had no signal.

"Actually think I'll check my email," he said.

"You have no connection," said Cynthia.

"What?" he asked spinning in his chair and clicking the icon to open his email client.

He stared at the message stating that he could not connect to the server.

"How did you know?" he asked.

"The spell I cast blocked off this room, including your internet connection. An easy way to infiltrate a shielded area, data connections like that. The nature of electricity causes too much havoc for magic to work in that manner, otherwise we would have been doing this in candle light."

Kyle grabbed his forehead with one hand and said, "Cyn, my brain hurts from this. All of this. A month ago I was a normal boring guy just living his life."

"You have always been yourself," she said, tilting her head slightly. "But you never knew what you really were. I knew that the day I first met you."

He shook his head and sighed.

Cynthia suddenly became aware of the fact her hand was on his shoulder, and she took a few steps back.

"Actually," she said. "It is getting late and you have a morning appointment, correct?"

"Yes," said Kyle.

"Then come here," she said walking over to the bed and sitting

231

down.

He hesitated a bit, but went over to her.

Cynthia unfastened the sleeve of her right arm and pulled the cloth back.

"Again?" asked Kyle.

She closed her eyes and whispered, "Just do this."

At his hesitation she added, "Please."

In a quick motion she pulled out the small dagger, sliced open her wrist and thrust it up at him.

The same feelings overwhelmed Kyle, filling him. And though he was in a place that seemed devoid of time, filled with the normal red and black mists, there was something different. There was a pain, outside of this, registering somewhere in his hand that began to pull at him as equally as he did her, and then her arm was yanked away.

His eyes shot open and he saw her leaning slightly against him, her left arm wrapped around his right, their fingers intertwined between them.

Breathing heavily she suddenly let go of his hand.

He opened and closed his right hand several times at the odd remnants of pain and tingling sensation in his palm that did not immediately disappear.

She sat there for a few minutes staring into her lap, at her bare hands, the fingers barely moving as the rest of her remained perfectly still. She glanced at him for a brief moment before fastening the button of the sleeve and putting on her gloves.

Standing, with her back to him, she said, "Have a good evening, Kyle."

He watched her walk across the room. As she reached his door, the walls, ceiling and floor wavered slightly. Opening the door she paused, then walked through, closing it behind her.

Chapter 08.11

Cynthia passed by Harry in the living room without him even being aware of her presence. The doors to the study opened as she approached and closed behind her, locking. Walking slowly to the center of the study she stood before Heather.

The Irish woman had spent the last several hours trying to free herself and eventually had given up and begun to think about what she really needed to do with Kyle. Suddenly, seeing Cynthia standing in front of her she could move again.

"Promise to never say anything about this evening." said Cynthia. "Or I will kill you, and every single person who has ever known you over the centuries of your life."

Every fiber of her being wanted to lash out at this girl, to rend her flesh, to eviscerate her, to drain her dry. But the ease that this Human had fought off Heather's attack kept her in check.

"I promise," said Heather.

"Upon the blood of your Clan?"

Heather wanted to take a step back, wondering how the Human knew that phrase, before nodding and saying, "Yes, upon the blood of my Clan."

"Then please leave," said Cynthia.

Heather nodded her head and faded from the room.

Cynthia walked over to the couch she had awoken upon this morning and sat down. She placed a hand on the cushion for a moment.

"What is the situation?" asked her father, stepping into the room whose firelight filled the area.

"There was an accident," said the maid. "She has been like that for almost thirty minutes."

Cynthia stared down at the lifeless body of the six month old white cat that lay in her lap, completely motionless. Both of her hands covered her friend's face, because his eyes were still open and the mouth was pulled back and frozen in terror.

The word sadness came to her, and though she recited the definition within her mind, over and over, she could not attach it to anything other than words.

As she stared at the lifeless body, she heard the clanking of some metal, then footsteps approaching, stopping a few feet away. Her father's leather shoes creaked as he leaned down.

"Now there, dear," he said in a comforting tone. "Did you have another accident?"

Slowly she nodded her head, eyes unmoving from the friend in her lap. Her only friend, who had been running around the room a short time ago. Then she had become upset, because Mr. Schwarzes had fought against her picking him up and bitten her hand. And now he lay lifeless in her lap, with her hands covering his face.

"It is alright," said her father. "Remember, you always have to remain in control, or these unfortunate incidents will occur."

The dark, charcoal covered end of the poker appeared over her friend as the hook grabbed the body and pulled it away from her. She watched Mr. Schwarzes' inert body being dragged away as the leather strap fell around her neck and tightened, the long wooden pole digging into the back of her neck.

Her father cradled the body of her friend as he said, "We shall have a proper burial for him tomorrow evening."

Cynthia nodded her head slowly.

"Now be a good girl and let Dieter take you back to your room," he said turning away from her.

As she walked across the room, the end of the pole pushing against the back of her neck, she heard the conversation, barely above a whisper.

"How sad," said the maid. "Please allow me sir."

Her father's words cracked slightly, and he coughed, before saying, "No, what is sad is that even if she recovers, she will never be able to be close to anybody, at least not physically."

Shaking off the old thought, Cynthia frowned and first removed her gloves, placing them carefully on the table, then her tall boots, which she set beside the couch. Reaching behind she unfastened her dress and let it fall to the floor. Stepping from it she bent down to pick it up, carefully folding it and setting it upon the table.

Lying face down upon the couch, her bare fingers caressing the leather, a sad look filled her eyes as her hand traced circles on the cushion.

The hand paused.

Forcing her eyes shut, she tried to go to sleep.

CONFESSIONS

Chapter 09.01

Kyle had parked his car and turned everything off except for the stereo that was playing a song that he liked. He closed his eyes.

Last weekend he could not even accept any of this, but after much coaxing, and discussions with Cynthia on Monday, that evening he had finally called Heather and they had spent every night since then doing training and teaching him the ways of this 'kind' he was somehow now a part of now. She had told him the name a few times, but he could not remember it, other than starting with an 'A', and felt too embarrassed to ask again.

Stepping from the car, he walked over to Heather, who was still watching his vehicle for some reason. He turned and watched it for a moment, wondering if there was something perhaps going on in the distance, but he could not see anything interesting.

"What are you looking at, Heather?" he asked.

Her sudden movement was slightly blurred and she was suddenly standing ten feet away from him, confusion filling her face.

"How did you do that?" she asked.

"Do what?"

"Appear next to me?"

"I walked over here."

"What has that Human been teaching you?" asked Heather, her voice defensive.

Kyle glared at her.

Heather paused and then bowed her head.

"My apologies, I did not mean any disrespect toward Miss Hapsburg, you simply surprised me," she said, regaining her composure.

Kyle walked over to her and placed a hand on her shoulder.

"Look, all of this is still hard to comprehend for me, but she has been a close friend of mine for ages, so please try to show some level of respect," he said calmly.

Heather looked away from him and said, "I understand."

"Wow, is everybody this serious and depressed all the time? Even though I don't know that much about this stuff, I wouldn't exactly call her a normal Human." he said, stepping away and placing both hands on the railing. "I know you didn't mean any personal offense so stop it. You're supposed to be training me and such, right? Come on, let's get started."

Heather looked up and froze at the care free smile before her.

It was the same smile her brother had always had, in his own laissez-faire manner, no matter what they were facing. And it was the first time she could remember Kyle smiling since her sister-in-law had died.

"My apologies, work has been stressful," said Heather quickly moving past him to open the door.

As they stepped into her house, Kyle walked into the kitchen and asked, "What happened?"

"Just doing some remodeling," said Heather.

Kyle stared at the shattered remnants of the cupboards and the large gaping holes in the drywall of the kitchen, noticing how most of the appliances were brand new. They had been meeting up in Los Angeles lately so this was the first time he had been to her house in a while.

"You sure nothing happened?" he asked, looking over to the dining room table which had a deep gouge in its previously pristine surface.

"Nothing at all," said Heather hesitantly.

"Of course," said Kyle. "So what is the lesson today?"

He asked this as he wandered into the dining room, a single finger tracing the gouge in the table that was still mildly sticky from what he guessed was a stain similar to the original table. He noticed that her old coffee table in the living room had been replaced with a new one, along with the love seat and chairs.

Her hand on his arm pulled him around.

"Today I shall teach you how to feed properly," said Heather.

"Properly?"

"Well, not quite, it takes a long time to learn how to erase short term memory, but there are ways to get around this so you can gain sustenance without killing your prey."

Kyle looked around the apartment, at the various signs of damage, then smiled and said, "As you wish."

Heather led him upstairs to her bedroom where a woman in her early twenties sat on the bed, unmoving. He did not recognize her.

"Do not worry, I shall erase her memory if anything goes wrong."

"If you say so," said Kyle, nervously.

Chapter 09.02

The office was large and spacious, filled with items that displayed the amount of power that the man who seemed to be in his late fifties wielded. He was in the middle of reviewing some paperwork when he paused, noticing a presence in the room. Raising his wrist, to note the time, he nodded slightly.

"Well, my dearest Cynthia, so good to see that you are as punctual as always," he said placing his silver pen, and papers, upon the desk.

"It is good to meet with you again, Lord Chancellor Solomon," she said bowing her head.

He placed his hand upon his chin, stroking his grey beard, then said, "Though I do find it rather unusual for you to involve yourself in our affairs."

"As I mentioned earlier, this is a personal matter," she said. "And I am most gracious that you agreed to indulge my request."

Standing from the desk, he walked around it as the door to his office opened and the man who entered pulled a fifty caliber pistol from beneath his coat and aimed it at Cynthia's head.

The response was instantaneous as she looked over and his arm was severed from his body while at the same time the barrel of the pistol was cut just before the trigger. The appendage and two pieces of the weapon came to lie several feet away.

Staring at his bleeding stump, the man in the suit managed to say, between painful gasps, "I heard somebody in here who was not one of us..."

"And I specifically told you I was meeting with somebody important and was not to be disturbed," said the Lord Chancellor.

Grimacing and holding the stump to try and stem the flow of blood he said, "My apologies, Lord Chancellor."

Waving a hand while walking back to his desk, the Chancellor said, "Please remove your appendage from my office."

"Of course," said the man in the suit, grabbing his arm and quickly leaving the room, leaving his broken weapon lying near the pool of blood on the fine white marble.

Pressing a button Solomon said, "The new individual, currently with one arm, have him detained immediately, and have a full evaluation performed as to why he came to be here and why he is unable to follow protocol. Have the head of security handle this matter personally."

"As you wish, Lord Chancellor," came the female voice from the speaker.

Nodding his head, he turned to Cynthia and said, "My apologies Miss Hapsburg, for the disturbance."

"No need to apologize, Lord Chancellor," she said bowing. "Please accept my apologies for the mess I have created."

"Again, please, Solomon is permissible," he said leaning back in his large leather chair. "And that is nothing to worry about. You are much kinder than I would have been with a hand gun pointed at my head."

"Of course," said Cynthia, inclining her head toward him.

"In regards to why you are here, there has been no news from the McClellan household in regards to your friend, they have been rather quiet, actually, and nobody on their Council or the High Council has been contacted regarding anything related to them," said Solomon.

Cynthia nodded her head slightly.

He paused a moment before saying, "As for your other request, I personally checked the archives, and there is no record of anybody two generations removed from our kind ever surviving an Awakening ceremony. Though it seems many have tried through the ages."

"Are you sure?" she asked, looking up at him.

"Very, unfortunately they lack the power of our blood, or our souls to survive, it is too diluted, and they usually die within one to two days," said the Lord Chancellor. "As such, you are quite certain that Jeoffrey McClellan's grandson has not died after being Awakened by Heather McClellan?"

"That is correct," said Cynthia.

"This is rather unprecedented then," said Solomon crossing his arms. "If he has survived, and there are no challenges to his birthright, I have found no reason why he could not enter into our society, with the proper training of course. There might be some political ramifications if this happens, due mainly to his Grandfather's choices, yet I will arrange for a smooth transition due to your request."

"Thank you, Lord Chancellor Solomon," said Cynthia.

He paused a moment, then said, "Honestly I did not want to mention this, but somebody has been snooping around in regards to you."

"Who?" she asked.

"An English gentleman, no real ties to any Council or the High Council," said the Lord Chancellor. "Unfortunately I cannot say more on this matter."

"I understand," said Cynthia. "Was any information disseminated about me?"

"Not to my knowledge," said the Lord Chancellor. "We have secretly worked with your family for many centuries, and you are a most valuable asset, especially after your accident. If I hear anything that I can discuss, I will let you know."

"As always Lord Chancellor Solomon," said Cynthia, bowing her head. "Thank you, I shall take my leave."

"Of course, Miss Cynthia," he said, returning the gesture. Looking up, she was gone.

Chapter 09.03

Kami threw her books and notes into her backpack and then carefully slid her notebook computer into the reinforced pocket before she stepped from the Advanced Computer Science class. Seniors passed her, both male and female, nodding solemnly to her.

"Good work," said the instructor coming up behind her.

"Eh," she said, dropping her head slightly. "Just strange being a sophomore and your assistant."

"No," said her instructor, patting her shoulder, "What is sad is the fact that you know so much more about this than me." He let out a slight laugh. "But I really appreciate your help."

"Sure, no problem," said Kami, pulling away from him.

"Need to meet my friend," she said running down the hall.

Kami was not comfortable with any of this, not even remotely.

Julien Giever

When, after a weekend of deliberation, she had finally mustered the nerve to talk to the Principle on Monday, about how bored she really was, the last thing she had expected was to become the assistant for the senior computer science class.

Let alone the fact that people two years older than her actually knew so little about computers.

Linux was mildly understandable, but the one girl who had no idea what a network was, or the fact she could store her file that was more than 1.4 megs there, instead of a floppy, and had no idea what a thumb drive was, made her brain twitch.

Honestly, Kami could not even remember when they made computers with floppy drives. Then she felt rather old at the realization she even had a couple 3.5 inch floppies with old data stored on them from her childhood, probably sitting in a box in her closet.

Kami came to the familiar row of lockers and stopped.

Stacie had just closed her locker and turned around to see she was surrounded by three girls dressed in cheerleading outfits. The one in the middle pushed her shoulder back into the locker.

"Hey little loser," said the cheerleader.

"Um, hi, Amber," mumbled Stacie looking at the ground.

"You haven't been doing my English homework lately, and that is a clear violation of our agreement."

"A... A... Agreement?" stammered Stacie holding her books close to her chest.

"Sure, the agreement that if you do my homework we don't beat you up."

"Uh, sorry," said Stacie. "I've just been kind of, you know, um, busy and stuff."

"Oh," said one of the other girls. "Been too busy with that freak new girl computer geek who suddenly became the teacher's pet?"

"I bet they're too busy getting it on, hot and heavy," said the other. "You make me sick."

"Yeah, what are the teachers going to think knowing you and the new girl are like that? Let alone our parents?" asked Amber smugly.

"Is that it?" asked the cheerleader on the left. "No boy will even remotely touch somebody as fugly as you, so you gone lez?"

"It's not like that," said Stacie.

"But you're not denying it either," sneered Amber. "Doesn't matter. That book report is due on Monday and I expect mine to be finished. Got it?"

An arm fell around Amber's shoulder, and she looked over to see Kami smiling at her.

"Hey there."

"Stupid little lezbo bitch, let me go," screamed Amber.

"You underestimate the power of those you call geeks," said Kami, barely audible. "Amazing what they can do, those you despise, they tend to tap personal conversations, emails, and even your fancy little cell phone. Something about a beer bottle from what I heard."

Amber paled, but said, "What the hell are you talking about?"

Placing her lips upon Amber's ear, she whispered, "I really do not have anything to lose, but if that info were to become available on a blog, or the audio clip popped up online, wow. Now leave me and my friend alone and go away."

The cheerleader tore herself from Kami, then glared at her. "You are so not worth it!" she exclaimed, then grabbed her two friends and disappeared into the mass of people.

Everybody else was staring at Kami, who stepped back and put her arm around the waist of Stacie, smiling at those around them.

"We need to get to class," said Kami.

Stacie's face was blushing as the crowd around them slowly dissipated.

"Wha... What did you say to them," asked Stacie.

Leaning over and whispering, while they walked, Kami said, "Just a rumor I heard the seniors talking about, but it seemed to work."

Stacie stared at the floor as they walked, and nodded her head, looking away from the one embracing her.

After their last class was finished the two of them stepped from the room and paused at the mayhem around them.

"Damn, I'm so glad the week is over," said Kami, stretching. "That reminds me, we haven't even talked about this weekend."

"No," said Stacie.

"OK then, we'll talk about it on the ride home."

"Sure," said Stacie.

"See you out front," said Kami heading toward her locker. "And for the thousandth time this week stop sulking."

"Yeah," said Stacie staring at Kami's back, then looking away.

Chapter 09.04

Caitlin was standing on the balcony of her house, watching the people below in the French Quarter of New Orleans as the sun began to set. She grumbled beneath her breath. All Human. None of her kind ever came here since that Human woman wrote those stupid books about an interview a decade or two ago.

She spotted a couple dressed in black, walking amidst the people below. Caitlin fought the urge to lure them into a dark alley and show them what they were pretending to be. Which would have been more viable decades ago, but modern forensics made such pleasantries rather dangerous.

"Pathetic," she muttered.

There was a knock on the door to her study.

She leaned inside and said, "Enter."

A man in his late sixties opened the door and stepped in.

"Mister Engle is here to see you, Ma'am," he said.

"Thank you Robert," she replied. "Please see him in."

He bowed and closed the door. A few minutes later the door opened again.

Entering and stepping to the side Robert said, "Mister Engle, Ma'am."

"Walter," she said smiling and walking across the room.

"Caitlin," said the man who entered. He appeared to be in his mid twenties, was dressed in a slightly dated designer suit, and had a heavy English accent.

"Thank you for coming," she said leaning up as they kissed each other's cheeks.

"A pleasure, as always," said Walter holding both of her hands.

"Excuse me, Ma'am?" asked Robert.

"Yes?" she asked.

"Shall I bring some refreshments?"

"Indeed," said Caitlin. "That couple I brought home yesterday."

"As you wish," said Robert closing the door.

"Please, have a seat," said Caitlin motioning to one of the finely carved chairs.

"Thank you," he said unfastening the button to his suit coat and

242

sitting down.

Taking her chair and crossing her legs, Caitlin asked, "It has been a while, have you been well?"

"Quite well," he said. "I got married about thirty years ago, have a son who is in his mid twenties, planning his Awakening ceremony some time in the next few years."

"I am amazed that you finally settled down," said Caitlin. "I am sure he is as dashing and extravagant as his father."

He laughed lightly and nodded his head.

"I take it you are still alone?"

She let out a soft sigh and said, "Unfortunately the younger generations of our kind have this twisted Lolita complex with me, and the older ones treat me more like a daughter than a lover. It is rather depressing."

"Aye, back when you were Awakened thirteen was a normal age to get married," he said looking into her eyes, his left thumb playing with his wedding ring. "Sad how times change."

"Indeed it is," said Caitlin, looking away from him.

The butler knocked on the door, and paused a moment before entering. He placed a silver tray on the table and lifted an unmarked bottle of wine, pouring the contents into the two fine lead crystal wine glasses. He returned the bottle to the tray and stood.

"Will you be needing anything else, Ma'am?" he asked.

"No, we are fine, thank you Robert."

Bowing, he excused himself, shutting the door.

"To old times then," she said leaning forward, the sound of the wine glasses connecting filling the room.

Walter lifted his glass and sniffed the dark red mixture, swirling it around. Taking a small sip he raised an eyebrow.

"Excellent," he said.

"I am glad you enjoy it," she said taking a sip from her glass. As she lowered it she asked, "Were you able to find anything?"

"Some information," said Walter. "Unfortunately that entire Human family line is exceedingly secretive, and those of our kind I inquired were unwilling to speak for the most part."

He reached into his inside coat pocket and pulled out an envelope. Leaning forward he handed it to Caitlin.

She took out the single page and began to read.

> The only known Cynthia Hapsburg was born to
> Adelbert and Charlotte Hapsburg in nineteen forty-
> seven, in Los Angeles, California. No further
> information about that child, and no records that could
> be found after exhausting all avenues of research.
>   It can only be assumed that the Cynthia Hapsburg
> in her early twenties is the granddaughter of Adelbert
> Hapsburg. She enrolled in a private school in
> Pasadena, California, eight years earlier from this year.
> There was no significant information about her either,
> but all other records seem in perfect order.

Caitlin read the next paragraph and dropped the piece of paper into her lap.

"Their family is actually registered as an ally to us?"

"Yes, strange that," said Walter. "Took a lot of prying to get that information. Apparently she is an accountant, and seems to have some rather high ranking members of our kind as clients. But nobody would say who. Though she is not officially listed, several individuals indicated that their family works with our kind. But nobody would say exactly how, accounting or otherwise."

"Curse God Almighty," hissed Caitlin, crumpling the piece of paper and throwing it across the room.

"Not good news it would seem?" he asked.

"This ruins everything," said Caitlin, her voice low, quiet, and filled with anger.

She stared out the balcony doors.

Heather had finally begun to train the worthless half-breed, now with this piece of paper all hopes of having the Council renounce Kyle were gone. She took a long drink of her wine, then smiled.

"Walter?" she asked. "If I were to ask you for a favor, one that might be frowned upon by the Councils, what would you say?"

"I would have to agree," he said, hesitantly. "After all, I still owe you for your help back in Paris two hundred years ago. Then again that is probably why you asked me to look into this."

"Very well then," she said. "We will travel to California tomorrow."

Standing Caitlin said, "But if you will excuse me, I have some preparations to attend to."

"Of course," he said standing.

"I shall contact you in the morning," she said walking over and opening the door.

"It was good to see you again," he said, pausing before her.

"It was a pleasure to see you also," said Caitlin placing a hand on his elbow.

Walter leaned forward and kissed her cheek before excusing himself.

She closed the door and walked to the middle of the room. Taking a deep breath she leaned forward and took her glass. Finishing off the contents, Caitlin poured more for herself.

Standing there she drank another glass before she felt confident enough.

Slowly crossing the room, Caitlin sat on the floor and placed the glass next to her. Pulling open the wide drawer she took out books until she reached the one on the bottom she was looking for.

She slowly paged through the book filled with aged letters, finally stopping. Caitlin put her hand on the plastic that preserved the old paper, and stared across the room.

She tried to stop the tears as she looked down to read the words. Yet she failed, raising a white silk handkerchief to her eyes.

Caitlin's finger traced the words slowly as she read them aloud.

12 September 1903

My Dearest Sister Caitlin,

Please accept my most sincere apologies for not contacting you sooner.

As for your concerns, they were completely unfounded. Though I spent several years with that Human woman I ended our relationship a few months ago. I know you fancy me the romantic, but there are some things that cannot be. Falling in love with a Human is one of them. Then again I wonder if we are even capable of truly falling in love with each other.

Perchance are you involved with that English gentleman you have fancied for so many decades? It would be a shame for you to lose yourself in our politics and pass on such a lovely young fellow. Though I hate to digress, I think he might do you well from what I have learned of him.

Of course, I am not trying to interfere, but at least please consider my words. Even though I may be a tad jaded, there is no reason for you to be.

As such, in regards to myself, please do allay your fears. I am still myself.

I would like to see you again soon. I am planning on moving to the United States of America in the next few years. It seems those rebels have a decent country now, so I have fancied myself to go there and see how it is. Heather has also expressed interest in joining me.

Please be well. I am thinking of you always.

Your ever loving Brother,

Geoffrey

Chapter 09.05

Kyle entered his house and closed the door, walking through the hallway to the living room where Thomas was watching television.

"Hey Thomas," he said.

Thomas jumped slightly and looked over. "My good man, how are you doing this evening?"

"Good," said Kyle, "Just getting back from a meeting. How are you doing?"

"Quite well, quite well," said Thomas smiling. "My secret ad went out yesterday so I am in eager anticipation of the results."

"Cool," said Kyle. "You seem to be back to your old self."

"Of course," said Thomas raising a hand into the air. "It takes more than a few setbacks to destroy a creative genius such as myself!"

Walking past him, Kyle shook his raised hand and said, laughing to himself slightly, "Keep it up."

Thomas dropped his hand and glanced over his shoulder, "Always."

Kyle went through the living room, and down the hallway to the study, and stood there for a moment, knocking lightly upon them.

The doors opened and he saw Cynthia standing there.

"Good evening, Kyle," she said. "How were your lessons?"

"It was kind of weird, but OK," he said.

She stepped forward and closed the door behind her. The empty hallway echoed with the sounds of the locks clicking into place.

"Shall we then?" she asked.

He nodded his head and they went to his room.

Kyle walked over to his computer chair and sat down.

Cynthia closed the door and walked over to Kyle, but did not sit.

"What happened today?" she asked.

"I learned I have fangs," he said, slightly shaking his head.

"Fangs?" she asked placing her hands before her, then behind.

"Yeah, it was really weird, and a bit unreal," he said. "Spent a couple hours feeding off some artist girl."

"Interesting," said Cynthia dropping her hands to her side.

"So what's up for tonight?" he asked.

"Undecided," she said. Cynthia turned away from him slightly.

"You know, Cyn," he said laughing. "Heather was a bit freaked out that I left my car and was standing next to her without ever sensing I did so. Your training must be pretty good."

"Perhaps," she said quietly.

"Are you OK?" asked Kyle.

"Why do you ask?"

"Don't seem yourself," he said. "You have been kind of distant all week, actually."

Cynthia walked across his room and stopped at the doors of the balcony, staring outside. It was a clear night, and the moonlight illuminated the back yard, the hill beyond was bathed in a cold blue light. She placed a hand upon the glass.

She heard Kyle stand and walk over to her, felt a hand upon her shoulder.

"Really, Cyn, you have me worried."

Dropping her head, she whispered, "You would worry about a thing like me?"

"Cynthia," said Kyle. "Of course. Why would you even ask that?"

She turned around and placed her hands on his waist.

"Can you please sit on the bed?" she asked staring past him and pulling away.

"Sure," he said, walking over and sitting down. "No training tonight?"

"No."

She turned and looked outside again, thinking of the words her father had said long ago after he had pulled her friend from her lap, in that room. Unsure if she even cared anymore, wishing she could.

Pulling off her gloves, she let them fall to the floor. After a minute she walked over to him. Beginning to sit on the bed she paused and stood. Turning she sat in Kyle's lap.

Cynthia could feel his body tense as she sat on him. Reaching up she released the latch of the choker around her neck and let it drop onto the bed, then unfastened the top three buttons of her dress. She took one of his hands that was tightly holding the blanket of his bed and raised it to her waist.

"This way, tonight," she said leaning her head to the side.

Kyle did not do anything.

Glancing up she saw that he had his eyes closed. Taking his face in both of her bare hands, she forced his face up before looking into his eyes as they opened, then nodded.

"If… If it hurts, tell me," he said in a quiet voice.

Nodding her head she pulled her hair out of the way, then put her arms around his back, pulling Kyle close to her, as she closed her eyes and her lips turned into a sad smile.

Kyle slowly leaned forward and placed his lips on her neck, then hesitated at the warmth of her skin and the feeling of her arms around him. He felt a hand on the back of his head push him forward. Closing his eyes he bit deeply into her.

The sensations overwhelmed him as he entered Cynthia. This was so different than that artist from earlier. That girl was this vibrant, yet the effervescent mist of red that flowed slowly and filled every fiber of his being with strength, resonating with the part of him that was as yet undefined.

But with Cynthia it was different. The red was more subdued, and hidden beneath that was this vast void of blackness that seemed to enter him and entwine everything inside him.

Yet it was more intense this time.

Something seemed different.

When he had first felt the sensation he had become lost, but now it became even more abstract within his mind.

Then he remembered Heather's warning not to become enraptured in the sensations. He focused his mind on the pulsing of the red. There was a brief flutter and it faded away. He concentrated harder, but there was nothing there now. Panic gripped his mind.

Kyle pulled away and stared at the limp body in his arms.

"Oh, god, no," he whispered to himself.

He shook Cynthia, and her head flopped around like a rag doll.

Kyle grabbed her face with one hand to hold it still, staring at the gaping wound on her neck.

But the wound did not heal.

"Cynthia?" he screamed at the motionless body in his arms.

Tears ran down his face as he pulled her listless body into his.

"No," he whispered. "No, no no no no no…"

His voice trailed off.

The hand that was around his neck slipped and fell to her side, hanging without intent, slowly moving back and forth like a pendulum, until it came to a stop.

Kyle was unsure how long they sat like that before he could even move, or try and form a cognitive thought. He laid her down in his bed and grabbed her wrist, then placed his head on her chest. No heartbeat, no breath. Kyle sat up slowly staring at her body.

His mind was numb. He leaned forward and checked again.

He stumbled over to the computer desk, grabbing his cell phone.

He should call Heather. She would know what to do.

He stared at the keypad, thumb hovering over the numbers, trying to form some thought in his head on how to operate the phone, and failed completely.

He had just killed one of his closest friends in the world.

He stared at her dead body on his bed, and dropped his hand, the phone falling to the floor.

In slow, shuffled steps he went back to the bed, sitting on the edge.

He stared at Cynthia's delicate face.

Reaching out he moved a few stray hairs from her cheek.

Kyle took one of her hands and held it in his lap, unable to even comprehend the situation, as he bowed his head, not wanting to accept what was before him.

Chapter 09.06

The two girls walked into Stacie's room, Kami closed the door behind them, and followed her friend over to the bed.

"Stac," said Kami, "what's really wrong?"

Looking up Stacie managed a faint smile and said, "Nothing."

Grabbing her shoulders, Kami forced Stacie to sit on the bed.

"OK, game over," said Kami leaning over her. "You've been moping all week and whenever I ask, you say nothing is wrong. I don't like seeing you like this Stacie."

"I don't want to talk about it," said Stacie as she reached over and grabbed her favorite stuffed Penguin, pulling it to her chest with both hands.

"Sorry, miss, but you have no choice," said Kami placing both fists on her hips. "I don't care what it takes. I'll turn off the lights and shine a bright light in your face and interrogate you, I'll tie you to your bed and subject you to ancient Chinese water torture. If neither of those work I will tickle you until you tell me."

Stacie let out a small laugh, looking across the room, then closed her eyes.

Kneeling before her friend, Kami crossed her arms on Stacie's lap and looked up at her.

"Please, talk to me," she said.

"It's just..." Stacie started. She looked down and then away from Kami. "There is somebody I like, but that person isn't interested in me, so I'm kind of sad."

"Who is he?"

"I don't want to say."

"Oh god," said Kami. "Is it that Ryan guy from calc?"

"That geek?" asked Stacie.

"Um, what do you think we are?" asked Kami.

"Oh, good point. But no, not him."

"Too bad, I've seen him watching you, but those types are too shy to ever say anything. Anyway, so who is it?"

"It doesn't matter."

"Yes it does, maybe I can help you."

"I doubt it."

"Come on, why won't you tell me?"

"Because," said Stacie raising her voice slightly. "Because you'd probably get mad at me."

"I'm not going to get mad at you, why would you think that?"

"Because of who I like."

"Just tell me, dammit."

"No."

"I'm not going to get mad, Stac. I just want you to be happy."

"That won't happen."

"Why? Why can't that happen? Who is this person that is making you like this?"

Stacie looked away from her, then said, "You."

Kami pulled away from her.

"What?" she asked.

"You," said Stacie in a whisper. "I think I am falling in love with you. But by that reaction I can tell I was right."

She fell sideways onto the bed, pulling her legs up, closing her eyes.

"You can leave if you want," said Stacie.

Crawling onto the bed, Kami put an arm around her.

"Stac," she said. "You mean more to me than that."

She just closed her eyes tighter and said, "Yeah, sure."

"Really, Stac, you mean more to me than a relationship," said Kami raising a hand and caressing Stacie's face.

"But what about these feelings I have for you?" asked Stacie, turning away slightly.

Kami placed her hands on Stacie's shoulders.

"It's OK, silly," said Kami. "But I really don't want to risk losing what we have. Sure, we could date, but if it ended badly we'd both be alone again, right?"

Stacie sat up and turned to Kami, pulling her close with both arms in an embrace.

"But," she said. "I… I want more than that."

Rubbing her face against Kami's, Stacie kissed her firmly and said, "I don't want to lose what we have, but I don't want to be alone any more either."

Kami closed her eyes as Stacie pulled her down onto the bed.

Chapter 09.07

Kyle was not sure what it was, but it felt like something stirred. Inside of him or near he could not tell. He opened his eyes and looked over at Cynthia, then shook his head, returning his gaze to the small, cold, white hand in his own.

Something pricked the palm of his hand.

He placed his other hand on top of hers and looked at her face.

Then he felt something push into his hand, this something that snaked up his arm and down into his chest.

Excruciating pain filled every single molecule of himself as he felt as if his very soul was being torn from his body, but the pain lessened suddenly as something connected with what was in him. It was a mixture of harmony and pain as they suddenly synched.

And at that moment he felt that thing leave him and her hand lightly grasp his.

Cynthia's eyes opened and she blinked several times as she took in a deep breath, the wound on her neck healing. Seeing Kyle she sat up quickly and wrapped her arms around him.

"Kyle," she said between quick breaths. "I did not die?"

"Uh, no," he managed to say.

"How… How… How long was I gone?" she asked desperately, pressing her face into his chest. "How many years?"

"Years?" he asked.

He felt her wet tears through his shirt.

"No, not decades again," she whispered pulling closer to him.

"Cyn," he said pulling her to him. "You were dead maybe an hour, I think."

Her body relaxed against his.

"An hour?" she asked.

"About," he said holding her tightly as the horror that had consumed his mind and body began to drain away.

"Cyn... Cynthia. Shit, I'm so sorry, Cyn," trying to not become emotional again. "I... I thought I...."

"Shhhhh," she whispered.

She was silent until her breath returned to normal.

"No, Kyle, it was my fault," she said. "I knew you were inexperienced with this and I let you take too much."

Kyle started to say something.

"Stop," she said.

They sat there holding each other for a long time before she even moved.

Cynthia slowly let go of him and pushed herself several feet away, her head bowed, staring at the covers of the bed, her arms still shaking mildly as if she was struggling to remain upright.

"May I ask a favor of you?" she asked.

"Sure."

"May I stay with you this night?"

Kyle was unsure what to say.

"Would that even be alright?" he asked. "You have a boyfriend, and I kind of have a girlfriend."

She raised her face and Kyle saw something in the normally cold, emotionless eyes he had never seen before.

Terror.

"Please," she whispered.

"Please do not make me be alone."

He could see her body shake as she looked up at him.

Staring into her eyes he nodded his head.

"Thank you," she said, closing her eyes and leaning forward until she was lying on his bed.

"Uh..." he started.

Cynthia simply shook her head.

After a while she spoke.

"Honestly I feel too weak to walk down to the study, to find something to wear," she said, her voice muffled from the covers.

Trying to think, Kyle said, "I think I have a T-shirt if that's ok."

She nodded her head.

"Are you sure you're ok?" he asked.

"I am never alright," she said, her head turning slightly to look at him. "But it seems I am still alive for some reason."

Kyle hesitated before standing and walking across the room to his dresser. He started pulling shirts out and tossing them to the floor, each of them colored or white, until he found the one he was looking for. Pulling it out, he paused for a moment, suddenly realizing it was the black T-shirt he had worn to the club several weeks ago.

"Here," he said walking over and placing it next to her.

"Thank you," she said, slowly raising a hand to grab the shirt.

"Do you need any help?," he asked.

Cynthia paused a moment, then said, "No, please excuse me."

He hesitated, then slowly stood to walk into the bathroom.

The little voice that constantly said he was going to go insane had become more quiet over the last week. As he came to accept the things that Heather had been telling and teaching him.

This new development made him question it again.

In the wall length mirror opposite him he could see Cynthia's reflection as the dress fell to the floor revealing her naked figure. Closing his eyes he kicked the door shut with his foot.

Chapter 09.08

Kyle was so lost in thought, some good, most bad, that he barely heard the words from Cynthia that he could come back into the bedroom.

Thankfully he had found a pair of sweat pants and a GITS:SAC shirt in the bathroom to change into.

He stepped from the bathroom and walked slowly across his room. Cynthia was lying on her back, beneath the sheets, with her eyes closed. Quietly he approached the bed and pulled the sheets back, then laid down, pulling them and the covers up.

He could feel her trembling.

As he turned his head toward her, Cynthia rolled over quickly and wrapped an arm around him. She pressed her forehead into his cheek and let out a long sigh as the trembling ceased.

Hesitantly he put his arm around her.

"Cyn," he said. "Sorry, but this is kind of weird, and wrong."

"Indeed it is," she said

Kyle's mind was a blur. He felt like he should say something, and struggling as much as he could, he could only manage to lay there with his best friend's girlfriend suddenly now wrapping her arm and leg around him.

"No, seriously, Cyn. I don't know what's going on, but, crap, what's happening? Ed has lamented for years about how you will not get close to him, yet now... Now..."

"My apologies," said Cynthia, pulling away from him to lie on her back.

She did not move, or say a word after that last statement.

Kyle laid there staring at the ceiling for a long time, unsure what to do or say.

Then he felt a tentative touch on his bare arm. It withdrew almost immediately. Several seconds later he felt tender fingers barely grasping his forearm, as she rested her head half an inch from his shoulder.

"I..." she started several times before stopping and repeating the letter several times.

"I was not always like this," she said hesitantly, then let go of his arm.

He lay there, trying not to look at her. Giving up and turning onto his side he placed a hand on her shoulder.

"We have been friends for a long time," said Kyle. "Almost like forever."

"Forever is a long time," she said.

He froze at her tone of voice, pulling away.

"Sorry, all this new stuff," he said.

"There was..." her voice faltered.

"There was a time, decades ago, when the former Cynthia Haps-burg was a happy, normal teenager in the middle of the last century, a fan of Elvis, wearing normal clothes, laughing and playing with her friends."

"What?" he asked, feeling one of her hands become a fist and rest lightly against his arm.

"As strange as it would seem from your perspective, at that point in time I was a rather normal fifteen year old girl," she said, in a slow, monotone voice, frowning slightly. "Unfortunately my family was not, as for many generations they had been involved in magical practices."

Her hand grasped his arm and she pulled forward slightly to barely rest her cheek on his shoulder.

Cynthia fell into silence, staring his throat, as he placed his right hand on her head lightly.

She did not move.

She did not even speak.

"Can you tell me what happened?" asked Kyle.

Cynthia did not move or say anything for over five minutes.

Then her head inclined slightly up, towards his, and she said, "If you want that information I can tell you. Though it is more like describing the life of another person."

Her head declined slightly, and he could feel her lips moving but he could not hear anything.

After a time, Kyle said, "Listen, if... Crap, I don't even know what to say at a time like this, honestly. I have no idea..."

"Stop," said Cynthia. "Nothing that happened to me has anything to do with you. "Please stop talking or thinking this is in some way your fault, as it is not."

"Sorry," he said.

He felt the fingers grasping his arm tighten slightly.

"These are the memories I have," said Cynthia. "I will do my best to recount them."

Taking a deep breath she began to speak, but the tone was different than the Cynthia he knew, the inflection seemed to be more of a younger person.

"For the most part, from what I remember before becoming this, I was mostly normal. Except for my family. Our line has a long history with Magic and the Occult. I grew up studying magic as a child. Simple things. Nice spells. But I knew the darker aspects my father studied. And being, in retrospect, a typical arrogant teenager, at that point in my previous life, I hated him for withholding that information from me.

"I knew my father's habits well. Before any major summoning he would lock himself away in the study for days, rarely coming out. But he would always emerge, for some reason, to spend the day with me and my Mother and my younger brother. He would eat dinner with us, and get a good night's sleep the day before he would perform any major ceremony."

Cynthia shook her head slightly. "I had been sneaking into the study and reading the books he had forbade for a year and a half. At this particular point in time, after he emerged from the study, I snuck in and recognized the tools, books and such as being necessary to summon something from another dimension. The older dimensions most, even like my father, never tried to access.

"So I made a plan. After all I wanted to impress him. He went to bed early that night, I did also. But I set my alarm for the middle of the night. When I awoke I took some of the charms and protections I had made and went down into the study, hiding myself away. Midday he came into the study and started preparing the spell. The sun set. He was still preparing."

She fell silent, then smiled. "He always talked to himself. It was so hard at times for me not to laugh out loud listening to him mumble about what he needed to do next. Several hours after the sun set he cast the spell. And I could feel it, this thing. I peered over the desk at the back of the room and beheld this black creature that was a mass of tentacles. But it was far darker than black, it was more like a void."

Letting out a long sigh, she said, "I should have known better. The one thing I had not done in my excitement was create a protective circle. Not that it would have helped. When I gazed upon this thing... When I looked at it my mind began to crumble, any semblance of sanity escaped me. In a panic I ran."

She raised her hand from Kyle's chest, holding her index finger and thumb apart.

"One inch. One inch to the right and I would have been out of the room, received a reprimand, probably had some time with a shrink, and would be an old woman with grey hair right now.

"Instead I ended up just inside the circle that restrained the creature. It lashed out and tore my soul from my body before my foot even touched the ground."

Cynthia trailed off and she shivered. She opened her mouth to speak, but did not say anything. The hand that rested on his chest grasped his shirt firmly.

"There are no words to describe what happened to me, the pain that filled me, the empty void that surrounded me and slowly ate away at the core of my being. Human minds are too simple to comprehend a creature as old and powerful as that thing was, and I shattered mentally. There was no time, no space, nothing. But I continued to fight against it, determined to somehow defeat this thing. Eventually I was able to overcome it.

"When I opened my eyes I was in my room, alone. I was still in a state of shock when the nurse came in and saw me sitting up in bed. She screamed down the hall for my father and rushed over to me, leaning over and putting a hand on my shoulder, asking me questions.

"I saw an old man walk in as I raised my hand and placed it on the nurse's arm. As our skin met I felt that darkness in me swell and enter her, drawing the nurse into me. She managed a low moan and fell over dead. I was still confused and looked up at the old man, only to realize that it was my father."

Shaking her head slowly, Cynthia said, "Twenty-six years had passed. My Mother had died several days after the accident when she tried to enter my mind and help me out of the coma. She went insane and killed herself shortly after that. My younger brother had died twelve years later, attempting an experiment he felt would help me."

"That's horrible," said Kyle, who then paused. "Wait, I don't understand, you said it killed you?"

Cynthia nodded her head. "When the creature killed me, my father had contained it, then called upon several powerful mages to help extract my soul from it. None of them had ever attempted to do something like that, and they had no way of knowing that the creature had already begun to assimilate my soul, so part of it was put back into my reanimated body.

"It took a while for me to be able to function in a normal manner. I could not touch people without killing them, had to re-learn how to speak, read, write, walk, eat. When I was functional a few years later, I moved to Germany and studied with some of the elder Hapsburg clan. Eventually I was able to control that part of myself, that darkness. I studied the dark arts, things nobody had studied for centuries or longer, to try and understand this part of me. It was during this time I learned about your kind, actually."

"And that is why you knew what Heather did to me?" he asked.

"Essentially, yes."

Kyle paused, then asked, "Then what happened?"

"After about fourteen years I returned here."

"But when I met you, you were in High School, right?" asked Kyle.

"Of course that is when we met," she said, her hand resting hesitantly upon his chest. "Please understand, after I awoke I had no emotions, they had been... Destroyed, lost, perhaps both. I thought that by being a teenager again I could learn how to talk to people, make friends, attempt to at least act like a normal person. So posing as my own daughter I enrolled in a private school. Became friends with Keiko, then met you some time later."

Cynthia paused a moment, then said, in her normal monotone voice, "Those are the memories I have of that time."

"And here we are," said Kyle raising a hand to massage his left temple, trying to make all the pieces fit in his head without making it hurt more.

He lowered his hand and placed it on hers.

"Thank you," said Kyle.

Cynthia pushed herself up and looked down at him.

"For what?" she asked.

"Being here, helping me," said Kyle "Telling me what happened."

She smiled, then a sad look crossed her face.

"I'm sorry," she said. "When I helped you the first time I did not know that part of me would go into you."

"That was a bit strange, but it's ok," said Kyle. "How could you have known?"

"I shall admit, though," said with a soft smile, "that when I found out it made me a little happy."

She sat up part way and placed both hands on his chest.

For Kyle, the darkness was always present, swirling around in the background of his existence. As she touched him, he became acutely aware of the darkness in her. Then the strangest sensation expanded through him as both seemed to synch and move in the same patterns. Staring into her eyes the definition of Cynthia and Kyle, the line that separated them as two different beings, began to blur.

He felt the dark tendrils enter his chest, while at the same time he felt tendrils from the hands on her arms enter her, and the line blurred even more for a moment.

Cynthia pulled her hands away, clutching them to her chest, moving backward from him.

Sitting up and leaning forward, Kyle put a hand on the bed close to her, making sure not to touch her, even though she visibly moved backward slightly.

"Hey," he said.

She looked away from him.

"It's OK," he said slowly. "What is it you told me? No matter what I am, I am still Kyle. So wouldn't that make you Cynthia still?"

Their eyes met and there was no way that Kyle would ever be able to convey in words the terror, loneliness, fear, and confusion that normally filled the cold and dark pupils he had known for so many years.

"And here I am complaining about having to drink blood," he said, smiling slightly. "Guess I have it easy."

Half a second passed before the look in her eyes returned to normal and she said, "Your attempt at humor is not amusing."

"I know," he said. Reaching forward and pulling her down with him, Kyle said, "Come on, we should sleep."

She nodded her head and curled into him.

Kyle tried closing his eyes, but everything he had received from Cynthia was racing through his system, filling him with more energy than he knew what to do with.

He opened his eyes and stared at the ceiling, waiting for her to fall asleep.

Twenty minutes passed and her breathing still seemed normal. Kyle took a deep breath and closed his eyes again, could not even fathom sleeping right now, and opened them to stare at the ceiling some more.

"Seems you cannot sleep," she whispered.

"Not really," he said.

"Neither can I," she said.

"Too much going on," he said.

Sitting up she placed a hand on his chest, smiling, and asked with a glint in her dark eyes, "Would you like a night cap?"

His eyes opened wide, then he looked to his left at the computer.

"Um, well, I mean, you see," he stammered.

Hitting his chest, she asked, "What is the word you seem to always use for stupid? Baka?"

Cynthia then hopped over him and landed on the floor.

As she walked toward his closet, Kyle watched her. She was

wearing only the T-shirt and something odd struck him.

Cynthia stopped and spun around.

"Of course I have legs," she said in a harsh tone.

Kyle jumped back and slammed his head into the wall.

"No, no, it's just that you always wear long dresses, and, and, it's just…"

He stopped. Even though she stood there scowling at him, she was blushing.

The scowl turned into a glare.

"You need to learn to contain your thoughts better, Kyle."

She spun back around and went to mini bar near the closet. Grabbing a bottle of bourbon she poured a glass and returned to the bed.

"Great, you can hear me think?" he thought to her.

"Only if you are thinking at me," she responded in his head, taking a sip then holding the glass up to him.

He took the glass and shook his head, staring out the doors of the balcony and taking a sip. Uncomfortable, yet not, at the person leaning against him who took the glass from his hand.

Chapter 09.09

Ed sat at a table in a dimly lit bar, staring at his beer. Two men dressed in black came up to the table, one of them kicking a chair into him.

"Bill, Shock," said Ed standing, leaning over and giving each a quick half hug. "Thanks for coming out."

"Hey, we're buds, right?" asked Shock sitting down.

"That and you'll be little use on the tour like this," said Bill.

"Damn, show the man some sympathy," said Shock throwing a pretzel at him.

"So what happened?" asked Bill, ignoring his band mate.

"Bah," said Ed finishing off his beer. "I think something is going on between Cynthia and my best friend."

"You think the Ice Queen is having an affair with Kyle?" asked Shock.

"Hey, I told you not to call her that."

"Well, she is," mumbled Shock.

Julien Giever

"I don't know," said Ed. "I don't know what's going on any-more."

"Want my honest opinion?" asked Bill.

Ed shrugged his shoulders then caught the waitress so they could order a round.

"This is one of those rebound relationships that got way out of hand," said Bill.

"Oi!" said Shock.

Frowning Ed asked, "Why do you say that?"

"Think of how you and Cynthia met," said Bill. "Back when we was in college, that gig got cancelled and you went home to find Cindy in bed with your music instructor. You go all psycho, but then a week later run into this cute dark and spooky High School girl and start dating her."

"So?"

"So," said Bill. "A rebound relationship turned into many, many years. Damn, man, I know she inspires your music, and that's cool, but you two don't seem to have much in common."

"Or talk, or even have physical contact," added Shock.

Ed glared between the two of them.

"Point is," said Bill. "It was nice and safe. You knew she wasn't interested in other guys. Deep down you probably know the two of you aren't right for each other, but you stay with her because you don't have to worry about something bad happening again."

Ed grabbed the new beer that the waitress had just set down and leaned back in his chair, thinking.

"Maybe you're right," said Ed.

"Just do me a favor and think about what I said. Call her up, tell her you need some space or... What's that other excuse chicks use all the time?"

"I need some alone time," said Shock rolling his eyes.

Leaning forward, Ed put his elbows on the table and began to spin his bottle around. Slowly he nodded his head.

On the other side of the partial wall that separated their booths the waitress stopped and asked the young blond woman with blue eyes if she needed anything else.

Pulling out several one hundred dollar bills, the girl said, "I'm set, just make sure they have a good night and a cab ride home. The rest is a tip. Tell them it was from an adoring fan."

Chapter 09.10

Parking the car, Keiko got out and looked up at the trees swaying in the breeze, smiling to herself. She looked back and raised a hand to block the morning sun.

Pulling out her phone she tried to call Kyle again but his phone went straight to voicemail. Sighing she dialed her sister.

A half-asleep voice answered.

"Eh? Keiko, hi," mumbled Kami.

"Hi, sorry I woke you," she said.

"Ugh, it's barely nine here in the states, you getting ready to fly back?"

"Actually I left a day early, am standing in front of the house," said Keiko.

"Oh, I'm not there, over at a friend's," said Kami, yawning loudly. "How was the trip?"

Leaning against her car she said, "Really good. Did a lot of thinking, had some adventures. Took about twenty rolls of film."

"That's good," said Kami. "I'm glad. You sound like yourself again. I was getting worried."

"Sorry, had a rough spot there," said Keiko. "Anyway, think Kyle would be home?"

Kami laughed and said, "Come on. You know him, he never schedules things before ten, especially on the weekends."

"That's right," she said smiling.

"Er, onee-chan?" asked Kami.

"Yes?"

"Can we chat later? I was up late last night and my pillow seems to be calling my name."

"Sure, sorry again for waking you, talk to you later."

"Bai bai," said Kami.

Keiko put the phone back into her coat pocket and walked to the front of the house. Unlocking the door with her keys she crept in, closing it quietly behind her. Tossing her jacket on the coat rack and taking off her shoes she went up the stairs and down the hall to his room.

Knocking lightly on his door, she opened it and walked in.

Kyle was laying on his side in bed, covers pulled up around his shoulders, watching her.

Clapping her hands she said, "Oh, you're awake, good morning, Kyle."

Kyle said, very slowly, "Hello, Keiko."

Walking over to his computer desk she kicked something. Reaching down she grabbed his cell phone and the battery off the floor and sat in the computer chair.

"No wonder it kept going to voice mail," she said putting the battery back and pressing the ON button. The phone lit up and beeped a few times. She leaned back and placed the phone on his desk.

"Um, Keiko, what are you doing here?" asked Kyle slowly.

"Kyle," she said spinning in his chair. "You have no idea. The trip began really crappy, so bad that I left my mom's house in the middle of the night. Then I traveled around, and some really weird stuff happened, and I did a lot of thinking about us and my job and what I want to do with my life."

Standing she ran over to the bed and sat on the edge.

"So come on, I want to take you to breakfast someplace nice and tell you all about it," she said.

Grabbing the covers she pulled them back.

Keiko saw a girl pressed against his back.

Her mouth opened, but she could not manage to say anything.

The girl pushed herself up and looked at her.

Keiko jumped backward and fell off the bed.

Chapter 09.11

As the bus came to a stop Thomas closed the unmarked black book and put it into his backpack. Per Harry's request, Corin had broken up their schedules so that they did not have to work the same hours, and Thomas had the last two days free.

Getting off the bus, he paused, nervous. Last night Harry had told him that Corin found out about the ad and wanted to talk to Thomas. But he would not go into detail.

"Let's do this," he said to himself raising his fist and walking down the road.

He turned and cut through the parking lot of the gas station.

Coming to the sidewalk on the other side he stopped. There were two news vans parked on the road, and a group of about fifteen people holding signs on tall sticks marching in a circle in front of Corin's gate.

As Thomas watched, a couple in their early thirties, dressed rather normal, pushed their way past the group who screamed that the two were spawns of Satan, going to hell, corrupting the youth of America with heavy metal music and other similar sentiments.

Running, Thomas managed to dodge his way through the group before they could notice where he was going. He caught up with the couple.

"Good morning," said Thomas.

"Morning," they said smiling.

Motioning with his hand Thomas asked, "What is all the commotion about?"

The man chuckled and said, "Bunch of zealots saw the ad for this place in the paper and organized a protest, got the media involved."

"Oh, that's not good," said Thomas looking down to the ground.

"Seems to be good for business," said the woman pointing down the driveway.

Looking up he saw a large group of people gathered on the lawn in front of the store sitting on blankets, in chairs, reading, talking with each other. As the three of them approached some of the people looked over and waved hello.

"It was nice chatting with you, but I need to go in," said Thomas raising a hand to wave farewell and running up the stairs.

He entered the shop, the bell ringing as the door opened, and he looked in to see several people browsing through the store.

"Thomas, come here," said Corin.

"Damn," he muttered to himself walking across the room.

"This way," said Corin pointing to the curtains.

Thomas went through.

Corin raised a copy of the LA Weekly and pointed at the large quarter page ad.

"Did you do this?"

Hanging his head, Thomas said, "Yes, sir."

He almost fell over as Corin slapped him on the shoulder.

"Good show, young man," he said. "Did you see all the people? I've already been interviewed by three different news stations and the LA Times. This is so much fun."

"You're not mad?"

"A little," Corin said laughing. "If you had shown me this ad I would have never approved, who knew it would generate such controversy? But Harry needs a break, so you should get out there."

"Sure thing, sir," said Thomas.

"Wait, here."

He handed Thomas a shirt that had in Old English type on the front, "Corin's Occult Shoppe".

"Several of our supporters out front had these made for us."

A smile crossed Thomas' face as he looked at the shirt.

Chapter 09.12

"I'm confused," said Keiko looking at the two of them.

Sitting up in bed Cynthia said, "That seems to be going around lately."

"This isn't what you think," said Kyle raising both hands.

"I don't know what to think," said Keiko sitting on the floor where she had landed. "Because I know that Cynthia has never even slept in the same bed with Ed, so this is... Strange. I was only gone a couple weeks, what the hell happened?"

Kyle looked over at Cynthia and their eyes locked.

"Never?" he thought to her.

"That is correct," she thought back.

"Wow, really? Oh, crap, what do we do?"

"Has Heather taught you how to manipulate people's minds?"

"No, we haven't gotten to that yet," he thought.

"How far back can it go?"

"Only short term memory as far as I know. What are we going to tell her?"

"I am unsure."

"You two are really creeping me out," said Keiko.

Kyle realized that even though he was just talking to Cynthia mentally, he had been using hand gestures as if talking out loud. Dropping his hands into his lap he let out a nervous laugh.

"Well, it's not like we're having an affair or anything," he said. "She just, last night, well, ah..."

Cynthia dropped her head and said quietly, "I am sorry, Keiko."

"What?" asked Keiko and Kyle at the same time.

Looking up into her friend's eyes, Cynthia said, "I knew how you felt about him, but over the last several weeks Kyle and I have been working together on some things. And we became closer. I am sorry if I have hurt you."

"What feelings?" asked Kyle.

Keiko stood and looked at the two of them as she unconsciously reached up and touched the charm around her neck. She thought about the decisions she had made. If she was wrong about Kyle, was she also wrong about her career?

She turned slightly as if she was going to leave, but did not move.

"Keiko, you OK?" he asked getting out of bed.

Looking over she saw Kyle standing a few feet away, Cynthia was just behind. Keiko leaned her head slightly and noticed something she had never seen before.

Taking several steps back Keiko looked between the two of them.

"I..." began Keiko. "I'm going to be downstairs in my room."

Kyle began to say something but stopped as Cynthia grabbed his hand.

Keiko's eyes opened wide when she saw that. Bowing slightly, she turned and left the room.

PASSING JUDGEMENT

Chapter 10.01

Caitlin and Walter appeared twenty feet away from a cabin in the woods.

He turned around and looked across the foothills to the cities of Los Angeles County in the distance and let out a whistle.

"I imagine that is a beautiful view at night," he said.

"Come on," said Caitlin walking toward the front door.

The inside of the cabin was one large room with a loft at the back above a kitchen. There was no furniture, no pictures, just a wide empty space.

"Might you have just purchased this place?" he asked.

"Yes, about ten years ago," she said.

"So what is the plan, Mon Capitan?"

Caitlin raised her wrist and checked the time.

"Heather should be meeting with Kyle soon," she said. "But I know that she has to go to her gallery early this afternoon. When they are finished I want you to be at the front gates of his house, stop him and bring that abomination here. Once you have delivered him go back to your family, I do not want you involved any further than that."

Walter let out a short laugh and said, "Always the woman with the plan."

"Somebody has to watch out for our family, and it sure as hell is not my sister," she said, scowling at the last word.

"But, please do tell, what will happen if the Council gets involved? I understand I am indebted to you to assist, but I do have a family to take care of."

"Walter," she said smiling and grabbing his elbow. "I understand your concern. That is why I have not told you anything that I am planning after that abomination arrives. Worst case scenario, you were doing a favor for a friend with no idea what was going to happen.

"But," she said smiling. "Best case scenario, all of this is quickly forgotten."

"Very well then, I am yours to command."

"Thank you, Walter," said Caitlin. "I think that you should go and walk through the woods for the next hour and a half so that I may prepare things here."

"Well in that case I think I shall pop over to Beverly Hills for some breakfast, have not been here in a while," he said, bowing slightly and then fading from the room.

She gritted her teeth and slowly walked around the cabin for a bit, pulling out a compass to determine true north.

Going to the back of the cabin, Caitlin opened up a suitcase and stared at the contents. Grimacing slightly she took the sheets of paper and began to review them. Setting the papers on the kitchen counter she began to pull vials and bags from the suitcase, muttering underneath her breath how much she hated magic.

Chapter 10.02

As the door closed, Kyle took a step forward but felt a hand pull him back.

"She is not running away," said Cynthia. "She is going to her room."

He looked over at her and asked, "What were you talking about a minute ago?"

"What do you mean?" she asked letting go of his hand and taking a step back.

"You mentioned something about her feelings toward me."

Cynthia did not say anything. She stared down at the floor, then turned around and began to inspect the contents of the bookshelf before her.

"Don't give me that silent routine," he said walking up to her. "What were you talking about?"

"That is something the two of you should discuss," said Cynthia barely above a whisper as she clasped her hands firmly. "Please do not involve me in that."

She heard him take a couple steps away.

"What the hell?" he said loudly. "What the hell?"

Cynthia looked over her shoulder to see Kyle staring at her.

"Not only do I have all this psychotic stuff going on in my life, things that are seriously pushing my concepts of reality and grips on sanity to their limits, but then... Then there's us, and I'm still trying to figure out these feelings I have for you. And now, to add fuel to the fire there's talk that Keiko has feelings toward me. The girl I have been longing after for almost six years has some kind of feelings about me and you won't say a god damned word."

"Let us not forget about Janice," said Cynthia.

"Argh!" he screamed throwing his hands into the air. "Yes, then there is Janice."

He spun around and his motions became even more animated as he paced back and forth.

"You know, there is this line. I don't know where it is, but it has been crossed. This is far beyond my call of duty and I am going back to bed. I can't take this any more. I am going back to bed and I am going to sleep and then I'll wake up from this surreal dream and I'll be some nobody computer geek sitting at his computer playing games wishing he had an interesting life."

"But, Kyle, your meeting," said Cynthia.

"No buts, going to sleep," he said raising a finger, and then jumping into bed, pulled the covers up over him.

She stood there and watched him.

Ten minutes later he was snoring.

Cynthia started laughing, pulling a hand over her mouth to quiet the sound. Reaching over, she grabbed a book and walked to the bed, picking up her phone and setting the alarm so she could wake him in time for his meeting.

Climbing over Kyle she sat down and positioned the pillow against the wall. Looking down at the snoring figure she pushed him onto his side. The snoring subsided.

Opening the book she began to read.

Finishing the first page, she turned it and began the second.

Half way down the page she stopped and looked at the person sleeping next to her, as a sad frown pulled at her face and she closed the book. Pulling away from him Cynthia shook her head and got out of bed, walking around it while tearing off the shirt she had slept in.

Quickly she got dressed, put the book and shirt away, then

grabbed her phone off the nightstand. Crossing the room slowly, she came to the doors of the balcony and leaned down to pick up the gloves off the floor, putting them on.

Walking over to the bed she picked up her choker, and slowly tied it around her neck.

At the door to his room she looked back for a moment before leaving.

Cynthia was sitting in the study, reading, when the alarm on her phone sounded. She went upstairs and sat on the edge of his bed, hands folded in her lap.

"Kyle," she said. "Kyle, it is time to get up."

Slowly he opened his eyes, blinked a few times and sat up in bed.

Standing, she took a few steps away.

"Sorry about earlier," said Kyle.

"It is understandable," she said, staring over his shoulder. "You have many things going on in your life at this point in time."

Throwing the covers to the side he swung his legs over the edge of the bed and stood, stretching and yawning.

"Thank you for waking me up," he said dropping his arms and smiling at her.

As he began to approach her, Cynthia took a step back. Kyle stopped and a look of concern crossed his face.

"What's wrong?" he asked.

"You should get ready," she said turning around.

Kyle watched her leave the room, closing the door behind her.

Chapter 10.03

"So, Emma, you ready for the show?" asked Heather pouring two glasses of white wine. She handed one to the young woman sitting on the sofa.

"Thank you," said Emma taking the glass and raising it. "I'm nervous, freaked out of my gourd, but here's to a good show."

Clinking their glasses together the two sipped their wine before Heather sat down.

"I'm still not sure about putting Hazy Yesterdays into the show," said Emma. "It doesn't really fit with the rest of my work."

"Worry yourself not," said Heather. "Though what you say is true, it does evoke more forcefully the emotions that are subtle in your other work. I am going to have it set by itself, still part of the show, but separate enough. All shall be fine."

"If you say so," said Emma twirling her wine glass nervously. "You're the expert."

"Indeed I am," said Heather. "Now, we have already reviewed the schedule. Have you decided what you are going to wear."

"Well…" Emma began.

A beeping noise sounded from the front door, letting her know somebody was at the front gate.

"Ah, that would be the Computer God," said Heather smiling and standing.

"You want me to leave?" asked Emma.

"No, no. Stay here. We are almost finished and he's a nice lad."

"Alright," she said.

Heather looked into Emma's eyes, and the girl became completely still. Waving a hand in front of the girls face produced no response, satisfied Heather went to the front door and opened it, pressing the button to open the gate.

A few minutes later Kyle stepped in and gave Heather a brief hug.

"You know," he said. "You really have to teach me that teleporting thing. You have no idea how much gas I've been burning lately coming down every day."

"That will take a while, unfortunately," Heather said closing the door and patting him on the shoulder. "It can take years to build up enough power to be able to move from place to place like that."

"Damn. So what wonderful lectures will you be imparting on me today?"

Laughing she said, "Sorry, Kyle, but knowing the history and laws of our kind is very important. Today we shall take a break and do some field work."

"Field work?" he asked.

"Follow me," said Heather leading them through the house to the living room.

Kyle glanced at Heather, seeing the unmoving girl sitting on the couch.

"Today," said Heather, "we shall practice mesmerizing."

She grabbed a pillow from the couch and threw it at Emma. It bounced off her head and landed on the floor, but the young woman did not move.

Picking up the pillow, Heather put it back.

"Normally I would show you by actually mesmerizing you, so that you could get a feel for what was happening. Unfortunately your mind is so locked shut I can barely detect it."

"Um, sorry," said Kyle, worried that Heather might discover the shield that Cynthia had taught him to build around his mind.

"Not your fault," she said. "Probably genetic. Remember, your Grandfather ended up with your Grandmother because he could not affect her mind."

"That's true," he said smiling.

"So what I need you to do is try to sense what I am doing to her. Worry yourself not about messing up or anything, I can go back and make her forget when we are done."

"I can try," he said.

"Very well then, let us begin. Stand near the entry there."

Kyle took a few steps back.

Heather stood before Emma and looked into her eyes. The young woman blinked.

"Emma, this is Kyle," said Heather raising a hand toward him.

Looking over and seeing Kyle, she shook her head slightly while standing and extending her hand.

"Sorry, must have spaced out there. Big show today. I'm Emma."

Shaking her hand he said, "I'm Kyle."

"Kyle here is the person who keeps my computer running and is teaching me how to use it."

"Wow," she said. "Good luck, I can barely get my email."

Heather caught his eye and nodded slightly.

"So, Emma," said Heather.

She looked over at the Irish woman.

Kyle focused his mind and tried to remember some of the things Cynthia had taught him several days ago. Her intent had been so that he could detect when people were trying to manipulate his mind, but he guessed it might help in learning how to do so also.

As the two woman's eyes met Kyle could sense the energy leaving Heather and entering Emma, and the changes in the young woman's brain that the energy created.

"We have about an hour to practice," said Heather. "Also, as I mentioned, she will not remember. So we shall sit, and you can engage her in conversation and practice for today."

"I understand," said Kyle.

He paid attention as Heather released Emma.

"Why do you not tell Kyle about your show?"

She blushed slightly and looked at Kyle.

He reached out and tried to emulate what Heather had done.

Emma seemed to lose her thought for a second and then said, "This is actually my first show..."

Kyle tried again as he made eye contact. In a way this reminded him of hacking a computer system, except in this case it was a person's mind. He tried not to worry about the moral issues that involved and concentrated again.

Her brows furrowed and she paused, looking away. "My first show. Well, at a gallery, I had several small exhibits when I was in college."

"Where did you go?" asked Kyle.

Their eyes met again. Modifying the hack a third time she suddenly became still.

Kyle leaned his head to the side, then reached out and tapped her forehead. No response.

"Hey, cool," he said.

"How did you do that?" asked Heather with a look of confusion on her face.

"Like you showed me," said Kyle.

"But in three tries?" she asked. "It usually takes days to learn how to do that properly."

"Huh, guess I'm a fast learner," said Kyle.

Heather regarded him for a moment, then said, "See if you can release her. If so, excuse yourself and go upstairs making a reason to fix my computer or something."

"OK," he said.

Looking back into her eyes she blinked.

"USC," said Emma.

"Nice school," said Kyle. "But, if you will excuse me, I have to go check out Heather's computer. It was a pleasure to meet you Emma. I hope you have a good show."

As they shook hands, she smiled and seemed mildly confused.

"Thank you, nice to meet you too."

Chapter 10.04

Cynthia closed the doors to the study, locking them, and turned around. She stood there a minute before slowly walking down the hallway, passing the entry to the living room, and finally stopping at the last door on her left.

She stared at the door a few minutes before raising a hand and knocking lightly.

The door opened.

"Cynthia," said Keiko.

"May we talk?" asked Cynthia.

Pausing a second, Keiko let go of the door handle and stepped back.

"Come in," she said.

Cynthia stepped forward, closing the door behind her.

In one hand, Keiko had a spray bottle of cleaner, in the other was a paper towel.

"The only time you are inspired to clean is when you have much to think about," said Cynthia in a quiet voice.

"After the trip and this morning, that's an understatement," said Keiko. "Sorry, please have a seat."

Walking over to the short Japanese table Cynthia sat upon the pillow on the floor and arranged her dress around her. Keiko set the spray bottle and paper towel on the desk and then sat on the floor opposite Keiko.

"I wanted to apologize again for this morning," said Cynthia.

Keiko regarded her friend a moment, then said, "You know, I did a lot of thinking about my life, my career, my feelings for Kyle when I was in Japan. I was actually going to confess to him today."

She noticed Cynthia tense visibly at the last sentence, and thought she saw tears begin to form in her eyes.

"Keiko," said Cynthia. "The few friends I have are precious to me, and I will not betray them. I know how you feel about Kyle. I wish the two of you the best."

"What are you saying?" asked Keiko.

Lowering her head, Cynthia said in a subdued voice, "I will not stand in your way."

Keiko said nothing for a minute, but only stared at her.

"I should be really mad at you right now, you knew how I felt about Kyle all these years, but I could never do anything because of that promise to my Mother. While in Japan I talked to her, and she released me from that promise."

"That is good to hear."

"Thing is, when I left his bedroom I was furious at the both of you. Then I started thinking. Yes I have these feelings, but I have been stringing Kyle along for all of these years, making him my pseudo boyfriend, but never making it real. Never committing. Knowing how he felt about me and using that to comfort myself when it was convenient for me."

Keiko trailed off. Reaching behind her she grabbed her soda and took a drink.

"I have known you over eight years. You never get close to people, and you never touch anybody. Even in all of these years dating Ed, I have never once seen you touch him. He has touched you, reached out to hold your hand, hugged you. But you never initiate contact."

"That is true," said Cynthia staring at the table.

"Then this morning I find you in bed hiding behind Kyle, pressed against his back. Right before I left, you were not just standing behind him, you were leaning against him, and then when he went to stop me you grabbed his hand."

"This is true also," said Cynthia.

"And I don't know what has been going on lately. That thing on the bed, when it looked like you two were talking but not saying anything was down right disturbing."

"I am sorry for that."

Keiko reached up and pulled out the charm around her neck, playing with it.

"Walking in like that was incredibly bad timing, but I think it showed me something," said Keiko, the words of Iizuka echoing in her head, as her heart struggled against the idea of losing her past, especially Kyle.

Cynthia did not say anything, she remained motionless.

"How do you feel about Kyle?" asked Keiko.

"That is irrelevant," said Cynthia. "As I said, you and Kyle can be together."

"Cynthia," she said. "I want to know. How do you feel about Kyle?"

Raising her head slightly Cynthia had a distant look in her eye as she thought about the night before, and the feelings she had this morning waking up in Kyle's arms. Because of what she was, being with another person like that had been relegated to her list of things that she would never be able to experience.

Smiling slightly, she said, "I feel... Happy with Kyle."

Keiko slowly placed the can on the table.

"Happy?"

Keiko did not move, she was staring at the wall beyond her friend.

"Unfortunately that would be correct."

Regaining focus, Keiko looked at her.

"Cynthia?"

"Yes?"

Keiko folded her hands in her lap and bowed her head slightly, then said, "I wish the two of you luck. I will not stand in your way."

Chapter 10.05

Kyle began to turn into his driveway and slammed on his brakes. A man in a suit was standing in front of the gates waving his arms. The man stepped aside and Kyle pulled up, pressing the button to roll down his window.

"Kyle, correct?" asked the man.

"Yes," said Kyle cautiously.

Holding up a hand in greeting, the man said, "Good afternoon, I am Walter. I apologize for intruding upon your day, but Heather sent me to get you. She indicated that there was something else she wanted to talk about before the show."

Shaking his hand quickly through the window, Kyle said, "Sure, no problem, where is she?"

"Actually, I can take us there immediately," said Walter.

"Alright, hop in and let me park," said Kyle.

Walter ran around the car and jumped into the passenger's seat.

Kyle opened the gates and drove up to the house, parking in the garage. As they were walking out he hit the button to close the garage door.

"Shall we then?" asked Walter.

Kyle nodded his head and Walter placed both hands on his shoulders.

Everything around them faded and moved away in a quick blur. A second later Kyle found himself standing in the foothills near a cabin.

Releasing Kyle, Walter said, "Heather is awaiting you in the cabin."

"In there?" asked Kyle.

"Yes, just let yourself in," said Walter.

Kyle turned to thank him, but Walter was nowhere to be seen.

Walking to the front door he opened it. There was a girl standing in the middle of the room. He entered the cabin and closed the door behind him.

He recognized her, from when he was in the bath tub, she had been standing near the door in Heather's bathroom.

"You are Heather's sister, correct?" he asked.

"Yes I am," she said. "I am Caitlin McClellan."

"A pleasure to meet you," he said walking toward her. "I am here to see Heather."

"She is not here," Caitlin said.

Kyle reached out with his mind and could only detect the girl before him, everything past the walls of the cabin became a blur. Heather was not here.

"When will she arrive?" he asked.

"Actually she shall not," said Caitlin. "A small change in plans."

"How do you mean?"

"This is not a meeting with Heather," she said smiling. "This is my challenge to your birthright."

"What?" asked Kyle.

"Oh, yes, I forgot," she said placing her hands behind her back and walking away from him. "You are being taught my half-wit sister."

"Heather?"

"Oh, the Human who wants to be one of us is brighter than I thought," she said clapping her hands gleefully. "I am impressed."

Kyle became nervous. Something was not right here.

"Asking one to prove their birthright is something that is not practiced much these days," she said. "Because most of my kind's laws and such render such formalities rather unnecessary. But it is still on the books, so I have the right to invoke it."

"What the hell are you talking about?" asked Kyle taking several steps back toward the door.

"Simply this," she said glaring at him. "I lost my brother because of that bitch Human Grandmother of yours, and you have no right to be one of us. So I am going to end this right now, and preserve what little respect my brother's name once had."

Kyle turned and ran toward the door. Caitlin appeared in front of it and leaned back. She reached up and turned the deadbolt of the lock.

"See, my brother told me he would never fall in love with a Human," said Caitlin. "Then he did, and because of that he died. And this day, I shall teach a pathetic half-breed his place in this world. Which is nowhere."

Faster than Kyle could see, Caitlin moved forward and hit him in the chest. He flew across the length of the cabin and slammed into the kitchen. He felt many parts of his body surrounded by warmth, then numbness, then Kyle felt normal again.

He reached out with his mind to try and find Cynthia, but again he found something blocking it.

Letting out a low laugh, Caitlin said, "I will not allow something as pathetic as you stain our family name."

Kyle stood and prepared himself.

Chapter 10.06

Cynthia did not move.

Keiko watched her friend, but after several minutes became concerned. Standing she walked around the table and sat on the floor, grabbing Cynthia's shoulders.

"Cynthia?"

The always dark eyes hesitantly looked up into hers.

"Are you saying that I can... That Kyle and I might... That I may be able to..."

Her voice drifted.

"Yes," said Keiko.

Keiko paused, then said, "I think, to have a good relationship, requires honesty. And I have been far from honest with him, with how I have used him. But I saw his reaction to you, when you grabbed his hand. I don't think I could ever get that response from him, no matter what I said, or did."

Cynthia pulled back slightly.

"Keiko, I do not want you to hate me," she said.

"Cyn, I meant what I said."

Cynthia raised her hands to her chest, then bowed her head. Placing a hand upon Keiko's she said, "I do not know how to thank you."

Keiko paused, in shock, and said "Um, just take care of him."

"Are you sure?"

"No, of course not, dummy," said Keiko. "But really, don't make me think twice about this."

Cynthia did not move for over a minute, because something felt wrong. Then Cynthia let go of Keiko's hand and nodded her head slowly, saying, "Thank you. I will take my leave now."

"What? Oh, OK."

At the door Cynthia turned and said, "I would like to hear about your travels, and what you are thinking, when you are ready."

Keiko nodded her head.

Leaving the room Cynthia walked down the hallway. She suddenly felt this sickness in her stomach and a disturbance that rippled through the core of her being. Stumbling, she held out a hand to the wall to regain her balance.

Something was wrong.

She reached out with her mind, trying to find Kyle. Nothing.

Closing her eyes she concentrated harder and was barely able to pick up a faint whisper of his being, but she could tell that there was a spell blocking it. Running down the hall and into the study she started grabbing supplies. The spell was not that strong, but it would still take her a few minutes to make the preparations to break it.

Another shock of pain hit her, and she felt the darkness within her begin to undulate.

Chapter 10.07

Concentrating, Kyle formed a shield around him like Cynthia had taught. It helped to lessen the impact of the blows that came at him faster than he could follow. Caitlin was incredibly fast, her moves a blur. She would be attacking him and then suddenly be standing someplace else.

"You're more powerful that I would have expected," said Caitlin jumping back twenty feet and regarding him. "But that just means I get to have more fun playing with you."

"Please, stop," said Kyle breathing heavily. He was having a difficult time healing the injuries she kept inflicting.

"Oh, and give me one good reason why I should."

"Do you think your brother would want this?"

Her eyes became slits and both hands became fists.

"Dare you to speak his name," she hissed. "You insolent bastard."

Caitlin was suddenly standing in front of him and grabbed his right wrist. In a quick move she raised his arm, while her free hand became a blur as it moved up, then she jumped back to where she had been standing.

The pain that struck him caused Kyle to fall to his knees. He reached up with his left hand and grabbed the stump where his arm had been. The darkness inside him began to undulate, expanding, and Kyle fought to keep it from consuming his mind.

"That's a pretty nasty wound," said Caitlin holding up his arm and waving it around. "Here's a pop quiz for you. How long does it take my kind to heal from a wound like that?"

Kyle leaned forward, holding himself up with his left hand, breathing heavily. Everything was becoming darker, his vision was beginning to become clouded.

"The answer would be one week," she said.

Almost everything was black for him, but he could still sense his surrounding somehow. His mind was barely in control now, it felt more like he was remote controlling his body from a distance in a very dark night without stars.

Caitlin began to speak, but felt the arm she was holding move.

Looking down she watched as it slowly evaporated in a dark mist until all she was holding was the sleeve of his shirt.

"What the?" she asked looking up at Kyle.

From his shoulder misty black tentacles emerged quickly, writhing over each other, expanding to form the shape of his arm. They solidified and the darkness faded, leaving only the bare skin.

"How?' she asked, stepping backward. "That is not possible."

He stood and looked at her and Caitlin almost fell to the ground.

His eyes were solid black.

"No!" she screamed. "This ends now."

She rushed forward and began a barrage of attacks.

Kyle was struggling to not be overcome with the darkness. Yet with it he was able to move faster than Caitlin, blocking every attack, and what few did hit him had no effect on his body.

She jumped away from him again and a thought entered his mind. Almost all of Caitlin's attacks were with her hands. He felt a welling of power inside him, then two dark tendrils shot from his hands, across the room, wrapping around her arms and constricting suddenly. The tendrils had returned to his body before her two arms hit the floor.

He felt the barrier that surrounded the house dissolve and he could sense everything beyond again. Something tried to push its way into his mind but he could not reach it.

Kyle had no control of his body now as he watched from a dark distance, his body moving of its own accord, the darkness wanting nothing more than to consume the individual before him. His body walked over to Caitlin who lay on the floor trembling, and he watched as he knelt down and placed his hands on her chest. The tendrils extended into her, and began to pull her power, her very being into him, absorbing everything.

She screamed in agony.

More of Caitlin flowed into him, he could sense her soul weakening, and yet there was a part of him, the darkness, that felt satiated by this.

Something pushed at the back of his mind again. This time harder. He felt a presence.

"Kyle! Stop!" came Cynthia's scream in his head.

He fought to control his body and managed to make the hands pull away from Caitlin. Struggling more he made himself stand.

He needed to get to Cynthia. She would be able to help him. He knew she was in the study, and wanted to go there. It suddenly occurred to him that he knew how to move himself there and everything around him faded away to be replaced with the sight of the inside of the study. Cynthia was standing near a table ten feet away.

He tried to take a step forward, but the darkness finally consumed him, and everything became black.

Chapter 10.08

Reaching out with her mind, Cynthia could sense that everybody in the house was asleep. Standing from the chair she walked through the study and up the stairs to Kyle's room. Inside she closed the door and went to the bed, sitting and placing a hand where he should have been sleeping this evening.

The hand became a fist.

From his closet she pulled out a large suitcase and set it on the floor next to his dresser. Going through the drawers Cynthia began packing his suitcase. When she came across the shirt she had worn the night before she paused and held it to her chest, closing her eyes. Setting it on the floor she finished packing the suitcase and slowly closed it.

In the bathroom she packed a travel bag with Kyle's toothbrush, shampoo, electric razor, and other necessities. When she was finished she turned off the light to the bathroom and placed the travel bag and suitcase near his door.

At his computer desk she unplugged his notebook computer and packed it along with all its cables and other supplies in the metal briefcase. Closing it she set it on the floor next to her and grabbed the mouse of his computer.

Starting a new email she placed her fingers on the keyboard and closed her eyes again, then began typing.

```
From:  Kyle
To:  Keiko; Kami; Cynthia; Ed; Thomas; JaniceA
Subject:  Unexpected Job

Hi everyone.  Hope you're well.

I know this is last minute, but I just had the
chance handed to me to fly to Ireland and do a
pretty big job.  Not sure how long I'll be,
maybe a week or two.  Am catching the red-eye
tonight.

I'll be in touch.

Take care!!!

--Kyle
```

Cynthia moved the mouse cursor and clicked on the send button. After she verified it had been sent she shut the computer down.

As she was walking to the door she saw the shirt on the floor. Picking it up, she put it in with the notebook, then grabbed the suitcase and travel bag. Double-checking everyone was still asleep Cynthia went downstairs and out into the night.

Opening the garage door she pressed the button on the remote and placed the bags into Kyle's car. Getting in she started the engine. A sad smile crossed her face as the theme song from one of Kyle's favorite anime series started playing, and she reached up, turning off the stereo.

Cynthia drove to the freeway and headed south.

Twenty-two minutes later she pulled up to the gates of Heather's house. The Irish woman was standing next to her open garage when Cynthia pulled up. Parking the car in the garage she got out and retrieved the metal briefcase from the back.

The garage door closed and Cynthia looked up at the moon which was ringed with a rainbow.

Heather began to speak, but stopped when Cynthia shot her a glance.

Nodding, Heather walked up to her and placed both hands on her shoulders. The two of them faded and reappeared near the front of Kyle's house.

Cynthia turned to walk back to the house, then stopped.

"Heather," she said in a coarse whisper. "Are you a religious person?"

"No," came the reply.

"Neither am I," said Cynthia. "But may I offer one piece of advise?"

"What?"

"If Kyle does not return soon, pray for the soul of your sister."

Heather did not say anything. A few seconds later she faded away.

Cynthia opened the front door and stepped inside. Walking back to the study she opened the metal briefcase and pulled out the black T-shirt. Closing the case she hid it away.

She began to tremble as she held the shirt. Clenching her hands into fists she forced herself to calm down and began to disrobe. Putting on the T-shirt she left the pile of clothes on the floor and walked slowly through the study to the center.

The coffee table had been removed.

In its place was a futon on the floor with Kyle's comatose body lying upon it. She stopped at the edge of the shield that surrounded the area, protecting Kyle from being detected by others. Cynthia raised a hand and created an opening for her to pass through. It closed behind her.

Lying down she placed her head upon his chest and held him tight, fear tearing her apart, knowing where he was and what he was going through.

TIME PASSES

Chapter 11.01

Keiko stepped out onto the patio and squinted against the morning light filling the valley beyond. Walking over to the table she stopped.

"Mind if I join you?" asked Keiko.

"Please, have a seat," said Cynthia.

"When did you start sitting out here?" asked Keiko setting her coffee cup on the table and sitting down. "You were never much of a fan of daylight."

"Recently."

"Did you see the email?" Keiko asked.

Cynthia dropped her head slightly, then nodded.

"Sounds like a cool job," said Keiko. "You see him before he left?"

"Yes, he came in to tell me the details, then said a brief goodbye."

"Oh, good, I'm glad you got to see him before he left," said Keiko. "Hey, want to hear about what happened to me in Japan?"

Her friend nodded her head. Then they heard the sound of a phone ringing.

Cynthia pulled out her phone and said, "Hello."

She nodded her head and said, "Yes."

There was a long pause, then Cynthia said, "That is probably for the best. Have a safe trip."

Ending the call, she put the phone away.

"It would seem," said Cynthia, "that I am now single."

"What?" asked Keiko.

"Ed has effectively terminated our relationship."

"Why?"

"He saw Kyle and myself come out of the study after talking all night. That seems to have made him consider the fact Ed and myself do not have an actual relationship."

"Sorry to hear," said Keiko. Then with a note of happiness in her voice she said, "But then that means you and Kyle can be together."

Cynthia looked down at the ground and said, "I suppose that could happen. But you were about to tell me about your travels."

Nodding her head, Keiko took her coffee and began to tell Cynthia about the desperation she had been feeling lately, leaving her Mother's house in the middle of the night and traveling around the country, the encounter with the fox spirit, then her travels with Noriyuki and the charm he had on his wrist, ending with Keiko talking to her Mother.

"A fox spirit?"

"As far as I could tell," said Keiko. "You ever hear of those things?"

"I have read about them in your country. In some stories they help people, in others they trick them."

"Which leads me to my problem," said Keiko.

"How so?"

"Well," said Keiko pausing. "Confessing to Kyle was wrong, so I am doubting my decisions regarding my career."

Cynthia looked over and said, "If you had not made the decision to confess, you would not have come into his room yesterday morning. By doing so you realized what you had been doing to him all these years and you let him go so he could live his own life. It may not be what you wanted to happen, but there was more than just you and your wants involved."

Keiko's shoulders slouched and she took a sip from the cup.

"Ouch, that hurts," she said. "But it's true."

"With that release, that means you can live your life also. All of these events would indicate to me a helpful spirit. In that case, your conclusions regarding your career are probably the best for you."

"Maybe you're right," said Keiko.

"If you choose that path," said Cynthia, "May I offer some advise?"

"Sure."

"Sell your house and move in here. It is not good to be alone, and you have made that house of yours a place to avoid people and life. Here there are friends and family who could support you through your transition."

Keiko pondered her words for a long time.

"Thank you, Cynthia."

"It is good that I was able to help."

Smiling Keiko stood and grabbed her empty cup.

"I'm heading back inside," she said.

"Have a pleasant morning," said Cynthia.

"I think I will," said Keiko. "Oh, and if you talk to Kyle, tell him I said hello."

"I shall," said Cynthia.

She listened to Keiko walk away and enter the house.

Fighting as much as she could, Cynthia failed and wiped the tears from her eyes with the end of the black silk scarf that was wrapped around her neck.

Chapter 11.02

Thomas closed the cash register and handed the customer their change, then wished them a good day.

A woman came to the counter and placed upon it a bag of mixed ingredients for a success spell, two bottles of scented oil, one for power and one for communication, and a book about using magick to attract a successful mate.

"Do you work here?" she asked with a touch of a New York accent.

"No," said Thomas. "Actually I work for the British Secret Service fighting the forces of evil, I just use this as a cover."

She started laughing.

"Sorry," she said. "Ask a stupid question, you know?"

Thomas nodded and began to type numbers into the cash register.

"By the way, saw your ad, that was just incredible," she said. "And the amount of press it got, very impressive."

"Impressive?"

"Yes, the ad," she said.

"Thank you," said Thomas. "I took a chance when I made it, but the ad seems to have worked quite well."

"You made that ad? Well, just so you know, I have a friend who runs an Ad Agency and she has it hanging on their Bulletin Board O' Inspiration," said the woman.

"I am honored," said Thomas smiling.

"Are you going to school for that?"

"Advertising? No," said Thomas. "Actually I finished school last year. Bachelor of Fine Arts."

"Impressive," said the woman.

"Not really," he said sighing. "The only job that qualifies me for is working at a museum."

The woman laughed and said, "Sad but true. Are you interested in advertising?"

"Ah, my friend," said Thomas holding out both arms. "I enjoy any form of creativity."

"Here then," she said opening her purse. "This is my friend's card. They don't have any openings right now, but as summer nears they usually start losing their college interns. And she mentioned that they might be looking for somebody new, so who knows?"

"Thank you," said Thomas taking the card. "Thank you very much. I am most sorry, I have not even introduced myself. I am Dunne, Thomas Dunne."

"Susan," she said taking his hand and shaking it.

After she had paid and left Thomas took the card and stared at it. A wide grin crossed his face and he raised both hands into the air.

"And so the path to greatness begins," he declared.

The two customers in the store turned and stared at him.

"Sorry, sorry, please continue shopping," she said dropping his arms.

He grabbed the phone and dialed the number. Best to make introductions now, while the ad was fresh in her mind, and set himself at the top of the roster for future interns.

Chapter 11.03

Kyle simply was. Or at least he thought he was. It was hard to tell, because of the endless void that surrounded him.

At first it had been pain. Such incredibly, massive amounts of pain that he had lost all pretext of himself. Eventually he had come to accept the darkness around him, and over time began to think that this vast nothingness was simply himself. Which was strange, because there seemed to be no time that he could tell. He was unsure what time was now that he thought about it.

He was Kyle, perhaps, but he was unsure why a vast expanse of darkness would be called Kyle. It seemed that he should have some memories, he was unsure why. When he went to look for these memories he found only more darkness. This was confusing.

The first time he felt the presence Kyle had become overwhelmed with fear and avoided it. There was only the darkness, so if something else was out there, that was probably not good, because he could sense that it was looking for him. The disturbance of the void caused pain and he did not like it and hid from this thing that was looking for him, hoping it would go away and let him be at peace.

After several more appearances, Kyle became intrigued by this thing that floated around the darkness looking for him. He was unsure what it was, but that presence was always looking for Kyle.

This last time the presence had done something different. It made pictures. There were a series of images of these two light colored creatures with four appendages and heads. These two people were shown sitting at a table, lying in bed, holding hands.

These images seemed vaguely familiar in a way that completely juxtaposed his current existence. But after the presence had left he became obsessed with the idea of memories and futilely sought them out.

Why did those images of those people bother him? Then he wondered what people were and how did he know that they were indeed people. He began to experience pain again, intense feelings of ripping and tearing in what he thought Kyle was. Settling back into the darkness the pain subsided.

Chapter 11.04

Letting out a scream, Caitlin opened her eyes. She stared at the white ceiling, then tried to push herself up and failed. Just outside she heard the sounds of the ocean.

Heather ran into the room and helped her sister sit up.

"Are you alright?" asked Heather.

"I have no arms, what do you think?" asked Caitlin.

"Good lord," said Heather inspecting her sister. "I have never seen you look this bad before. Here."

Sitting behind her sister, Heather pulled Caitlin back and offered her wrist. Caitlin closed her eyes and took the offer, drinking for a long time until Heather finally pulled her arm away.

"I still feel weak," said Caitlin.

"What the hell happened?" asked Heather holding her sibling close with both arms.

"I tried to kill that abomination," said Caitlin.

Heather pulled away and stood from the bed.

"You tried to kill Kyle?" she asked frantically. "Why?"

"To preserve the legacy of my dead brother."

"Then why did you help me Awaken him?"

"Because I did not expect Kyle to survive. But there is a much larger problem."

"What?" asked Heather.

"He is not one of us."

"Caitlin, I know you hate Jeoffrey for choosing to become mortal and marry a Human, but Kyle is still blood. He is Awakened now, so is one of us."

"You do not understand, you simpleton," said Caitlin leaning slightly. Waving her stumps in the air she lost her balance and fell forward.

Rolling onto her back Caitlin said, "He is not one of us. He did things our kind cannot do. I tore off his arm and he regenerated it immediately. His eyes were solid black. He was much more powerful than me."

"Have you considered Cynthia?" asked Heather. "She may have cast protective spells on Kyle, perhaps even defensive ones."

Heather was about to say something, then stopped, looking away. The feelings of being devoured from within, and the promise stopping her.

"Not any magic I have ever seen," said Caitlin.

"Well, considering that some of the books I saw in her study, that may not be too surprising," said Heather laughing and trying to forget that feeling.

"No, that is not it, he is not one of us," said Caitlin glancing down at her chest and remembering the feeling of being slowly consumed from within. She shivered.

Heather was staring out the window and said, "Kyle is one of us now. Both the Council and High Council have confirmed, and approved it somehow. If you do not want to accept him, because of what our brother did, you have that option. Just forget Kyle exists. But considering the state I found you in, I do not think it would be wise to cross Kyle or Cynthia again."

"I'm going home," said Caitlin closing her eyes and fading from the bed.

Chapter 11.05

Keiko stepped from her bedroom on Monday morning and the first thing that caught her attention was the smell of food and coffee. She was half way through the living room when her sister ran past.

"Sorry," said Kami disappearing into the kitchen.

Walking in she saw Kami and Harry arguing.

"Why?" asked Kami.

"Because breakfast is the most important meal of the day," said Harry. "I cannot fathom how you believe eating such rubbish will give you the energy you need to get a decent education."

"You're not my Father," she said leaning on the table. Making a weird face she added, while looking at his floral print apron, "And not my Mother."

"No, but Master Kyle asked me to help watch over you in his absence," said Harry. "You have ten minutes before Miss Stacie arrives, I would suggest you begin eating."

Muttering to herself, Kami sat down and began to eat the meal before her.

"My apologies for the spectacle," said Harry. "Good morning, Miss Keiko. Would you like me to prepare you something?"

Pouring herself a cup of coffee, Keiko asked, "You talked to Kyle?"

"No," said Harry putting down the morning paper he had been reading before the altercation with her sister. "Miss Cynthia relayed the message to me the other day."

"Ah, OK," said Keiko walking across the kitchen. "Hey, Kam, get all your homework done over the weekend?"

Kami rolled her eyes and said, "God, yes. What is with you people? Can't I live my own life?"

"Not 'til you're eighteen," said Keiko smiling at her sister.

"Great, thanks a bunch."

"You know, Grandma's place isn't that bad," said Keiko. "Pleasant, relaxing, and the school is only ten miles away. Would make for a relaxing walk every day."

"I get the point," mumbled Kami taking another bite of the waffles and glaring at her sister.

As Keiko reached the doorway Harry asked, "Are you sure you would not like something to eat?"

"I'm fine now," said Keiko over her shoulder. "I'll eat in a bit."

"Very well then," said Harry.

"Thank you, Harry," she said leaving the room.

Stepping into the living room she saw Cynthia sitting out on the patio. Going outside she sat down at the table and looked over at her friend.

"Good morning," said Keiko.

Cynthia nodded her head.

Looking closely, Keiko asked, "You don't look so good."

"I have been having a hard time sleeping lately," said Cynthia taking a sip of her coffee.

"Wow, Kyle being gone affecting you that much?"

Closing her eyes, Cynthia placed the coffee cup slowly on the table and said, "You have no idea."

"Hey," said Keiko. "Don't worry. He'll be back before you know it."

"I hope so."

Turning her head slightly Cynthia looked at Keiko and asked, "Is today the end?"

Letting out a small laugh Keiko sat back in her chair and stretched her legs. "Yep, today is the day. I am going to the owner of the agency and will end it all."

"Have you considered my suggestion?"

"Yeah," said Keiko. "I just wanted to talk to Kyle before I did anything."

"I see no reason why he would object," said Cynthia. "You already have a room here. Plus there is the issue of your agent."

"What do you mean?" asked Keiko paling. She steadied the hand holding her coffee. She had never told Cynthia, or anyone, how Jonathon actually treated her.

"From the way you have talked about him, and other incidents, it would seem that your agent may not be the most mentally stable individual. He may not take your leaving well."

Looking into Keiko's eyes, Cynthia said, "If he is that unbalanced, it may be unsafe for you to live alone. Please use caution."

"I... I will," said Keiko. "Um, I should go write my resignation. Is the network still up?"

"Yes," said Cynthia turning and staring out at the trees. "The printer is online and has paper in it."

"Cool," said Keiko standing. "Try to get some sleep, OK? I'm worried about you."

"Thank you for your concern," said Cynthia softly.

Keiko hesitated, then walked over and placed a hand on her friend's shoulder. Slowly Cynthia nodded. Walking back inside, Keiko went into the kitchen.

Standing in front of the open refrigerator she thought back to that breakfast with Noriyuki and decided to make Miso soup for breakfast. It seemed appropriate, considering what she was going to do today.

The instant Miso turned out moderately well. But it was good enough to bring back fond memories and raise her spirits for the tasks at hand.

Cleaning everything and placing them in the dish washer, against Harry's insistence that he could do so for her, she went back to her room and turned on her notebook. As it booted she returned to the kitchen for another cup of coffee.

Sitting back in front of her computer, making sure the wireless connection had been established, she grabbed a stack of papers from the drawer of her desk and read over her contract, doing some calculations on the computer. Satisfied that the results that matched what Cynthia had come up with yesterday she began to type. When finished she reviewed it and then printed two copies.

Walking upstairs she paused at the closed door of Kyle's room before walking in.

Keiko took the pages from the printer and looked around. The images from Saturday morning flashing into her head. Keiko was still confused, wondering what could have happened in two weeks to affect somebody she had been best friends with for over eight years so much.

Her shoulders slumped and she walked over to Kyle's computer chair and sat down.

It was still somewhat disheartening. If only she could have told him sooner. Her mind raced with hundreds of if situations over all the years, times she wished she could have said something, anything to him. She shook her head.

Rushing out of the room she went downstairs and took a shower. Back in her bedroom she pulled out her best business suit and hung it over the top of the door of the closet.

Staring at one of the letters Keiko could not help but smile. Folding both of them, she placed the letters in two envelopes. Checking to make sure everything was in order, she called the office and asked for Jonathon's assistant.

"Jonathon William's office, this is Greg, how may I assist you?"

"Greg? This is Keiko Nakamura, how are you doing?" she asked.

"Very well for a Monday," he said with a smile in his voice.

"Um, please don't tell him I called. But I was wondering if he was going to be out of the office any time today?"

"Actually he seems to be missing," said Greg.

"He was due back from Europe a couple days ago, wasn't he?" asked Keiko.

"Yes he was," said Greg with more of a smile in his voice. "But he did not return and has not contacted the office."

"Oh no, what if something happened to him?"

"Honestly, I cannot say that would be a bad thing," said Greg. "You know quite well what type of man he was."

Involuntarily Keiko shivered and asked, "You sure he went to Europe?"

"Yes. I drove him to the airport myself."

There was something in his tone of voice that chilled Keiko.

"Um, Could you transfer me to Mr. Labarre?"

"Of course, Miss Nakamura, please hold on."

"I am sorry, but Mr. Labarre is unavailable at this time, would you like to leave a message?" asked the assistant.

"Clair? It's Keiko Nakamura," she said.

"Oh, Keiko, how was your trip to Japan?"

"I had a great time. Visited with my family, traveled around the country, took a ton of pictures."

"That's great to hear," said Clair. "Mr. Labarre is in a meeting right now, anything I can help you with?"

"Actually, yes," said Keiko. "Is there any way I can meet with him today?"

"Oh, let me see," said Clair.

Keiko heard the keystrokes in the background.

"Unfortunately he is really, I mean really booked today," said Clair. "Would Wednesday be ok?"

"Actually, this is something I need to take care of today," said Keiko. "It's very important."

"Sorry, but like I said, he has meetings out the wazoo today, and tomorrow is just as bad."

"OK," said Keiko. "I mean this is really important. As in I will get you and your husband into the finest restaurant in Beverly Hills on Friday with reserved seating in the VIP section kind of important."

"How much time do you need?" asked Clair.

"Fifteen minutes, max," said Keiko.

"Huh, imagine that," said Clair. "His ten o'clock just rescheduled to Wednesday. I'll put you in for ten then."

"Thank you so much Clair," said Keiko. "Oh, and your dinner is on me."

"No sh... I mean, yes, not a problem, thank you for calling," said Clair. "Mr. Labarre, your ten..."

The line died.

At ten o'clock Keiko parked her car. At five minutes after ten she was standing in front of Clair's desk.

"Good morning, Keiko," said Clair.

"Good morning to you, Clair," said Keiko, winking at her. "Thank you again."

Standing, Clair smiled and opened the doors to announce, "Miss Nakamura is here to see you."

The elderly man stood and walked around his desk to meet Keiko half way across the room.

"Please, have a seat," he said patting her hand and leading her to the fine leather chair.

Instead of sitting behind his desk he sat in the chair next to her.

Pulling one of the envelopes from her case, she paused momentarily.

"Well," he said glancing from the envelope to Keiko. "I would assume this is not a social call."

"Unfortunately not," said Keiko.

Holding the envelope in both hands she said, "After much consideration, I wish to terminate my contract with your agency."

"Hmmmm," he said stroking his chin. "You do not have the disposition of somebody who has been offered a better contract."

Lowering her head, Keiko said, "No, I simply wish to leave the modeling business."

Extending a hand and placing it on one of hers he asked, "Why would you want to do that?"

She restrained herself from pulling away.

"It is..." she began. She felt his withered fingers grab her hand firmer. "It is just that I have decided to leave this line of work and do something that will make me happy."

She dropped her head, prepared for an onslaught.

He let go and folded his hands in his lap.

"I would guess that is a letter of resignation."

Glancing up she said, "Yes, it is."

"Why?" he asked.

"Because, honestly, I am miserable," said Keiko. "I just want to live a normal life. When I started all this I thought it would be fun. But it's not. I'm sorry."

"And what about your contract?" he asked, standing with his back to her, staring out the windows.

"It is detailed in my resignation," said Keiko. "I am prepared to buy out my contract."

Turning around with one eyebrow raised he asked, "Buy out your contract?"

"Yes, sir," she said. "I have just over a year on the contract, which comes out to a little over a million dollars."

He sat on the edge of his desk.

"And if you leave, what will you do?"

"Photography, sir," she said.

He leaned his head to the side and said, "Photography?"

Dropping the envelope into her lap, she looked down on it and said, "Yes, Mr. Labarre, I have loved photography long before I ever became a model."

"Hmmmm," he said.

There was a long pause.

Keiko tried to remain still, picking up the envelope in her lap.

"You know, Miss Nakamura?" he asked. "I have seen many faces walk in and out of those front doors. But very few people. You are one of those people. Even after the success you have achieved, you are no different than the day Jonathon brought you into this very office."

He walked forward quickly. The envelope she was staring at was snatched from her hands.

"Accepted," he said.

Keiko looked up at his smiling face.

"But on one condition."

Keiko did her best to hold back the fear that consumed her mind.

"What?" she asked.

"When you get a decent portfolio together, please contact me," he said. "Because it would be a pleasure to work with you again."

The fear in her abated. Standing she held out a hand.

Mr. Labarre reached forward and gave her a hug.

Patting her back, he said, "Please, Keiko, I wish the best for you."

Keiko did not feel like her feet were even touching the ground as she said her farewells to Clair, then floated through the halls to the desk outside of Jonathon's office. Greg was in the middle of a phone call and Keiko stood a few feet away, waiting for it to end.

"Sorry about that," said Greg. "Is there anything I can do for you?"

"I am leaving the modeling business," she said. "When he returns, please give him this letter of resignation."

Taking the envelope from her hand he placed it on the desk and put both hands on it.

"Keiko, I am glad you were able to escape this," he said. "I hope you have a good life."

"Thank you," she said, taking a step back from the melancholy look in his eyes.

Chapter 11.06

Stepping into the house Thomas turned and said, "Thank you again for the cab ride home."

"Not a problem," said Lucy. "I've been meaning to come over. Seems like a lot of things have happened while I was taking care of some other things."

"Tell me about it," said Thomas, closing the door. "Various happenings at the establishment where I work, Kyle flying off to Ireland for some mysterious job, Ed leaving to stay with his parents before his band departs for Germany, Keiko leaving modeling. And I suspect something might be going on with Kami and her best friend."

"Dang," said Lucy, "That's quite a bit for a few weeks."

"Ah well, that is life, is it not?" asked Thomas flashing a grin at her.

Nodding her head, Lucy glanced down the hallway and saw Kami and Keiko sitting on the couch watching the television. Neither of them had noticed them entering the house.

"Wait here," said Lucy putting a finger to her lips. "Shhhh."

Quietly sneaking down the hall, Lucy came up behind the couch without either girl noticing her. Harry, sitting in the chair, glanced up from the mystery novel he was reading and raised an eyebrow. In a graceful move Lucy leapt over the back of the couch and landed sitting next to Keiko.

The two jumped and let out startled noises.

"Lucy!" cried Keiko giving her a big hug.

"Hello, Keiko," said Lucy embracing her tightly, then pulling away. Leaning forward she waved at Kami and winked while saying, "Hey cutie."

"Um, hi," said Kami blushing slightly and returning her gaze quickly to the TV.

"You seem to be doing really well," said Lucy putting a hand on Keiko's arm.

"Yep, yep," said Keiko. "I quit modeling a few days ago and am going back to college soon."

"Nice, and I take it you finally had that talk with Kyle?"

"Nope. No point, he found somebody better, and I'm happy for him."

"That college girl he was dating?" asked Lucy.

"No, Cynthia."

Pulling her head back in shock, Lucy said, "What? Cynthia? I never saw that coming. Then again I suck with relationships."

"They seem to get along pretty well," said Keiko.

"Speaking of, is she," began Lucy, "Oh, there you are."

Cynthia was standing in the doorway.

Harry suddenly threw his book to the side, jumping out of the chair, in a defensive position.

Cynthia and Lucy simply stared at him for a moment.

"Good evening, Lucy," said Cynthia.

"How do you do that?" asked Harry, his fists in the air twitching. Nobody responded.

"Actually, can you excuse us?" asked Lucy to everybody in the room. "I need to talk to Cynthia for a few minutes."

"Sure," said Keiko and Kami.

"Wait!" exclaimed Harry as they left the room.

"Have you ever thought about meditation to relieve your stress?" asked Kami. "You're always wound up."

Harry stared at the backs of the two females leaving the room, then walked over and picked up his book from the floor, before returning to his chair to read it in silence.

Cynthia led Lucy down the hall, the doors to the study unlocking and opening as they approached. As they entered, the doors closed behind them.

As Lucy stepped in she glanced at the shelves of dolls with black eyes and said, "You know, that's really spooky."

Cynthia led them around the corner and into a small cubby at the front of the Study.

"What did you want to discuss?" asked Cynthia.

"What happened to Kyle?" asked Lucy.

"He is on a business trip in Ireland."

Lucy's eyes narrowed and she said, "Bull. Last Saturday I was in Spain and I could feel him. His power seemed to go off the charts, then he disappeared. I've searched all over this little planet and cannot sense him anymore. Is he dead?"

"No, he is not dead," said Cynthia.

"Then where is he?"

"Are you familiar with other dimensions?" asked Cynthia.

"Yes," said Lucy putting her finger on her cheek. "But honestly since we got kicked out I have just been here. Well pretty much."

Nodding her head Cynthia motioned for Lucy to follow and went to a large book. Flipping through the pages she stopped on one that showed an illustration of a tentacled monster with a description in an ancient language underneath. On the opposite page were other monstrosities illustrated with notations underneath.

"I've heard of this dimension, nasty place from before we came to exist," said Lucy. Then her face paled, "Oh, please tell me Kyle is not there, his kind is much weaker than us."

"No, he is not there exactly," said Cynthia. "Wait, even you cannot sense it?"

"Sense what?"

"Kyle."

Laughing, Lucy said, "My little dark one, I can barely sense you exist, and your mind is a blank to me, which is quite a feat, let me tell you."

"I understand," said Cynthia glancing at the dark creature illustrated on the page as a slight frown crossed her lips. "Thank you for coming over, but I have work to do."

"Wait, you're kicking me out?" asked Lucy.

"Yes."

"But what about Kyle?"

"You do not have information that can help. And I have more research to do."

"Cynthia, what happened?" asked Lucy.

Turning away from her slightly Cynthia said, "As I said, thank you for visiting."

Lucy stared at her, then reached out and placed a hand on her shoulder.

"I'll ask around, maybe some of my brethren know of that place, or might be able to help you, " said Lucy.

"Thank you," said Cynthia.

Turning, Lucy left the room.

Chapter 11.07

Lifting her arm, Janice checked the time on her watch. Grabbing her cell phone off the bed next to her she checked to make sure it had a signal, and out of paranoia checked her voice mail to find no messages. Rolling over onto her stomach she saw that there were no new emails.

Sighing heavily she began to re-read the chapter of her new course book. This was probably the twentieth time she had started reading this chapter, unfortunately she could not concentrate.

After reading ten pages and not knowing what she read, the alarm on her cell phone rang and she turned it off. Checking the phone for messages she found none. Checking for email she found none.

Rolling off the bed she walked across the small room to the decrepit pressboard kitchen table that had seen much better days in its many years of existence. Picking up the teddy bear holding a red heart she hit the animal on the top of it's head and then set it carefully on a stack of newspapers.

Pulling off the tag with Kyle's name on it she tossed it onto the floor and opened the box of chocolates. After devouring half of them she went back to her bed and laid down on her stomach, staring at the screen of her computer for a few minutes.

Opening the web browser on her computer she accessed her MySpace account, then clicked the link to enter a new blog entry.

February 15   12:07am

Oh yay. Happy valentines day to me.

I took it off of work, and skipped my classes. hung out here all day. I know K. is in ireland but I was sure that he would at least call or email or somthing.

But nothing. what a waste of a day. I hate this.

looks like I screwed up yet another relationship.

Chapter 11.08

Everyone was asleep. Pulling the metal briefcase from hiding, Cynthia took out the notebook computer and connected it to the phone line. Dialing an Internet Service Provider in Ireland she logged on and typed a brief message from Kyle.

It was his weekly update to his friends that he was really busy, but having a good time in Ireland, enjoying mass amounts of Guinness, and hoped to be home some time soon.

That was the third message she had sent out. And after all these weeks of research she still had no idea how to bring him back.

Closing the notebook she placed it back in the briefcase and hid it away.

Taking off her clothes she put on the black T-shirt and slowly walked through the aisles of books to the center of the study. Passing through the shield she lay next to the comatose body and closed her eyes, entering the darkness, trying to find him.

After all this time her efforts seemed futile. She knew that Kyle was avoiding her, she knew what he had done. Escaping the pain he had melded into the darkness.

Several hours later she gave up. Exhausted, she opened her eyes and hit his chest.

"What did you always say? Baka?" she said hitting him again lightly.

She stood and wandered the circle inside the shield several times. Kicking the magical shield with her foot, the momentary shock of pain was a pleasant change. She walked back over to Kyle and sat next to him, unsure if she could exist like this for another day, a year, or even twenty-six.

Placing both hands on his chest she whispered, "Kyle."

Kneeling next to him, her hands as they were, she closed her eyes and remembered a similar situation less than a month ago, the only night she had truly not felt alone. A brief moment where she believed she could be with another and live life instead of just existing.

Her brows furrowed and Cynthia opened her eyes. Looking at how she was sitting, where her hands were.

A slight smile crossed her lips.

Staring at Kyle she could sense the overwhelming darkness inside of him. As she concentrated, the patterns of movement of that darkness within him began to synch with hers. At first she began to slow it down, but then made it swirl around faster and faster.

She felt the tendrils enter him.

Chapter 11.09

The presence had been here again. He was still curious about it, but not enough to actually make contact, it was too painful. Whenever he thought about something like that he was full of pain, and he did not like being in pain.

After a while the presence disappeared, and he settled himself back into the void that he was.

Anything was better than the pain and torment that ripped through him whenever he tried to think.

Yet there was one lingering word.

"Stop!"

Nothing made sense within this void of nothingness. But that voice, the one screaming the one word seemed to create a juxtaposition as he felt the presence start searching for him again.

Everything shifted suddenly. It was kind of like he became in synch with the screaming voice, and that presence as everything began to move faster somehow.

Two strange snake-like things entered the darkness and hesitated for half a second before racing toward him. Kyle wanted nothing more than to evade, but he did not. He held that word within his thought, focusing on it, using it to give him the strength not to move.

Both of them hit Kyle and he felt himself moving.

He was strained, being pulled away from the comfort of the void he knew. Then he was someplace else. Kyle tried not to think, but this place was part of something that he had longed for all of the times he had tried to seek those things called memories.

The darkness began to fall away from him.

He saw a body through something he knew were eyes. There were two small hands upon what he realized was a chest.

He was inside the presence.

As the darkness melted away, suddenly he began to remember.

He was being pushed away. Back to the other side, back into the body he had seen.

But there was no need to become part of the darkness again.

The pain to his eyes, as he opened them, made Kyle flinch. Blinking several times he slowly raised a hand and placed it on hers.

He heard her start screaming his name, over and over.

Sitting up he felt cold hands on his face. She was asking more questions. In a way they made sense, but not enough for him to understand.

Then all of his memories suddenly flowed into him, and into what he knew as his body.

Raising his eyes, he looked into hers, and she stopped moving.

Fighting the weakness within him, and the weakness that filled every fiber of his being, he lifted up both hands and pulled her to him, holding her close, as he rested his face on the top of her head.

"How long was I gone?" he managed to say in a voice that cracked.

Her tight embrace relaxed slightly as her cheek brushed against his and she whispered, "You were only gone three weeks, Kyle."

He nodded his head slowly.

Chapter 11.10

Kami and Stacie walked into the kitchen and saw Keiko reading a cookbook at the table.

"We are officially free," said Kami taking off the coat of her school uniform and slinging it over her shoulder.

Keiko looked up and said, "Not really. You still have two more years of school, then don't forget about college."

Grumbling something under her breath, Kami said, "I'm going to grab my things."

"I'll stay here," said Stacie sitting down.

"So whatcha doing?" asked Stacie.

"Planning a dinner to celebrate Tomas' new job on Monday. Harry has to work, so I volunteered to cook."

"That's really nice," she said.

"Yeah, he's a little strange, but a good guy when you get to know him," said Keiko.

"Oh, tell me about it," said Stacie rolling her eyes. "You have no idea how much Kami used to complain about him when she first moved in here."

Keiko laughed and said, "Yeah, oh trust me, I heard the stories."

Putting both hands on the table and leaning forward Stacie asked, "Did you hear what happened between him and his dad?"

"No," said Keiko.

"OK, this is what I heard from Kam, anyway, he called his dad the other day and told him about the new job," said Stacie. "And they talked a bit. His dad seemed really happy and said that Thomas could have all his money and stuff back. Then Thomas told him that they could talk about it in another year, that he wanted to see how well he could do on his own. Personally I think he's trying to impress that brainiac physics girl he's dating."

"Damn," said Keiko. "From what Kyle said he used to be a spoiled little rich kid."

"He says he's living his dream, or starting to," said Stacie.

"That's good to hear," said Keiko smiling and playing with the charm on her necklace.

They heard the front door open and then close, and heavy boots approach from the entry.

"Yo," said Ed walking into the kitchen and then stopping. "Did I interrupt anything?"

"Nah," said Keiko. "Just talking about Thomas and his new job at the Ad Agency."

"Ah, that," he said, wandering over to the fridge and grabbing a beer. "So Keiko, you still coming to my gig in Hollywood tomorrow?"

"Of course," she said, as she suddenly began to read the cookbook intently.

"Sweet," he said walking past them and pausing at the doorway. "Just make sure to bring some of your cute college friends."

"You wish," said Keiko not even looking up from the cookbook. "Like I would introduce any of my nice friends to the likes of you."

Laughing Ed said, "You know they like the bad boys."

"Dream on," she said, flipping the page.

As he was leaving he said, "Hey, Kami, have a good trip."

"Yeah, thanks," she said passing him.

Kami walked back into the kitchen and said, "OK, I'm all set."

Glancing over, Stacie saw the black travel case slung over her shoulder and moaned.

"You're bringing your laptop on a family vacation?"

"Technology is my lifeblood," said Kami. "I'd be a neurotic mess if I spent a week away from a computer."

"God, what am I going to do with you?" asked Stacie standing from the table.

"Oh, trust me, I have plans."

Stacie turned bright red.

"TMI," said Keiko raising a hand, continuing to read the cookbook.

"That always gets her," said Kami laughing and stepping forward to take Stacie's hand.

"Have a safe trip," said Keiko. "Oh, and Stacie, your parents have all our numbers, right?"

"Yes they do," she said.

"See you next week!" exclaimed Kami waving a hand and leading her girlfriend out of the kitchen.

Chapter 11.11

Kyle had remote control of a client's computer, and had just finished changing some settings when he heard a knock on the door. He motioned with his hand for them to come in.

"There you go, Mr. Cryder," said Kyle talking on his cell phone. "Glad I could help. Yes, you have a good weekend too."

Looking up he saw Kami and Stacie.

"You two out for your little family vacation extravaganza?" he asked.

"Oh, please, onii-chan," said Kami.

"Yep, we'll be back in a week," said Stacie.

"Alright, have fun then," he said. "Take a lot of pictures."

"Will do," said Kami as the two of them turned and headed out the door.

They left saying, "bai bai," as they did.

Checking the time on his phone he shut down the computer and walked over to the closet. Pushing some of the long black dresses aside he grabbed a long sleeved dress shirt and pair of slacks. After he changed he put on a pair of dress shoes and a suit coat, thought about a tie, then decided against it.

He went downstairs, to the kitchen.

"I think we'll be heading off soon," said Kyle.

Keiko jumped and looked over at him.

"Dammit," she said. "You're picking up some bad habits from Cyn." Looking him up and down she added, "Including wearing black all the time."

He smiled and said, "Sorry, didn't mean to startle you. Anyway we won't be back until tomorrow, maybe Sunday."

"You two and your get away weekends," said Keiko laughing.

"Hey, there's a whole world out there to enjoy," he said.

"I know, I know. Just funny, would have never guessed but you two make a really cute couple."

His face became somber.

"Don't ever let her hear you say that," said Kyle.

"Trust me, she won't."

"Excellent, well, you're in charge here, Ms. Nakamura, call if you need anything."

"Yes sir," she said making a mock salute.

Kyle smiled at her, then walked through the house to the study. Cynthia was sitting at the far end of the long table, looking over some documents.

"Please allow me just a few more minutes," she said.

"That the paperwork for the new office?" he asked.

"Yes," said Cynthia. "I want to assure everything is in order before we sign off on it."

"Thank you," said Kyle, kissing the top of her head.

She did not react as she turned to the next page.

Wandering through the study, to the center, he laid down on the leather couch, closing his eyes. The only sound was that of papers being shuffled on occasion.

Some time later he felt a hand on his shoulder and two lips upon his. He opened his eyes as Cynthia pulled away. He lay there and stared up at her for a time until her eyes narrowed. Laughing, he stood and held her close, closing his eyes.

They faded from the room and appeared in an alley surrounded on either side by worn bricks. Stepping out into the street they paused and watched the sun rise over the Paris skyline.

After a pleasant breakfast they spent the rest of the day at the Louvre Museum, then had dinner at a small bistro.

Later, as they walked through the night-time streets that evening, Kyle paused as they came around some buildings and he saw the Eiffel Tower. Staring up at it he felt Cynthia put her arm around his waist and lean against him. Putting his arm around her, Kyle pulled her closer.

AUTHOR'S NOTES

I originally wrote Greetings & Farewells back in 2002, which is honestly a different life for me. The anime section in Suncoast was at best several feet wide and few here in the States had even heard of manga. My, how times change. I had attended my first Anime Expo convention in 2001, and after finding such diverse and different characters, storylines, and even culture, I set about writing this book.

Originally I had wanted this book to be a manga. Sadly, though I had been in Commercial Art in High School, I became frustrated trying to draw what I saw in my head. So I turned to what I knew best. Writing. I had been writing for many years as of then, but had never tried writing a novel. So I wrote everything down, and then it kind of sat there on my hard drive. Self publishing, even in 2002, was a very costly prospect.

Then Life happened.

Years later I found myself at a new company and a co-worker asked me if I wrote. She told me about how she had written several books and how she had published them.

I seriously considered making major revisions and changes to this book, but after a lot of consideration I decided against it. This book reflects who and what I was creatively back in 2002. And the next one I write will reflect more of who I am now, so I look forward to sharing it with all of you. And, please feel free to drop by JulienGiever.com for more information.

I want to thank all of you who have read this book.

If you didn't catch that page before the Contents, I am releasing this under Creative Commons, so you don't have to worry about Big Brother if you want to pass copies of this to your friends. Full versions of the whole book are online. Personally I want to thank all of the staff from BoingBoing.net for not only providing great content, but also to one of their contributors, Corey Doctorow. He helped me overcome my 20th. century views on personal creations and copyright.

Writing this book was a solitary venture. I did not have any editors, advisors, or consultants. Yet this work would not be possible without the many people who have helped me in my life.

First off my father who let me be myself, and who did his own thing. Hell, a guy who gets a Masters in weaving can definitely show one how to think outside the box in this society. Also for my mother who worked hard to raise myself and my sister, I thank you for everything.

To Christian, Aaron, and Rob... Not only did you introduce me to the world of Anime and Manga, in one of the worst points of my life you saved me in more ways than I could ever explain or hope to thank you for. I miss you guys and hope to shed my hermit ways soon.

My mentor and teacher from when I first moved here to California, Nick, I still carry many of the lessons you taught me. And the same goes to my brethren, Christine and I R Raven.

Many thanks also to Meilena for her moral support and guidance in getting me to finish and publish this book.

Also I have to thank all my friends at Anime Expo. These last few years being on staff have been great and I look forward to next year! And to everybody in the Dance department, what more can I say, other than you are the best.

Rhiannon, though the last several years have been hard, please know you are always in my thoughts. I have worn the necklace with the Rhiannon's Knot since before you were born, every single day.

Until the next time...

Julien Giever
September 2008

www.ingramcontent.com/pod-product-compliance
Lightning Source LLC
Chambersburg PA
CBHW060424030726
47495CB00003B/731